Praise for

THE LOST LEGENDS
of NEW JERSEY

"The Meadowlands, the diners, and Atlantic City are all here, but Reiken invests them with an almost mythic beauty.... Smart, unsentimental, and elegiac... This is a wise book filled with people a reader cannot help but care for."
                                        —*The Boston Globe*

"A witty novel that bribes us to accept its painful moments with the sheer delight of unlikely romance."
        —*The Christian Science Monitor,* "Noteworthy Books of 2000"

"Reiken has written a wonderful, wonderful book. By turns funny, poignant, clever and sad, *Lost Legends* is almost unerringly original.... Reiken is an inspired storyteller, shifting gracefully from ethereal to earthy, and then meshing the two.... Part of the reason Reiken's stories are so engaging is that he is so good at drawing characters that are multilayered, familiar and yet totally individual.... You find yourself wishing that Reiken's beautiful, affecting writing and his haunting characters and their stories could go on and on."
                                        —*The Philadelphia Inquirer*

"[Reiken] strikes a restrained balance between mysteries and matters of fact.... By the conclusion of this complex, engrossing novel, the title no longer seems the least bit funny."
                                        —*Time*

"What's distinctive about Reiken's book is not so much the period detail—Bruce Springsteen on the boom box, the summertime Jersey shore, the local diner—although he nails these targets with a sharpshooter's eye. Nor is it the effortless unfolding of the plot. What's singular here is the author's ability to conjure moments of dazzling joy out of a mournful story. Love blooms around pain, humor peeks out behind tragedy, and beauty, most unexpectedly, shines through the mundane." —*The Baltimore Sun*

"What a pleasure to read a novel and forget that you are reading, to forget that this is not your life and these are not your people. Frederick Reiken's wondrously appealing second novel contains the confusion, hurt and hope of real life. Its particular time and place become ours.... A beautifully told story of bad choices, good intentions, and the price of intimacy." —*Chicago Tribune*

"By turns deeply romantic, funny, and tragic, *Lost Legends* explores how more often than not we are the forces that get in the way of finding our true loves. Although this truth might not deliver the same sentimental payoff as a five-hanky movie classic, Reiken charts the longings and fears of his characters with such emotional acuity and unadorned language that a different kind of satisfaction arises: a bittersweet recognition of how people really work.... Reiken reminds us that when good literature comes along, it feels, like true love itself, as if something legendary is occurring." —*The Washington Post Book World*

"In his affectionate but tough-minded second novel, [Reiken] captures the poetry of the New Jersey condition, circa 1980, with a rare precision. Whether he's depicting the mournful uneasiness of two siblings on a last moonlit bike ride or the bewilderment of an estranged father giving himself over to the healing power of a Jacques Cousteau special, Reiken knows how to charge the quietest domestic scenes with consequence and emotion." —*The New York Times Book Review*

"Magical . . . poetic and evocative . . . Reiken has a gift for exposing a character's pain and letting him grapple with it, know it, and learn to live with it. . . . The mysterious achievement of Reiken's second novel is to affirm rather than shake our faith in love." —*Newsday*

"Frederick Reiken, in this wonderful new novel, is tracking the way that something shifts inside us whenever we fall in love: how we are altered, how we become different under its spell. His story is about the eternal hope for a matching of souls, and the reality of making do with a mismatch. His scenes are crisp and clear, wise and knowing, funny and moving—a miraculous balancing of tone and theme." —Charles Baxter, author of *The Feast of Love*

"Frederick Reiken has woven a magical story as entrancing as *Le Morte d'Arthur*, the Sir Thomas Malory tale that becomes a touchstone for [protagonist] Anthony's emotional quest. As evocative of suburban life as the best work of Philip Roth or John Updike, *The Lost Legends of New Jersey* is accessible to adults and mature adolescents everywhere and is one of the finest novels published this year." —*Los Angeles Times*, "Best Books of 2000"

"The gentle empathy for the intricate muddle of family and romantic relationships that distinguished Reiken's accomplished debut, *The Odd Sea*, is also a dominant feature of this considerably more ambitious successor. . . . Reiken knows the territory of emotional commitment and confusion as well as anybody writing today. Beautiful stuff." —*Kirkus Reviews* (starred review)

"In Reiken's dazzling second novel, young Anthony Rubin's eyes are opened to love, adultery, despair and the constellations that burn over the Jersey Shore. . . . Imbued with pathos and humor, hope and longing, this is an imaginative love story that flows with graceful clarity toward an affecting conclusion." —*Book*

"A lovely, sad tale. Frederick Reiken has delivered a memorable second novel about a young man's journey to maturity in a family marked by emotional upheaval during an era characterized by rootlessness."

—*The Wall Street Journal*

"With a Springsteen-shaded touch of Camelot... This novel confirms that Reiken is a talent to track. *Lost Legends* is a work of compassionate perception."

—*The Newark Star-Ledger*

"This sweet, sad second novel from Frederick Reiken is about loss, all right, the loss of love and trust and the sudden, preposterous absence of those on whom we depend to supply them. But it is also a story about the passages life imposes and about how we stumble through them, groping not so much for lessons as for toeholds.... Reiken time and again demonstrates an observant eye for the passing scene and a passionately lyrical heart."

—*The Miami Herald*

"Elegiac and unsparingly direct, funny and poignant... A beautiful story about loss, hope, and survival."

—*Publishers Weekly* (starred review)

"I've fallen hard for Anthony Rubin, boy next door extraordinaire—the Sandy Koufax of high-school hockey and a character J. D. Salinger could envy. This is a gem of a novel, so endearing, so true and wry that I didn't want to let it go."

—Elinor Lipman, author of *The Inn at Lake Devine*

"Reiken's writing captures Bruce Springsteen's elegiac style, and the novel's characters are the broken heroes found in nearly every Springsteen song.... A tightly woven book... Reiken writes thoughtfully, but he lets his ideas run quietly under the surface of the narrative. A master of show-don't-tell, he demonstrates in his writing that actions can speak louder than words, even in literature."

—*The Memphis Commercial Appeal*

"Reiken's second novel merges the ordinary and the mythological in the suburbs of New Jersey.... Reiken seamlessly combines stark realism with fantasy in this exceptional tale of love and loss."

—*Booklist* (starred review)

"The writing itself is lucid and the characters complex.... This is part of Reiken's gift: rendering people, even the ones who do not always behave as well as they should, likable enough to make the reader care about them.... A perfect end-of-summer-into-fall book for the beach. Literature buffs who spend more time reading about the ocean than swimming in it will be pleasantly surprised by this complex look at adolescence and the influences that affect it."

—*The Orlando Sentinel*

"Like Raymond Carver's short story 'What We Talk About When We Talk About Love,' Reiken explores the various stages of love without lapsing into simple definitions.... Reiken is able to take ordinary people and render them extraordinary in their tragedies and victories."

—*San Francisco Chronicle*

THE LOST
LEGENDS
of NEW JERSEY

THE LOST
LEGENDS
of NEW JERSEY

Frederick Reiken

A Harvest Book
Harcourt, Inc.
San Diego   New York   London

Requests for permission to make copies of any part
of the work should be mailed to the following address:
Permissions Department, Harcourt, Inc.,
6277 Sea Harbor Drive, Orlando, Florida 32887-6777.

www.harcourt.com

Any resemblance to actual people and events
is purely coincidental. This is a work of fiction.

Library of Congress Cataloging-in-Publication Data
Reiken, Frederick.
The lost legends of New Jersey/Frederick Reiken.—1st ed.
p. cm.
ISBN 0-15-100507-9
ISBN 0-15-601094-1 (pbk.)
1. Family—New Jersey—Fiction. 2. New Jersey—Fiction.
I. Title.
PS3568.E483 L67 2000
813'.54—dc21   99-057774

Designed by Lydia D'moch
Text set in Electra
Printed in the United States of America
First Harvest edition 2001
A C E G I J H F D B

CONTENTS

PART IV

THE LOST
LEGENDS
of NEW JERSEY

PROLOGUE

THE DAY MY MOTHER left Livingston, New Jersey, she threw rocks through most of Claudia Berkowitz's windows. When I think about it now, of course, it's nothing. I've heard of people who go crazy and buy guns. Take that woman from Parsippany, the one who ambushed her husband with his girlfriend. She found them in her bed and shot them each once in the leg. Holding the gun to her husband's head, she made him slap his girlfriend Rita in the face until she cried. She made him call Rita a slut, then fired a bullet through Rita's temple. So, when you think about it, throwing rocks is not too big a deal.

Of course, it was strange being down there playing Ping-Pong with Jay Berkowitz. I remember saying, "Jay, I think there's someone throwing rocks through all your windows." We went upstairs and saw my mother. It was a sunny day in August. The sun was going down over the house across the street. My mother's hand was filled with stones from the rock garden by the driveway. I watched her hurl one and a window smashed right near me.

I could hear my father yelling from the upstairs window. "I'm here to pick up Anthony," he was saying.

My mother kept throwing rocks until her arm got tired. Then she crumpled to the lawn and I could see she was hysterical. I could see that she was blocking out the world the way she sat there and cried, and as she cried I just kept staring through a hole in the Berkowitzes' window.

✦ ✦ ✦

I ask my mother where the beach is.

"About a mile from here," she says. "Although it's probably going to rain."

"I like your pond," I say. "Anyway, it's too late for the beach."

I'm tired from the flight and now I'm sitting on the couch with her two cats.

She says, "I just want to make a dinner. Something nice, where we can talk."

I say, "That's fine."

"I'd like to hear about things."

"Fine."

"Maybe we'll make some sort of plan. We'll take a trip—down to the Keys."

"I like it here," I say.

My mother steps into the kitchen. She pulls a pan out from the cabinet. The cats think it's dinner so they run into the kitchen. Through a glass door across the room, I watch the sky over western Florida. Soon my mother is talking softly to her cats.

✦ ✦ ✦

When she cried on the Berkowitzes' lawn she was somehow beautiful. She fell down onto her knees and never covered up her face. She had her hands pressed to the ground where she was kneeling, barely moving. She kept on crying and I told Jay Berkowitz not to watch.

He asked me whether my father was in the house and I said, "Jesus, Jay, you heard him just yelling." He asked if his mother was there too and I said, "What are you, Jay, an idiot? You think my mother throws rocks through people's windows for the hell of it?"

My mother cried and the tears kept coming. Her lips were trembling but her hands still did not move. She didn't punch the ground, slap, or tear out pieces of her hair. I watched her face through the glass and hated her, and loved her, both at once.

There was glass all over the Berkowitzes' hallway. I could hear my father yelling, saying, "Jess, please just go home!"

She just kept weeping with both hands at her sides, motionless, unclenched. She wept until her face was wet, but still she didn't raise her hands to wipe her cheeks.

✦ ✦ ✦

I can hear her chopping onions.

"Mom," I say, "do you want me to set the table?"

"Yes," she says, "set it."

I brush by her in the kitchen and I pull out two plates and a pair of carved wooden animal napkin holders. There are lions, leopards, hippos, gazelles, rhinoceroses, zebras.

"I'm giving you the leopard," I say. "I'm taking a rhinoceros."

"How's your book, the one you're reading?"

"It's very good," I say.

"It's gonna rain in about ten seconds."

"So?"

"Just telling you."

I don't answer.

"Sometimes it scares me," she says. "The lightning. Though it's beautiful from in here."

I look outside and I can see the palm trees blowing. The pond is rippling and soon the sky is darker than the earth. It starts to rain and the drops seem thick. They smack the roof and pound against the cobblestones. Tiny brown lizards run around my mother's patio, and there are toads, enormous toads the size of softballs.

✦ ✦ ✦

I think I wanted to hear her scream, to see her thrash around or move like some crazed animal, but she just sat there. She sat there quietly with tears running down her face. Like it was her lawn, her life—What did it matter that her kid was right inside there playing Ping-Pong? What did it matter that her husband was up there screaming out the window? At least she never had sick thoughts—unlike that woman in Parsippany. That sick, crazed woman bought a handgun and she practiced on a range. She left her husband wounded and bleeding, his girlfriend Rita dead beside him. Two hours later police discovered the woman's car at a nearby Pizza Hut. They went inside but couldn't find her. When the detective arrived they found the woman sleeping in her car.

✦ ✦ ✦

"Anthony," she says, "the silverware."

"I'm watching the rain," I say. "Give me a second, please."

"It's rain," she says, and then I hear her running to her bedroom, looking for the cats, making sure that they're inside.

"Please let's sit down," she says. "It's nothing. We get these storms here every day."

I hear my mother coming toward me. The rain makes splashes on the patio. The drops are the size of marbles.

"Why are you standing there?" she asks.

I say, "Because, I like rain."

"Please," she says, "the fish ..."

"Give me a second."

"Why?"

"I want to feel the rain."

I slide the glass door back and then the water pelts my chest. I step outside and cross the patio. Water is dripping down from palm leaves. The grass is soft, mushy, slimy on my feet. When I look back I see my mother trembling.

"Anthony!" she yells. "Please, you're sopping wet now!"

"A second," I say, and watch the lightning.

✦ ✦ ✦

She drove across the Berkowitzes' lawn. She made circles until the yard looked like a racetrack, and the treads were deep, ruts. The ground was soft because Claudia was obsessed with watering her lawns.

After she left, she drove straight down to western Florida. And it made sense, her being by the water. My mother was very comfortable around water. She loved the Jersey Shore, where we spent four summers. She loved the jetties. She could walk over the slick rocks and never fall. She liked to talk to the scraggly fishermen. She would go out there in the evenings, sometimes wearing the fancy clothes she'd worn to dinner. Then she'd come home with her skirt looking like Saran Wrap. Her blouse would cling to her breasts like film. My father had to make a choice then: Be confused or let it go. Most of the time he let it go. He'd take her hand, lead her upstairs. We'd hear them showering and talking in the bathroom.

✦ ✦ ✦

"I just want us to have a pleasant dinner."

"The fish is good," I say.

"Tell me what's happening with you."

"There's not too much," I say. "Not a whole lot more than what I've told you in our phone calls."

"I'm your mother," she says. "There are things you can tell your mother, such as—do you like school, do you have a girlfriend?"

"School's okay," I say. "No, I don't have a girlfriend now."

"How is your knee?"

I say, "It's good."

She looks down at her plate, and for a second she seems weak, as if her face is about to drop into her fish. She cuts into the sole, then she looks up and says, "I'm sorry."

I say, "There's nothing to be sorry for."

"I'm sorry," she says. "Anthony, I'm so sorry."

My mother stares down at her plate. She puts her fork down. When she looks up her eyes seem frozen, like she's lost. It's been three years since she left New Jersey. I always wish I had some sort of newsreel of my life. Because I want to show her *everything*. I want to go back in time. To find some doorway back to all the things I don't know how to tell her. I watch a tear slip down her cheek and I say, "Mom," but then she's running from the table.

✦ ✦ ✦

When I watched her drive away I hoped that she'd explode. I hoped she'd go drive off a bridge and disappear. Or that she'd move somewhere else and just become another person. I wished I could say that no, she never did these things, she's part of the PTA.

I told my friends that my mother just went crazy once with rocks. It's hard to know what really happened. I sometimes think I should have walked out from the Berkowitzes' house. I should have done a lot of things, but I just stood there in the hallway. I stared at my own mother through a small hole in the window, and as I watched her drive away I could feel part of us both dying.

✦ ✦ ✦

"Anthony," she says.

I turn around. I'm on the porch, watching the sky now that the rain has stopped.

"Anthony," she says. "Hey. We have to try to work this out."

I say, "It's hard. I've really missed you. But then I sometimes have no feelings."

She says, "I know how you are, remember?"

"I think I get it all from you."

My mother nods, purses her lips. She says, "So what do you want to do about this visit? I really was looking forward to this week."

"Me too," I say. "I think it would have helped if Dani came."

"Her summer's different now that she's in college."

"What was it like when she came last summer?"

"It went fine."

My mother closes the screen door and stands in front of me. I start to feel it again—the feeling that I want to go back in time.

"I'll take you snorkeling," she says.

"Where?"

She says, "Key Largo. I have a friend who has a cottage there."

"I've never snorkeled."

"It's pretty easy."

I look outside and watch the pond.

"Mom?" I say.

"What?"

"There is a lot I want to tell you."

"We have all week," she says, with her voice calm, the way it gets when she's not afraid of things. I watch two ducks land on the water. I see a cloud that looks like someone's ear. "It's good you're here," my mother says, her voice too quiet now to tell what she is thinking. She takes a seat on the chair next to me, and suddenly there is no need to talk.

PART ONE

CONSTELLATIONS

Summer 1979

ONE SUMMER many years ago, the Rubins and the Berkowitzes were out on the porch of the house they rented on the Jersey Shore in Allenhurst. It was a moonless night and stars were rising out from beyond the fold of the horizon. Two constellations kept on growing, almost like trees.

Anthony Rubin watched the ocean. Each time another star popped over the horizon, he readjusted his idea of just what the shapes resembled.

First he saw something that looked like a big panther. Then the shape turned into a box kite.

Claudia Berkowitz lit a cigarette. She turned to Anthony's father and said, "Michael, you were a Boy Scout. Shouldn't you know the constellations?"

"He was too busy chasing Girl Scouts," said Jess Rubin, Anthony's mother.

Michael stood up and said, "Well, I can at least tell you what I learned from my great-uncle. He sold scrap metal. We used to visit him in Binghamton."

"Michael, you're drunk," said Jess. "Sit down."

Claudia smiled and said, "Wait, I want to hear this."

"These are the Yiddish constellations," Michael continued.

"Somebody stop him," said Claudia's husband, Douglas, but no one did.

Anthony's father raised his hand. He pointed up to a bright zigzag of four stars. "Right there," he said. "We can see the shiny belt of the Yenta, Miriam." He pointed lower, to a cluster of stars that looked like a falling teapot. "And below Miriam, down on the horizon. That's Ira Nusbaum, the Swindler. Good thing that bandit's 40,000 light-years away."

He moved his hand across the sky and then picked out another random cluster.

He said, "And here, to the north, we can see Maury, the Disappointment. This constellation was named after my third cousin, Maury Rosenthal. You'll always find it near the luminous Sophie Schatzberg, also known as the Great Kvetch."

He paused and Claudia chimed in, "Wait. I think I'm seeing Howie Grossman, the Great Schlemiel."

"That's very good," Michael said. "Do we all know the myth of Howie?"

"Michael, enough," said Jess.

Anthony saw that his mother's eyes were incandescing with silent anger. He wondered whether she was offended. She'd been raised Orthodox and had gone to a yeshiva as a girl. But she'd stopped going after sixth grade. She had renounced all that yeshiva had tried to teach her, not to mention her parents' orthodoxy. When asked, his mother always claimed to be an atheist, and so he could not fathom why the Yiddish constellations made her angry.

"Poor Howie dropped the Torah during his own bar mitzvah," Michael continued.

"Such a schlemiel," Claudia said, and raised her cigarette to her lips.

"To keep him out of temple on High Holidays, God gave Howie his own place in the night sky."

Jess yelled out, "Stop!"

She glared at Claudia and rose. She crossed the porch and descended the wooden stairs, down to the sand. Anthony's father followed after her. When he caught up with her they stood talking on the beach for a few seconds. Then Jess walked off and headed down the shoreline.

Anthony knew where she was going. In recent weeks she'd spent half of her time out on the jetty. She sat alone, watching the ocean. She sometimes sat so far out that she got drenched by the spray of waves. Anthony saw that his father was returning, a web of stars hanging directly above his head as he walked back. When he stepped onto the porch, he said, "She's fine. She's just going to the jetty." He grabbed his drink and went inside to wait for her in their room.

Later that night, Anthony and Jay Berkowitz were out wandering the Asbury Park boardwalk. It was just one beach away from Allenhurst, and the boys often went there several times a day. They were with their closest down-the-shore friends, Bradley Kalish and Andy Sullivan. They all played Skee-Ball for a while, then walked the boards, acting like jerks, as they often did.

Andy Sullivan was a stud—long white-blond hair and blue eyes. Having him with them seemed to give the foursome license to talk to any pretty girls they saw. Not that they knew what to do when girls would actually respond. They were all thirteen, except Jay, who was eleven.

At some point they returned to Allenhurst, went down to the beach, and midget-wrestled. They had seen tag-team midget-wrestling on television. Now they had given themselves names. Jay was Wizard Eyes. Bradley was Laughing Man. Anthony was Puckhead and Andy was Dr. Death. They'd be announcers while they wrestled and always staged impossible situations. They would announce things such as, "Wizard Eyes, in a brilliant move, has ripped Dr. Death's arm off." Andy would then have to wrestle with one arm behind his back.

That night while wrestling, Anthony saw his mother. She'd just come off the nearest jetty and was walking back toward the house. He saw the stars in the sky above her. In some strange way his mother seemed like a constellation. He was about to run off after her, ask her why she got upset about the myth of Howie Grossman. Then Andy decked him. Jay jumped on top. He yelled, "And Puckhead is now crushed by a double dogpile!" Bradley dove in and yelled, "But Laughing Man...now mutilates Dr. Death and Wizard Eyes!" Anthony squirmed out from the pileup, rolled, and looked again for his mother. He tried to find her in the darkness, but she was gone.

+ + +

During that summer they all became junior lifeguards. They got paid five dollars an hour. It was Andy's idea. His older brother, Shane, was the Allenhurst Beach lifeguard. Shane started out as a junior life-guard—at least, he claimed to have. Anthony couldn't remember there ever having been such a thing as the junior lifeguards in the past.

As junior lifeguards they didn't do much lifeguarding. From time to time, Shane would take one of them up on watch. Mostly he took Anthony's sister, Dani, who was fifteen and just starting to fill out her bikini. She got more lifeguarding instruction from Shane than anyone, though she wasn't an official junior lifeguard. She wouldn't take part in the main junior lifeguard duty—cleaning the beach.

It was their job to get up at seven every morning and sweep the beach for whatever garbage the tide had brought in the night before. They'd get old sneakers, plastic bags, strange cans, occasionally a T-shirt. They also found lots of nonjunk—pieces of coral, dead starfish, shells, and that amazing ocean phenomenon known as sea glass. They would find rounded, opaque glass in colors ranging from dark brown to green to lavender. Anthony always thought it miraculous that broken glass could be transformed into these gems that lined the shore of Allenhurst Beach each morning.

One day they woke up and found tar balls. It seemed another amazing ocean phenomenon, but not something they really wanted to keep. The balls were sticky and gross, though they looked hard, almost like marbles, when they washed up in the tide line. All through that week Anthony, Jay, Bradley, and Andy collected the balls with shovels.

They gathered hundreds of balls each day, while never knowing what they were or where they came from.

In July they woke one morning to find the beach covered with syringes. It made the news—hundreds of plastic little syringes without needles. Apparently, they'd been illegally dumped at sea. The syringes were reported from Sandy Hook all the way to Manasquan.

People were frightened of the syringes, which came in heavy for a week or so. Each day the junior lifeguards collected them by the bagful, all of which were turned over to the Environmental Police. For Anthony it became a kind of mission. From seven to eight each morning, he gathered them up as if his life depended on it. Despite the fear most people had, he knew the empty syringes were quite harmless. He always trusted the magic of the ocean to make things safe.

There was a night during the Syringe Tide, as they called it, when the four boys were all out playing Skee-Ball at the arcade on the Asbury Park boardwalk. To his own stupefaction and even mild discomfort, Anthony found that he couldn't miss. He barely tried, it seemed, yet almost every ball he rolled up the ramp jumped gently and arced right into the small bull's-eye, worth fifty points.

During one game he scored a rare, perfect four hundred. The machine spit out a very long strip of win tickets. He turned uneasily to Bradley, who was playing in the lane next to him.

"Hey, check this out," Anthony said. "A perfect game."

Bradley rolled his ball and got a thirty. He said, "No way," and turned to Anthony. He eyed the win tickets, which hung all the way to the floor. He said, "Hey Andy, check this out. Rubin just scored a perfect game."

Anthony glanced around for Jay. The last he'd looked, Jay was playing three lanes away.

He said, "Where's Jay?"

"Beats me," said Bradley. "Maybe the wizard boy went to do some math."

Andy said, "Jesus, check out all those tickets."

Anthony grabbed them and stuffed the tickets into his pocket. He turned to Bradley and said, "I'll be right back."

He started searching the arcade. He traversed three rows of Skee-Ball lanes and wove his way through all the rake-a-prize machines. He walked around the corner by the fun house, looked across the room toward the squirt-gun balloon clown game. He had the inexplicable sense that he'd find something, and he did.

He saw his father standing next to Claudia. She was leaning over the railing, her big butt staring Anthony in the face. His father's hand was resting on her back. She held a squirt-gun and was squirting at the mouth of a plastic clown. A red balloon was inflating out of the clown's head.

One balloon popped. It wasn't Claudia's. A little freckly-faced boy on the end had beaten her. Anthony sprinted out of the arcade before they turned.

He found Jay wandering by the railing. He ran up wildly and said, "I saw them."

Jay said, "Me too."

"It wasn't anything," said Anthony. "They're in there playing that stupid clown game."

Jay nodded. Anthony could not tell whether Jay was denying or confirming the assessment. Jay said, "Let's go down to the beach before they see us."

They weren't Asbury Park junior lifeguards, but it was bright from all the boardwalk lights and easy to find syringes. They gathered them out of habit, dropping them into an empty popcorn box they pulled out of a trash can. When they hit Allenhurst Beach they kept on walking. They passed their house and barely looked. They got as far as the next town, Deal, then something happened. As if some magical wind were blowing, the ocean sky grew clear and dark, and filled with stars.

"Holy shit," Jay said. "They're even brighter than that night your father did the Yiddish constellations."

"There's Sophie, the Kvetch," said Anthony, and pointed.

Jay said, "That's actually part of Cepheus, the King."

"How do you know that?" Anthony asked.

"I bought a star chart. I've been learning."

"You bought a star chart?"

Jay said, "Yeah. They have them on sale at the Shop Rite. My mother bought them for my brother and me. You should get one, or else you could steal Stuart's. He'd never notice."

It turned out Stuart, who was eight, had already lost his star chart. The next day Anthony bought a star chart of his own. For a few weeks he and Jay walked the beach at night and learned whatever summer constellations they could find. Sometimes they couldn't match a cluster to the chart, but Jay explained that there were many more stars than people would ever name. Jay said he'd read long ago in *Ranger Rick* that there were more stars in the universe than grains of sand on the whole earth. When Anthony thought of deserts, this seemed impossible. Most nights in Allenhurst they were lucky if five constellations were visible.

Late one sultry July night when Anthony got up to use the bathroom, he could see part of a constellation out the window. Framed by the windowpane, it looked just like a map. He moved closer, to see it all, and quickly realized it was Scorpio. As he picked out the constellation's brightest star, Antares, he noticed the sound of breathing from below.

When he looked down he saw his father and his mother. Out on the porch his dad was kissing her neck and unbuttoning her baggy flannel shirt. He kept on watching, thinking maybe he was dreaming. It almost didn't make sense that his parents would be kissing. Anthony kneeled and let his chin rest on the windowsill. There was a glow from the other porch lights, and an ocean wind that carried their breaths and sighs up to the window.

He saw his mother push his father's head back. He saw her slide the flannel shirt off of her shoulders and then draw his face into her bosom. Her assertiveness amazed him. He kept wondering if somehow it were Claudia in disguise. But she was too tall and too agile, too lithe and sprightly in her movements to be Claudia. He saw his father kissing her breasts while his mother laughed and caressed his head. They both seemed happy, or else they were both drunk.

The next morning, she seemed calmer than she had for all that summer. She didn't go out to the jetty. She read and listened to the radio on the porch. At noon she asked Anthony and Dani if they wanted to go for burgers at the Windmill, their favorite restaurant. They all piled into her blue Honda and drove to Long Branch.

It was Dani who finally asked the question. They were eating on the top deck of the converted windmill, the lowest blade of the wooden rotor angling off to the right of Dani's head.

She said, "So Mom, what's going on?"

Their mother looked up from her burger.

"What do you mean?" she asked.

"She means you've been kind of a nervous wreck all summer," Anthony said.

She put her burger down and said, "I had a scare. There was a chance that I had cancer of the cervix."

"And you found out it isn't anything?" Anthony asked her.

Their mother nodded. She said, "Last night."

"Everything's fine then?"

She said, "Everything is fine for the time being."

"You must have been so scared," said Anthony.

"It would have been okay to tell us," Dani said.

"I didn't think so," she said, and took a sip of her Diet Coke. "I always knew it wasn't cancer. Still I was trying to get ready, just in case."

✦ ✦ ✦

During the second week of August, the fecal coliform count got so high that all the beaches closed. Apparently, there was some sort of flesh-eating bacteria in the water. Shane Sullivan claimed that the bacteria came from raw sewage that had been dumped into the ocean. He also claimed that it caused human skin to molt and come off like a crab shell.

The beaches stayed closed for six days. Anthony, Jay, Bradley, and Andy midget-wrestled and became denizens of the Asbury Park arcade. One rainy afternoon the four boys stood around the prize counter.

They discussed prize options and what they planned to cash in all their win tickets for come Labor Day. Andy and Bradley both wanted the Muhammad Ali boxing gloves. Jay, who had barely any tickets, said he would probably go for the plastic back scratcher. After much deliberation, Anthony found that the only thing he liked besides the boxing gloves was a ceramic winged horse that was actually a coin bank. When he pointed the horse out, Jay said, "That's Pegasus, from mythology, just like the constellation." They had seen Pegasus several times while starwatching that summer. Somehow this incidental correlation settled things. Anthony nodded and said, "Yeah, that's what I'm going for."

That was also the week Bradley started them listening to Bruce Springsteen. He had just purchased a small boom box. He had four Bruce tapes and swore that his oldest sister had once sat right next to Bruce at a bar in Sea Bright. He started toting the boom box everywhere, playing all songs as loud as possible. One day while blasting the album *Born To Run*, Bradley suddenly stopped walking. He turned the volume down and looked at his friends dramatically. Then he said, "We are walking through Bruce's songs."

Jay and Anthony immediately got their parents to buy them *Born To Run* on cassette. They started listening to it religiously, and soon they knew every cryptic word of "Jungleland." Anthony found that *Born To Run* evoked a sadness, that certain songs were almost cinematic. Each time they listened to "Thunder Road," all of the lyrics would unfold again inside him. He'd always see a screen door slam. Then he would picture some wondrous girl named Mary, her dress waving as she danced across the floor of their house in Allenhurst.

Toward the end of that week of the closed beaches, they even had one Bruce-related miracle. They met two Teaneck girls, Denise and Jackie. The girls approached while Bradley was blasting "Rosalita" on his boom box. They started singing along and saying things like, "Totally awesome song!" Both went for Andy, of course, but he played soccer. Just a day after they met the girls, Andy left the shore in order to go to soccer camp in Maryland. This made things easier and soon they were all hanging out together on the boards.

Denise and Jackie were best friends. Jackie was fragile and quiet. She had short light brown hair and a gaze that always caused Anthony to wonder what she was thinking. Meanwhile Denise seemed the quintessential Jersey girl. She had thick black hair and plump breasts and would call out "Jinx!" whenever she and another person spoke the same word at the same time. Then she would punch the person's arm until the person named five movie stars or beer brands or whatever Denise asked for. Likewise Anthony always had to say "safety" if he burped, otherwise Denise would say "slugs" and then start punching. She had three brothers, which explained her sort of tomboy roughhouse nature. She even liked to midget-wrestle. Both she and Jackie got their own names, the Big Babe and Psycho Kitty.

There was an afternoon when Anthony wound up alone with Jackie on the boardwalk. He had a crush on her by then. Jackie was eating cotton candy. They were both leaning against a railing, talking and watching small children ride the Asbury Park carousel. He got his guts up and placed his hand on hers.

She didn't move her hand away, but also did not respond to his bold gesture. They continued chatting as Jackie ate her cotton candy, her captured hand still clasping the metal railing. Finally Jackie pulled her hand back. She held out the purple cotton candy and said, "Want some?" He took a bite.

She said, "You're Jewish, right?"

He nodded.

"Then why the heck is your name Anthony? I've never met a Jew named Anthony in my life."

"I had this cousin," he said. "Anthony Spignatelli. He was half Jewish, half Italian. He died two months before I was born. Until then my parents planned to name me Eric, or else Jill."

"How did he die?"

"It was a mystery."

"They have to know."

"They say they didn't."

He took her hand again. For a few seconds Jackie stared as if assessing the situation. Anthony smiled, clasped her hand tighter. "I barely know you," she said, and pulled her hand away.

Allenhurst Beach reopened on a Sunday in mid-August. By then Anthony, Jay, and Bradley were getting bored with being junior lifeguards. They'd make one garbage pass in the morning, then they would run off to find Denise and Jackie. The girls belonged to The Breakwater Club in Elberon. They had a freshwater pool and a snack bar, unlike Allenhurst. They had a shuffleboard court, and Anthony loved shuffleboard.

Because of Denise, they would always do laps in the swimming pool. Denise was big on self-improvement and was always pointing out the benefits of their various activities. Swimming laps helped both your muscle strength and cardiovascular capacity. She applied this logic to other things. For instance, midget-wrestling was good for learning how to defend yourself. Having to say "safety" after you burped taught you to think fast, or not burp. Playing shuffleboard honed your hand-eye coordination. Weaving through people while jogging on the boardwalk was good for quickness. Anthony found this way of thinking to be contagious, though Jay did not. Once while star-watching, Anthony said, "It's teaching us to *see* better." Jay said, "You think I really care how well I see?"

One afternoon they were all getting ice-cream cones and milkshakes. The nicest thing about The Breakwater was the charge account. Denise and Jackie charged everything to their parents. When Jackie's younger sister, Lizzy, got her cone, she took one lick and the ice cream fell. Anthony happened to be standing right beside her. Without thinking, he reached out with his left hand and caught the ice cream. Denise said, "Wow, you're like Mr. Lightningfast Reflex." He placed the scoop back on Lizzy's cone.

An hour later they went body-surfing in the ocean, having conveniently forgotten that one week before the water was filled with flesh-eating bacteria. Anthony tended to get cold fast. After five minutes he was shivering uncontrollably. He caught a wave and missed the crest, so he got crashed, as they always put it. The wave's force slammed him against the sand, twisted him here and there, and then pulled back. He rose and trudged out of the water. He could feel sand inside his bathing suit. So he walked over to the tidal pool by the jetty, and there he crouched in the shallow water to get the sand out.

He saw a blue-claw crab move past his feet and tried to catch it. He saw the starfish that always magically appeared in the tidal pools. He felt a tap on his left shoulder, turned around, and there was Jackie.

She said, "I followed you."

Anthony said, "I see that."

She stared in that sexy way that always made him want to know what she was thinking. So then he said it. He said, "Jackie, what are you thinking?"

She said, "Guess."

He said, "You want to look for crabs?"

Jackie said, "No."

She stepped into the tidal pool, sending a crab scuttling in Anthony's direction. It disappeared and then Jackie was beside him.

"I want to kiss you," she said. "That was so cool when you saved my sister's ice cream."

"You want to kiss me because I saved an ice cream?"

She never answered. They started kissing as they stood in the tidal pool. He'd never kissed anyone, though clearly Jackie had. Her touch was practiced, tender and delicate. She kept on pressing the tip of her tongue to his, then pulling back and saying, "You taste good."

They kissed in the tidal pool for about five minutes before Bradley, Jay, and Denise ambushed them. They didn't see their three friends until they were running at them through the shallow water. "Break it up!" Denise yelled. She jumped on Jackie. Soon they were all tag-team midget-wrestling. Jackie and Anthony teamed up and went for Denise. They pinned her down and made her name five Democratic presidents. That day they also invented a new move they called "the starfish."

To do the move required a tidal pool and abundant starfish. During a pin, the winner quickly grabbed a starfish and rammed it into the loser's face.

✦ ✦ ✦

Just before Labor Day weekend, Anthony's mother got arrested. It was a weekday. Anthony's father and Douglas Berkowitz were each at home that night in Livingston, which was an hour's drive from Allenhurst without traffic. Sometimes they stayed there on weekday nights instead of braving the Parkway after work.

Both Jess and Claudia got tanked at a bar called Tides, which was in Belmar. On the way home, Jess was pulled over in Asbury. She was arrested for drunk driving and locked up in an Asbury Park jail cell. All four children were there when Claudia returned in a kind of frenzy. She said the officers acted like rough jerks and had left her standing on the roadside. Clearly as plastered as Jess Rubin, she had walked back because she figured she'd get pulled over if she drove.

Michael arrived an hour later, after receiving his wife's phone call from the jailhouse. He explained the situation to his children. Then he and Claudia went out. Anthony didn't know what to feel. He kept on thinking that his mother was somehow part of a Bruce Springsteen song. She was behind bars in the Asbury Park jailhouse. She'd had a cancer scare and wouldn't laugh at Yiddish constellations. Maybe it wasn't as mythical as "Jungleland," but it still seemed too confusing to be reality. He also knew that his mother would freak out when she got home.

The children sat around the shore house all that evening. They watched *The Sound of Music* on TV. They played Monopoly, the beach way—using sea glass in place of the plastic houses and hotels. They had lost most of the parts long ago, one night in Livingston when Dani got mad and threw the whole game at her brother's head.

Three hours later, Anthony's father returned with Claudia. He said that bail would not be posted until the morning. Anthony asked if this meant his mom would spend the whole night in a jail cell. His father said, "Unfortunately, yes."

Claudia told them not to worry. Dani yelled, "Why! It's your fault that she's in there!"

"It's no one's fault," said their father, and made Dani apologize to Claudia.

Still there was something completely off about the way Claudia was acting. Anthony sensed that she was secretly quite thrilled with his mother's fate. He couldn't read his dad as easily, but he seemed calmer than he should have been. They left the room, sat in the kitchen, and drank vodka.

Later that evening, Anthony saw them leaving. He was out on the porch with Jay. They had their star charts. It was the first starry sky they'd had in weeks. He watched them skip down the stairs and onto the sand below him. Before he thought very hard, he called out, "Going to see the Yiddish constellations?"

His father stopped and looked up. He said, "Anthony?"

He said, "Hi. I'm out here watching stars with Jay."

"I'm taking a little walk with Claudia," said his father. "Just down the beach, to calm our nerves. Then we have to go get the other car."

He said, "Okay," and understood for the first time that they were guilty. He watched them go and turned to Jay.

He said, "Our parents are definitely screwing."

Jay said, "I know," and shined a flashlight on his star chart. He turned it off and then looked up at the sky. "It took you this long to figure it all out?"

"My mom's in jail," Anthony said. "It's like she's locked up while they do this."

Jay said, "She is locked up," and shined his flashlight on the chart again. He shut the light off and then pointed. "Right there's Pegasus," he said. "Do you still plan to get that bank?"

Anthony fell asleep that night before his father returned with Claudia. He tried to slough the whole thing off as a bad dream. At about six he heard a car pull up. He heard the front door opening and closing.

Soon he could hear his parents' voices. When he went down, they were sitting in the kitchen. His mother's elbows rested on the table and her forehead was pressed into her hands.

She looked up and said, "Honey?"

Anthony stepped into the kitchen and said, "Hi. Are you okay?"

"Fine," she said. "It was a very comfortable jail cell."

"We're talking," said his father.

He said, "I have to clean the beach."

He went upstairs to get dressed. He woke up Jay and they went out to do their Allenhurst junior lifeguard beach sweep. That morning Bradley didn't show up. For a few minutes they waited by the lifeguard chair. Then Jay suggested they get to it before a garbage tide floated in.

They found the usual plastic bags and beer cans. They stamped down seafoam in the places where it looked gross. They found a tennis ball in the tidal pool by the jetty. Anthony picked it up and noticed dozens of starfish lying placidly beneath the shallow water. He said, "Hey, look. They're making a constellation."

Jay said, "It's Miriam, the Kvetch."

"You mean Sophie."

He said, "Whatever."

Jay reached down into the water and grabbed a starfish.

"Don't even think it," Anthony said.

Jay said, "Think what?" and was all over him in a second.

They midget-wrestled. Jay kicked wildly. Anthony got hold of his arms and pinned him easily. He grabbed a starfish and pressed it to Jay's face.

Jay yelled, "Okay! I think I'm lying on twenty starfish! I might kill them!"

He pushed Jay's face under the water. For one strange instant he truly felt like drowning him. Somehow Jay managed to kick him in the groin.

Jay squirmed away, brought his head up, and screamed, "You psycho!"

"What's your problem?" said Anthony. "I just dunked you."

Jay coughed up water, looked up, and yelled, "You psycho! Someone should throw you in jail just like your mother!"

"I'll fucking kill you!" Anthony yelled, and lunged at him.

Jay rolled away in the shallow water. He grabbed his garbage bag, got up, and darted out of the tidal pool. He yelled, "You'll never fucking catch me, you psycho idiot!"

"I'm sorry!" Anthony yelled, suddenly realizing he was a psycho idiot.

Jay yelled, "I don't accept your apology!"

He turned and ran down the beach with the green garbage bag. With his free hand he gave Anthony the finger. He held it up over his shoulder while he ran.

Around nine, when Anthony got back, he learned his family would be leaving the Jersey Shore that afternoon. His father had already begun packing. He talked to Dani, who said Mom had a nervous breakdown while making pancakes. She was now sitting out on the jetty. Anthony went outside and found his father cleaning out the car.

He said, "It's Labor Day. We can't stay here three more days?"

His father turned and said, "You know how your mother gets."

"But I can't go," Anthony said. "I met . . . a girlfriend. I also haven't cashed in my Skee-Ball win tickets."

"You have the day," his father said. "We leave for Livingston at five."

Even though Jackie wasn't really his girlfriend, Anthony searched for her, maniacally. In the course of just that morning, he jogged up to The Breakwater Club three times. He felt a panic but reminded himself of how he was improving his heart and lungs. After the third time he ran home and called Bradley, who said that Jackie must have gone yachting with her family. He yelled, "Since when does she have a yacht!" Bradley said, "Hey, take it easy. I'm just joking."

He packed his suitcase and made a final trip up to The Breakwater. He left a note with one of the club's cabana boys. The note explained that he unexpectedly had to leave, but that he hoped they would talk soon. He gave his phone number and home address in Livingston. He signed his name and at the bottom wrote: *Please call!*

In his last hour at the Jersey Shore, Anthony went alone to the Asbury Park boardwalk. He'd counted out all of his win tickets and had tied them with rubber bands. Had he not tried to drown Jay that same morning, he knew Jay might have lent him the forty-seven tickets he still needed. But by then Jay had disappeared with his mom and brother. They'd gone to Long Branch to see a movie called *The Champ*.

At the arcade, he told the man he had four hundred fifty-three tickets. He asked for the winged-horse bank, which cost five hundred. The man suggested he take a frog bank, which cost less.

He said, "It's ugly. Can't you just give me the winged horse?"

The man said, "No."

"But I've been saving for it all summer."

"We're not a Burger King," the man said. "You can't always have it your way."

In the end, he wound up handing all his tickets to a long-haired boy who passed by on the boardwalk. He looked to be eight or nine and held a hockey stick, which was why Anthony had noticed him in the first place. He jogged right up to the boy and said, "Do you play Skee-Ball?"

The boy nodded.

"Then take these," Anthony said. "I don't have time to cash them in."

The boy said, "How come you don't just keep them for next summer?"

He said, "Just take them," and handed him the bag.

The boy said, "Thanks."

He said, "For forty-seven more tickets, you can get the winged-horse bank which is Pegasus, from mythology. He even has a constellation. You'd need a star chart."

The boy just nodded, then Anthony took off.

He could see Loch Arbor and then Allenhurst Beach ahead of him.

He smelled the tangy smell of ocean, which made him sad. He jogged with high steps, for no reason—the way he sometimes did with Jay when they were imitating football. Two girls made fun of him as he passed, but he didn't care that he looked ridiculous. He knew that running this way improved his balance. He also knew that he would never be coming back.

JOEYLAND

October 1979

CLAUDIA BERKOWITZ was feeling a bit wicked, so she looked Michael Rubin in the eye.

"Vodka?" she said.

Michael stood in the doorway to her kitchen. He had just come to pick up Anthony after making his evening rounds at the hospital. She hadn't seen him since late summer, when the Rubins had abruptly left the shore house.

"I told Jess I'd be back by nine," he said.

Claudia glanced at her watch. She said, "It's not even eight-thirty. You have time."

Michael seemed nervous, but he sat down. She took the vodka from the cabinet.

"So where is Douglas?" he asked.

"He's in Chicago until Monday."

She poured vodka for them both and lit a cigarette.

"It's so annoying with the whole world quitting smoking," Claudia said. "Lately I feel like the last smoker left on Earth."

He said, "It suits you."

She said, "Maybe."

She ran her hand along his arm.

She said, "I'm sorry again about the Asbury Park fiasco."

He said, "You're not sorry. I'd rather not discuss it."

"Okay, what's new then?" she said. "We haven't talked in five weeks."

He said, "Not much. I'm having trouble with my interns. They're all too slow."

She placed her cigarette in the ashtray.

"And how is Jess?" she asked.

"The same as ever."

She slipped her hand under the table. She rubbed his leg for a few seconds and thought of tall, aloof, and unpredictable Jess Rubin. They'd met eight years before at an awful barbecue, when Jess insulted one of Douglas's friends by pointing out that his tie was garish and ridiculous. Claudia stood beside Jess and had agreed that the tie was hideous. They were both twenty-eight-year-old parents with young children. She'd offered Jess, who still smoked back then, a cigarette. Later that evening they'd gotten stoned in the host's bathroom.

She said, "I'll check on the kids. Stay. I'll be right back."

Michael nodded. She brushed her hand through his hair and rose.

She went upstairs and found Stuart playing with his Action Jackson doll and his stuffed animals. He'd wedged a fox inside his Action Jackson jungle fortress. An armadillo was balanced on the roof.

"What's going on?" Claudia said.

Stuart said, "Foxy is talking to Action Jackson. Arny's just waiting for the Platzmans."

"Who are the Platzmans?"

Stuart said, "Action Jackson's friends."

"You silly boy," Claudia said.

She smiled and left him playing on the carpet. She went into her own bedroom, where Jay and Anthony were sprawled out on the bed and watching *The Six Million Dollar Man*.

She said, "Your father is here, Anthony."

Both boys were lying so their faces were ten inches from the television. She sometimes yelled at Jay for this. Anthony turned and said, "Could you tell him that we're halfway through the program?"

"Alright," Claudia said. "But please come down when the show is over."

Claudia stepped into her bathroom, rinsed off her face, and combed her hair. She slipped her diaphragm in mechanically. She thought of Jess Rubin being frisked by police and handcuffed. Jess started weeping the second they latched the handcuffs on her wrists.

I am a sadist, Claudia thought, as she left the bathroom. The thought of Jess being handcuffed was arousing, to say the least. Not to mention the sight of the leering cop sizing Jess up as he administered the Breathalyzer. He must have walked into the Asbury Park station and yelled, "Jackpot!" It wasn't every day he got to book a pouty, attractive, well-proportioned mommy from the suburbs.

"No other shows," she called out, and continued past the transfixed boys.

She went downstairs and found Michael. He'd crushed the cigarette out and had pushed the ceramic ashtray across the table. She stepped behind him and swiveled his chair around so that he faced her.

"What are you doing?" Michael asked.

She said, "I'm going to fuck you in my kitchen."

+ + +

That same night Claudia dreamed of Joey Malinowski, her high school sweetheart. It was a strong dream in its feeling, although abstract in its plot. She was young. Joey was built like a bear. She jumped into his arms. They were together in the past, yet her awareness in the dream had remained grounded in her present life in Livingston. She knew her husband and kids were near. She had not left them. She felt her life as it was now, and yet she knew that in some real way, she and Joey had never been apart.

She dreamed of Joey with regularity. When the dreams came just before she woke up in the morning, it sometimes took half the day to shake. She'd recall Christmases and Catholic school and all the other things she'd hated. She'd feel her blue-collar past as a crass Polish girl. She would feel Joey and think it wasn't all that bad.

This proved to be the case that Sunday. She found herself watching boxing and then bowling on TV. Inside her head, she saw the sycamores and maples that lined the streets of Elizabeth, New Jersey. She saw her mother in the driveway, carrying groceries—Polish foods like kielbasa and pierogi, which she despised.

That night she called up Michael before going out to the Shop Rite. She wasn't sure why she was calling. Maybe to break the spell of Joey or perhaps just to be destructive. She called at home, on the special phone line for his patients. When he picked up after three rings, she said, "It's me."

"Is something wrong?" Michael asked. "You shouldn't call me here."

"If Jess walks into the room, prescribe me Valium. I'm feeling pretty wound up anyway."

"Are things okay?" he asked again.

She said, "I need some eggs and milk."

"What do you want then?"

She said, "I want you to meet me at Shop Rite in ten minutes."

"It's almost nine."

She said, "Just go there. Tell Jess you're going out to get some milk."

"I bought milk yesterday," Michael said.

"Maybe you'll have to spill it down the drain."

When she arrived, Michael was waiting outside the Shop Rite. She was aware of the clothes that she was wearing. A brick-red turtleneck under a loose cardigan. Tight jeans with a braided belt. It occurred to her that all she had really needed was to be seen by him. Dreams of Joey had the peculiar effect of making her feel invisible. But Michael's gaze seemed to restore her. If nothing else, he made Claudia feel powerful and alive.

"What's going on?" he asked. "Do you need to talk about last night?"

"Talk about what?" she said. "Having extremely quiet sex on a vinyl kitchen chair?"

He said, "I thought that maybe something had happened. One of your kids found out."

She laughed.

"I just wanted you with me while I shopped," Claudia told him. "I need some things and I'd like you to be my helper. Grab a cart."

He found a cart outside the door and followed Claudia with obvious discomfiture. "Kiss me," she said, as Michael turned into the produce aisle. She rubbed up against his side and said, "Or else I might explode."

He kissed her cheek and said, "We're in a supermarket."

"But you're still thinking about ripping all my clothes off, right?"

He said, "I'm always thinking about ripping off your clothes."

She said, "So what do you do at home? Do you think of me when you're touching Jess?"

"I never touch Jess now," he said. "Even before things got this bad, she mostly hated to be touched."

"And why is that?" Claudia asked. "Sounds like some pervert might have nailed her as an eight-year-old."

He said, "I think it's a lot simpler."

"How is it simple?"

"For a long time Jess hasn't liked me, or her life."

Claudia placed a bag of apples in the cart.

She said, "Delicious."

Michael said nothing.

"It's a joke," she said. "They're called Delicious apples."

"Where are we going after this?"

"Maybe we'll drive to Northland Park."

"Anthony knows," he said.

"How?"

"I can just tell that he knows what's going on."

"Well," Claudia said. "It's not as if he won't need years of therapy already."

"We have to be more careful."

"About what?"

Michael said, "Everything. We need to watch the things we do."

"Don't delude yourself. We're reckless."

She grabbed a butternut squash and placed it in the cart.

"Please," Michael said.

"What?"

"Can you agree to be more careful?"

"Why?" Claudia said. "You just told me that the cat's out of the bag. You should enjoy this while it lasts, because it's probably going to end soon."

"And just how soon?" Michael asked.

"I guess we'll see."

✦ ✦ ✦

When she woke up again the next morning, Joey was there, all around her for a moment. They'd been together in that place she knew existed, though she never could fathom how she arrived or left.

Inside her head she always thought of it as Joeyland. It was a place she could escape from, though it never went away. She didn't feel it every moment, but it was chronic, and it kept growing. The more the years went by, the wider and more expansive this place became.

That afternoon she was in her car, a new Mercedes. Claudia smiled to herself when she realized that the passenger seat was still adjusted back as far as it could go. She moved it forward again with the automatic seat control. She looked around for other evidence of Michael. She was driving to Newark Airport to get her husband, but she was early. His plane from Chicago was not landing until four.

She drove along Route 24 past Millburn. She passed the Parkway and soon came upon the exit for Elizabeth. She had an hour to kill, so she pulled off. Soon she was cruising her old streets. Now it was mostly black and Latino. When she was growing up it was all Polish Catholics and Jews. She passed the three-story house she'd lived in. She saw a cat sitting out on the front steps. She made a pass by the apartment Joey had rented with his brother. When she was waitressing in Newark, she'd slept there more than she slept at home.

He had a poster of a boxer above his bed, and it was gross. The boxer's face and hair were coated with rheumy slime and sweat and blood. His mouth was open and she could see a plastic mouthguard, which for some reason was the grossest thing of all. One Sunday morning, before church, Joey had played some loud song about a boxer on his stereo. He'd put his boxing gloves on and danced around the room. After a while he faced the poster. He started acting like he was boxing with the boxer. She sat and watched him, cheered him on, yelled things like "Knock his goddamn head off!" And for the one time in her life that she could remember, Claudia knew that she was wildly in love.

One afternoon when they were lying around naked in his bedroom, Joey picked her up and carried her to the kitchen. He put her down on the kitchen counter and then fed her purple grapes. He placed each grape in her mouth with colossal tenderness. He slid his fingers around her lips while she was chewing, sometimes pressing them just hard enough to hurt. She spit the pits into his hand. Joey kept saying she looked sexy when she spit. He fed her grape after grape, and she felt safe there, in Joeyland. She felt as if this was a place that she belonged to.

They'd been engaged for three months when she met Douglas at the restaurant. He'd started coming in to eat alone and always asked for her. One night he left her a folded note with his standard 50-percent tip. Claudia stashed the note in her tip jar. Four hours later, when the restaurant closed, she read it. The note said: *You, Claudia Nowicki, are the most beautiful woman I will ever lay my eyes on. I can't stop thinking of you at home or at work. I love you. Will you marry me?* Inside the note, Douglas had left his business card.

She knew with Joey she'd have six kids and always drive a big blue station wagon. She'd drink canned beer and spend Sundays watching football. Joey would own her and love her and beat her up if she deserved it. By fifty-five there would be so many grandkids she'd have trouble remembering their names.

The next night at the restaurant, she saw Douglas. She didn't mention the note. She tried to act as if she'd never seen it. He asked her questions about the specials. He said he'd had a very long day at his office. Later when Douglas was paying for his dinner, Claudia watched him open up his wallet. She never saw what he had inside but made her choice right at that instant. She cleared his table and thought: Fine. Now I am going to be rich.

On her own twenty-second birthday, she told Joey it was over. He kept on screaming things like, "Baby, it makes no sense!" By his reaction, she knew she might as well have shot him. She knew he probably wasn't smart enough to ever fully recover.

As she was leaving his apartment he yelled, "You're crazy!" She didn't turn. "We're like two angels who are made of the same air!" Joey screamed. This was the most beautiful sentence she'd ever heard from a human mouth. "We're like two angels!" he screamed again, or almost shrieked it, as she walked out. She didn't know where he'd found those words. He was a young, dumb boy who liked to box. She lay in bed that night, weeping, hearing his words over and over. But the next morning she felt resolved. She picked the phone up and called Douglas at his office.

Claudia drove around for longer than she meant to. She found it strange to know these streets so well, yet feel like she was lost. Most of the stores were gone. The people were gone. There wasn't anyone around who'd ever heard of Joey Malinowski.

She could see spots where they'd walked and kissed. She noticed places where they'd had fights. Once they had stood right out on Center Street, screaming insanely for half an hour. She was concerned that Joey had a thing for her blond-haired cousin, Lucy Kowalczyk. "Tell me you don't want to fuck that little bitch!" she kept on screaming. Finally Joey literally tackled her and carried her back home.

Just before Claudia headed back to the highway, she happened upon a spot where they'd once put maple fruits on their noses. Claudia recognized the giant maple. She stopped the car and killed the engine. She saw brown bunches of its winged fruits hanging off the naked branches. The tiny fruits also littered the cracked sidewalk. When she stepped out, she had the sense that she could be anywhere.

They're called samaras, she remembered. She'd learned this word from her own children. So she and Joey had put samaras on their noses. They had walked with their samaras, until the fruits slipped off and helicoptered down to whatever landing spots they found.

She crouched and saw that many wrinkly, brown samaras lined the sidewalk groove. She picked one up and tried to put it on her nose. It was too dry, of course. Claudia found that she couldn't even peel it open. A car rushed past and she felt self-conscious. She let the samara fall to the cement. Then she felt dizzy and strange, yet oddly lucid in her thoughts. She tried to promise herself that, somehow, she had not wasted her life.

IN AND OUT
OF MOONLIGHT

May 1980

DANI WAS PACKING in her room. In the morning she would be leaving for a summer in Barcelona. Anthony stood beside the sliding door, stared out through the glass, and dreaded Dani's absence. Lately their mother had gone into a withdrawn phase, and sometimes Dani was the only one who knew how to deal with her strange moods.

One afternoon the month before, he had come home and found her crying in the kitchen. "Tell me a joke," she had said. He wound up telling her the interrupting cow joke. She smiled and thanked him, though she didn't seem to laugh. Dani walked in, took one look at her, and said, "We have to get out of the house." That was a Friday, and Dani had convinced her to take them bowling. They bowled three games and by the time they were done, her mood seemed calm and less distracted. While they were driving back a song she used to love came on the radio. It was called "Groovin'," by a group called the Young Rascals, from the sixties. She sang along and each time the song came back to the word "Groovin'," she held her hand out like a microphone for Anthony and Dani to join in.

Now his mother was upstairs reading her bulky textbook for psychology. It was past six and his father was still working at the hospital.

Dani was nervous, Anthony knew. He assumed it was because she hated flying. Outside a full moon was rising in the daylight. The sky was blue and the moon seemed to be balanced on the top of a nearby house.

He called, "Hey Mom?"

She called back, "What?"

He said, "Come down and see the moon."

"What?" she said. He heard her rising. She came halfway down the stairs, holding her textbook. She had her hair up in a clip, but was still wearing the kick-pleat skirt and Oxford shirt she'd worn to class that afternoon.

He said, "I thought you'd like to see the moon."

She walked down into the den, where he was standing.

She said, "Your sister wants to go out to the Claremont Diner for dinner. She wants to see that weird glass in the new atrium."

"What weird glass?" Anthony said.

She said, "It's green. And now they're suing. Because the glass makes people's faces look disgusting."

"Did Dad get home?" Anthony asked.

She shook her head. She put her textbook down on a speaker and mussed his hair up. As happened sometimes, he was surprised by her affection. She had a way of doing that—suddenly zooming in with a powerful, gentle warmth.

"Will he be home soon?" he asked.

She said, "I doubt it. We'll go without him."

"So look at the moon."

She looked.

He said, "It's sitting right on top of the Kaufmans' roof."

"*Hal'vanah kehpanim halohatot b'togah,*" she said.

"What's that?"

His mother laughed and said, "It's Hebrew. Something your aunt Leah made up. In yeshiva, when we couldn't speak in English, she used to make up all this poetry in Hebrew. I always think of that one line when a full moon's out."

"What does it mean?" Anthony asked.

She said, "The moon is like a face that glows with sadness."

✦ ✦ ✦

To Anthony's amazement, the Claremont Diner atrium's new green windows really did give everyone the complexion of a ghoul. Besides the pallor, all blemishes and pimples were accentuated. He could see wrinkles he never knew his mother had. Dani was thrilled by the green glass and kept calling it "the world's most colossal fuck-up." Meanwhile Anthony was more entranced by the full moon, which he could see through the green windows as they waited. He started thinking of lines of poetry himself, though not in Hebrew. One was *The moon is like an eye over the Claremont.* He didn't say it but kept chuckling when he thought it.

They were seated at a table near a window looking out over Bloomfield Avenue. A busboy brought them out a pickle plate, along with the diner's trademark Claremont salad. A tangy variant of coleslaw, it consisted of cabbage, carrots, cucumbers, onions, and red vinegar. Anthony hated it and always wondered why the Claremont salad was so famous. People would say things like, "The genius is the onions." His mother sometimes bought containers of Claremont salad to bring home.

"No, thank you," he said, as Dani passed the Claremont salad. Instead he took a pickle from the pickle plate. He placed it down with the plastic tongs and felt his mother like wild nettles inside his gut. Years ago, they'd had a fight at the kitchen table. He'd started crying because he wasn't hungry. She had dumped half a container of Claremont salad on his head. Sometimes she blew like that—just lost it. There was no way of predicting when she would blow. Last time it happened was in Allenhurst, the morning after she'd been arrested. He'd been out cleaning the beach and hadn't seen it, but Dani told him she'd gone berserk.

Dani and Anthony ordered hamburgers and milkshakes. Their mother ordered a club sandwich. Then she smiled to herself, or else the menu, and said, "I'll also have one of your egg creams."

"What's an egg cream?" Anthony asked, when the waitress left them.
She said, "It's basically chocolate soda."

"Is there an egg in it?"

She said, "No."

"Abbey Roth's father sometimes makes them at their house," Dani
said.

"I've always liked them," said their mother. "We used to get them
after games when I was a cheerleader."

It was a strange thought, always, to imagine his mother as a cheerleader. She didn't seem like the type who'd have school spirit. She barely
ever talked about her high school years. But Anthony had seen dozens
of pictures. She had filled up several albums that sat out in the hallway
bookshelf. One was all sports clippings and team photos and black-and-
whites of every cheerleader. He had seen shots of his mother waving
pom-poms, mouth wide open as she yelled some defiant cheer. Shots of
her doing kicks in midair, her long legs taut and toned with muscle.
There were shots of his mother twirling, one funny shot of two boys
crawling under her skirt. He assumed that Grandpa Ira and Grandma
Hannah, who were both dead now, had never laid eyes on those pictures.

He had once asked his father about Mom's cheerleading. His father
told him something frightening—that when Mom became a cheerleader, her parents threatened to rip their clothes, cover their mirrors,
and act like she was dead. Why rip their clothes and cover mirrors? His
father said these were the Orthodox rules for mourning a family mem-
ber who had died. Anthony knew his grandparents did funny religious
things, such as using Kleenex in the bathroom on the Sabbath, so they
wouldn't have to tear the toilet paper from the roll. On the Sabbath
they also wouldn't answer phones. They had their lights set up with
electric timers and they would yell if you ever flipped the light switch.
All that was *melachah*, Grandpa Ira had explained to him. On the Sabbath you refrained from any form of work that fell within the thirty-nine
categories of *melachah*. You couldn't comb your hair or bite your nails
because these fell into the category "shearing." You couldn't kill any
insects found on vegetables. Killing a nonthreatening animal would fall

into the *melachah* category "slaughter." All this made sense in some peculiar way to Anthony, although it seemed like more work than actually
working. If nothing else, it was fun, like a big puzzle to remember
while at Friday night dinner at your grandparents'. Still it seemed crazy
to think that they would mourn their living daughter's death for cheerleading. He told his father he didn't ever want to go there if they'd done
that. His father promised, at least three times, that they had not.

When the drinks came she slipped her straw into the egg cream.
Anthony watched his mother's face as she stared into the drink and
stirred it. The egg cream's presence seemed to make her calm.

"So how's your class going?" Dani asked her.

She said, "It's fine," and looked up from the egg cream. "Right now
we're reading about IQ tests. Isn't that stupid? But this is introductory
psych. When this is done I can take the higher-level courses."

Dani said, "How long until you're a psychologist?"

Their mother laughed and said, "A long time. I should have started
this years ago."

Anthony watched her sip her egg cream. He wondered whether
she'd also ordered them on dates with his father in the sixties. Then
for no reason he could think of, he said, "I would have thought Dad
would be here." He felt alarmed the instant the words slipped out of his
mouth.

"It's okay," Dani said. "He said he's driving me to the airport in the
morning."

"He's off with Claudia," said their mother.

Anthony felt his insides doing somersaults. Dani stared at their
mother, wide-eyed, and said, "You know about... *that*?"

"Come on," their mother said. "I'd have to be blind not to."

"But then how can you..."

"What? Stay with him?"

Dani nodded.

"It's not much different than it's always been."

Dani said, "*How* is it not different?"

"I wish I never brought this up."

"But you just did," Dani said.

"Well then don't worry. I'm okay with it. I know it won't go on forever. And if I'm not okay I'll let him know."

Dani said, "How can you be okay with it? And, I mean, how long have you known?"

"Listen," she said. "I've always understood that my marriage to your father was a mistake. I knew it a few weeks after our wedding. I guess I could have stopped everything right then. But I still loved him and I didn't have the strength to break his heart. Soon you two came along, and here we are. I don't have the energy to change things. At least not now I don't. I'm just too tired."

+ + +

"Dumbhead, get up," Dani said.

Anthony opened his eyes and picked his head up. He'd gone to sleep on his top bunk. Dani was standing halfway up the bunk-bed ladder. As he rolled back, she climbed the rest of the way and sat with her legs hanging over the bed.

Anthony looked down at his clock radio. He'd tipped it up onto its back so he could see it.

"It's two A.M.," he said.

She said, "Thank God I have a seven-hour flight."

"Have you been packing?"

She said, "I'm packed. I've been just staring at the walls."

"You shouldn't worry..."

Dani said, "Quiet," and touched his leg. She rarely spoke this way—seriously—to Anthony. Yet lately Dani had started to seem more serious about everything. She'd started writing her real name, Danielle, on schoolwork. She'd studied for the chemistry achievement test like a madwoman. She took her sophomore-year finals early, so she could head off to Spain in May. And since the winter she'd been dating Bobby Tannenbaum, who was president of her class.

She said, "In Spanish this year we read a book called *El Camino*. It means 'The Path.'"

He said, "So?"

"So, I'm telling you—if you'd listen," she said. "The whole thing takes place the night before the character is going away to school in some big city. He has to go in order not to be stuck being a cheese-maker like his father. He reviews his whole life while having bad insomnia. His past seems better than the road that lies ahead, and he feels miserable."

Again Anthony said, "So?"

"So, I'm the opposite," Dani said. "I've been up feeling the opposite of *El Camino*, but it's still scary, like I'm still doomed."

He felt too tired to make the leap of logic she required.

He said, "You want to be a cheesemaker?"

His sister laughed and punched his leg. She said, "Thank God I always have you to be a dunce brain."

Anthony sat all the way up. He saw that Dani was fully dressed and wearing shoes.

He said, "What's wrong? You look afraid."

She said, "I am. That's what I told you fifteen seconds ago."

"And you're afraid of your own path?"

She shook her head and stared across the bedroom. Light from the full moon was falling on the wall above his dresser. She touched his leg again and said, "Let's go ride bikes."

"It's two A.M."

She said, "Indulge me. You won't be seeing me for three months."

"You should try sleeping."

She shook his leg again.

"Come on," Dani said. "You're getting up."

It was two-thirty by the time they got their ten-speeds out the back door of the garage, across the backyard, over the fence, and back around to the street. Both of their parents were light sleepers, so they moved with the stealth of cat burglars. They walked their bikes past a few houses and jumped on.

They glided down Cherry Hill Road and turned on Tanglewood. They followed Tanglewood to Fellswood and then Fernwood, turning on streets that now seemed strangely far away. They flew down Crestview Hill and Longacre, back up Ashwood, out to Melrose. They kept on riding, wherever the roads led them. Anthony pedaled very hard to stay with Dani. She had long legs and a swimmer's explosive power, since she was one. She was five-feet ten-inches tall, just like their mother, and at five-nine Anthony felt like a shrimp beside her.

The moon was bright and they rode in and out of moonshadows. Some of the shingled roofs seemed silver. The dark windows seemed like quiet, knowing eyes. When they came out onto East McClellan, they saw the Kelbys' house. Anthony pictured Craig and Jamie Kelby sleeping. They were both normal and would never be up this late.

When they hit Livingston Avenue, Dani turned left in a wide arc. He wasn't sure where she was leading him, if anywhere. There were no cars on the street and Dani rode on the center line. They passed by Harrison Elementary, where they had both endured their first six years of school.

Dani turned right onto Congressional Parkway, a residential street that led to Northland Park. She pedaled hard around the turn and kept on pedaling down the hill. This was the older, post-World War II section of town. Houses were smaller and much uglier. The trees were tall, the shadows darker.

He pedaled hard around the turn like Dani, but then he coasted down the final portion of the hill. He looked around and could see flashes of things he knew he would not remember—beneath his tires the trellised shadows of crisscrossing branches; the moon-bleached road that looked as if it were made of light. He felt the wind and the moon and a sense of freefall that reminded him of the Kiwanis Carnival Ferris wheel. He assumed they'd break into Northland Pool, but she didn't turn there. She kept on riding to where Congressional dead-ended at the ballfields.

Dani turned onto a walkway. There was a sign that said No Bikes, but they ignored it at three-thirty in the morning. They weaved around the benches that had been placed along the center of the walkway. Then Dani stopped beside the biggest field, the Treat Field, and leaned her bike against the chain-link fence.

He followed Dani onto the field. Both of his legs felt taut and tingly from the riding. He had the urge to slide headfirst into second base, and so he did.

When he got up from his slide, Dani yelled, "What the hell are you doing?"

"Stealing a base!" he called back, although there were no actual bases except home plate. Dani stood staring for a moment, hands on hips, but didn't answer. She turned around and walked into the dugout.

He jogged to third and then home, then went into the dugout. He found her sitting on the bench in a spot of moonlight so bright she could have read a book there.

But she was crying. She sat frozen, both hands pressed to the bench, with silent tears dripping down her cheeks. He stepped over to where Dani was sitting. He felt clumsy because he couldn't really hug her. At sixteen Dani was not the type of sister you could hug. He touched the small of her back and told her, "Hey, it's okay."

She laughed morosely through her tears and wiped her face with her shirtsleeve.

She said, "It's not okay, you dunce brain." She opened her mouth to say more, but then closed it. She shook her head and said, "I'm sure we'll both be fine though."

He said, "At least you'll be in Spain tomorrow."

She said, "I'll be in Spain today."

"You know, you're missing Jay's bar mitzvah."

She said, "It hadn't really entered into my plans."

"Jay said it's going to be an undersea theme. That should be neat. The rest will probably be miserable."

"Jay's a weird kid," Dani said. "Pretty soon you won't be friends."

"Why wouldn't we?"

Dani shrugged, then wiped her eyes again. She said, "In three months I doubt you'll have to ask that. And if things start going crazy, you can call me in Barcelona. I'll leave the number. Of course, I'd rather not even hear it. I'd rather find out about it when I get home."

He said, "Like what things would go crazy?"

Dani said, "Obvious things."

"Like what?"

"For all I know I'll get back and find Dad living with his favorite Polish shiksa."

"She converted."

"Don't be an idiot."

"Mom said she's fine with it. You heard her."

"She's not fine with it," said Dani, and looked away, toward the moon.

Anthony looked at the moon as well. He thought: *The moon is like a face that glows with sadness.*

He said, "You know what?"

"What?"

But he did not recite their aunt Leah's poetry. Instead his brain suddenly filled with premonition. For the first time in his life, Anthony conceived of his parents' marriage ending. And though he tried to shake the idea from his thoughts he found it stayed there, bare and obvious, as if this were something he'd known forever.

THE GIFT
OF ANTICIPATION

July 1980

LOOK! BACK THERE on Livingston, New Jersey. Michael Rubin is on his way to the Village Bakery. He feels the privilege of the morning, warm, July; he is thirty-nine. He's walking down Mount Pleasant Avenue, passing the car wash, Eppes Essen restaurant, Firestone Tires. He stops briefly by the window of the music store, Frank Richard's. He surveys the instruments in the window. He starts to think of his own clarinet, which sits in the hall closet. He hasn't touched it for ten years. More.

We make decisions, Michael thinks. He knows his father, the idealist, still faults his lack of courage. "What about Juilliard?" Max asked when Michael told him he'd won a scholarship to Hahnemann Medical School, in Philadelphia. "What about music and joy and beauty and all those things?" Michael was married. He told his father he was planning to have children. Soon he would have to support a family. "Support a family?" Max had yelled. "You plan on joining some fancy country club? Driving some fancy expensive car? You don't need much in this world, Michael. You have a wife who doesn't care if you make money. I saw you dancing around like a meshuganah at your wedding. You want to support your beautiful wife, then go on and play your clarinet."

It was true. He had played clarinet at his wedding. During the hora he pranced around like the pied piper. Even Jess's frigidly cold parents had followed after him in the line. Later he'd serenaded their table with several *Fiddler on the Roof* songs. The allusion seemed appropriate, given the scene in which the second daughter, having agreed to marry a non-Orthodox Jew, seeks her father's blessing. Of course, he gives it. There's a large difference—demonstrated later in the movie—between betrothal to a secular Jew and a non-Jew. So far as Ira and Hannah Adelman were concerned, Michael was not the ideal son-in-law. But they had not disowned their daughter. They had just grumbled a lot and prayed for her.

Near the end of the wedding party, he played "Moon River" for Jess. She cried and laughed while she was crying. After he finished she wrapped her arms around him. "Get me out of here," she whispered. She was undressing him in the limo before they'd pulled away from the small crowd that had assembled outside the catering hall. "Just drive around," she told the driver, who was taking them three miles to a Holiday Inn in Springfield. She was staring into Michael's eyes as she said this. She was undoing his belt, his pants. Just drive around.

Michael crosses Trocha Avenue. Of all preposterous things, the Eppes Essen deli was out of bagels. He had intended to get a dozen bagels, along with lox and the chive cream cheese that Jess likes. Someone had cleaned out Eppes Essen and nothing else would be delivered until Monday. So he decided to walk down to the bakery, to buy doughnuts as a substitute for bagels.

He passes Norman Florist and the movie theater. He feels alert and strangely energized despite waking at five that morning to take Anthony to his hockey game. This was the price for deciding on no shore house. Anthony playing summer-league hockey. At least the games were all at South Mountain Arena, in West Orange. His fall-winter traveling team, the Essex County Chiefs, played everywhere. On any given Saturday morning, he could be down in Ocean County or halfway across Long Island. Yet it was Michael's idea to get him playing hockey in the first place. What a decision. Who knew what hockey parenting would be like? Actually Jess knew and she warned him. Jess always had the gift of anticipation. She told him, "Fine, let him play hockey. Wake up at five on your days off, but just don't ask me to do the driving."

Still Jess would wake up as she had that Sunday morning. It always meant a lot to Anthony. She'd come downstairs and perform one of her hockey spells in the kitchen. She would have Anthony stand with his eyes closed. She would pick out a few spices from the spice rack and then throw them on his head. That morning she had given him star anise. She said to keep it in his hockey bag while he played. "What's it for?" Anthony asked. She told him, "Face-offs." She used to make up spells for Michael. Silly, beautiful little spells. For his medical school comps, she'd sent him off with crushed hibiscus in his pockets. "What's it for?" he had asked, the same as Anthony. It brings a hobgoblin to whisper all the answers in your ear.

Oh, Jess. The unapproachable Jess Adelman. When he first met her she was holding a canoe paddle. They were both counselors for a Metro West Jewish Community Center trip on the Delaware. She had glanced over while he was gaping, her eyes expressive. Michael stepped toward her. He waved and smiled.

She said, "You swagger."

"My name is Michael."

She said, "What is it you want?"

"Just to say hi."

"Okay, then say it."

"Hi."

"I'm Jess."

He said, "I know."

Michael was one of the main trip organizers. He was nineteen and going into his sophomore year at Rutgers. Jess was just seventeen and supposedly from an Orthodox Jewish family. She didn't seem very Orthodox to Michael. After they talked, Michael pulled aside one of the other counselors from her town.

Orthodox parents, yes. At least they claimed to be. But she herself?

Not even close. Jessica Adelman was a cheerleader. She smoked cigarettes at the diner after games. Was she a prude? I'm afraid not. She'd
once gone down on some star of the basketball team, even though that
guy was dating her best friend. Her older sister was like that too, but a
lot smarter. She kept a lid on things. She always did what her parents
wanted. Now Leah Adelman had married some real *macher* from a very
wealthy family. He worked on Wall Street. They kept kosher. She was
pregnant at nineteen. Her younger sister? Forget that. She might as well
have been a goy for all her Orthodox Jewish upbringing. Michael took
in this information and mulled it over. Then he made sure to arrange
that he and Jess would be in the same canoe.

He quickly learned that Jess was different from most people. She
had strange gifts, confusing problems. Her behavior was almost always
paradoxical. If Jess did wild things, she did them very quietly. When
she felt happy, it almost always made her afraid. Even before they married, Michael had known he was choosing someone difficult. But he
was also choosing someone extraordinary. That had always been his
dilemma—which way to go. Should he protect himself or go for what
seemed magical and dangerous? In many ways he had protected himself. Even at nineteen he was planning to be a doctor.

Jess! He has just left her at home with Anthony. Although she's
never really bothered to figure out the rules of hockey, she always talks
at length with Anthony about games when he returns. She knows a
handful of hockey phrases. That morning she asked Anthony if the
goalie had made any miraculous kick saves. Anthony told his mother
no, but he'd won almost every face-off. He also had two goals and one
assist. Anthony poured a glass of milk and chugged it. He was trying to
gain weight. He hoped to play first-line varsity for Livingston as a ninth-
grader. He chugged a second glass of milk. Jess asked him how many
times his line had done a power play. He told her, "Mom, you don't *do*
a power play, you *have* one." Anthony took an almost visible delight in
these conversations. Unlike his analytical hockey talks with Michael,
these conversations clearly had nothing to do with words.

Michael turns the corner by the Shop Rite. He sees the Lions Club park, a backyard-garden-sized plot with a small monument. Once he and Dani had been clowning around after shopping. Dani said, "Hey, let's go to Lions Park." They crossed the lot and stood next to the monument. "What a great park!" Dani said. "This is so fun!" Unlike her brother, her sense of humor was always cynical. She was a realist, just like Michael. Meanwhile Anthony and Jess were the family poets. They were both sensitive and more vulnerable. They both guarded their sense of wonder about the world. They were also the family jocks. Though she had no interest in team sports, Jess herself was a gifted athlete. She was a natural at most water sports. She could ski slalom and hold onto the tow bar with one hand. As a high school cheerleader, she had moves that bowled him over. Her legs and hips were so powerful it unnerved him. The way she kicked and twirled and twisted had an ease to it, a sublime dignity and confidence, the source of which Michael could never figure out.

He passes by Silverman's Stationery, where Dani was once caught shoplifting. She'd stolen bubblegum and a Barbie doll from Silverman's. She'd gotten caught with her friend Jane Rosenberg. They were both twelve. The owner, Silverman, called up Michael and said that next time he'd press charges. He lectured Dani that night, sternly. She cried and Michael wound up holding her in his arms. She said she didn't even like Barbie dolls, which was true. When she had dolls as a little girl, she mostly broke off their limbs and buried them in the yard. "I'm not a *criminal*," Dani kept saying. Michael assured her that she wasn't. Still he was not sure that Dani wouldn't steal again. All he was sure of was that Dani usually wasn't the type of person to get caught.

Just as he reaches the Village Bakery, a car pulls up in the space beside him and honks so loudly that he jumps. When Michael turns he sees Claudia's tornado-gray Mercedes. That's what she told him the color was. It looks more brown, kind of metallic. She has the sunroof open, a tank top on, dark glasses, a just-lit cigarette in the hand that holds the wheel.

She rolls her window down.

"Hey, handsome."

He walks up to the window. He quickly runs things through his mind. Jess in the kitchen, talking with Anthony. Dani in Spain until late August. A plausible full hour to buy doughnuts, given the bagel impasse. Ten twenty-five A.M. on a Sunday. Claudia looking like the Wicked Witch of the West.

"What are you doing here?" he asks.

"I saw you walking. I thought Anthony had a hockey game."

"We just got back," Michael says.

"So fancy this. An unpremeditated meeting."

"I'm buying doughnuts," he says.

"You feel like taking a short ride?"

He looks at Claudia and feels queasy. At home his wife of seventeen years is in the kitchen with his son. His wife who now hates to be kissed. The times they've made love in five years Michael can count out on his fingers. His wife who sometimes wakes at night, sits up abruptly, and starts yelling out words in Hebrew. Who he will hold against his body as she trembles and calms down. Who he can hold only then, while Jess cries softly and says, "I dreamed I was in Hell again."

What kind of hell? She never answers. She kisses Michael and says, "I'm sorry I'm so wrong for you." He says, "You're not wrong." She will laugh and ask him, "How did this disaster become our lives?"

He'll say, "I love you," and Jess will laugh again. "Oh Michael, you just don't see things." She'll kiss him gently on the cheek and he will ache to press his face into her bosom. She'll lie back down, curl up tight, and pull the covers all the way over her head.

"Wait here while I go in," Michael tells Claudia.

She says, "Hurry. I was just going to the car wash. Everyone's home."

"Your car looks clean," he says.

"I went. That's where I saw you. You were going into the Eppes Essen deli."

"They had no bagels," he says.

"Scandalous."

She takes a drag of her cigarette.

"I'll be back out in just a minute," Michael says. "Will you be waiting?"

She says, "We'll see."

He goes inside, stands in the line. He thinks of Claudia's soft ass. He imagines fucking her again in her tornado-gray Mercedes. He thinks how Jess and he, in their twenties, once had sex while going through a car wash. How it was silly and it was magical and afterward he felt happy. How with Claudia he feels angry, almost belligerent, and weak.

The Village Bakery line is long, but now he will absolutely need to bring home doughnuts. And what a sham, Michael thinks. It's not as if Jess doesn't know what's going on. She's never said it out loud, but Jess knows everything. He is sure of this. Jess's sense of intuition tends to verge on ESP.

There was the time at the animal shelter in East Hanover. She had warned Michael not to take the basset hound that Anthony and Dani fell in love with. They overruled her. Two days later, the shelter called. They said the dog's former owner had been in Florida, on vacation with his family. The man's cantankerous father had been house-sitting. He'd brought the dog to the pound because it barked too loud when cars passed. Now the wife and kids were in hysterics. The man was terribly sorry and offered to pay any amount of money necessary to get their basset Abigail returned.

What had Jess known? She never said. They let her pick out another dog. She chose a quiet, depressed-looking four-year-old pit bull. Michael was wary because he knew pit bulls were unpredictable, particularly strays who wound up in a pound. Dani and Anthony had their eye on a Dalmatian puppy, Barney. Jess took one look at the Dalmatian and said, "This dog is trouble. We should take Nellifer, the pit bull. She'll be wonderful." They acquiesced to Jess and took the pit bull. Nellifer lived for five more years before she came down with lymphoma. She was the sweetest, most charismatic and soulful dog that Michael had ever known.

Most notably, and most eerily, Jess had experienced immediate, visceral hatred of Janice Kellerman, Dani's now infamous first nursery-school teacher. To Michael the woman seemed completely normal, if not a bit too cloyingly sweet. After a week Jess had pulled Dani out of the Westwind Nursery School, which was just up Route 10 in Livingston. For that whole year Jess drove her all the way to the Playhouse Nursery School in West Orange every morning. By the time Anthony went to nursery school, the woman Jess had loathed on sight had been fired. She'd been at Westwind two years and rumor had it she'd been fondling little children in the coat room. There were no formal charges made by any parents, but Westwind's nursery class enrollment had dropped by half.

"Christ, what a doughnut line," says Claudia.

Michael turns and finds that she's beside him. He smells her breath, a strangely arousing mixture of stale cigarettes and Wrigley's Spearmint gum.

"Use some bravado," Claudia whispers. "It's not as if we have all day."

"It's just four people," Michael says.

She says, "A smooth talker like you should be able to think of something."

There is no way he will finagle cutting a doughnut line.

He says, "No."

"What a good citizen," she says, and rolls her eyes at him. "I'm going over to Silverman's to buy cigarettes. I'll meet you back out at my car."

"Want any doughnuts?" Michael asks.

She says, "I don't allow my children to eat that crap. It's solid lard."

"See you outside then," Michael says.

She pats him lightly on the ass. She leaves the bakery and he's still not sure she'll be waiting when he comes out. He's heard her talk about her past affairs enough to know this whole thing will be jettisoned, at some point, in an instant.

He considers the fact that Jess would know, without a doubt, whether Claudia will be waiting. She claims she always knew when boys would stand her up on dates in high school. But will Jess know when he comes home what he's been doing? Will she see Claudia's aura glowing around his body? He understands that his actions are abominable. He has done things he could never have imagined. Claudia here and there. Motels. His office. Bathrooms. Her son's bar mitzvah. He hopes to God Jess only knows all this abstractly. That she is not aware of each specific instance and its details.

Where had it started? Their demise. Was it when Michael first crawled into bed with Claudia, one afternoon at the shore house while Jess was playing on the beach with all the kids? Was it a year before that, when Jess said sex with him mostly made her want to cry and disappear? Or was it two years prior to that, when Michael asked Jess why their sex was never dirty anymore? "'Cause I'm not dirty," she responded. "You want dirty, rent a video. Go buy *Hustler* magazine." He tried to kiss her that night in bed and she yelled, "Don't touch me!" She grabbed the blanket and took Nellifer and slept out on the couch.

Was it the day of the Bicentennial? When they were watching Operation Sail from Lanny Eisenberg's Fort Lee highrise. He had been talking about the *Esmeralda*, a former torture ship from Chile that was passing down the Hudson. He had read all about the *Esmeralda* in the paper. Then he was talking about the Israeli raid on Entebbe. It had happened just the night before. Jess threw a drink in his face and told him that he talked too much. She looked at Lanny, who seemed appalled, and asked him why he was such a priggish asshole. He dried his face off, grabbed the kids, and took them home.

Or was it 1969, in late July, the day of the first moon landing? They had been married for six years. On this rare Sunday off from his residency, he woke up early and had memorized the clarinet part for the first movement of Mozart's Clarinet Quintet in A Major. He learned the piece straight from the record, which he'd been playing over and over in the living room.

He knew Jess loved it. It took less than half an hour to get the whole thing down. He went upstairs to their room with his clarinet. She was in the bathroom. He began playing the relative minor solo right outside the bathroom door.

Jess said she'd be out in a second. Something seemed wrong with her voice, so Michael asked what she was doing. In the same off voice she said, "Nothing!" He tried the doorknob. She'd locked the door, but he used his weight and easily broke it open.

Still holding the clarinet, he entered. He found Jess squatting naked in the bathtub, clutching her bloody left arm with her right. There was a towel draped over the tub beside her, and she appeared to be very much in control of the situation. Stifling his panic, he placed the clarinet on the sink counter. He crouched next to her and said, "What's going on?"

In an embarrassed but composed tone, Jess said, "I do this sometimes."

"Do what?"

She said, "I cut myself sometimes. It's nothing serious. It's not deep."

"You've done this before?"

"Not since our wedding."

"When?"

"I used to do it from time to time in high school. I haven't needed to since then, but I do now."

He took the towel and applied pressure to the wound.

"You don't know what it's like," she said. "I sometimes feel like there's so much pressure inside my head that it might blow up. Or even worse, I don't feel anything. This calms me down, helps me release."

He took the towel off, saw the raised cut on her forearm. It wasn't bleeding anymore. He saw a patch of faint hairline scars all nestled in that same area. He had first noticed them long ago. He'd never thought to ask Jess what they were.

"What did you use?"

"Glass. It's in the wastebasket."

"Was the glass clean?"

She said, "Of course."

He found the hydrogen peroxide, Bacitracin, gauze, adhesive tape. Jess just stayed crouched there in the bathtub. She seemed calm as he wrapped the wound. He filled the bathtub and she sat with her arm resting out of the water. He took a washcloth and cleaned a spot of dried blood off her hair.

Michael was terrified after that. But was it fear for her or for himself? Was he embarrassed that Jess was secretly a basket case? Or was it fear of a greater magnitude—fear that in Jess's eyes their marriage had turned into an irreparable problem?

All day he drank straight-up scotch and followed Jess around the house. That afternoon, as they watched the moon landing, Jess fell asleep while lying in his arms. It was a frightening juxtaposition—Dani, age five, staring wonderstruck; Anthony, age three, on the floor, more absorbed in playing with his Fisher-Price parking garage. Jess lay asleep in his arms as Michael sat there feeling his secret terror. He watched Apollo 11 touch down and kept wondering what to do.

So far as Michael knew, she never cut herself again. She went to therapy. She was twenty-six years old. Once when he asked, Jess said she had outgrown it. Instead she rolled around in the garden, spent whole days weeding. She would come in so caked with dirt that water coming off her body in the shower would turn dark brown. There were her episodes. Her unpredictable outbursts. Her depressions. Her sudden canceling of vacations. Her tremendous fear of marionettes and clowns. There were the sexual complications, a list of things he could not do and certain places he could not touch. The list kept growing until it more or less included everything. But no new scars appeared—or none that he could see.

When at last it is his turn at the Village Bakery, Michael asks for a dozen doughnuts. He chooses four Boston creams, four honey-dipped, four jellies. A young girl places them in a bakery box and ties it with a string.

He pays and heads outside to look for Claudia. For those few seconds of uncertainty, his heart races. He finds her waiting, seat tilted back, lying face upturned under the open sunroof. Her eyes are hidden behind her black-framed glasses.

He pulls the door open. She sits up.

She says, "The great American father."

Michael slides in. He slams the door closed.

He says, "We better make this quick."

"Where to, James?"

He says, "Anywhere."

"You'll have to be a little more creative."

"Go to that office building by Friendly's. No one should be there on a Sunday."

Claudia slides a cassette into her tape deck. A form of torture. Neil Diamond. Twenty-four hours of straight Neil Diamond would surely kill him. She pulls the car out and cuts behind the Shop Rite to Mount Pleasant. He sees Frank Richard's, Heritage Diner, St. Peter's Church, Friendly's—all of these places burned indelibly in his memory. Claudia turns into an empty lot and pulls behind the building. She kills the engine and Michael slides the seat back.

"Don't crush those doughnuts," Claudia says.

He puts the box on the floor behind the driver's seat.

Once upon a time, during his last free week in summer before starting his internship at Saint Barnabas, Michael was playing his clarinet. They had just moved into a condo across the street from the hospital. That morning Jess had brought the children to her parents' house in Millburn. It was a hot day in June, and she had been outside lying in the sun.

Michael looked up while he was playing and there she was, greasy with tanning oil. A frilly teal blue string bikini, a Time-Life book about dolphins in her hand. Michael stopped playing and just stared at her in wonder. Even after four years he sometimes marveled that this drop-dead gorgeous woman was his wife.

She said, "Don't stop. Play me a song." He wet the reed with his lips, decided. He began playing the Beatles' "When I'm Sixty-Four." She crossed her arms and cocked her head. He moved around, wielding the clarinet expressively as he played. He got dramatic and ended with a flourish. She dropped the book and stepped up close.

"Was that a question?" she asked. "You want to know how I'll feel when you're sixty-four?" He hadn't thought about the words. He hadn't meant it as a question. But he said, "Well, what do you think?" Then he was scared because he sensed that she would know.

She started unbuttoning his shirt. "I'll always love you," she said gently. "Whether I'll need you? Hard to say. Whether we'll still be to-gether, I don't know. Right now I want you." She took the instrument from his hand. She laid it carefully on a chair and then turned back to him. She took his belt loop in her finger and pulled him toward her. She said, "Don't ever stop playing your clarinet."

Five months later, Anthony was talking. Michael was working hundred-hour weeks and thriving in his delirium. Jess still seemed thrilled to be the mother of two children. In Michael's memory, they were happy.

Now, as he steps out onto Fellswood Drive with a box of dough-nuts, as his fatigued legs touch down on the street around the corner from his house, as Claudia gives her wry smile and says, "Best to Jess and Anthony"—now, as he feels lassitude and sadness, as he feels glutted and yet somehow still empty—he tries to see himself, his fu-ture. He cannot.

SANIBEL

"MOM?" I SAY.

It seems like dawn and now the light has turned the white walls of this bedroom pink and yellow. I see a circular stained-glass window and understand that I'm not dreaming. When I sit up in bed, I see that she is there.

"What?" I say. "What time is it?"

She says, "Five-thirty. I was just watching you."

"I was sleeping."

She says, "I know."

"I had a dream about a dolphin."

She says, "What happened in the dream?"

"I can't remember." My eyes focus on my mother. She's wearing jeans and a faded orange T-shirt, the exact same clothes she wore last night. She's drinking coffee, the steam rising around her face.

"Go back to sleep," she says.

"I'm wide awake now."

She says, "Roll over. You'll fall asleep again in a minute."

She leaves the doorway. I don't roll over. I take *Le Morte d'Arthur* off the night table. I hear my mother wandering around, doing some dishes, feeding her cats. She reappears in the doorway and says, "What's this book you're reading?"

I say, "King Arthur. I got it as a present." I hold the book in the air. "I'm at the part where Guinevere meets Lancelot."

"So now you're up?" she says.

"I'm used to getting up from hockey."

"Then come on out to the porch," she says. "Maybe we'll get an early start."

We're having breakfast on the porch, looking at maps, when she brings up Sanibel. It's on our route down to Key Largo. A slight detour off the highway.

She says, "I'm thinking we should stop there."

I assume she's joking.

"Just for an hour or so," she says. "We could have lunch. Then we'll keep going."

"Why would you want to?" I ask.

"It kind of haunts me."

"What would we do?"

"We'll take a walk on the beach. I'd just like to see what the place looks like."

My mother stares at me, her eyes conveying something, maybe sorrow. I think of Sanibel, the normal things. Beach Frisbee. Collecting shells. I also think of my mother's jacket, which she lost. I think about our last night there and can recall the smallest details. I tell her, "Sure, it would be fine. You haven't gone there since you moved?" She shakes her head and I sense that she's been waiting—God knows why—to make this trip back to Sanibel with me.

+ + +

We had a dinner plan the last night of our Christmas week in Sanibel. It was 1973. We had a window table reserved for five o'clock at a restaurant called the Pelican Rest. We hadn't eaten any lunch and we were starving. We also wanted an ocean view to watch the sunset. The place was right on the beach, maybe a mile from our motel. When we got into our rented car, my father headed the wrong way.

"Where are you going?" my mother asked.

She had a skirt on. Over a black top she was wearing a thin gold jacket. My sister had convinced me it was made of real gold leaf.

"We're all dressed up," she said. "We'll miss the sunset."

"We won't miss anything," said my father. "It's a surprise."

He drove for a few more miles. Then he turned into the Ding Darling Reservation. He paid three dollars at the booth and said, "We'll finally see some gators."

Dani and I had been whining about alligators all week.

"We're wearing nice clothes," said my mother. "Can't we come back tomorrow morning?"

"It will be quick," my father said. "We won't be getting out of the car."

"Do they like Tic Tacs?" I asked.

I started shaking my container of orange Tic Tacs.

"Don't be an ignoramus," said Dani.

At that time Dani's favorite word was "ignoramus."

"Close all the windows," my mother said. She began searching around the center console for a button. The rented car didn't have an automatic window lock. It was a low-end four-door Ford. It also didn't have automatic door locks. So Mom leaned back in the front seat and crossed her arms over her chest. She punched the cigarette lighter in and then we should have just stayed quiet.

Dani whined, "Mom, you just said that we can't open up the windows."

She said, "You can't. Blame your father."

She took a cigarette from her purse.

"I hate smoke!" I yelled. "Now we won't be able to breathe!"

She turned around and stared at me with something far from anger. In her green eyes, I could see something more like pleading. It was as if she were saying—Please, just let me be.

———

On the drive down to Sanibel we listen to the radio. The sun's still low on the left side of the car as we drive south. I keep on fiddling with the stations. She has a tape deck but it's broken. I ask her why she hasn't fixed it, since she owns a lot of tapes. She says these days she doesn't listen to much music. She has no patience with the radio, and all the music on her old tapes makes her sad.

I say, "What *do* you do these days?"

She says, "I told you. I'm still a bartender."

"I mean what else. Besides work."

"I took this job so I can scuba dive all day," she says. "Right now I'm working on my Divemaster. After I log a hundred dives, I can take courses to become a dive instructor."

"Will you quit bartending after you get your Divemaster?"

"Probably not."

"You think you'll always be a bartender?"

She says, "Hey Anth, I promise there's a plan. I want to go back to school full time. Not in psychology though. I'm switching. I want to get my degree in marine biology. I also want to study the Kabbalah. There's a center that offers courses in Kabbalah, right in my town."

"I thought you hate all of religion."

"Kabbalah's different. It's not so literal."

"But you're an atheist."

"Not lately," she says. "So tell me something about you."

"Like what?" I say.

"Well, you never tell me who you're dating. You must have girl-friends. Start with that."

"I've had one. Sort of."

"Why is it sort of?"

I say, "She wasn't really my girlfriend. Now she's gone."

"It's not that girl from the shore."

"No."

"Someone from school?"

I nod my head.

"Someone I know?" she asks.

I tell her, "Juliette Dimiglio."

My mother seems surprised at first. Then she just nods and says, "Of course."

✦ ✦ ✦

Dani was doing mazes when we came up on the gators. I saw two other stopped cars and touched her shoulder. One man was leaning out his front window, snapping photos.

"There they are," my father said.

Two giant lizards were lying motionless, just above the sandy bank of a little pond.

"Right where that man in the lobby told me," said my father. "He wasn't lying."

Mom said, "Okay, now can we go before we miss our reservation?"

"Look at those gators," Dad said.

My mother leaned back and stared out the front windshield.

I said, "That one looks like he's sad, or maybe dead."

Dani said, "Maybe he's a fake. He almost looks like he's made of plastic."

Mom said, "Okay? Did we see enough?"

I said, "Let's go before we're late."

"How many times in your life do you see a gator?" said my father.

He was right. We all should have been more excited. Alligators were all we had been talking about in Florida. Even our mother had seemed interested in alligators. She'd sent her parents an alligator postcard.

We all stared for another minute. I smelled the smoke from my mother's cigarette. I had a mouthful of Tic Tacs to combat it. One of the gators took a step forward.

"He's a real gator," I said. "He moved."

Dani said, "Okay, I think I'm getting hungry."

My father put the car in gear but continued watching another moment. He said, "Just sitting by the road. Two giant gators. Can you believe it?"

I knew my mother was ready to explode.

As we drove away, she rolled the window down. I felt the rush of cool air and raised my head so the air got to my nose. We'd driven in less than a mile to see the gators, but the access road was one way, so we had to keep driving through the Ding Darling Reservation. My father said the access road was just five miles, but it was one lane and the speed limit was fifteen. To make things worse we got behind a slow-moving van with people staring out windows through binoculars.

My mother started crying, very quietly. I clenched my fists and prayed for the five miles to pass quickly. We hadn't gone another mile when something ruptured the front tire of the rental car.

"This is a joke," my mother said.

"It's just a tire," said Dad, and pulled the car over. "We have a spare. It's no big deal."

I said, "At least we didn't break down by the gators."

"There could be alligators anywhere," said Dani.

I said, "But probably we'd see them."

"There are no gators here!" yelled my mother. "Just a lot of moronic people!"

We'd broken down at a marked stopping point for bird-watchers. At least six cars were parked in a roadside pull-off. My mother got out of the car and said she needed to use the bathroom. It was a bird blind, though. My father tried to tell her.

She headed off toward a square gray structure that had long open slats so people inside could look out. As always she moved fast, with strides that seemed too quick for her long legs and languid spirit. We watched her walk down the road in her black sandals, short skirt, and gold jacket. Dani said, "Mom looks like a movie star in those clothes."

Dad popped the trunk and found the tire, jack, and crowbar. He removed his nice shirt and got to work. I stood there watching him jack the car up, amazed to see the weight of the whole thing rising. He said, "Remember, when you crank, it's righty tighty, lefty loosy." Then Dani pointed out a strange bird in a tree beside the water. The bird was sitting on a branch with its wings spread out, like it was hurt.

After he'd pulled off the bad tire, we left our father and approached a pair of bird-watchers by the water.

"That's an an-*hinga*," a man said, and spread his arms just like the bird. "They have less oil than most water birds in their feathers, so they get waterlogged. They use the air to dry their wings."

He pointed out two more anhingas in another tree. Their coloration and shapes blended with the branches. They reminded me of the Can You Find the Hidden Animals? game on place mats at Don's Restaurant in Livingston.

The man said, "Some people call anhingas the water turkey."

Dani said, "So, could you eat one on Thanksgiving?"

Our father yelled out that the tire was changed. We thanked the man and jogged back to the car. We saw our mother standing near the bird blind. In her nice clothes, she looked extremely out of place there. Not like a movie star so much as some space traveler who had come out of the future and was now lost.

She was scaring away the birds. People were yelling at her to either leave or get inside the blind.

Someone yelled, "Go back to your car!"

My mother turned and gave the entire bird blind the finger.

"Bitch!" someone yelled.

Dani said, "Neat, the building's talking."

A woman stepped out from the blind and said, "Hey Goldy, what's your problem?"

Mom was much taller and seemed enormous beside the woman. She kept on staring with rapt astonishment, as if amazed that there were actually real people behind the blind.

✦ ✦ ✦

"Look at the water," she says.

I have been looking. I still remember this Sanibel Island causeway. As we drove over it in our rental car ten years ago, my sister was busy doing mazes. She brought the maze book with her everywhere that vacation. Back in New Jersey, months later, I found it in the kitchen. She had done every single maze, even the ones that spanned two pages. Beneath each maze she'd signed her name in the flowing script of a proud fourth-grader. Both of her i's were always dotted with big round circles.

My mother drives through town, past all the shops and what appears to be a new hotel. We see a sign that says DO NOT FEED THE ALLIGATORS. I look around, but no gators are in sight.

We take a left, toward the Gulf, and then we drive along a road beside the water. The sea is calm and shorebirds float along with wind currents. We come upon a very classy-looking restaurant called the Pelican Rest. It looks quite different from the picture inside my head.

"I don't remember that whole deck part."

She takes a sip of her now cold coffee and says, "It's probably an addition."

I say, "Last time you were here you had that jacket. The one you lost."

"That piece of junk," she says, and laughs. "I can't believe you would remember."

"It was gold," I say. "And shiny."

She says, "I guess it did stand out."

"How did you lose it?"

She says, "Did I?"

"You didn't have it when you came back."

"I don't remember much of anything. That's why I wanted to come back here."

We take our shoes off, roll our pants up. I watch a pelican crash down into the sea.

✦ ✦ ✦

When we arrived at the restaurant that night it was past seven. The sun had set. We'd lost our table by the window, but they said they could still seat us if we waited another twenty minutes. We all sat down at the bar and soon a hostess came to get us. Mom said, "No, Michael, forget this." She turned around and headed out the door.

We all went after her. Dad tried reasoning. She said, "Fuck you," and tied her jacket around her waist. She was just thirty years old then. I was seven. Dani was nine. She headed off into the dark with her too-quick strides before we knew what was going on.

Dani yelled, "Mom, don't be an ignoramus!"

She stopped to take off her shoes but did not look back.

"Just go inside and hold the table," our father told us.

He jogged off after her, so Dani and I went in.

Dad returned almost half an hour later. Dani and I had ordered Shirley Temples and shrimp cocktails. We'd told the waitress our parents were outside fighting. Dad said Mom needed to walk things off. He said she'd be back before the main course came and ordered her the swordfish. Her untouched plate sat on the table right beside me. Throughout the meal we kept acting like she'd be back any second.

In all we spent more than three hours at the restaurant. We searched the beach awhile but couldn't find a trace of her. We resisted the maître d's recurring offer to report our situation to the police.

As we drove back to the motel, Dad kept insisting there wasn't any reason to worry. This was not the first of our mother's episodes, though the strangest. But not to worry. He said she wouldn't go very far. He dropped us off and then drove back to the closed restaurant.

I fell asleep that night, but Dani kept her light on and did mazes. When I woke early the next morning, she was still at it. She had been doing mazes all night. I put on clothes and found my father on the phone in his motel room. He'd given in and was now calling the police.

Our mother walked in fifteen minutes later. We had already missed our flight, which was at nine. I was in their room reading *Strange but True Hockey Stories*. Dani was lying on the bed, still doing mazes. My father sprang up from the bed when the door opened and she appeared.

"Jess," my father said, and stared at her.

"I'm so sorry," was all she said.

"You lost your jacket."

My mother nodded. Her clothes were covered with sand and sorrow seemed to ooze from her tired body.

"Are you okay?" he asked.

"I'm fine. I need a shower."

"We were all worried."

She said, "I know."

Then she stepped up to him and wrapped her sandy arms around his body. My father held her and we seemed to have survived this. An hour later, we were heading to the airport.

✦ ✦ ✦

"Hey," she says. "Right *here*."

I see my mother. Her jeans are soaked to the knees. She's walking up the beach, toward a stone wall. I watch her long legs and high hips and the faded back of her orange T-shirt. She says, "Come on," and so I follow. The sun feels warm on my face and I feel calm.

My mother stands on the small stone wall. I climb up next to her and stare down at the sand that rests beneath us.

"This is the place," she says.

"What place?"

"The place I slept. Somewhere around here."

She puts her arm around my shoulders. I feel cold, but I also feel the sun.

"Just a few feet behind this wall," she says. "It sheltered me from the wind."

Now I lean into my mother's side. We both stare down at a patch of sand. Inside my head, as in my dreams, I see her sleeping in her gold jacket. I see her waking at dawn, rising, throwing the jacket into a calm sea.

PART TWO

LOST MOTHERS

October 1981

THE AMBULANCE CAME in the dead of night, while it was pouring. Dani had been the first to hear the siren and wake up. She went to Anthony's room and found him sitting up in bed. When they went in to wake their father, he was already up and staring out the window. By then police cars, at least four of them, had pulled into the neighbors' driveway. "It's the Dimiglios," he said. "Looks like someone finally shot our neighbor."

Anthony's thoughts went first to Juliette Dimiglio. She was a junior. Anthony worried that she'd been killed. His father dressed and went out with his black Christian Dior umbrella. They watched him standing out with another neighbor, Mrs. Leff. Then he was helping them because he was a doctor. They saw him talking to EMTs who had just wheeled the stretcher out from the garage. No one was rushing, it seemed. Anthony knew someone was dead. He couldn't see who was lying on the stretcher, but he saw Juliette behind it, her long hair drenched.

When their father returned, Dani and Anthony were waiting in the kitchen.

"It was Isabella Dimiglio," he said. "She went down into her garage and blew her brains out."

Anthony saw things, two pictures. He saw Isabella Dimiglio wearing roller skates. He saw brains.

"I heard the shot," Dani said. "But I just figured it was a backfire from a car, or else a dream."

"She had a sad life," said their father. "I saw her once at the hospital. She came in with a black eye and a broken rib."

"Her husband hit her?"

"Let's go to bed."

"Wait," Anthony said.

"What?"

"What was it like seeing Isabella Dimiglio dead?"

"I see dead bodies every week."

"But she's our neighbor."

"Now she's just dead."

+ + +

There were stories about Isabella Dimiglio. She'd been a dancer, people said. Vince Dimiglio had first met her in Las Vegas. Or else he'd met her in New York, where she was dancing in a short-lived Broadway show. No one had ever gotten the story straight.

Some people claimed she had been a prostitute—that Vince Dimiglio had won her in a card game. She had been sent to his room in some hotel, and he had fallen in love with her on sight. Others claimed that he had rescued her when he found her lying half-dead on a park bench in New York.

There were also stories about Vince Dimiglio. Everyone said he was some sort of gangster. A very minor gangster, though. Because his house wasn't big. The Dimiglios seemed to live a normal life. Anthony sometimes saw Mr. Dimiglio mowing his lawn. He had seen Mrs. Dimiglio jogging. He'd seen her roller-skating all around their driveway. She had white skates with little pom-poms. She could skate well, which gave some credence to the dancer/Broadway show theory. She'd just skate up and down the driveway, forward and backward, sometimes balancing on one leg.

The Dimiglios never gave out candy on Halloween. They kept their porch lights off and no one answered if you rang. Each year Anthony imagined gangsters doing "business" inside, although he'd never learned what Vince Dimiglio did. Various theories had been thrown out, including hit man. Anthony's father said it was more likely that Vince Dimiglio just sold window frames or cement. One thing was certain—he was not in the league of "Richie the Boot" Boiardo. New Jersey's most famous Prohibition-era ganglord, the now ninety-year-old Boiardo had lived in Livingston for years. His fortresslike estate sat on a western-facing slope above Beaufort Avenue. Once a flamboyant, dangerous mob boss, he had become a fabled recluse. He supposedly spent most of his time working in his garden, which, rumor had it, had been fertilized by some of his former rivals.

Several times, while driving by, Anthony's parents had stopped to stare up the steep, winding, double-gated Boiardo driveway. Outside the wrought-iron fence there were stone pillars with carved lions. The house itself, which they could only see a part of, was made of red and white imported Italian stone. The estate was known to have a working crematorium. Boiardo once claimed it was simply an incinerator used for burning garden refuse, but many mobsters had alluded to his private iron-grated furnace. One even noted Boiardo's generosity—he was willing to take bodies from almost anyone. Anthony sometimes wondered if there were mobster bodies buried in the Dimiglios' yard. Among other things, they seemed to get more dandelions than anyone. They also hadn't planted any backyard trees.

In school that rainy day Anthony kept thinking about the suicide. How had she done it? Had she gotten up to pee and decided: Now I'll put a bullet through my skull? Had she rolled over, kissed her husband, and headed down to the garage? Had she been beaten up that night? Had she been drunk?

He tried imagining what it felt like—finding your mother dead and bloody. He wondered if, horrific as it was, it might be better than having a mom who lived in Florida. A mom he spoke to but hadn't seen in a year. A mom whose absence seemed to be everywhere. Inside the house, in every cabinet, he found her. She would pop out sometimes and startle him with her absence.

That evening when Dani came home from swimming, she told him, "Juliette Dimiglio was with Tommy Lange at Friendly's after his football practice. Bev Glasser saw them. They were in Tommy Lange's Firebird, making out."

"I didn't see her at school," said Anthony.

"Well she was majorly messing around with Tommy. Same day her mother killed herself. That's so creepy."

Anthony thought about this, and for some reason the thought was very visual. He could see clearly in his mind the sight of Juliette making out with Tommy. Then he imagined her mother's brains. He thought of his friend Craig Kelby's brother, Jamie, who volunteered on the Livingston First Aid Squad. He owned a flashing blue rotator light, which stuck magnetically to his car roof. He sometimes liked to pull his friends over for a gag. Once when Anthony was at Craig's house, Jamie had told them that EMTs carried a spatula tool for picking up people's brains. He said they kept it with all their other tools in the ambulance. Anthony never knew if this was true.

"Bev says hi," said Dani. "You know, she's doing the 200 I.M. this year. She trained a lot over the summer and got faster."

"Bev Glasser said hi to me?" he asked.

"She likes you."

"She's a senior."

"And you're the latest hockey hero now, remember? Get a clue."

"Tell her hi," Anthony said, still wondering why Bev Glasser would acknowledge his existence. She had been swimming for years with Dani, but she was cold and aloof and rarely smiled. He'd always liked the way she looked and had once sat by her at Temple B'nai Abraham's junior service on Yom Kippur. During the service he had been goofing around and talking with Barry Brumberg. At one point Bev had turned with a stern look on her face and told them both to "Shhhh."

Right after dinner, Anthony went upstairs to try and write up his chemistry lab report, which that week had to do with moles. He was good in chemistry, acing it, but still he didn't understand what a mole was. All he knew was that in lab they'd counted beans. Navy beans, pinto beans, lima beans, kidney beans, and others. Somehow it had to with moles. And for some reason there were always 6.02×10^{23} particles in a mole.

But now he didn't know what a mole was and the write-up was due tomorrow. At times like these he always felt like calling up Jay Berkowitz. Jay understood things like moles and what they had to do with beans. He hadn't called Jay for a year, though. Not since a few days after his mother smashed the windows. He'd called to see if Jay wanted to play street hockey. Claudia wouldn't let Jay speak. Anthony told her he'd call back later, but she said not to. She said he wasn't allowed to talk to Jay or set foot on the Berkowitzes' property in his lifetime.

Now the Berkowitzes no longer lived in Livingston. They had moved to West Orange in July. One afternoon just before the school year had started, Anthony rode his bike to Shadowlawn Drive to look at their old house. It was the first time he had been there in a year or so. He hadn't ridden his bike on Shadowlawn since the day of his mother's episode. Of course, the windows had been replaced. The grass had grown back on the lawn. Still in his mind he could see everything as ravaged and smashed and ruined. He knew it wasn't quite *The Shining* but felt a ghost there. He wondered whether whoever bought the house could sense it.

Anthony got up and stared out his bedroom window. The rain had just stopped and the air was misty. He saw the jungle gym in his yard. It was so rusted that you couldn't really climb on it. He saw the garden, which had been fallow for the first summer Anthony could remember. Now there was catmint and rhubarb everywhere, still living in October. Both of these plants grew by themselves and no one picked them.

He spied Juliette Dimiglio on her back steps. The steps led up to a wooden deck with a barbecue. In all the years the Dimiglios had lived next door, he'd never seen them use the barbecue. But he saw Juliette

there often. She would go out to the back steps to smoke or listen to her
Walkman. It was a spot where she must have felt invisible, since from
ground level a small wooden gate and the handrail mostly shielded her
from view.

Juliette was sitting with her head in her hands, staring down at the
slatted gate below the steps. Her clothes and hair looked wet. She sometimes did this—sat outside on her porch when it was raining. When she
was little she used to walk around her yard during summer showers.
She would sit down and intentionally get drenched. For such a sullen,
edgy person, Juliette had some endearingly silly habits. She used to
spend hours outside making dandelion chains. Or she would wander
around picking all the dandelion clocks, blowing clouds of their downy
seeds into the air.

Now that he saw her, Anthony had the urge to go outside and talk
to her. He wanted to ask her things like how she felt and what it was like
finding her mother dead.

But he did not go out and ask. He'd never had an actual conversation with Juliette in his life. Once on a whim, though, he had hooked
up his special fire-escape ladder. He had climbed down to the backyard from his window right in front of her. It was a late spring afternoon and Jay was over. Anthony was eleven. That year he'd gotten the
chain ladder on Chanukah and would practice high-speed fire drills
all the time.

When Jay saw Juliette on her back steps, he said, "Dare you to do a
fire drill." Anthony knew Juliette would think he was a moron, but he
was not the type of boy to resist a dare. So he climbed down to the
ground and up again while Jay made sure the ladder hooks stayed tight
against the windowsill. As he crawled in and rolled onto his bedroom
floor, they both cracked up. They got hysterical. Jay said that Juliette
had watched as Anthony was climbing—that she was probably *still
watching*. Anthony grabbed his World Cup soccer ball and threw it out
the open window. Jay yelled, "You're crazy!" He threw a hockey stick.
Anthony threw his sneakers. Jay threw a sweatshirt and then Anthony

heaved down his entire wicker hamper. When they looked out again Juliette was gone.

+ + +

Sometimes Anthony saw his mother in his dreams. They always seemed to be walking on some suburban street he recognized, though no such street existed in the world. He would stand with her and somehow, even there, she would be leaving. Disappearing, almost, though in his dreams she would never be quite absent. It was as if, within these dreams, he'd slipped inside some oceanic version of her body.

It was so strong that there were times when he would wake in the night and think: Now I can feel you. Are you here? He'd feel her bleeding out of the dream and filling up his bedroom. He'd wander downstairs and look out at Cherry Hill Road in the moonlight. In that half-floating state Anthony would picture things. Her Cat Woman costumes on Halloween. Her enchantment with Jacques Cousteau specials. Her excitement when she played volleyball at the pool.

Still she would always seem part stranger. There were parts of her that always seemed detached and faraway. Some of his friends said she was "hot." They always liked to trick-or-treat when she would come to the door as Cat Woman. Even his hockey coach, Bill Marino, had noticed his mother once at a school fund-raiser. Coach Marino clearly had a crush on her. Throughout ninth grade, the year she left, he had deflected his coach's recurring inquiries as to why she never came to games.

And always Anthony wanted answers. He wanted some logical story to explain why she was gone. So he invented the explanations. He tried to think of her the way he thought of characters in legends. But he was always doing that, making things up, trying to see how it all might fit into a legend. He didn't understand why he did this, because New Jersey was not legend. It was the armpit of America, according to most people. Still he saw everything around him as a legend.

———

It took a day but then the story became the talk of Livingston High School. Mrs. Dimiglio had blown her brains out with a semi-automatic. Where did she get a semi-automatic? What *was* a semi-automatic? She was a battered wife whose life was very sad.

Anthony kept on getting questions about rumors. Every half hour people asked him things like—Did her "clients" come right to the house? He felt an urgent need to protect her. He'd tell them Isabella Dimiglio skated on her driveway. He'd say she skated very well. He'd say, "The woman was not a whore. She was just sad. Her life was sad." But still he wondered if she had ever been a prostitute. He found it hard not to keep wondering things like that.

Two mornings after the suicide, her obituary ran in the *Star Ledger*. Dani found it and said, "Check this out. Mrs. Dimiglio got a whopping five-sentence obit." She then proceeded to read the piece aloud:

Isabella R. (Marinetti) Dimiglio, 41, of Cherry Hill Road, died early Monday morning at her home. Born in Nutley, she moved to Livingston in 1969. She leaves her beloved husband Vincent; beloved daughter Juliette; brother Luigi Marinetti, of Nutley; and two sisters, Camille Brazzi, of Short Hills, and Francesca Giordano, of Hoboken. The funeral will be held Friday, 9 A.M., at St. Michael's Cathedral Church, Nutley. Mass of Christian Burial to follow at Hillside Cemetery, Belleville. Viewing hours Thursday noon-5 P.M. and 6-9 P.M., Hopping Funeral Home.

"What about her dancing?" Anthony asked. "It doesn't say anything about the Broadway show?"

"Guess not," Dani said. "It also doesn't say that she was a prostitute. It doesn't even mention that she killed herself. What's the point?"

"I thought that Catholics can't be buried in Catholic cemeteries if they kill themselves."

"They can't," Dani said.

"It said she's having a massive Christian burial."

"Cut it, both of you," said their father.

Dani said, "Why? She was just our dumb ex-hooker neighbor."

"She had a sad life," said their father.

"I'd say pathetic is the word."

"Stop," their father said.

Dani said, "What, were you hoping to score with her since now that other hooker, Claudia, won't speak to you?"

"Danielle, enough!" he yelled, and struck the table with his fist.

Dani moved back and wound up stepping right on Roger, their black Lab, whom they'd acquired from a shelter that past spring. When Roger yelped, she turned and kneeled beside him.

She said, "I'm sorry Dad, okay? I wish you'd find another girl-friend."

"That's not your problem."

"Who said it was?"

Dani began petting Roger, who had rolled onto his back. She scratched his chest in the spot that always made his foot go wild.

"Mrs. Dimiglio probably wasn't a hooker," Anthony said, and stared at Dani.

She just stared back and said, "Looks like we'll never know."

That afternoon there was dry-land training for the hockey team. They ran two miles, did sprints, and then ran "stadiums" up and down the bleachers. They also did push-ups, sit-ups, and other calis-thenics led by Assistant Coach Baldwin, who taught history and ran marathons.

Then Coach Marino handed out the raffle books and said they each had to sell two hundred tickets if they wanted to go to Minnesota for the Breck School tournament in February. They all wanted to go, of course, even though they had lost by at least five goals in every game the year before. In fact, they barely ever won a game in New Jersey. But Coach Marino said it was good experience, since Minnesota had the best hockey in the country. The coach was fond of doing important things, like having individual water bottles. His next big plan was to get last names on the jerseys.

After the dry-land training Anthony went to Friendly's with half a dozen people from the team. As they walked in, Anthony's linemate Dave Delaney saw his girlfriend, Miranda Dixon. Part of the group went to sit with Miranda and her two other pretty friends. Anthony sat with Will Smithson and Brian Kane, the goalie, who was the only other Jewish player on the team.

At some point Anthony got up to use the bathroom. There was a door that led into a small hallway that had a cigarette machine and one for biorhythm readouts. Using a birth date and the current date, the machine produced a card with a graphed rating of things like luck, romance, family, health, and driving. He'd gotten hundreds of readouts in his life, many with Jay in years past when they were riding their Schwinn ten-speeds around town.

As he stepped out of the bathroom, he was thinking he would ask Brian and Will over to play street hockey. Then he looked up and found that he was standing face-to-face with Juliette Dimiglio.

She had just put in a quarter to get her biorhythm. In her left hand she was holding a pack of cigarettes. Juliette looked once at him, then quickly looked back down at the machine. She slipped the cigarettes into the pocket of her boyfriend's Livingston Lancers football jacket. She moved a strand of her dark blond hair behind her ear.

Anthony stood there, attempting to say something. He couldn't think of anything simple enough. All the ideas inside his head were so enormous that no words fit through his mouth.

Finally Juliette looked up and said, "Hi Anthony, how are you?"

It amazed him that she had spoken. It amazed him to hear that she knew his name.

He said, "I'm good."

The machine spit out her biorhythm. Juliette reached down for the card.

"How'd you score?" he asked.

Juliette glanced downward. "Looks like I'm off the chart in luck and driving." She laughed and held the card where he could see it. He saw the two lines Juliette was talking about. All of the others were about average, except health, which was pretty high.

"Well," she said, and slipped the card into her pocket. "Someone's waiting for me outside."

"Have a nice afternoon," he said.

She said, "You too."

Juliette stepped past him, through the door. Anthony looked at the machine. He saw her birthday. A few months ago: July the twenty-ninth. He wondered how she had celebrated her birthday. He wondered if her now-dead mom had made a cake. He couldn't move because his whole body felt frozen. He felt as if he were standing in a dream.

Then Helen Ludwig and Shari Gross walked in. They were both sophomores. They almost clocked him with the door. Shari said, "Anthony jockboy Rubin, buying cigarettes?" He shook his head and said, "No way."

Without thinking, he stepped back inside the bathroom. He could hear the two girls putting money in the machine. He heard the knob being pulled out, snapping back in, a pack of cigarettes hitting metal.

After they left, he went back out. He looked once more at the settings on the biorhythm machine. Then he set the machine for his own birthday. He put a quarter in and watched as the needle sketched his biorhythmic peaks and valleys. There was a "clunk" when the machine finished, and then silence. Anthony grabbed the card and found that he'd scored high on all but family and driving.

ANTHONY SELLS
JULIETTE A RAFFLE

October 1981

DURING THE VIEWING HOURS at the Hopping Funeral Home, Juliette found herself cornered by Aunt Camille, her mother's younger sister. In Camille's voice she could sense tension that she knew stemmed from her father. Just about everyone on the Marinetti side of the family held him responsible for the suicide. People like Aunt Camille and Uncle Gino wouldn't speak to him.

"You poor girl," Camille said. "How are you doing?"

Juliette said, "Fine."

"Have you been crying?"

She said, "Not much. I guess I'm just not very sensitive, or something."

Camille said, "Well, you're just like me."

Juliette liked her aunt Camille, who'd always treated her very nicely. Unlike her mother, Camille would sometimes take her clothes-shopping. They would eat lunch at the fanciest mall restaurant. When Camille smoked cigarettes, she'd always offer one to Juliette. Meanwhile her mother, who also smoked, constantly badgered Juliette to quit.

Aunt Camille had a rich banker husband, Frankie. They had bought Juliette several expensive presents. The opal earrings were a gift on her fifteenth birthday. The silver jewelry box was an embarrassing gift last Christmas. When Juliette opened it, her mother had seemed flustered and then angry. She had said, "What the hell? This probably was lying in her attic."

Juliette knew better. During one mall outing, Juliette had admired the silver box. She had mentioned to Aunt Camille that it was gorgeous. She even knew the exact price.

"How's school?" Camille asked.

She said, "I'm passing all of my classes, with straight C's."

Camille smiled and said, "Well, you could have A's if you tried harder. Of course, it's not the Marinetti way."

She said, "My last name is actually Dimiglio."

Camille said, "Yes, but you are *such* a Marinetti. Just like your mother, at least before she married Vince the bricklayer and tossed her life away."

"Pop was already doing office stuff when they married," Juliette said.

Aunt Camille nodded. She glanced across the room toward the spot where Juliette's father recently had been standing.

Camille said, "Izzy was so talented. You should have seen her doing ballet as a kid. I was so jealous. Then she grew up and got the Marinetti figure. You can't have that and do ballet. And all those guys start thinking that they own you just 'cause they see you. She could have still done something with her dancing. She just didn't know how to deal with guys."

Juliette waited for Camille to make another comment about her father—and his reaction to the Marinetti figure—but she did not. Camille reached into her purse. She pulled out an almost-finished pack of Certs.

"How are the boys?" Juliette asked.

"Wilder than ever," she said, and held the breath mints out toward Juliette.

Juliette took one and said, "Little Frankie looks a lot like you."

"He's turning into a little monster."

"He'll grow up fine," said Juliette, though she knew both boys were spoiled beyond repair.

"That reminds me," Camille said, and put a Certs in her mouth. "Frank Sr. and I discussed this yesterday. We know your pop's not in great shape, with all the gambling and now this."

She nodded toward the outer room, where her sister's body was displayed.

"You could live with us for your last two years of high school. We'd help you get into a college, and we could pay for your tuition. Today a girl has to go to college. At least she does if she wants to marry a smart man."

Juliette was trying to think of what to say—how to explain that she was fine with her lousy father. To explain that it really wasn't his fault that Isabella killed herself. But before Juliette could speak, Camille said, "Think about it, okay? We'd have such fun. We'd be like sisters."

Juliette thanked her but gave no hint of a reaction to the idea.

Camille said, "Hey, you know I love you. You call me any time you want to talk about it more."

She left Camille and found her father with his two brothers, Sal and Lonnie. He raised his arm up when he saw her and she stepped under it. He brought it down over her shoulders, looked at his brothers, and said, "Give me a few minutes with my girl here."

Lonnie and Sal walked away, toward where the cider and cheese and crackers were.

"I'm going home," Juliette said. "I have a headache."

"How are you planning to get home?"

"I'll either walk or take your car. I could come back here at nine to pick you up."

He said, "Alright," and took his keys out of the pocket of his jacket. He said, "You haven't even looked at Isabella."

"Maybe I have," she said, although she hadn't.

He said, "I know you. Let's go take a quick look."

Juliette followed her father into an anteroom, where Isabella's dark-stained casket lay unattended. She had avoided looking at her mother.

She knew her mother was stone dead, prettied with make-up. It all seemed pointless. She also feared that the gunshot to the head would have somehow caused her face to seem distorted. She guessed her mother would have felt the surprise of agony in that half-second of life after she pulled the trigger. And that the muscles of her face would have frozen in an expression of deep pain.

"Poor Isabella," said her father, as they stepped up to the casket. To Juliette's surprise, her mother's gaze looked peaceful. The expression seemed that of someone watching her favorite show. The gunshot wound had been cleaned up well. One of her sisters had put a rosary in her hands.

"Your sad old mother," her father said.

Juliette said, "Yeah, she must have been even sadder than we thought."

He said, "Look, Julie, we're gonna be okay. I've got some money coming in, then we'll get out of here."

Juliette said, "Pop, that's what you've told us ever since I was five years old."

He said, "You trust me, you hear?"

Juliette said, "So, where would we go?"

"Maybe out West somewhere. Las Vegas. No. Maybe Palm Springs, California. It's always hot and you got an artificial lake there in your yard."

"What about Kansas?" she said. "They have tornadoes. We could wind up in the Land of Oz if we get lucky."

"Don't be a wiseass."

Juliette stared down at her dead mother.

She said, "They did a good job. Her face looks nice."

✦ ✦ ✦

As she drove home she wondered why she had not cried once since the suicide. She knew her mother always meant well, though she pushed Juliette in ways that were annoying, at times infuriating. "You have to stop acting like me," her mother told her, over and over. She wanted

Juliette to be a straight A student and go to college. She wanted Juliette to meet nice boys from good families. She got upset every time Juliette went out in a tight sweater. In recent years they had barely talked, and when they did it was often nasty. Now Juliette could not help feeling an overwhelming sense of guilt.

From time to time, Isabella threatened suicide. Juliette would say awful things like, "Just don't screw it up and become a vegetable." She never really thought her mother would go through with it, much less buy a gun and shoot herself. In some ways, her life had seemed to be getting better. At least five years had passed since the last time Pop had hit her. She'd joined a knitting club and learned how to make mittens. She'd even taken up jogging, though to Juliette this hobby had seemed absurd.

Juliette turned onto Fellswood Drive. As she was going around a curve, she saw the back of a green Livingston Lancers letter jacket. A boy was walking on the road, so she veered over to the left. She passed by him and glanced up at the rearview mirror. Anthony Rubin. As she had figured. For two days she had seen him selling raffle tickets in the neighborhood. The day before he'd gone up Cherry Hill Road and hit every house except for hers.

Anthony Rubin had lived next door to her ever since they were both little. For years she'd seen him walking the strange pit bull that had died. She'd seen his birthday parties out in the backyard. She'd seen him playing street hockey in his driveway. Or he'd have friends over for endless games of Wiffleball and Nerf football. Juliette laughed as she thought about her boyfriend describing people who played Nerf football. "Nerf football is for fuck-face fairy dipshits," Tommy would say.

Then again Anthony was supposedly a big hockey star. He was all-state in ninth grade and set some goal-scoring record. Hockey could get pretty physical, from what Juliette had observed. When she saw hockey on TV, it seemed like all the players did was punch each other's faces in.

Juliette turned onto Tanglewood. She started wondering what the prizes for the raffle were. Maybe a typewriter like the one prize that her mother had ever won. It was third prize in a drawing for the Lions

Club. She jumped around like a little girl when someone called and said she was the lucky third-place winner. Then Isabella signed up for a typing class at Seton Hall. It seemed like a good thing. For the first time in about ten years, she took an interest in something other than soap operas.

Unfortunately her father came home stinking drunk one night. He couldn't stand the sound of typing, and when he walked in he found Isabella typing in the kitchen. Juliette came down just in time to see him cream the thing. To see him throw it on the floor and kick the keys apart with his boots. Her mother quickly yanked the plug out so he wouldn't get electrocuted. After that her mom collapsed and began to sob.

The truth was Juliette hated the sound of typing. She was glad she'd never have to hear the annoying hammering of those typewriter keys again. But she felt sorry for her mother, sorry this hobby ended up the way it did. Juliette had hoped that one day someone would invent a noiseless typewriter. She would have bought one for her mother as a present. This had been her secret plan. It was a stupid plan, she knew, and now it obviously didn't matter.

Juliette turned up Cherry Hill. She pulled into her driveway but didn't open the garage. She wasn't sure why she'd left the wake. She didn't really have a headache. She was just sick of speaking with her relatives. Talking to Aunt Camille had been too draining. Her aunt Francesca's twin daughters drove her crazy.

She lit a cigarette and remained in the car. She wondered whether Anthony would come home soon. She knew he drooled over her. It was funny, though somewhat creepy, to catch him staring at her out his bedroom window. At school she sometimes saw him staring when she was holding hands with Tommy. It cracked her up. He was so clean-cut. He seemed to have such a boring and clean-cut life.

✦ ✦ ✦

The next morning, before the funeral, Juliette's father got a phone call. Juliette was standing in the kitchen with her long dress on. Out the window she saw children walking to school.

He took the phone into the den, so that the cord stretched as far as it could and seemed on the verge of popping out of the wall. Juliette tried hard not to listen, but she heard him say, "Don't worry. I'll get the vig or at least most of it, okay?"

There was a silence, then he said, "Hey, I said I'm good for it. Could you let me go to my own wife's funeral?"

Juliette knew her father had a gambling problem. She also knew that he was talking to a loan shark. She guessed he'd gambled away some money he should have used for several months of house and car payments, and that the interest he had to pay on the illegal loan he took was breaking him.

Long ago he'd been a bricklayer. In certain ways it seemed more logical than the job he'd held for almost twenty years. He worked a desk job for a labor union. His office was in a run-down section of Jersey City. She'd been there once and his job had seemed preposterously boring. All day he sat at his desk and answered phone calls. He drank black coffee and yelled at people on the phone.

"No," her father said. "You can breathe easy. It's all coming."

Juliette sensed that the person calling was not willing to breathe easy.

"Look," he said. "Give me a day or two, then send them over. I said I'm good."

She left the kitchen, went upstairs, sat on her bed, and waited for his holler.

✦ ✦ ✦

At the funeral home, her aunts and other relatives were all bawling. She had not seen many of them crying during the viewing hours. Now on the morning of the funeral, something had changed and they were all carrying handkerchiefs.

She said hello to Aunt Camille, who kissed her cheek but did not look once at her father. Her aunt embraced her, hugged her tightly. Camille let go and wiped her eyes. "Oh Juliette," Camille half sobbed. "How can we bury my big sister?" She kissed her aunt and walked away, then she could feel something. She understood her mother was gone forever.

She left her relatives and went into the room with the open casket. It would be closed soon, she knew, and she suspected this would come as a relief. She made her way across the room, unsure why she would want to view her mother's face again. But still she let her eyes fall on Isabella. To her bewilderment, the expression on her mother's face seemed different.

It did not seem calm the way it had the day before. It also wasn't pained the way she had expected. Somehow her mother's face had taken on a haughty look. Her mouth seemed scornful, if not mocking. The expression seemed to radiate disdain. Juliette guessed the change was due to subtle shifts of her limbs and features. Perhaps the floor had been shaking slightly every time someone walked by the casket. Perhaps the calm face had simply been the work of a skilled mortician. She sensed that this was Isabella's true expression, underneath.

At the church, Juliette looked around for Tommy. She didn't really think he'd come, so she was not surprised when she didn't see him. People were milling around a wide room with their funeral faces on. Juliette saw her uncle Gino standing beside his much-too-skinny wife Antonia, both of them wearing very affected looks of sadness. She saw a young couple she didn't know approaching them. The man was heavyset, strong, balding. His twenty-five-year-old wife was blond and beautiful. Whoever these two were, their expressions seemed so contrived that Juliette felt like punching them.

She left the room and ducked into the church, which was still empty. Her mother's casket had been brought in. Now it lay closed, up near the alter, its dark-stained wood catching the glint of some unseen light source. Juliette stood near the back wall. She stared at Jesus on his cross and the church's two large stained-glass windows. She wondered whether she could skip the dinner at Camille's house. She hoped that Tommy would at least show up and take her out. She felt a rush of something odd, perhaps despair, for Isabella. She felt a puzzling desire to see her mother's face again. She also knew that she would not.

People began filing into the empty church room. She turned and looked around for her father. When she saw him Juliette walked over and took him by the arm. She led him up to the front row, where they sat down without a word. He had a handkerchief out and he was crying. His face seemed innocent and boyish as he wept.

+ + +

That afternoon, after the burial, Juliette was upstairs in her bedroom. She was watching Anthony Rubin out the window. He was working the houses on their block, probably hitting up all the people who had not answered their doors two days before. The sky was overcast again and it would pour soon. She wondered whether he would continue selling the tickets in the rain.

Downstairs her father had two visitors, the collectors. They had come early, so Juliette had locked herself inside her bedroom. Tommy was picking her up at five o'clock, supposedly. She kept on watching the driveway for his Firebird, ready to sprint downstairs and slip out through the garage.

She lit a cigarette and spied Anthony on a doorstep down the street. She saw the back of his Livingston Lancers hockey jacket. Some stupid moron stood beside him, handing him money. She watched him ripping a ticket from the raffle book, shaking the man's hand, then jamming the book of tickets into his pocket. She laughed and thought of his expression when he had practically walked into her at Friendly's. He'd stood there gaping, his mouth open, as if he'd suddenly gone dumb.

The front door slammed. She saw the loan sharks heading down the walkway. They both wore stupid-looking hats like Al Capone or something. She hadn't seen them in a while, which was a good thing, since they both were total pigs.

Now she saw Anthony across the street, two houses down, walking in his quick, determined way to another doorstep. She watched the men get in their car. They stayed a long time before the engine started. They looked as if they were counting money, although they could have been just listening to the radio. She heard the engine finally start and watched to make sure they didn't bother Anthony as they left.

Downstairs she found her father pouring himself a bourbon. One of his eyes was all puffed out. He barely looked at her as he sat and downed the bourbon in one swift gulp.

She said, "Oh shit, are you okay?"

He told her, "Yeah. They got their point across."

"What was their point?"

He said, "That's none of your goddamn business."

Juliette ran tap water on her cigarette, then tossed the soggy butt in the garbage. She sat down across the table from her father and said, "Your face, it looks like hell."

He said, "I told you to go over to Camille's house. I oughta clobber you for being here."

She said, "I told you I'm not going to Camille's house."

He said, "Next time you see them come, you get your ass out the back door."

"You told me six," Juliette said. "It's five-fifteen now. Tommy was picking me up at five. He's fucking late so what the hell more do you want?"

Her father stared at her. He was a large man who could throw things such as tables across a room.

"You keep your mouth shut," he said. "These guys are amateur little fucks, which means they might act stupid if they see you, understand?"

Juliette nodded.

"It's a tense time for me," he said. "I owe this little bit of money. Right in the middle of it all your mother decides to blow her head off. Last thing I need is that one of these two goombahs gets an itch for you, right?"

"I get it."

He looked away and poured another bourbon. She saw his eye and felt afraid. She said, "Hey Pop, you should ice your eye. Okay if I make you up an ice pack?"

"I sure could use one," her father said.

Juliette walked over to the freezer and pulled two ice trays out. She banged each one on the sink to get the cubes out, then refilled each tray carefully with water and put them back. She took a plastic Ziploc bag from the drawer beside the kitchen sink, filled it with ice as her father downed the bourbon. Then she said, "Here Pop, take this." She held the bag until he reached for it. She watched him press it to his eye.

"You're a good kid, Julie," he said. "You got some cigarettes lying around here?"

"There's a pack somewhere," she said, turned around, and opened the same drawer where the Ziploc bags were. She didn't see any cigarettes, so she opened another drawer. There she found magazines, clipped coupons, matches, gum wrappers, *Soap Opera Digests*. She grabbed a matchbook and slid open another drawer. A pack of Marlboros sat inside. She took them out and placed them on the table. The doorbell rang. With great relief, she said, "That's Tommy."

Juliette sprinted up to her bathroom. She washed her face, combed her hair, and put on lipstick. She tucked her T-shirt tight into her jeans. She ran downstairs, then up again. She looked once more into the mirror. She combed her hair one more time, then shook it out and decided it was hopeless. She raced downstairs, opened the door, and found her neighbor, Anthony Rubin, with a book of bright blue raffle tickets in his hand.

She stepped outside and quickly slammed the door shut.

She said, "Anthony."

He looked right at her the way he always did, half enraptured and half ready to throw up.

"I'm selling raffles," he said. "I've been to every house on the block. I thought I might as well stop here, too."

She didn't answer.

"I can just leave."

"What a salesman," Juliette said. "Shouldn't you try at least telling me what the prizes are?"

"Right," Anthony said. "Okay. You know, my father says the key to selling is excitement. He says you always should act thrilled to be a salesman. My sister says the key is to be pushy. I'm still not sure which one works better."

She said, "You really are an awful salesman."

She pulled the door open and stepped in, but he kept standing there. She was about to slam the door in his face when Anthony said, "Sorry about your mom."

"What?" she said.

"I watched the ambulance out the window. I'm really sorry. It looked awful."

"That's not a topic for conversation."

"Well, I'm still sorry," he said. "I'd better go."

"Jesus Christ," Juliette said. "Aren't you going to say the prizes?"

"It doesn't sound like you want to hear them."

Juliette said, "Look, I'm really tense. Could you please humor me and tell me the damn prizes?"

"Okay," he said, and checked the raffle book. "First prize is an RCA color television. Second's a Hoover vacuum cleaner. Third is free dinner at Bonvini's Family Pizzeria."

Juliette said, "Wow. Hard to beat those."

"I know they suck," Anthony said. "But it's to raise money for the hockey team."

"Money for what?"

"We have this tournament in February. We're raising money to help with airplane fares to Minnesota."

"Sounds like a pretty pathetic cause."

He said, "It's hockey. That's the cause. If you like hockey, then it's worthwhile."

"How much are they?"

"Two dollars."

She said, "Two dollars for one ticket? And the third prize is a dinner at Bonvini's?"

"They have good mussels marinara."

"You order mussels at Bonvini's?"

"I don't like pizza all that much."

"You really are strange," she said, and kept on staring. She saw a white scar on his chin. Behind his head she saw a brooding sky with clouds so dark they almost looked like velvet.

She said, "It's going to start pouring any second."

He said, "I know."

"So how'd you get that scar?"

"This one?"

Anthony touched his chin with the book of raffle tickets.

Juliette said, "Yes. Did someone hit you with a stick?"

"Actually, no," Anthony said. "When I was seven I fell down at a swimming pool. I was hurdling a chaise lounge, and my foot caught. My chin landed on a bottle."

"That's a dumb story."

"It's what happened."

"Then you should change it."

He pointed under his right eye and said, "See this one?"

She saw a thread of a scar that was barely noticeable.

She said, "It looks more like a zit."

"Well, it's a scar and it *did* come from a hockey game," he said. "My first year playing, before they invented face masks. The Chatham Boro goalie flipped the puck into my face. I was rushing in to try and block his clear, and so he flipped it."

He hit his face with the raffle book to demonstrate.

"The puck bounced off me and went right into the net—my second goal of the game."

"Your face was bleeding from the puck?"

He said, "I had to go get *stitches.*"

"Nice," Juliette said, and wondered why she was still standing there. She said, "So, I guess hockey's kind of dangerous."

"Not really," he said. "Now we have face masks. And most of the time it doesn't even hurt when you get checked. Haven't you noticed the way players get right up?"

She said, "I've never been to a game."

"Well you should come," Anthony said. "Three weeks from Thursday's our opener against Brick Town."

"My boyfriend doesn't really like hockey."

"Go without him."

She said, "Maybe."

He slipped the raffle book into his pocket and seemed afraid of her again. Somehow this fear made her all anxious and wild with feelings that made no sense.

Juliette said, "So, don't you want me to buy a raffle?"

He said, "Not really. I just wanted to say sorry about your mother. I meant to tell you the other day in Friendly's. I'm glad we finally got to talk."

She felt surprised, even startled, that he could say something that simple and intelligent. Of course, there hadn't been any actual point to talking. She truly doubted they would ever talk again.

"Me too," Juliette said.

It began raining.

"I guess we're nine years overdue."

"More like fourteen," she said, and took her wallet out. She found two dollars and said, "Go home and fill my name out. I think you know my address. You'd better get out of this rain."

"I don't mind rain," he said.

It started pouring.

"Please take the money before I kill you."

She placed the two bills in his hand, but he kept standing on her doorstep.

He said, "Hey Juliette."

"What?"

"Come out here."

"In the rain?"

"I know you like the rain," he said.

His hair was wet now and dripping down his forehead.

"God, you're a weirdo."

"Are you coming?"

She said, "Why would I?"

Anthony shrugged and she stared quizzically at her neighbor. She knew that Tommy had stood her up. She guessed that Anthony was nuts.

She said, "I must be going crazy."

Then she stepped out into the rain.

He said, "You're not," and for some reason she felt lighthearted, despite everything. She smiled at Anthony. She felt rain. She raised her arms out to her sides and let it soak her.

LOST MEADOWS

October 1981

ANTHONY WAS STILL thinking about the Rush concert, trying to understand why the final encore, "Red Barchetta," made him so happy. His sister, Dani, was in the backseat with her head on Bobby Tannenbaum's shoulder. Josh Stern was driving and doing his best to act as if he knew where they were going.

They were about to be lost. That much was obvious. Josh had tried taking a shortcut that he claimed would avoid the traffic after the concert. Instead of waiting in the long line to get on Route 3 from the sports complex, he'd taken the one exit no one seemed to be going near. "This is amazing," Josh said, as a ramp fed his mother's Saab onto a winding two-lane road. For a few minutes, they were heading toward the skyline of New York. But then the road veered to the right and the whole universe seemed to vanish.

Giants Stadium, Brendan Byrne Arena, even New York disappeared behind tall marsh grass. They drove beside a wall of reeds, through mist and ominous-seeming swampland. Anthony figured a dumped body would appear along the roadside any second.

"We're in Secaucus," said Josh. "I think."

Dani said, "Shouldn't we just turn around and wait with the other cars?"

Josh said, "Don't worry. If we can cross this swamp I'm pretty sure we wind up at the Turnpike."

They all knew better, but still they hoped Josh knew where he was going.

"I loved that final song," said Josh.

"That song was weird," Dani said. "It's like some fascist thing's going on. And then that video they had going of a car chase. What was that?"

"The whole song's set in the future," Anthony told her.

Dani said, "So?"

"When he escapes across that bridge, it's like a doorway back into the past."

Josh said, "I love when Geddy plays that bass solo. He's such a talented musician."

"I'm thinking maybe he's a eunuch," Dani said. "His voice is so high it's kind of frightening."

Anthony was about to start defending Geddy Lee when they hit a pothole. But it was more than a pothole. It was like dropping into a ditch. Josh hit the brakes, which left the car almost suspended, nose angled down into the hole. He tried to floor it in reverse but the car was stuck. It wouldn't budge.

"Let's lift it out," Josh suggested.

They all got out and tried to lift it. The nose was wedged in such a way that moving the vehicle was impossible.

Dani said, "Great, here we are."

"We'll have to call Triple A," said Josh.

"We're in the middle of the damn Meadowlands," said Dani. "It might be days before anyone can find us."

"Someone will pass," Josh said.

A fog was settling over the meadows. Anthony smelled the giant garbage mountains in Kearny, so he knew the Turnpike couldn't be that far.

"Is it safe?" Dani said.

"What?"

"Being stuck here. Even the fog smells."

Josh said, "I don't think we have a lot of choice."

"My friend Marc Aaronson comes here to bird-watch with his dad," Anthony said.

Dani said, "Thanks. When we get home we'll plan a field trip."

"Don't be a bitch," Anthony said. "I'm just saying that it's safer than it smells."

Dani said, "Well, I don't feel safe. Shouldn't we turn on the hazard lights or something?"

Josh turned his hazard lights on. Within that blinking reddish glow, the foursome stood on the road beside the car. If nothing else, it was a warm night, maybe sixty-five degrees out. They were all wearing Rush concert jerseys except Dani, who wore a short denim skirt, a turtleneck, and loafers. Josh put a Rush tape in and they stood around the car listening to "Tom Sawyer." About halfway through the song he turned the tape off and said, "Jesus, what the hell are we gonna do?"

"I could make it to Giants Stadium in half an hour," Anthony said. "I could jog. It's probably three miles."

"That's a dumb idea," said Dani. "You could get lost."

Bobby said, "I could go with Anthony."

Josh said, "We'd better stick together."

"Oh what the hell," Dani said. "Nothing like hiking through the Meadowlands at midnight."

Bobby smiled and said, "Hey. At least you didn't wear your clogs." He put his arms around her shoulders and she leaned into him. After a few seconds she looked up and said, "Okay, is there a flashlight in the car?"

Josh searched the trunk. He produced a six-volt flashlight with no bulb. He rifled through his mother's glove compartment, where he found a single penlight.

"This one works," Josh said, and shined the tiny flashlight. "And we have these."

He held up his mother's fluorescent-green reflecting jogger wrist bands.

"Anyone want them?"
Everyone looked at Anthony.
He said, "Sure."

✦ ✦ ✦

The fog had settled thickly over the meadows and the road. Each time they stepped through another cloud wall, Anthony felt the surreal moisture on his face. Then just as quickly as they had entered, they would step out into clear air and the pale moonlight that illuminated the endless marsh grass. Soon all the meadows began to seem like a new planet they'd discovered, and despite Dani's apprehension, he felt strangely happy to be lost.

After an hour, they'd walked far enough that Giants Stadium should have at least been visible. They kept on going, assuming it would pop up any second. Another half hour passed, and even Josh understood that they'd screwed up.

"We must have missed a turn," said Dani.

Josh said, "There wasn't a turn to take."

"Can someone promise me we're not going to spend all night here?" Dani asked.

"Let's just keep walking," Josh said. "I'm sure we'll see something soon."

By Josh's voice Anthony knew he was getting nervous. It was past midnight and they could have been almost anywhere. Anthony scanned the roadside for some marker or clue or meaning. He saw a rise and said, "Look, the ground seems higher than the road."

"He's right," Bobby said. "It's higher."

"Were you two planning to make camp?" asked Dani.

Bobby said, "No, but maybe we can see something. I've also had to pee for about an hour."

Josh said, "I wouldn't go up there if you paid me."

"It looks okay," Anthony said. He thought again of Marc Aaronson and his father. Marc said they'd driven out to East Rutherford once at dawn. They had seen egrets and great blue herons as the sun rose over a place called Walden Swamp. Now Anthony saw the rise in the land and wondered what was up there. He saw a path that curved off to the right and vanished behind marsh grass. The way it curved drew his eye into the unseen.

"I'll go with Anthony," Bobby said. "We'll check it out."

Dani said, "I'll just stay right here and avoid cancer."

"I'm with Dani," said Josh, and handed Bobby the penlight.

Dani said, "Please don't touch anything that's glowing."

Anthony followed Bobby up into the meadow. They went beyond the bend in the curving path, and he looked back just to see that they were now no longer visible from the road. Within that mist and the thread of light from the tiny flashlight, he vaguely worried that they *would* find a vat of radioactive sludge. But when the path opened into a wide meadow, all they could see was a stretch of desiccated, yellowish chest-high grass.

"Looks fine to me," Bobby said.

Anthony said, "It actually looks nice."

He took a few steps out into the meadow. He looked around for Giants Stadium but saw nothing except the sweep of the wide field. Just as he wondered if they'd stumbled on the last pristine meadow in the Meadowlands, he felt his knee connect with something solid.

"Shit," he said.

"What?"

"I just banged into something."

Bobby shined the tiny flashlight toward the spot where Anthony was standing. Anthony pushed aside some grass, which revealed the flared end of a white marching-band tuba.

"What the hell is that?" Bobby said.

"It's an old tuba."

Bobby stepped closer and shined the light down into the tuba's mouth. He kicked the instrument, knocked it over. Anthony saw that the base was rusted and caked with dirt. The middle section was designed to curl and fit around a marcher's body. Somehow the tuba resembled a giant snake.

They both unzipped their flies and peed beside the instrument. Other animals came to mind—a baby elephant, a small hippo. Anthony watched the beam from the flashlight as it fell onto a patch of grass ahead of them. He was only mildly surprised when something glowed and reflected the light back.

"Check that out," said Bobby, and stepped toward it. He crouched down until Anthony could no longer see the glow.

"What've you got?" Anthony asked.

Bobby held a rusted, slightly bent trombone up. He let it fall and said, "I think that we've discovered a band graveyard."

They started searching around the meadow. Though most lay hidden beneath the dry grass, the dead instruments were everywhere. They took five steps and discovered the black remains of a badly damaged clarinet.

A few more steps and they found a cymbal. Bobby lifted it by its handle. On the ground beneath it, the cymbal left a perfect circle of bare earth. Just past the cymbal they found a shadowy mound that proved to be a pile of majorette hats. They were all rotted. Bobby and Anthony didn't touch them.

"Maybe the mob knocked off a whole marching band," said Bobby.

Anthony laughed as Bobby pushed aside grass and shined his light onto a bass drum. "Man, check that out," Bobby said, and caressed the drum as if it were some lost medieval relic. He pulled more grass away and shined the penlight onto the drum's face. Anthony saw three dark green letters: LIN.

"You think it came from the town of Linwood?"

"That's all the way down by Atlantic City."

"What about Linden?" Anthony said.

They heard a noise and saw the fog-muted glow of headlights above the marsh grass.

Bobby said, "Shit, that's a car. Let's go."

They both charged back across the meadow, dodging the instruments with the agility of two soldiers sprinting across a battlefield. By the entrance, Bobby hurdled the dead tuba. Anthony followed, catching part of it with his foot but still not falling. They both raced down the path to the roadside, where Josh and Dani were both flailing their arms wildly above their heads. Bobby ran up and shined the flashlight toward the vehicle, a truck. Anthony held up his wrists to catch the headlights. He kept on staring at his wrists, trying to see the fluorescent glow.

✦ ✦ ✦

An eighteen-wheeler slowed beside them and then groaned to a full stop. The driver turned out to be a woman. She looked to be about thirty-five. She had a hardened but pretty face, a cold expression, but watchful eyes. Her hair was tied behind her head in a long blond pony-tail. She leaned her head out of the window and seemed tired.

"What are you doing?" the woman yelled above the engine.

"My car broke down up the road," Josh yelled. "We were trying to walk back to Giants Stadium."

"You would have walked most of the night. Another five miles, you come to my father's landfill, which is closed."

"We didn't see any turns."

"It was a mile ago. By the tower."

"We didn't even see a tower."

"Okay, get in," the woman yelled. "I'll call a tow truck and take you back to your car. On the way, I'll show you where the turn was."

"Do you own this dump right here?" Anthony screamed up to her.

"What?" The woman looked down and saw the reflector wrist bands. She yelled, "Who are you, Jimmy Connors?"

He yelled, "They glow in the dark. We thought they'd help. So do you own it?"

Anthony pointed to the path.

"You mean that field with all the instruments?"

Anthony nodded.

"Jocko McCarthy does," she said. "So do you all want to get in or would you rather stay here with the instruments?"

They all climbed into the truck's cab, Dani and Anthony squashing Bobby and Josh's laps. Bobby politely asked the woman questions. He won her over. She said her name was Morgan, and that they weren't the first dumb rich kids she had rescued in the meadows. She said she'd spent her childhood living in North Arlington. She had a half-brother who had messed himself up on drugs. Now she drove trucks for her father. She said his name was Bob Lafleur.

"Like Guy Lafleur?" Anthony asked.

Morgan said, "Who?"

He said, "He plays for the Montreal Canadiens. When he retires he'll make the Hockey Hall of Fame."

"I don't watch hockey," Morgan said.

"Are you Canadian?"

"No, American." She pointed. "Right over there is where you missed the turn."

Anthony craned his neck to see over Dani's shoulder. A two-lane road wound into misty darkness.

"How did we miss it?" Josh said. "How could we *not* see that road?"

In a pleasant enough voice, Morgan said, "Well, I'd say you're fools."

Anthony watched the truck's odometer. To his surprise, more than six miles reeled off before they got back to Josh's car. Morgan slowed down and stopped the truck so that her lights shined directly on the angled-up rear bumper. She killed the engine and the meadows suddenly seemed hauntingly silent and unfamiliar.

"I'll take a look," she said. "If you're just stuck I can pull you out."

They all hopped down from the cab. Morgan was wearing the kind of heavyweight full-body suit that mechanics often wear. Josh asked her whether she was also a mechanic. She said, "Yup."

Morgan climbed down into the giant pothole. She slid beneath Josh's car and assessed the situation. Anthony heard the sound of her flashlight tapping metal. All he could see were the work boots on her feet.

After five minutes she climbed back out. She took a seat at the pothole's edge. Her hair had started to come loose, so she reached back to redo the band that held it. She turned to Josh and said, "Looks like you busted your front axle."

"What does that mean?" Josh said.

She said, "An axle. It's broken. Know what an axle is?"

"Something serious?"

Morgan said, "Man, you rich kids from the suburbs."

She let her thick blond hair out to its full length. She retied it. She smiled pleasantly at Anthony. He stared as if Morgan were some sort of truck-driving Meadowlands fairy princess.

"It's the supporting shaft that the wheels rotate on," said Bobby.

Dani said, "Looks like we're marooned."

"That's one way to put it," Morgan told them. "I'll make a call to Ernie's Shell station on Route 3. They have a flatbed."

"Are they with Triple A?" asked Josh.

She didn't answer. She walked back over to her truck, grabbed some handle, and hopped up to the cab. She took her CB off its holder. She looked away to the side while she was talking. When she was finished she started the truck, pulled up, and leaned her head out the window.

"Someone will be here soon," she said, once again yelling above the engine. "They won't be able to fit all of you in the tow truck. I can give two of you a ride."

"I'll stay with Josh," Bobby yelled.

Dani and Anthony started walking toward the truck.

"Can it be fixed?" yelled Josh.

Morgan looked down and yelled, "Sure. Won't run you more than two hundred. Maybe one-fifty. Ernie will get to it next week. He's pretty good that way."

This seemed to break Josh's spirit. He still had hopes, Anthony knew, that some mechanic could fix the car in twenty minutes that same night.

Dani and Anthony climbed up into the cab and slid in beside Morgan. She put the truck in gear and pulled forward. She said, "I need to find someplace to turn around."

They went around a sweeping curve. About three-tenths of a mile ahead, there was a sign that said TO NJ TURNPIKE. Neither Anthony or Dani made a comment.

"Are you two brother and sister?" Morgan asked them.

Dani said, "Yeah, how did you know?"

She said, "It's easy. I can tell by the way you act around each other."

She turned around on a roadside pull-off. In the distance Anthony saw a stream of headlights from the Turnpike. After the time spent wandering in nothingness, the cars were startling. He watched as Morgan's strong arms steered them through the turn.

They passed by Bobby and Josh, who waved. Morgan waved once and did not stop.

She said, "You're lucky to have a boyfriend like that guy back there."

Dani said, "Thank you. His name is Bobby."

"You'd be surprised how hard it gets to find a decent guy," Morgan said. "My last boyfriend I thought was pretty decent. He turned out to be a drunk."

She put the radio on and fiddled with the tuning dial. She settled on a station playing a song by Billy Joel.

"Do you have a girlfriend?" Morgan asked Anthony.

He said, "No."

"Why not?"

Dani said, "Anthony's too busy having a crush on our mobster neighbor."

"Her name is Juliette," he said. "She's not as awful as you think."

Dani said, "Juliette would eat your heart for breakfast. Don't you know that?"

Morgan laughed and said, "I actually think he does."

"I wouldn't let her," Anthony said.

He pictured Juliette's moody eyes. Her pouty mouth and her pretty nose. He had now talked to her twice in school since the day she bought a raffle ticket. She acted sweet with him, and playful. She always asked if she won the vacuum, even though she knew the drawing wasn't until January.

Dani said, "Hey, what did you mean about those instruments?"

"There's lots of trumpets and things," said Morgan. "It's a whole marching band's worth of stuff."

"That's really strange," Dani said.

"Every piece of junk has to wind up somewhere."

"But it's not like instruments go bad."

Morgan said, "Why would you tear Penn Station down? Can either one of you tell me that?"

"What do you mean?" Dani said. "I was at Penn Station last week."

"Not that Penn Station. The old one."

"There was an old one?"

She said, "Of course there was an old one."

She slipped her hand into a small purse on the dashboard. For one ridiculous second Anthony wondered whether she was reaching for a handgun. Her hand emerged with a pack of Juicy Fruit gum. She took a stick and passed the pack to Dani.

"They tore it down in 1964," Morgan continued. "Then the whole station, all its columns, were dumped out here. It was this gorgeous work of modern architecture or something. I've seen the columns. A bunch got dumped in this one field that my father's friend owns."

Dani unwrapped a stick of gum. She said, "How come they tore it down?"

"I guess they wanted something new, or something bigger," Morgan said.

As if on cue, Giants Stadium rose above the meadows at that moment. The lights were brighter than the moon. The New York skyline reappeared.

"Thank *God*," Dani said, and handed Anthony the gum. "I just hope Bobby and Josh get rescued."

Morgan said, "Ernie's on his way."

"I hope Josh isn't driving Bobby crazy."

"I wouldn't worry," Morgan said. "Your boyfriend seems like he can handle things."

"He's pretty great, huh," Dani said.

Morgan smiled and blew a tiny bubble with her chewing gum. Then she said, "Yeah, if I was your age I'd be jumping him in a second."

Dani said, "You and the whole world."

"I knew a guy like him," Morgan went on. "Sammy O'Toole, he lives in Philly now. I must have been insane to let him go. And I can tell you. You should take it from me. Don't ever let that boy out of your sight."

Dani looked over at Anthony, smiled, and didn't answer.

Morgan said, "Hey, Little Miss Smarty Pants. You listening?"

Dani said, "Yes. I think I heard you."

"Don't let that boy out of your sight."

"It's not that easy," Dani said. "We both applied to different colleges."

Morgan said, "Man, you rich kids from the suburbs."

As they turned onto Route 3, Anthony saw that the lot outside the Brendan Byrne Arena was deserted. If they had waited in the line of post-concert traffic, he knew they'd all have been lying in their own beds now.

"There's Ernie's flatbed," Morgan said.

Anthony watched as the truck zoomed by. Then his gaze was drawn back out into the shadowy, fog-swept meadowland. He saw a Days Inn and two other buildings looming over the marshes. He wondered where in that enormous expanse of darkness he'd been walking.

Morgan dropped them off at the Shell station. She was long gone when Ernie pulled in with Josh, Bobby, and the Saab. Dani had called their father and explained the situation. It was past two and he'd been worrying. He'd called up Bobby's and Josh's parents, and was now coming with Josh's father to pick them up.

Bobby hopped down from the truck and looked at Dani, who'd closed her eyes and sat dozing on a bench. Anthony elbowed his sister gently. When Dani opened her eyes and saw him, she yelled, "Bobby!" as if they'd been apart for months. She sprang right up and walked directly toward him. Standing in front of a super unleaded gas pump, Bobby opened his arms wide.

Anthony saw the words "Moving Pictures" on Bobby's Rush shirt. Then Dani's body covered up the words. She slipped her arms up to his neck. They started kissing within the eerily bright light of the Route 3 Shell station. A kiss flashed through Anthony's mind: a girl named Jackie he once kissed at the Jersey Shore.

Josh called out, "Hey, should we get all of this stuff out of the car?"

Bobby and Dani chose to ignore him. Dutifully, Anthony headed over. Josh was there searching through the documents in the glove compartment. As Anthony crossed the strangely lustrous asphalt of the Shell station, he glanced once more back at his sister and Bobby Tannenbaum. They were still kissing but the scene possessed a different feel, a sadness. It was already, he sensed, part of the past.

GOODNIGHT KISS

November 1981

ON THE BALLFIELD Tommy Lange was beating up a blue-eyed math whiz named Roland Malnick. He'd cornered Roland by the backstop. Roland was standing on home plate with about fifteen people watching.

People called the kid Roly, since he was fat and was always falling down in gym class. In the boys' bathroom, he had been peeing beside Lance Silver, who Roland knew from the accelerated math class.

He'd said, "I'd love to grab those mangos on Juliette Dimiglio."

Lance had said, "Roly, I think you should stick to math."

"She looks like such a total slut. Did you just see her?"

Lance said, "No."

"I bet she blows every guy she sees," Roland said. "I'd love to put it right between her mangos."

Ten feet away Tommy Lange was taking a crap inside one of the bathroom stalls. Juliette stood waiting in the hall, where the photography class exhibit covered seven bulletin boards. She stared at photos that depicted "Life in Livingston, New Jersey." This was all bullshit, she was thinking. Life in this stupid town, for her, was not these quiet streets and leaf raking and firemen's parades. Most days she sat around watching football practice, waiting for Tommy. Waiting for five-thirty, when he'd spread-eagle her in his Firebird. Then she'd return home sore and sweaty and get yelled at by her father. She'd go outside on her back steps, smoke a cigarette, and wonder who she was.

Now Juliette stood watching as Roland Malnick quaked with fear. It was a warm day for November. It looked like rain again. She didn't move or speak or cringe as Tommy grabbed the frightened boy. She continued watching, expressionless, as Tommy slammed the boy against the earth.

Tommy said, "Juliette, come over here."

She walked over and stood beside him.

"You wanna hit him?"

"No."

"Why not?"

She didn't answer.

Roland tried running, but Tommy grabbed him, almost comically. He picked Roland up and lobbed him face first back down to the ground. Juliette walked away from Tommy, but he yelled, "Stay here, Juliette!"

Roland got up, his nose bleeding. His cherubic face had turned bright red. Tommy took one of his sneakers off and then told Roland it was time to chew on leather.

"Open up wide," Tommy said, and jammed the sneaker into Roland's mouth. Juliette began walking away again. Tommy said, "No, Juliette, stay here. I want you to stay where Roly can keep staring at your mangos."

Like an automaton she stood there, almost as if she had done all this before. She dropped her book bag on home plate. She slid her purse up to her shoulder and stared at Roland without expression.

Tommy said, "Chew on that shoe. Good boy. Soften that leather up."

Tommy asked Roland how it tasted. He suggested Roland recall that taste next time he wanted to stare at Juliette. The boy kept chewing the shoe, crying, wondering when it would all stop.

Tommy said, "Okay, give the shoe back." Roland timidly held it out. Tommy took it, slipped it on. Then he said, "Thank you, Roly-Poly." All this seemed humorous for a second, until suddenly Tommy flattened him and left Roland writhing in pain. Juliette darted over, knelt beside him, and said, "Roland?"

Tommy yelled, "Leave him!"

He reached over Juliette and lifted Roland by the shirt. Compared to Tommy, the boy looked tiny. His bright eyes seemed to glow with terror. Now Tommy punched him in the gut and slammed his body to the ground again. Clearly in shock, Roland looked up.

He said, "Stop hitting me. I'm hurt." He held his chest as if it had been broken. Tommy said, "Okay, Roly-Poly, here comes one last goodnight kiss."

Juliette said, "Wait. Tommy, come on."

Tommy said, "What, it's almost over. I'm finishing this little pukehead off."

"You know, you're like a goddamn pit bull. You'll wind up killing the fucking kid."

Tommy said, "Roly-Poly should know better. Now he does. So let me finish him."

"He's finished," said Juliette, and dropped her purse beside her book bag. She stepped in front of Roland. She looked at Tommy and said, "Enough."

"Oh, come on," Tommy said, and grabbed Juliette by the waist. He lifted her up confidently, with firm hands, the way he might lift a football. He turned and placed her at his side. Then he said, "Roly, keep your eyes open. I want you to see my fist."

Juliette said, "Wait, Tommy. I'll do it."

"What?"

"I'll finish this. I'll hurt him. But at least I won't kill the fucking kid."

"Are you serious?"

She said, "Yeah."

Juliette walked over to Roland, who curled up as she approached. He clutched the earth and began trembling now as Juliette knelt beside him.

She said, "You poor stupid kid. You gotta know that my boyfriend's got a mean streak. You gotta figure I'm not standing outside the bathroom for my health. You're a math brain, for chrissake. Where was your brain this afternoon?"

Roland said, "What are you gonna do?"

"I'm gonna hit you," she said. "'Cause if I don't, my stupid boyfriend will wind up putting you in the hospital."

"I don't understand this. I don't think this is fair."

Juliette said, "Roly, life's not fair. That's why you have to watch your mouth. I'd say you've definitely had some crappy luck here. But sometimes that's the way it goes."

"You're gonna punch me?"

Juliette nodded. She said, "Believe me, it's the biggest favor I could do for you."

"Do you punch hard?"

She said, "Maybe. Let's stand you up and get this over with, okay?"

It started raining as she helped him up. She lifted the boy carefully, almost tenderly. Beside her, Roland looked like a shapeless blob.

The rain got louder and smacked the ground, spattering in small splashes. She pushed her hair behind her ears as she stared at Roland and said, "Sorry about this."

"I really can't accept your apology."

"That's okay," Juliette said.

Turning to Tommy, she said, "I want you to stop acting like a shithead. So if I do this, will you stop?"

"Stop what?" Tommy said.

"Picking on harmless kids."

Tommy said, "No, but if you'd clobber him, we could get out of this fucking rain."

Already Juliette's hair was drenched. It fell down over her face as she leaned over him. Under her breath she said, "Hey listen, I'm really sorry. Next time just don't be such a fucking idiot."

"You're the idiot," Roland said quietly. "You're the one whose mother died because she was a prostitute."

A tremor passed through her body. She let his collar go, then grabbed it again. She slammed him back against the ground and pressed one knee against his chest.

"Where the hell did you hear that?"

"That's what people say."

Keeping her voice low, she said, "My mother was *not* a prostitute. She shot herself. You better watch your fucking mouth."

Juliette was shaking, trying to keep herself from hurting him. She felt like gouging his sad eyes out.

She said, "My mother was clinically depressed, you understand that?"

Roland looked up with a hateful gleam, his blue eyes almost twinkling. He said, "Your father's a dumb mobster who screwed up with someone's money. They made your mom become a whore again, so she shot herself."

For one instant Juliette stared at him, bewildered. Then she kneed Roland in the groin with all her might. She pulled him up off the ground and threw him down again, face first. She kicked his ribs and he started moaning. She turned him over, squeezed his face, until he looked more like a fish.

Juliette said, "What, do you have a death wish? Are you crazy?"

He couldn't answer. She felt raindrops. She pressed Roland's face into the mud and screamed, "Goddamn it!"

Roland was holding his groin, writhing, and then Tommy was standing beside Juliette.

He said, "The poindexter pissed you off. What did he say?"

She didn't answer.

"He say something about your tits again?"

Juliette said, "Yeah, this little kid is fucking nuts."

"You laid him out," Tommy said.

She watched as Roland clutched his groin. She heard his anguished breaths and watched as tears went gushing down his face. Juliette suddenly felt absent. She felt as if she were made of air, as if she wasn't actually in her body.

She could hear Tommy yelling at Roland, telling the boy to start running unless he wanted to lose his teeth. Somehow Roland got up.

His face was muddy and the blood from his nose was all around his mouth. Clutching his ribs, he grabbed his book bag and hobbled off as Tommy shouted at him maniacally. It started raining even harder, and then a bolt of lightning flashed across the sky.

Everyone watching went for their cars. After a minute it was just Juliette and Tommy beside home plate.

Tommy said, "What, Juliette? You clobbered him."

Juliette sat down, crossed her arms.

Tommy said, "Juliette, what's your problem?"

She said, "Just stay here."

"It's pouring."

She said, "Then leave me the hell alone."

Finally Tommy picked her up. He said, "Okay, get on your feet. I'm putting you on your feet."

She felt her feet touching the ground. She stared at Tommy, sizing him up. She watched the rain drip down his face and mat his bangs against his forehead. Then she said, "Tommy, you're one scary motherfucker."

"Can we get out of here?" he said.

She reached down for her purse, but stopped. She knelt beside it and breathed deeply. Then she laced it around her shoulder.

"Is this slow motion?" Tommy said. "Can we get out of this fucking rain?"

"Can you shut up for one second!"

"No."

"Tommy, *please*," she said.

"What? I'm leaving in ten seconds, with or without you, so come on."

"You really are a fucking asshole."

He said, "I am when you act like a dumb bitch."

"Fuck you," Juliette said, and it took all her strength to rise. She understood that she despised him. She wondered why it was so arousing. She knew she'd probably wind up screwing him in his Firebird until dinnertime. She breathed in deeply, grabbed her book bag, and said, "Let's go."

THE INVISIBLE WORLD

November 1981

THIS IS THE SITUATION, Michael. Your character may die. Not physically. Just in spirit. It sometimes happens. The successful secular Jewish professional who tries to do right but is plagued by his unconscious, internal contradictions.

Who can fault your very reputable aspirations? You have succeeded. You are identical to every other suburban doctor in Essex County. But now your wife has moved to Florida. You don't even have a girlfriend at the moment. It's nothing strange, nothing provocative or original. And yet you find you walk on eggshells. You're drawn to women who make no sense for you. You keep on wanting all these women who, in some way, you can't have.

What about Dr. Jenny Walsh, the twenty-seven-year-old pediatrics resident? She acts so sweet to you and guileless at the hospital. She will sit down with you in the hospital cafeteria. She would go out with you because she just got dumped by Andrew Allston, the cocksure surgery resident who seems to believe he's God. There is an opening right now. You could date Dr. Jenny Walsh. She'll be excited for two months, maybe three. Then she'll say why would she want to be with someone twice her age. She plans to move back home to Seattle anyway. You'll say that twenty-seven plus twenty-seven isn't...but the point is not the numbers. Then you will long for Dr. Walsh. For her young body. Her mousy face. Her short blond hair.

She has big hips, like Jess. Maybe that's it. There is nostalgia riding here, though Jess was taller and much prettier. Sometimes you think you had it all with Jess. Except her interest, of course. And empathy. But now you see these firm wide hips. The way she slouches as she does paperwork in an alcove. Her aloof poise and her cold, vulnerable demeanor. Her sleep-deprived, incessantly weary gaze. You'll see she's lonely and strangely drawn to total bastards like Drew Allston. You are not nearly such a bastard. Despite the obvious transgressions, you're a nice man at the core. Generous. Whether that's weakness or an asset is still something you debate.

You are there late, having come in after Rose Weissman, a family friend and longtime patient with chronic kidney failure, was admitted. You stood with the nephrologist Sidney Rossner, reviewing Rose's medical history. Rose is delirious, a one-hundred-and-four fever. You discussed treatment and called Dr. James Seabrooks, a vascular surgeon who's coming in to remove the infected access graft. Rossner has moved her to I.C.U., where he is now giving Rose dialysis with a temporary catheter. You have some paperwork. Seabrooks will be here soon. It's eight.

Dr. Walsh arrived at six and will work all night in the E.R. She has a bed down the hall where she may sleep a few hours come three A.M. She has said hi to you. You're waiting for a lull so you can chat. There is a lull right now, of course, but she's absorbed in her own paperwork. So you're there waiting the moment when she walks over and says hi to you again.

You will die, Michael. You understand. You will kill yourself at forty by longing for Dr. Jenny Walsh, a lightweight version of the women for whom you've killed yourself before. There is a new wife out there waiting for you, certainly. She is divorced and has smart teenage kids like you. She dresses well, very elegant. Successful. A professional. She is attractive, in a grown-up way. She'll understand you and, imagine this, the things you can provide will make her happy.

She'll like your gifts, the car you drive, and your strong work ethic. She'll like your latent romantic temperament, your responsible and practical-seeming nature. She will accept your mild sexual eccentricities. She can be dirty and will be glad that it excites you. Perhaps fortunately, she'll never want to have sex in public places. She had good role models for parents. She can communicate, imagine. She will tell you when and exactly why she's angry. You'll respect her.

But of course Jenny is right here. She's a looker. And those hips. She is crossing the Emergency Room in front of you. She's wearing glasses today, not contacts, which sometimes give her bad reactions. You wave to Jenny and she waves back in a way that seems ebullient. Something about you clearly wakes her up.

What would your kids think? Dani is seventeen. Closer to Jenny's age than you are. Even Anthony is closer to her age. They are still mad at you in ways they have not even begun to figure out. Probably not a good thing to bring a twenty-seven-year-old blond home. And Jenny looks twenty-three. She is athletic. Though in the right clothes, and those glasses, she could easily look thirty. They could get used to her, you think. They'd wind up liking her for the three, possibly six months it would last.

You should go home now. You're done for the day. Rose Weissman is in I.C.U. Seabrooks is probably there already and only needs to speak with Rossner. Dani and Anthony have eaten TV dinners, but you can still get home in time to bring them Häagen-Dazs chocolate chocolate chip.

Possibly Jenny will have a break soon. It's an unusually quiet night in the E.R. You see a nurse taking vital signs from a heavy boy with a black eye, a split lip, and a defiant facial expression. Jenny steps over to examine him. She has a pencil behind her ear. You always like that. She is that fine-featured, type-A shiksa dream girl, though she's probably an ice-cold fish in bed.

It would be nice to see your kids tonight. Bring them the Häagen-Dazs. See if Anthony burned the house down. This month your son has decided he will learn to cook what he calls "real food." This now that

TV dinners seem too boring. And now that, God knows why, the kids won't use the charge account you set up at the Eppes Essen deli. You keep reminding them. They won't go.

You also try to come home early at least once a week and cook for them. Things like poached salmon and asparagus don't fly. They only seem to like the things Jess used to buy. Whole, already roasted chickens straight from Shop Rite. The gourmet ravioli stuffed with cheese and mushrooms, also from Shop Rite. Dinner has never been a hallowed institution for your family, but now there seems to be a blatant lack in spirit. Part of the problem is, of course, they miss her. She hasn't called now for three weeks. You've told them both, several times, "No news is good news." If she were missing or dead, you'd know. Jess always does things her own way and she will call them when she's ready. You said all this although you're probably more frazzled than your children. You still imagine you can somehow win Jess back.

Dani and Anthony can both get very passive-aggressive. Dani's aggression can also be the opposite of passive. She sometimes makes cracks about Claudia, who you've not spoken to in a year. You've heard she's sleeping with Al Schoenfeld, the runty millionaire who developed the Newstead section of South Orange.

Why aren't they mad at Jess? They should be furious. In every sense of the word, they've been abandoned. The answer's obvious. Because you're here. Thanks to your presence, you are someone they can be mad at. Thanks to her absence, Jess is alternately Greek tragedy and saint. They don't hate you. Not a bit. In fact they like you, but they still blame you for everything. You aren't blameless, you know, but there's more to it. You also know it's best to let them vent their anger and lay their blame.

On occasion, you will feel hints of forgiveness. The night when Anthony cooked omelets, everyone laughed so hard you knew they couldn't possibly stay mad at you forever. The eggs kept sticking but Anthony kept trying. After the third attempt you took them out for pizza.

Another night he made a variant on the McDonald's Egg McMuffin. You all sat down, each with an English muffin sandwich of one fried egg, a piece of sliced ham, and a wad of melted cheese. They tasted fine, but this was dinner. He had not made any side dish to go with it. "I'm still starving," Dani said when you all finished, five minutes later. She and her brother began searching the kitchen cabinets and cupboards. They brought out Saltines, bittersweet chocolate morsels, an ancient can of sliced pears in heavy syrup. You kept suggesting going for pizza again, but both kids seemed to enjoy the ad hoc scavenging. They made you eat a soggy Saltine with a sliced pear, Skippy peanut butter, and raisins. It was disgusting, but you felt that this was penance.

Dr. Walsh steps out and appears to be done looking at the boy. She smiles at you, walks over to where you're standing, and says, "How come you're here this late?"

A longtime patient, you explain. Her name's Rose Weissman. She's sixty-eight. Friend of the family. She's up in I.C.U. with a high fever, an infected bovine artery graft access, and blood pressure too low for standard hemodialysis.

"Will she pull through?" Dr. Walsh asks.

The odds are good. Within an hour, she'll have the access replaced. Broad spectrum antibiotics should take care of the infection. Her nephrologist, Sidney Rossner, is the best.

"God, I'm so tired," says Dr. Walsh. "I have a break now, twenty minutes. You feel like grabbing a cup of coffee?"

You tell her sure and you both head off to the medical staff lounge.

Then it's the two of you in the coffee lounge. "That was upsetting," Dr. Walsh tells you. "That last patient. That little boy."

You say, "It looked like someone hit him with a baseball bat."

She says, "At first it just seemed obvious. His timid mother there, so nervous. The boy would not explain what happened. I started asking about the father, where he was. But the father's dead."

"You think that woman beat her kid up?"

She shakes her head and says, "No. Someone at school beat him up, but he wouldn't tattle. That's what his mother told me after. Nothing was broken, thank the Lord."

She starts to tell you about the other kids she's seen like this. These kids who always get beat up in school and may develop the same psychological patterns as the victims of ongoing abuse at home. It's quite a problem, you agree. Jenny is young and still has passion about ethical quandaries and polemics. You know she'll lose it. She'll go dead inside at some point. But here she is, twenty-seven and impassioned. You adore her.

You change the topic and ask her how her cat is. "Oh, Chloe's fine," she says. "She gets so mad sometimes. She snubs me when I get home from long overnights in E.R."

Then Jenny smiles a tired smile and says, "I enjoy talking to you, Michael. You're a good listener. Or maybe I just like seeing your handsome face."

You smile and thank her. For some mysterious reason, you do not take this lead and ask her out. You start to feel things. Inexplicable. Nothing related at all to the situation. You feel how much you miss Jess. And it's not Jess only. You miss your brother, Daniel. You miss your mother, who always loved you more than Daniel. You miss your mostly boring childhood in Fair Lawn. Daniel played saxophone and you played clarinet in the school band. You always loved him and tried hard to take care of him. You were oblivious, of course, and didn't do this well.

When Daniel died, your father cried for months, then wrote a book that a small Jewish-affiliated press published. Your father called the book *The Invisible World*. It was a memoir all about Daniel's leukemia, about facing the impossible—losing a fourteen-year-old son. You recall reading this book and wondering how your father could write this down. He explained treatments, play by play. He described Daniel in every phase of his short life.

You don't remember much else, except the title, what it meant. That when a son dies he goes on, though he's invisible. How every day, your father found a way to talk to his invisible, dead son.

You know he still does this each day. He talks to Daniel. He also talks to his dead wife now, even though they never got along. You know you're much more like your mother. You are restrained. The voice of reason. Not so preoccupied with absent things and people. Mainly you'd like to be in bed with Dr. Walsh right now. And yet you still have not attempted to ask her out.

Maybe you're not so restrained after all. There were the years, after he died, when you continued Daniel's journal. You found the journal one night while you were looking through Daniel's coins and stamps and baseball cards and autographs. You started reading. The last entry was made three weeks before he died.

What will happen to me? wrote Daniel. *How will things be after I'm dead? I just hope everyone's okay with it. I can't believe I won't be able to watch the Yankees.*

He seemed so calm in this last entry, but you knew better. There were some nights when he got panicky and hysterical. He would go up to his room and cry so loud it sounded more like screaming. Both of your parents would try hard to console him, but they could not.

For a few years you made intermittent entries in Daniel's journal. It was your own way of talking to your dead brother. You never told anyone. You took the journal from the house when you moved your father to the Pine Manor Home for the Elderly. The journal still sits in the sock drawer of your dresser. You never look at it now, but if your house was burning down you'd surely grab it on your way out.

You wrote: *It's spring now. You've been dead five months. The Yankees play their first game tomorrow. That cute girl Susan who you always had a crush on said she misses you. I saw her walking yesterday after school and gave her a ride home.*

You wrote: *The Yankees are looking strong again. They're in first place by eleven games at the All-Star break. We saw the fireworks and you would have really liked the grand finale. There were some greasers and one of them was Terry, that guy who pitched on your team in Pony League. He's still short but he acts like he would kill you if he felt like it.*

You wrote: *Exactly one year since you died. Today we had the unveiling of your gravestone. Dad got crazy because they somehow got your birthday wrong. It says Feb. 17 instead of 14, which means Dad's 14* looked like a 17 on the form he gave the place that made the gravestone. The gravestone place said they can fill it in and fix it but now Dad plans to get a whole new stone made.

You wrote: *Hey Daniel, it's your birthday. You would have been sixteen and probably still a virgin. I'm just kidding. Dad brought home strawberry tarts, your favorite. It's snowing out. It's always strange to have your birthday along with Valentine's Day. I have no Valentine, if you're wondering, so don't feel bad. I applied to Rutgers and last week I got a call from the guy who runs the orchestra.*

You wrote: *I sometimes can't believe it's 1959. And now it's almost 1960. They put the new stone in the graveyard and got your birthday right this time. We all put little rocks on your gravestone. Mom also brought a ton of flowers.*

You wrote: *I finished my first year of college today. I took exams in chemistry and Shakespeare. Chem went okay but Shakespeare was all essays. I got blitzkrieged, as you used to say. You know how bad I am at essays. How did you get all those writer genes from Dad when I got none? And what's the deal with this Fool guy in King Lear?*

You wrote: *You wouldn't believe the girl I met canoeing. Her name is Jess and I want to marry her. She is gorgeous! Tall. Green eyes. And what a body. She let me kiss her on the bus ride. She's seventeen and lives in Millburn. I keep on praying she feels everything that I feel. I'm in love.*

You never wrote again in Daniel's diary after that. You met Jess Adelman. Then you stopped. You're still not sure how the two things are connected. You sometimes feel very guilty, as if somehow, through your laziness, you lost touch with your brother. Other than naming your first-born child after him, you basically ignored his nonexistence.

Lately you think that maybe you should start talking again. Maybe you wouldn't write in the journal. It would be strange to have a gap of so many years. But you should talk to him, perhaps the way your father does. You really should tell him all about the things that went on with Jess. And if you talk to your brother, Daniel, then why couldn't you also talk to this other woman—the still invisible, more suitable, second great love of your life? Your *b'shert*, as your father called it. He always loved that Yiddish word, *b'shert.* You look at Dr. Jenny Walsh and feel quite sure that she is not your Fated Other. Still you feel certain powerful things that draw you to her. You also notice she's still waiting for you to speak.

"I love our conversations too," you say.

Despite the lameness of this noncommittal comment, she smiles sweetly. She says, "Thank you. That's nice to know."

Now you're right here and you can feel how in her mild-mannered way she will still manage to somehow kill you. How she'll turn frigid and detached in ways that will make you crazy. How it will surely not be worth it, even if you get to touch her gorgeous ass.

It's now or never. You choose never. You will feel baffled by this choice later. You sip your coffee and talk pleasantly with Jenny. She's very good at this—being pleasant. You reach the point where she knows you will not ask her out. She leaves.

So, you go home. It's still the same. You ache for someone, not Jenny Walsh. Someone you feel inside, who ceaselessly eludes you. You've always carried around this magical anticipated romance. It's like a cloud, Michael, that keeps on moving with you all your life. Someone like Jess appears. The cloud comes down. You throw it over Jess. Then she becomes your cloud, embodied. You can feel everything through her. Soon she won't hold the cloud. You throw it down on Claudia. After Claudia, you're left with the cloud again. Now until someone new appears this cloud is longing. If she appears, the cloud may turn, just for that moment, into joy. But when is love just love and not a cloud, or is it all just cloud? You step back into your house. You hear the kids in the TV room. You picture Jenny at the hospital and feel like you would die for her. You take your coat off and call, "Hey, I brought home Häagen-Dazs."

ROMEO AND JULIETTE

November 1981

WHEN JULIETTE WALKED IN, she found her father huddled over the kitchen table. He had just poured a glass of bourbon and hadn't noticed that she was standing there.

She said, "Hey Pop, is something wrong?"

He didn't answer.

"Pop..." she said.

He turned.

"What the fuck are you doing home?"

"Tommy got hurt today in practice. So I came home. He hurt his shoulder..."

He yelled, "Goddamn it, Julie, get out of here."

She said, "I'm tired. I can't lie down in my own bed?"

She watched the glass, ice, and bourbon smash against the kitchen wall. She saw him rising and coming toward her. So she ran.

"Get the fuck out!" he yelled. "The goddamn Dino boys are coming any minute."

She ran upstairs and felt like crying but no tears came. She ran fast. Up to her bedroom for her jacket and gloves. She threw her purse onto the bed and sifted through it. Wallet, gum, cigarettes, make-up...shit. She'd lost her brush again. Forget it. She saw her father in the doorway.

She yelled, "I'm going, okay? Just let me pass you. I'll walk right past, then out the door."

"You have five seconds," he said.

She began walking. He let her pass, but then he followed right behind her. She was almost to the door. She felt his hand grip her shoulder and screamed, "Leave me alone! Goddamn it!"

He said, "Hey Julie, what's your problem?"

His hands seemed huge and she smelled the bourbon. She said, "I'm trying to leave, okay?"

"You take your mother's car," he said. "You don't come back till after nine."

Juliette nodded. He pulled the door open. She knew something was really wrong. She stepped outside and began running down the cobblestones. At times like this she always wished she could just vanish.

Or become someone else entirely. Maybe become her neighbor Anthony. The Rubins' house looked empty. She assumed that they had all gone to his hockey game. It was the first game of the season, against Brick Town, she remembered. That was what Anthony had told her three weeks before when she bought a raffle ticket.

Until that moment she'd never really planned on going. About the last thing she had ever planned on doing was watching ice hockey. She hated all sports, except football, because Tommy was the fullback. What the hell did that mean—fullback? She turned the key, pulled down the driveway. Maybe she'd do that, go watch hockey.

And so she drove, very slowly, to the South Mountain Arena in West Orange. West Orange was one town over from Livingston. The rink was next to the Turtle Back Zoo. She'd never been inside the zoo, though long ago her mother would sometimes ask her if she'd like to go see the animals. Now Juliette could not help wishing she'd said yes on one of those occasions. Two or three times Isabella had gone to the zoo all by herself.

As she pulled through the light on Northfield, she saw the rink. It was all lit up. She hadn't been inside in years, ever since one winter day when Isabella took her skating. Isabella was a good skater. Juliette had rented skates, held hands with her mom, and fallen on her butt every time her mother let her go. They took a break at some point and drank hot chocolates with whipped cream. They also shared an apple Hostess fruit pie. That day her mother seemed very beautiful. Coral red lipstick, sky blue sweater, white wool mittens. Juliette recalled how Isabella warmed her cheeks with those itchy mittens. How she had groaned with relief after she finally took her skates off. Back in the car, Juliette had joked about how bad she was at skating. Her mom had laughed and said, "Your father can't skate either. I tried to take him one time. He's like a wrecking ball."

Now Juliette wondered how long her dad would hold on to the dying Chevy Nova. It was still littered with Isabella's gum wrappers, cigarettes, lip balms, and magazines. She could see traces of her mother all over the stupid car. There was also an overpowering smell of mildew. Isabella was perhaps the biggest slob Juliette had ever known.

It was dusk when she coasted into the wide lot and parked a little way from the rink's entrance. She saw the zoo across the lot. She started wondering if she could manage to get inside the zoo and wander. Of course, she'd probably get arrested. Given the way the day was going, it wouldn't be much of a stretch. First Tommy hurting his shoulder during practice, then Pop upset and waiting for the loan sharks. It was just one of those days when crappy things happened. She guessed that it didn't really matter what she did.

She grabbed her purse and stepped outside. The air was cool but still pleasant. They'd had what seemed the warmest, rainiest fall in history. She crossed the lot and soon Juliette was standing before the zoo's locked entrance. She peeked inside but could not see anything except one sign with arrows showing the way to different animal exhibits.

She saw the penguin logo, the cougar logo, the bat logo. She started wondering about the animals. What the hell did they do at night? It was so quiet that it was strange to think the animals were in there. By the zoo's entrance she sat down and tried imagining she'd turned into an animal.

Now she felt good, in a strange way. She felt as if she had almost managed to disappear there. She sensed that no one on earth knew where she was. She let her purse slide off her shoulder, to the blacktop. She lay back and felt the cold ground on her neck.

Juliette sat up, took out a cigarette, and noticed a half moon across Northfield Avenue, behind McDonald's. The moon was rising, she assumed. She used to think the moon was part of the sun. This had seemed logical. No. She knew there wasn't any logic there at all. She'd once suggested this in third grade. Her teacher thought Juliette was trying to make fun of her. She'd had to stay after school and discuss "gross insubordination."

There was a path, Juliette realized. It circled around the zoo along a fence. Juliette got up and walked the path, hoping to see some of the animals. She saw the kiddie train and a food stand. She saw a bird cage. Some of the birds were moving.

She kept on walking around the zoo, skimming the wrought-iron fence's vertical black bars with her left hand. It made a noise that scared the birds. She took her hand down and walked slower. She walked so slowly that her footsteps made no sound. She closed her eyes now as she walked, and when she opened them she saw penguins.

Then Juliette saw something else, a person: a young boy. She'd been so silent that this boy had yet to notice her. He seemed intent on whatever he was watching, and he stood maybe thirty feet away.

His face was pressed against the fence. He held the bars with his hands in such a way that he resembled a prisoner in a jail cell. She took a drag of her cigarette and kept watching the silent boy. Then she said, "Hey. Hello." He pulled his face back and turned, but did not answer.

She said, "I'm Juliette. What's your name?"

He said, "It's Romeo."

She already felt like hitting him.

She said, "Well Romeo, what are you doing here?"

He said, "Staring at the yaks."

"Did you see those penguins?" she asked. "They're over there, to the left."

He said, "Of course I've seen the penguins. Do you think I'm blind?"

She said, "Hey listen, I'm just trying to be nice here, okay? I can be mean if you want, okay?"

He said, "Okay."

"How old are you?"

"Fourteen."

"You look younger," she said, and took another drag from her cigarette. She looked away as she exhaled smoke. When she turned back, she found him staring.

He said, "You shouldn't smoke, you know."

She said, "Well, thank you. I didn't know that. Glad you told me."

He kept on staring at her face.

Juliette said, "What? Do you have a problem?"

He said, "You're Juliette Dimiglio. You're a junior. And you live next door to Anthony. Anthony Rubin, right?"

She said, "That's right. So what's your name?"

"Jay Berkowitz." He kept staring. He said, "You go out with Tommy Lange the football star."

"That's right."

He said, "Your mother just died. I'm sorry."

Jesus Christ, Juliette thought. This stupid kid knew her whole life story.

She said, "I'd rather we didn't talk about my mother, okay?"

"Fine."

He took his eyes off of her, finally, and looked back at the yaks.

"So how do you know Anthony?" Juliette asked. "He's in tenth grade."

"I'm in ninth," he said. "I skipped a grade. We also used to be good friends."

"You and Anthony were friends?"

He said, "Our parents did things together. We used to spend summer vacations at a shore house we all rented. It was Anthony, me, his sister and my brother, and all our parents. Two years ago, our last time there, we were both Allenhurst junior lifeguards. Over that summer we also learned the constellations."

Juliette said, "How?"

"We both had star charts."

She imagined Anthony and Jay Berkowitz as lifeguards. She couldn't picture it. The idea seemed impossible. The star charts yes, but lifeguards no.

"Do you go to Livingston?" she asked.

He said, "I would have, but we moved. And by the way, I also know about Roland Malnick. I still talk to Donna Ginsling and Lance Silver. Last year we were all in gifted math with Roland. He really is a little weasel, but it's still weird that you supposedly helped your boyfriend almost kill him."

"I didn't mean to," she said.

"You accidentally punched his face in?"

Juliette said, "Look. That stupid kid said some dumb stuff. I think he called me a slut when my damn boyfriend was basically right next to him. Then I was trying to help that little...idiot. I said I'd hit him just so Tommy wouldn't kill him. I would have tapped the kid, you know? He started saying nasty things about my mother."

"He's such a weasel," Jay said. "It's still weird though. You're pretty lucky you didn't get suspended. I would have told."

"Good thing we weren't beating you up."

"I would have definitely filed criminal charges and then *sued* you."

She rolled her eyes and said, "Hey genius, you don't sue for assault and battery."

Jay told her, "Actually, you do. People can sue for civil damages in addition to the criminal prosecution. I won't tell, though, so don't worry."

"I feel much calmer now."

"I'm also not afraid of you, if you were wondering."

"I wasn't."

The boy turned back to the yaks. His bowl-cut hair was long in back and Juliette decided that she liked him. She liked being here with this edgy little nerd brain. She said, "Hey Jay, do you mind if I just stare at these yaks with you?"

"No," he said, so she walked up next to him and gazed through the metal bars. She saw three yaks standing motionless. They looked like statues.

"They're from Tibet," said Jay.

"I didn't know that."

He said, "Behind them, way back there, is the tapir. You can see him."

"Where?"

He pointed and said, "Behind the yaks. He's in another cage, way back there."

She strained her eyes but could not see anything except fences and signs.

"I still don't see him," Juliette said. She bent her head down to Jay's eye level and said, "Where?"

Jay put his arm around her back. He pointed and said, "Follow the direction of my finger. It's pointing right between his eyes."

She looked again. She found it frustrating. She said, "You should have brought binoculars."

"Look harder, okay? Keep trying."

She said, "Forget it, another time."

"There may not *be* another time."

She said, "Don't worry, it's not important. I don't care all that much about this tape thing."

"Tapir," said Jay. "And he is probably the most interesting animal in this place. He used to live in South America. He's worth seeing."

"Guess we'll have to break into the zoo then."

Jay said, "Fine."

"You're kidding."

"No. There's a perfect place. I first noticed it two months ago. It's so perfect that it's *amazing*, like someone planned it. All we have to do is climb a tree."

"Forget it," Juliette said.

"Why?"

"I'll split my pants if I start climbing. These jeans are tight as hell."

"Then split your pants," he said. "It's worth it."

"What are you talking about?"

"Come on."

"Do you break into this zoo a lot?"

Jay told her, "No. But I walk around here all the time because I live a block away. By now I know we won't have any trouble. This zoo's so broke they never have security guards. They also don't have an alarm."

The kid was crazy, Juliette thought. But still she followed him. She was laughing. She even let him take her hand. She led him up to the far side of the yak cage.

"This is the tree," he said. "A silver maple, by the way."

"That's good to know," Juliette said.

Jay slapped the trunk of the small tree.

"He's pretty solid," Jay said.

She said, "He's tiny. His branches look like twigs."

"We can get right down to the roof of that little yak hut. Isn't it perfect?"

Juliette said, "Yeah. You sure you really want to do this?"

"Positive," Jay said. He made a stirrup with clasped hands and said, "I'll hoist you. Just step on here."

Juliette stepped onto the stirrup, but Jay couldn't really lift her.

She said, "I don't think this is working."

"Then grab the tree and use your arms."

Juliette jumped and grabbed onto the lowest branch of the silver maple. She felt his hands and then his shoulder on her rear end, pushing her up. It didn't help, but he kept pushing. She was wearing Frye boots, and they didn't grip the tree well. She pulled her body up with her arms. She got her legs over the branch, arched her way up, and found her balance. Then she said, "Hey, I'm okay. You can stop pushing me, okay?"

She climbed on up to another branch and saw that she was higher than the fence.

Jay said, "Just throw your purse and jump down to that hut thing."

She let the purse fall to the ground. She hadn't closed it. She saw an eye pencil bounce out. She turned to Jay and said, "You coming?"

"Just a minute," he said, and sounded nervous.

He tied his shoelace. Then he tried jumping for the branch but couldn't reach it. Juliette dropped to the lower branch and held her arm down. Jay grabbed on but she couldn't pull him up, so he let go.

Juliette said, "Wait." She hung from the lowest branch and jumped down to the ground again. She said, "I'll lift you up. I'm taller." She clasped her hands the same way Jay had, made a stirrup, and he stepped on.

Jay was embarrassed, she could tell, because she lifted him up no problem. She hoisted Jay to the first branch and he sheepishly took hold of it. He said, "Okay," pulled himself up. He quickly climbed to the higher branch and said, "I'm good."

Juliette pulled herself up to the lowest branch again. Jay said, "I'm jumping onto that hut thing," and sprang down to the flat roof of a wooden lean-to. She was relieved to see that he didn't crash right through it. Juliette climbed up to the second branch. She hung her legs down and let go. She landed next to Jay and saw that the lean-to's sides were put together with crisscross latticework.

Jay said, "I'll show you how to break your fall by rolling."

"We can just climb down the side. It's like a ladder."

Jay said, "Don't worry," and leapt off.

He hit the ground and rolled immediately. He kept on rolling— about three rolls. Soon he was halfway across the cage. When he got up, he looked around and brushed his clothes off. He said, "Okay, Juliette. Make sure to roll."

"I think I'll climb down."

"It's a piece of cake to jump it."

"But so is climbing," Juliette said.

"You should just jump."

She saw her purse on the ground, thought what the hell, and hoped she wouldn't break her ankle.

She said, "Alright, you win. I'm coming down."

Juliette jumped and Jay yelled, "Roll!" So Juliette made sure to roll. One roll was plenty, she decided. She pressed her hands to the ground and felt the smooth dirt of the yak cage. As she stood up, she said, "Don't yell. You'll wake the yaks."

Jay said, "They're up."

Juliette looked around. She saw them. One yak was staring at her calmly. The other two yaks were huddled close together, as if talking.

She said, "Alright, little Romeo. Let's go and see your friend the tapir."

"Grab your purse," Jay said.

She quickly grabbed it.

He said, "Don't worry about the yaks. They never charge, though they could gore you with their horns if they really wanted."

"How reassuring," Juliette said.

She let him take her hand again and this amused her. Why did she like it when this peewee held her hand? They walked together past the yaks. They climbed a chain-link fence and stepped out of the cage. As they touched down on the blacktop path used by zoo patrons, Jay said, "You might want to check your shoes for yak shit."

She said, "You're kidding. I mean, we *rolled* in it."

"I didn't see any," Jay said. "And I was looking."

Juliette checked the bottoms of her boots. They both seemed clean. She followed Jay down the blacktop path.

She said, "What else? Will we go swimming with these penguins?"

He said, "The water's way too cold."

They passed the penguins. Juliette glanced up and thought about her father. She felt a startling jolt of terror but blocked it out. She saw the glow from the rink lights and remembered Anthony was in there. At the next cage Jay stopped and said, "Okay, so here he is."

Juliette gazed at this odd animal, the tapir. She took one look and thought: Christ, who would invent this thing? And how the hell did it wind up in New Jersey?

It had a snout, like a pig. Or maybe even like a rhino without a horn. But cuter than a rhino. Juliette thought: Yes, he's kind of cute. She saw him wandering round his cage, meandering here and there. He seemed quite purposeful though really there was no purpose whatsoever. No hay to eat, or insects. He just kept combing the soft dirt with his snout, looking for something. She kept on watching him and realized she was fascinated. She felt entranced by this stupid-looking tapir.

"He's pretty active," she said.

"He's nocturnal," said Jay. "Are you?"

"Sometimes I think I am," she said. "Sometimes I'm up all night worrying about nothing."

"Then you're nocturnal. So am I."

"Why are you here?" Juliette asked. "Why are you wandering around the zoo on a Tuesday night?"

He said, "I'd rather not go into it. But I can tell you why I'm nocturnal."

"Go ahead."

Jay said, "I sometimes get insomnia. Ever since I skipped fourth grade. That's not the reason, of course. I didn't get insomnia from skipping the fourth grade."

"Great," Juliette said. "Now can you tell me why you're here?"

"I said I'd rather not go into it."

"What if I'd really like to know?"

"It wouldn't matter," he said.

"Well, I guess you'll always be a mystery."

"So why are *you* here?" Jay asked.

She slid her purse down off her shoulder, then she remembered: the eye pencil. It was still lying in the yak cage. She'd have to get it. If she could find it.

"Well?" Jay asked.

"What?"

He said, "I asked you why you're here."

"I came to watch the Livingston-Brick Town hockey game. Your

friend Anthony invited me. But when I got here I didn't feel like going.
I walked around."

"He *invited* you?"

"Yes. I bought a raffle ticket from him about three weeks ago."

"And you were going to watch Anthony play hockey?"

She said, "Well, sort of. Let's just drop it, okay?"

"Okay," Jay said. Then he was down tying his shoe again. Juliette
watched the intent expression on his face as he pulled the laces tight.
She turned away after that and gazed again toward the bright lights
from the rink.

"So what's Anthony like?" she said, and wondered why she would
ask this question.

"Anthony's nice," said Jay. "I like him. We don't talk much now,
unfortunately."

"Why not?"

"Because we don't."

"Did you guys fight?"

Jay told her, "No. But things just happen. I can't explain it. You'd
really like him though, I bet."

Jay flashed a melancholic smile, then turned away and said, "Excuse me for a second."

He began sneezing. He sneezed five times into his hands.

"I have allergies," he said when he was finished.

Juliette unzipped her purse and produced a Kleenex.

"Here," she said.

Jay took the tissue. She slid a cigarette out and held it between her
fingers. She didn't light it. She didn't even really want it. She watched
as Jay blew each nostril individually. When he was finished she said,
"Jay, you're very cute. Do people tell you that?"

He said, "No."

She slipped the cigarette back into the pack. She took her gum out
and said, "Want some?"

Jay said, "No thanks. I really hate gum. No offense."

She started laughing and threw the gum back in her purse. "You have to chew gum if you smoke," she said. "Or else your breath smells really terrible."

Jay said, "I know. My mother smokes. My father sometimes does, too. He likes cigars."

He crumpled up the tissue in his fist. She watched him drop it. He let it fall onto the path.

She said, "It's lucky I ran into you."

"Why is it lucky?"

She said, "I might have been really lonely. I might've wound up watching hockey."

"Hockey's not bad," Jay said.

"I'll take your word for it."

Jay said, "You know, me and Anthony used to watch you, in your yard. We always liked when you walked around picking dandelions."

She said, "That's funny. I used to do that. I loved picking them and blowing all the seeds off."

"We used to think you were like a TV star or something."

She said, "So what do you think now?"

"Well, now I know you," he said. "Now I can see that you're really smart. You're also beautiful, of course. I mean, you are—you're like a princess, which is what Anthony always said."

"Anthony said that?"

"Yeah. He'd say, 'Hey Jay, don't you think Juliette is beautiful, like a princess?' Then I'd say, 'Yeah, but she's really not your type and her dad might kill you.' No offense."

"No offense taken," she said, and laughed. "I also doubt Pop would have killed him, though way back then I guess he was much crazier."

"Has your dad killed people?"

Juliette groaned. She told him, "No. He's not a gangster."

Jay said, "He's not?"

Juliette said, "No."

"What does he do then?" asked Jay.

"He has an office job."

"A mob office?"

Juliette glared at him but didn't feel much anger for some reason. "I'm not lying to you," she said. "But if you make another crack like that I'm leaving."

"It's just surprising," said Jay. "Who would have thought your father works in an office? Does he take business trips?"

"It's not that kind of office."

"My dad is always taking trips. I never see him."

Juliette looked at him. At his eyes.

She said, "Your eyes. They're different colors."

"Thanks for telling me."

Even in this light she could see it. His left eye was a soft blue, almost turquoise. The right eye was a dull gray, as if the color had been washed out.

She said, "They're beautiful."

"Could you stop staring at my eyes now?"

"If you stop asking about my father. Should we go wander around this zoo?"

Jay shook his head. He said, "There isn't much to see besides the tapir."

"I've never seen the place though."

He touched her arm. He had guts. He didn't even think twice about touching her.

He said, "Hey Juliette. I'd really like to sit here, by this tapir. I'd like to sit here with you for just five minutes. Is that possible? I don't care if you smoke or chew gum, go right ahead."

She said, "That's nice, Jay. Sure. I'd love to sit here."

She smiled and sat down on the path, though Jay kept standing. She liked his body. He seemed compact, just like the tapir. She liked his eyes, particularly the gray one.

She said, "Hey Jay, will you sit down?"

He said, "Just tell me. Is Tommy nice to you? Is he a nice guy or an asshole?"

"He's an asshole," she said, without much thought. "He's probably the biggest fucking jerk I've ever met."

"How's he a jerk?" Jay asked.

She said, "He cheats on me all the time, with stupid cheerleaders. Thinks I'm blind."

"Do you cheat on him?"

She said, "Not yet."

"You shouldn't cheat," Jay said. "It wrecks things."

She said, "I know," and pulled out another stick of gum. She unwrapped it. She said, "With Tommy, there's nothing left to wreck, though." She placed the gum in her mouth and began to chew.

She said, "Hey Jay."

"What?"

"You can sit down here already. Will you sit down here?"

Jay sat down.

She pulled him close and laced both arms around him. She said, "Don't worry. This isn't cheating."

He said, "I know."

She ran her fingers through his hair. It felt so soft—softer than Tommy's. She heard the tapir move. Cars passing out on Northfield. She heard his breath.

"So won't you tell me why you're here?" she asked again.

"I just like zoos."

"I know there's a real reason."

He said, "Of course there's a real reason. And I know you have a real reason. Some of your make-up's smeared."

"It is?"

"Were you crying before you saw me?"

"I didn't think so. Let's just drop this."

Jay said, "Don't worry. I don't care. And if you really want to know, I always come here when my mother has this guy over. His name is Al something. He's bald. He's always wanting to show us card tricks, even when it's the last thing you'd want to see."

Juliette laughed.

"It isn't funny," said Jay. "It's bad enough that he comes over every time my father goes away on business. We always tell him the wrong card and screw his tricks up. He doesn't care."

"Sounds like an idiot," Juliette said.

"Okay, I told you. Can we stop talking?"

She said, "Of course."

Jay hugged her tightly and pressed his face into her shoulder. The hug surprised her. He was strong. She didn't think she had ever been hugged harder in her life.

"You feel good," he said.

"You, too."

"I have to go," Jay said, releasing her.

He slid back on the blacktop, smiled uncomfortably, and stood up.

"You're really leaving?"

"I have to get home and help my brother with his science project. He's doing a report on the marsupials. You know what they are?"

She said, "No."

"Like kangaroos and koalas. They all have pouches. That's how you know."

Juliette rose. She said, "I'll drive you."

He said, "I told you. I live right near here. Through the woods and down the block."

"I'll drive you anyway," she said.

"I'd rather walk. But thank you for the offer."

She said, "Don't mention it."

"You should feel free to keep sitting here."

"Maybe I will," Juliette said. "It's kind of nice here by the tapir."

"I knew you'd like him."

"I do. I'll see ya later."

Jay held his hand out. They shook hands, which seemed peculiar. Then he said, "Bye."

He walked away, climbed the low fence, and crossed the yak cage. She saw him come up to the lean-to, climb up the latticework, and crawl onto the flat roof. She guessed he wouldn't make it back up to the maple tree. She was already moving to help him, but Jay jumped up and managed to reach the branch on his first try.

So she sat down again, by the tapir. She watched Jay hoist himself up, brush his pants off, hop to the lower branch, and jump. She saw him roll, three or four times, and then brush himself off again. He tied his shoelace once more, rose, and looked at her through the vertical metal fence bars. Juliette waved.

He yelled, "YOU LEFT SOME OF YOUR MAKE-UP IN THE YAK CAGE."

She yelled back, "THANKS."

"SOME SORT OF PENCIL."

She yelled, "I KNOW. DON'T SCARE THE YAKS."

"WHAT'S IT FOR?"

"WHAT?"

"THE PENCIL."

"FOR MY EYES."

"I'LL SEE YOU LATER."

She said, "GOODNIGHT," and then "Goodnight" again, much softer, to herself. She watched as Jay walked away. She just adored this little kid. When he was gone, she was still smiling. Then it hit her— something hollow. The feeling lasted just a moment, then it was gone.

Juliette stayed there by the tapir, smoked a cigarette, and waited until another half hour passed. Then she stood up and hopped the fence into the yak cage. She passed the yaks, who were now clumped together, sitting. She found her eye pencil just below the maple tree. With purse slung over her right shoulder, she climbed up the latticed side and made her way to the flat roof of the lean-to. From there she grabbed a branch, swung up, and scissored her legs around the skinny maple bough. She pulled herself up to the next branch and just sat there for a moment. She breathed in deeply before descending. When she jumped down to the ground she landed crouched and did not roll.

Juliette followed the path back to the parking lot, checked for police, then crossed the blacktop to her car. There were three sparrows under the car, eating some Crackerjacks. This seemed absurd and somehow frightening. She said, "Hello, little birds." She felt like crying.

Instead she took out her lighted compact mirror. She saw a black smudge of mascara beneath one eye. She found a make-up sponge and wet it with saliva. She wiped the blotch off. She still could not remember crying once that evening.

She leaned back against the Chevy Nova. She saw the sky and a few faint stars. She knew her mother liked the stars. Isabella liked a lot of things. She liked the zoo animals and art museums and pizza. She even liked the man she married.

Juliette wanted to drive home, but still she didn't. She was afraid, so she kept staring up and wishing she could walk into the sky. She was jarred out of her thoughts by the loud slam of a side door to the ice rink. When she looked over she saw three hockey players crossing the wide lot. They carried sticks and their equipment, and she looked hard to see if one of them was Anthony.

Her heart was racing as she stood there. She assumed that this was why she'd waited there — she *wanted* to speak with Anthony. Now she remembered buying the ticket, and how he looked at her: afraid. Afraid and yet compassionate, desirous, but afraid. The boys drew closer. Juliette kept standing there. She saw that their letter jackets were from Brick Town and not Livingston. One of the boys yelled out, "Hey babe, who you waiting for?" She said nothing. She turned and got into her car, where she smelled mildew and stale cigarettes. She knew she'd have to find a way to clean this car.

She took the long way, through the county-owned South Mountain Reservation. The road wound down past a reservoir, then into a forested area lush with hemlocks. She'd always found something false about these woods sandwiched between the endless suburban neighborhoods. Soon she came out at the South Orange Avenue intersection. She took the right and headed toward the mall.

Coasting down the hill toward Don's Restaurant, Juliette thought again of Isabella. She understood that she never liked her, but that she should have. It was so obvious. She was good. The problem was, she was also stupid. She'd let a thankless asshole own her. Still Juliette managed to keep loving her thankless asshole of a father.

She wondered how her life would be if he really was some sort of gangster. She also knew he was too much of a baby to really be one. An angry, tough-guy baby boy who just liked gambling. Whose older brothers once beat him to a pulp when they caught him running numbers for some Jersey City bookie named Moriarty. It was a story he sometimes told, how Sal and Lonnie scared him straight. She knew she'd stay with him, at least for another year or so. She knew she wouldn't have stayed with Isabella.

It took her close to half an hour to drive home this way. She cut past the mall to Hillside Avenue, then came back on Route 10. She took the turn beside the Hopping Funeral Home, where just three weeks before she'd been to her mother's wake.

She turned on Fellswood and started feeling very nervous. She took the curve at low speed and turned on Tanglewood. When she turned left up Cherry Hill, she saw the porch lights from her house.

She drove up slowly and did not turn into her driveway. She kept on going, doubling back where Cherry Hill Road intersected Thurston Drive. She scanned her house again when she reached it and then felt certain that the loan sharks were long gone.

She parked the Chevy by the garage but didn't get out right away. She sat inside with the engine on and she was praying. She prayed for something more than this emptiness, which in the last few days had begun to swallow her. She prayed that everything would be fine when she went into her house.

As she stepped out of the car, she felt a wind against her face. It was gentle, almost sultry. Far too warm to be November. Juliette ascended the front steps. She spit her gum into the azaleas. She pulled the storm door open, inserted her key, stepped in.

"Pop?" she called out.

She got no answer. Juliette went into the kitchen. A smear of darkened blood had stained the beige linoleum kitchen floor. A metal toaster lay on the floor, and there were bread crumbs in the blood.

Juliette yelled, "Pop, are you upstairs?"

She raced upstairs. His door was closed and she burst through. The light was on and her father lay on his back. A wet blue towel covered his face.

Juliette said, "Pop?"

He didn't answer. So she walked over to him, shook him. Her father groaned and then she knew he was alive.

"Pop," she said. "How come they clobbered you? Why the hell do they keep pounding your face in?"

"They're scum, Julie," he said.

"They'll wind up killing you."

He said, "I gave them the last of what I owed them, even the principal. It's all done."

She took the towel from his face. Both of his eyes were swollen shut.

"Christ," she said.

"Don't worry. We're getting out of here."

"When?"

He tried to sit up, but could not.

Juliette said, "What, did they break all of your ribs while they were at it?"

He said, "I'm fine, Julie. We're leaving this place, soon."

Juliette yelled, "When!"

"Soon," he said again, in a voice much calmer than what Juliette was used to. "I need some ice for my face. And while you're down there you'll bring me up the bourbon, right?"

She nodded.

He said, "Hey Julie, there's no problem. We got no reason for any worries."

"Why did they hit you if you gave them back the money?"

He said, "Look, kiddo, I'm just a little black and blue here. These tough-guy jerks just like to hit because they can."

Juliette went downstairs. As she was filling a bag with ice, she felt her legs give way beneath her. Somehow she found herself sitting on the floor beside the toaster.

She rose again, went to the sink, and threw some water on her face. She grabbed a sponge and bent down to wipe the blood up. As she was doing this, something came over her. She recalled the way her mother used to sing while she cleaned the kitchen. Stupid songs like "Amazing Grace" or "Michael, Row Your Boat Ashore." How she would close her eyes while singing, and how she'd sometimes sing almost in a whisper. She heard the rise in her mother's voice, and then a hush.

ATLANTIS

AT JAY'S BAR MITZVAH, Claudia was wearing a black dress. She had a necklace on with diamonds and her hair was done up in a special way. She wore black heels and sat with her legs crossed under the table.

She sat there smoking, the same Parliament Lights she always smoked. The pack was lying next to her bread plate, which had a plastic starfish right beside it. Every place setting had either a piece of coral or a plastic starfish. All of the centerpieces had cutout cardboard fishes and squids and octopuses and sea fans.

The party was held in Temple B'nai Abraham's reception hall. My sister, Dani, was off in Spain. The Lenny Lionel Band was playing and my mother was out improvising the steps of some new line dance. She was with Jay's uncle Hal, who also didn't know the line dance. In her high heels my mother towered over Hal.

I watched my father sit down next to Claudia. She turned to face him, then switched her cigarette to her farther away hand. They started talking and Jay's little cousin, Katie, tapped my shoulder. "Let's do the line dance," Katie said. So I got up and danced with Katie Berkowitz. As we walked out my mother waved. We both waved back and Katie said, "I think your mom's been having a few drinks."

———

She dives under now. I watch her. Pinching her nose with her thumb and pointer, she kicks down with her fins and soon she's far below me. We're in the Keys and it was her idea to come here. Now she's a diver and takes trips with the Reef Explorer Girls, her dive group. In the past year she's been to the Cayman Islands and Bermuda. She can reel off all sorts of facts about each fish, coral, or eel in her reef field guide. I tried to learn at least some fish on our drive down.

She passes through a school of tiny yellow fish I can't identify. She glides above a much smaller group of striped ones, which I know are sergeant majors. She reaches out with her hand to touch the coral. She does not look up or wave as she circles round this massive head of coral. Inside my head I see the sea-blue tablecloths at Jay's party, the plastic fish surrounding all the flower bouquets, the giant cake with glass sea creatures. I see my mother gliding up again, then down and out of sight behind the coral. And for a second I'm thinking—What if she were Jay's mother? What if Claudia were mine?

Not that I ever really liked Claudia Berkowitz. But even if I never liked her, there was something about her I respected. Maybe because she was someone you always had to watch your step with. For instance once, when I accidentally broke a window with a baseball, she came outside and got extremely angry. We had just watched the Mets blow a game against the A's in the World Series. She made us come inside, put work gloves on, and sweep up all the glass. Meanwhile she picked up the phone and ordered a new window. When it was ordered she called us both into the kitchen.

She started shouting at Jay about how this opaque, ridged sidelight window would cost two hundred dollars to replace. She looked at Jay and asked if he felt good about throwing two hundred dollars in the garbage. Jay didn't answer, so she grabbed him by the arm. She yanked him toward her and then whacked him four or five times on the ass.

Jay started crying and Claudia said, "You think that's all you get for a two-hundred-dollar window?"

Jay whimpered, "No," and tried to walk away. His mother kept holding onto his arm.

"You think that hurt, wait till your father gets home."

She began spanking Jay much harder, as if she really wanted to hurt him.

I yelled out, "Wait, Jay didn't do it. I threw the ball to first base when he wasn't looking. He was John Milner and I was trying to be Bud Harrelson."

She hit Jay two or three more times, then let him go.

"Were you?" she said, glaring at me. "And who is Bud Harrelson?"

"He's the shortstop on the Mets."

"And do you think you're a pro ball player, Mr. Rubin?"

I said, "We just like to pretend."

She grabbed my arm and yanked me toward her kitchen table. The *Star Ledger* was sitting out there. With her free hand she found the sports section. She placed it on the table right in front of me. She said, "I want you to look hard at this paper, Mr. Rubin. Let me know if you see your name there on the sports page."

"Why would I?" I said.

She pushed my face down toward the paper and started hitting. In a cold voice she kept on saying, "Find your name yet, Mr. Rubin?"

When I got home that night I told my parents. As expected, my mother went bananas. She started cursing wildly at Claudia. My father calmed my mother down and called the Berkowitzes. He wound up talking with Jay's father for an hour. At one point I heard him say, "Claudia really shouldn't have hit him." When he got off, he said, "Look, honey, that's how she is. Doug says she didn't hit him hard."

I can hold my breath underwater close to a minute. So can my mother. Still every time she dives down I start to worry, which makes no sense. She likes to go down near the bottom and look up at the fish above her. She seems incredibly comfortable underwater, a lot more agile and untroubled than Jay's mother or any person I can think of ever would.

Now she is rising toward the surface, kicking lightly with her fins, one of her hands down at her side. She gives me the "okay" sign with the other. I make a circle with my pointer and thumb and tell her "okay" back. I continue watching her lithe body as she approaches. The bright lavender on the shoulders of her wet suit almost glows.

Now she's beside me, blowing water out her snorkel. She pulls the snorkel from her mouth and says, "Hey Anth, there's an underwater cave down there. I want you to come see it."

I tilt my head into the water. I look around but I don't see it. I see some rocks, which maybe have a cave in them. It looks too deep, at least twenty feet under. I pick my head up.

"It hurts my ears," I say. "When I dive down that far, it makes them hurt."

"'Cause you don't hold your nose and equalize the pressure."

I say, "I'm terrible at equalizing pressure."

"There's a big cave down there," she says. "But you can go through so it's really like a tunnel. We can swim through."

"To where?" I say.

"Just through."

"What if I can't hold my breath that long?"

"You can," she says. "We'll be down less than thirty seconds. And, you know what? We'll do a practice. We'll just go down and take a look, so you can practice and get a feel for where we're going. I bet it takes us twenty seconds."

I see her face. She seems excited. I say, "Okay," and I remember why I miss her. Who else would take me through an underwater tunnel?

On the practice dive, she leads. She points her body downward. Her long legs follow and I watch as she submerges. I dive down after her. I'm pinching my nose and blowing out much harder than I need to. I can't decide which hurts more, this blowing out or the pressure if I don't.

I keep on following her down, below the coral mound, past sea fans, and then right through a patch of dark brown tubelike sponges. She glides toward rocks where I suspect we'll find the tunnel, and we do. It's very wide and maybe ten feet long. Inside I see a million fish. There is bright light on the far end, behind the silhouettes of sea things. It looks like something from a movie. Some sort of doorway into another world.

✦ ✦ ✦

At Jay's bar mitzvah my mother basically got plastered. Even during the hora she was dancing, though she has often expressed her loathing for the hora. But she loves dancing and has a natural grace and rhythm. She also has no inhibitions when she's bombed.

Claudia Berkowitz was also part of the hora. She smiled calmly as we raised Jay till his head almost banged into the chandelier. She didn't seem at all worried that Jay might hit it, which had happened at one bar mitzvah that I went to, David Solomon's. It didn't cut David's head, but when he hit it his father crashed right through the circle and broke the hora up. He even threatened to sue the Glendale Lawn and Racquet Club, but never did.

The hora ended and we put Jay down. Everyone went back to their tables for dessert. I saw my mother sitting with Claudia. They were both smoking beside two untouched pieces of chocolate cake. By then my mother had mostly quit, though she still smoked now and then in party situations. I always worried she'd start smoking again for real, but she never did.

I felt relieved when Uncle Hal came by and dragged my mother back out to the dance floor. She had her shoes off and was dancing in her stockings. She was still three inches taller than Uncle Hal. My father took the chair next to Claudia, who I could tell was quite drunk as well. He started talking but she didn't seem to hear him. She kept on watching my mother and Hal, her brother-in-law. I looked around and got the sense that very few of Claudia's Polish-Christian relatives had come.

I didn't notice when Claudia and my father left their table. I had been talking with Jay's friend Donna Ginsling, who was pretty. Then I was eating my piece of cake when Mitchell Weintraub came up and asked me if I wanted to sneak down to the temple's game room and play air hockey.

We were the only eighth-graders at the bar mitzvah. Mitchell's father and Douglas Berkowitz worked together as investment bankers in New York. The Lenny Lionel Band was doing Motown and my mother was out there with no shoes on, going wild. So the idea of leaving was appealing, although Mitchell could be annoying. He talked nonstop about his dad's twelve-cylinder convertible Mercedes.

We knew the temple because we had both gone there for Hebrew School. So we snuck out and took the stairs down near the bathrooms outside the party room. On the first floor it was dark, and it felt strange being down there by the classrooms, none of which I had set foot in since my own bar mitzvah.

In pitch-black dark Mitchell and I crossed the main room where they held the junior services on High Holidays. Then we came to the hallway with the candy machines. It was easy to stick your arm up them and steal things, but we'd had so much food and cake we didn't bother.

We heard the soft hum of a soda machine and faintly the sound of drums from the Lenny Lionel Band. Then we turned into the Hebrew School's game room, which had no door. Mitchell Weintraub turned the light on. Claudia Berkowitz was arched back against the pool table. Her long black dress was bunched up around her waist. My father froze when the light went on. He turned and saw us. Then Mitchell yelled out, "Holy shit!" and flipped the light off.

I recall running up the stairs with Mitchell Weintraub. He kept on saying things you wouldn't have thought possible, such as "Shit, I think your dad was doing her. That was cool." Ten minutes later, I saw Claudia back upstairs and dancing away to Motown. I was surprised she took that long. And then my father slipped back into the party room. He looked around for my mother, spotted her dancing to a Supremes song. He quickly crossed the room and sat down at his table.

Later that night, when we got home, she was still plastered. She locked herself in the downstairs bathroom. I was awake and I could hear her throwing up. Then she stayed in there, even after Dad came down and asked her to come out. He wound up getting a screwdriver from the kitchen, picking the lock, and carrying her upstairs. After he put her to bed he came back out and found me in my room.

He said, "Antonio, I'm sorry. We'll talk tomorrow."

I said, "Why?"

He said, "Because, I think we should."

I said, "Forget it."

"Forget what?"

"I don't want to talk about all this tomorrow."

He said, "You might," and tried to be a gentle father. But at that moment I just wanted him to leave.

I said, "Hey Dad, don't you know that Mom knows *everything*?"

He stared right at me. He said, "Yes."

"*Yes*?" I said. "You know?"

He said, "I'm going to break things off with Claudia."

I asked him, "When? Will you break things off tomorrow?"

He said, "Soon."

✦ ✦ ✦

My mother points to a barracuda. It's hovering near the surface of the water, maybe twenty feet away from us. It is a medium-sized cuda, purplish silver, moving past.

"He won't bother us," she says, as she treads water.

I say, "I'm not afraid of harmless barracudas."

"Some people are since they look scary," she says, and tips up her mask to clear the water out.

"His face looks screwed up," I say. "He's kind of sad-looking. Maybe he's depressed."

She laughs and says, "Okay, you ready?"

I put my snorkel in and nod.

"You feel okay about this?"

I take my snorkel out.

I say, "It's easy. I could see how long the tunnel is. And all that light on the far side was kind of cool."

She smiles tenderly at me. She says, "You know what we always do before we go down under on our dive trips?"

I shake my head.

"We say, 'Okay, let's find Atlantis.' It's kind of silly."

She puts her snorkel in and smiles around the mouthpiece. Then she points down.

As we descend, we pass by parrotfish and bar jacks. We glide down through an enormous school of round blue fish I don't remember from the reef book. They're very flat with tiny fish mouths and much bluer than the water. They all move slowly, as if hovering, faces with quiet, gentle expressions. They look like fish someone would make up in a dream.

I keep on blowing out my ears until we reach the tunnel's entrance. I let my hand fall to my side and I'm amazed that my ears feel normal. I am amazed that I am twenty feet underwater with my mother—that of all places, anywhere in the universe, we're here.

I watch the light on the other side, but still the tunnel itself seems dark until I enter. Then I'm surprised that I can see things. Fanlike bristles sticking out like feathers in the coral. Spiny black urchins on the roof of the cave above me. Now I kick hard and can feel a sort of passage. I stretch my hands out to part a moving wall of fish. I see two angelfish with stripes and have the sense that I am following these angelfish. Just as I think this, the angelfish disappear.

When I pass out of the underwater tunnel I half expect to see Atlantis. I look around for a lost underwater city. I see a reef with endless fish and sponge and coral. I keep on kicking and turn up toward the water's surface. I rise much faster than seems possible. It feels as if I'm being pulled up toward the air. As I break through the ocean's surface, I blow the water out my snorkel. I breathe in rubbery-tasting oxygen and tilt my mask to clear it.

My mother surfaces beside me. She blows the water out her snorkel, takes it out of her mouth, then breathlessly says, "God, did you see that school of tang on our way down?"

"You mean those blue ones?"

"Yes."

I say, "They're pretty hard to miss."

She slides her mask up on her forehead and says, "Oh honey, that was great."

I push my mask up just like hers and tell her, "Thanks."

She says, "Thank *you*. Was it so awful?"

I say, "No."

"Good," she says, and puts her mask down. "Let's go dry off and have lunch. Do you feel hungry?"

I say, "A little."

"Well I'm half starved," she says. "I'm ravenous. I could probably eat a sea cucumber."

I start to laugh. Then I just look at her, my mother. Her arms move slowly, calmly, as she treads water. She smiles carefully at me. Now in her smile I can see a kind of grace. Where has she been and what is this smile made of? I can't know. She puts her mask down, sticks her snorkel in. She turns away and starts kicking toward shore.

PART THREE

LOVE

December 1981

As MICHAEL RUBIN PASSED by the Saint Barnabas Hospital snack bar, he caught sight of Leah Kleinfeld, his ex-wife Jess's older sister. She was sitting at the counter, drinking a Coke and reading the *Star Ledger*. He peeked his head in without thinking and said, "Leah?"

Leah looked up and seemed slightly embarrassed. Then she said, "Hi Michael, how are you?"

He said, "I'm fine."

She said, "I'm visiting someone."

"Who?"

She said, "A friend in intensive care," and smiled bitterly. She said, "I have a dying friend."

"I'm sorry," Michael said. "How long has your friend been here?"

"Just since last night," Leah said, and looked away.

Michael stared in the way he knew he shouldn't. Leah was shorter than Jess, heavier, and bustier. She was wearing an unzipped jacket over a ribbed turtleneck sweater. He'd always wished that Jess was as voluptuous as her sister.

"Are you okay?" he asked.

She said, "My friend had a stroke. A bad one. He's mostly dead."

He said, "That's hard. I'm very sorry."

"His family's getting ready to grab the plug."

He smiled inwardly at Leah's misuse of the expression. It was a habit of hers, a tendency to alter familiar phrases and clichés. He'd always blamed it on yeshiva. Unlike Jess, Leah knew every prayer and could speak Hebrew. She could cite the Talmud and Torah. Michael suspected that somehow this capacity caused her to mix certain English expressions up.

And unlike Jess, she was still Orthodox—a very low-grade, selective orthodoxy, which was closer to a conservative orientation. She had married Barry Kleinfeld. He was a Wall Street executive who'd grown up in the town of Maplewood. Leah had met him at some shul-related function toward the end of her senior year of high school. Michael had always felt quite sure that she did not love him.

"How are your children?" Michael asked her.

She said, "They're fine. How are Anthony and Dani?"

"Dani just applied to college. Can you believe it?"

"Both of my girls are at the University of Chicago."

He wondered why the University of Chicago. He didn't ask. He remembered kissing her.

Once at a mutual friend's winter holiday party years ago, when he was already carrying on with Claudia Berkowitz, he and Leah had found themselves alone in a hallway, waiting for the bathroom. They'd just been talking about their kids when Leah looked up and said, "What's that?"

"Mistletoe," he said.

"Who would have known?" said Leah. She'd smiled a playful, sarcastic smile and said, "Hey, mistletoe."

Then they had kissed.

"And how are you?" Michael asked, now wondering whether he should sit down with her for coffee.

She said, "I'm awful. You?"

"That pretty much sums it up."

"Well then, get out of here," said Leah. "We'll both just make each other miserable."

He understood that he wasn't going to sit down with her. He smiled and said, "It was nice seeing you." Leah smiled back—a sweet smile infused with a faint but obvious hint of irony. She waved and looked down at her newspaper. He continued watching her for a moment, thinking she'd look up one more time, but she did not.

Later that evening, while he was passing intensive care, Michael glanced in and saw that Leah was sitting there. She sat alone but for the nurses and the stroke victim, whose hand she was now holding to her cheek. He saw the wires around the inert man's body. He heard the blip-blip of his heart on the electrocardiograph machine and felt a small eruption of understanding. He considered stepping into the room, but instead walked faster down the hall.

When he got home that night—as he sat dreading Anthony's latest experiment, some sort of macaroni with Campbell's cream of mushroom soup thrown in to enhance the flavor—he again thought about kissing Leah under the mistletoe. He'd left the party with Jess an hour later. Jess was drunk and fell asleep in the car. Awake in bed that night, as Jess lay curled up with Nellifer, the pit bull, Michael experienced a feeling he knew was longing. Leah had felt so alive and vibrant when they kissed that he found it hard to believe Jess and she had come from the same parents.

After the kiss, Leah had taunted him. She'd poked his chest and said, "So, I must be evil. I've just smooched with my little sister's doctor husband. The Jewish clarinet-playing internist. Every nice Jewish girl's wildest dream. Of course my parents still say, 'Too bad he's not Orthodox.' Although with Jess they were even lucky to get a Jew."

Michael said, "Well, I guess I've just smooched with Jess's wiser, slightly evil older sister."

"I guess you have," Leah said. Then she had smiled in a surprising way. Her smile seemed nurturing and gentle. In a soft voice, she'd said, "And, I guess you blew it."

"Blew what?" he said.

"You're cheating on her."

"Jess told you that?"

"No, but it's just obvious. Who can blame you? Jessica never knows what she wants."

Leah leaned forward and kissed his cheek, then wiped the lipstick off.

She said, "You also like kissing me, a lot."

"I may have married the wrong sister."

Leah stared at him. For one moment he thought he could see her joining him, agreeing to do what he knew was crazy. Then she said, "Well, Dr. Rubin. Maybe you'll learn something from kissing me."

Michael said, "What? What would I learn?"

"For instance, why I wouldn't wreck my life for you."

"Why wouldn't you?" he said, his tone more urgent than he'd intended.

She said, "Oh, please."

He said, "No, really. What if I told you I could love you?"

Leah had laughed, shaken her head. She had looked coldly into his eyes. "You're just some doctor," she had said. "A confused clarinet-playing doctor. I liked watching you play clarinet at your wedding. It's maybe what I liked about you most. You also have the sort of confidence and posture I find sexy. But you have no idea what it is to love."

✦ ✦ ✦

A few days after the encounter at the snack bar with Leah, Michael was crossing the Saint Barnabas parking lot. He'd just walked over to Nettie Ochs, the last extant apple orchard in Livingston, and rather odd in its incongruity to the hospital. To appease his children's almost irrational love of apple cider, Michael had picked up two half gallons, which he now carried like dumbbells in his two hands.

He saw a woman sitting on the rear bumper of her car. It was Leah, he realized quickly. She was crying. His first instinct was to keep walking. He changed his mind at least three times and then turned into the row of cars. When she looked up and saw him coming toward her, she wiped her eyes with her sleeve and said, "Oh, Christ."

"Did your friend die?" he asked.

"Not yet."

He said, "I saw you the other night in I.C.U."

"Yeah," Leah said, still wiping her eyes. "I saw you walk by a few times. I guess you caught me or whatever. So did you come here to bring me apple juice?"

He said, "It's cider. From Nettie Ochs."

Leah burst wildly into tears. He quickly placed the two plastic containers on the blacktop beside the rear tire of her car. Then he stepped closer and stood in front of her. He touched her gently on the arm. He said, "I'm here. You're not alone." Leah stood up from her car's bumper and said, "Just hold me or I'll die."

He put her arms around her back as, almost violently, she buried her whole face into his chest. She let out raspy, primal sobs. She clawed his back and her whole body was convulsing.

"It's okay," he kept on saying. He was supporting the entire weight of her body. When the fit passed, she pulled away from him. She turned and put one hand on her car for balance.

"My God," she said, and breathed in deeply. "I can't believe Pauly's going to be gone."

He said, "How long have you been seeing him?"

"Twenty-six years," Leah said quietly.

"Twenty-six years?"

She said, "I've never loved another man. I was sixteen when I asked him to the Sadie Hawkins dance."

He said, "Paul Haney? The one you dated during high school? He owns that dealership in South Orange."

"He's Irish Catholic," Leah said. "My parents would have disowned me if I married him."

"I know."

"Now his whole family's in there," she said. "His wife and forty-seven children."

"I can't believe it," Michael said. "We bought a car from him. That's when Jess told me he'd been your boyfriend. I don't think Jess ever knew what was going on."

She said, "Of course Jess didn't know. Nobody knows except my therapist, three I.C.U. nurses, and now you. I had a perfect, justifiable affair going. That's what I told myself anyway. I didn't run it past any rabbis, but now I know there's no such thing. 'Cause there's a price, you know, for loving this way. For loving someone *this much*. And it's just crazy . . . to be this lonely. I'm so scared of this. I don't know what I'll do."

"You have your family," he said. "Your family includes me."

Leah said, "Right," and laughed maniacally. She said, "And she shall run after her lovers but she shall not overtake them. And she shall seek them but shall not find them. Then shall she say, 'I will go and return to my first husband!'"

"What's that?"

She said, "The Bible!"

"I mean what part."

She said, "Who cares! Paul was my husband even if I never married him. I have a family, sure. They're all at *home*. Twelve miles away. They're in Montclair and I'm staying at a Motel 6 in Union. And you know what?"

"What?"

She said, "They think I'm down in Florida, with Jess!"

"Have you been speaking a lot with Jess?"

She didn't answer. Leah sat down again on the bumper. He understood she had not been speaking a lot with Jess.

He said, "So what have you been doing? Just hanging out at the Motel 6?"

She said, "I sit there, watching television. Or I sit here, like a ghost. I wait around for Pauly's family to leave the hospital. I've taken all the nurses into confidence, just to spend an hour each day with his brain-dead body. There isn't anything they can do. If they unhook him he'll stop breathing."

He said, "I'm sorry."

"Don't be sorry!"

"You're getting angry."

"I feel like killing you and everyone in the universe!"

"Hey," he said. "Listen. Why don't we go for a cup of coffee? I can call up and we'll find out when his family leaves. We can come back here to see him when they do."

"You should get home."

He said, "Don't worry. I'll call my kids. We'll get some coffee. Then we'll come back here."

"I'm a disaster," she said. "Why would you want to be around me?"

He said, "You're Jess's older sister. I'm just trying to be your friend."

They went to Todd's, a little diner on Northfield Avenue. It was two doors down from Temple B'nai Abraham. Leah kept joking about breaking into the synagogue to pray.

They ordered coffee. Michael got up to call his answering service and then check on Paul Haney at the hospital. There was a message to call Anthony, so he called him. Anthony wanted to know whether yeast would die after sitting in a closet for several years. "We're baking bread," he explained. "I found this pack of dry-active yeast. What does that mean, that it's dry-active?" Michael said probably it had died. He said he'd stop on his way home and pick up fresh yeast at the Shop Rite. He said goodbye and dialed the switchboard at the hospital. He asked for Gretchen, the head nurse.

It took awhile before she picked up. Michael said, "Hi, it's Dr. Rubin. I'd like the status of Paul Haney in I.C.U."

She had him hold the phone a moment while she checked records. When she returned she said, "Mr. Haney expired this evening. His family gave their consent to let him go."

"Are they still with him?" he asked.

"Yes, they're with the body."

Michael said, "Thank you."

He hung the phone up, took a breath, pulled out five dollars. He walked over to the table and laid the money down. He said, "Let's get back to the hospital."

"Are all the Haneys gone?"

He said, "No."

Leah stood up. He'd never seen a human being look more vulnerable.

Leah said, "What? You think..."

"He's dead," Michael said. "They signed and let him go this evening."

A tear slipped down Leah's cheek. She turned away and looked intently at the wall, almost as if she could see through it. Unlike before, she now cried silently, without moving. Big wet tears streamed down her face, but her whole body froze like a dancer in tableau.

She cried like Jess, of course. That strange, unnerving way of crying. Michael stepped up and wrapped his arms around her. He pulled her close and held her tight, though she stayed frozen. When he released her, she said, "It feels like I just died, too."

At the hospital, all of the Haneys were still milling around outside the intensive care unit. Michael checked things out while Leah waited in the snack bar. He counted six children in all, as well as siblings and in-laws and Paul's mother. Their family physician, Jacob Katz, was there discussing the situation with Mrs. Haney, whose eyes were swollen and very red.

When he went back to the snack bar, Leah was standing at the entrance with her arms crossed.

"All of his family's still around," he said, and caressed her lightly on the arm.

Leah said, "Yeah, I'm sure they'll be here half the night."

"They have to move him," Michael said. "They're waiting for the people from the funeral home to come."

Leah's face took on a fatigued and angry-seeming expression. She said, "Oh Christ, Michael, I don't know what to do."

"Do you have to see him?"

Leah said, "Yes. Can't you just clear them all away for at least five minutes?"

He said, "I doubt it."

"Then what good are you?"

"It's not an easy situation."

Leah said, "Guess I'll make a scene. Luckily Paul's wife is a dingbat."

He said, "Just wait another minute. I'll see what I can do."

Michael headed down the hall again. He felt nervous. But as he passed through a cluster of Paul's relatives, he grew aware of his own power and authority. He turned the corner and went into I.C.U. None of the family members were inside.

He saw Paul Haney, still on the table, all of the breathing apparatus disconnected from his body. He remembered seeing Paul many years before, the day they bought the car from him. He was a blond-haired man whose smile and warm blue eyes had won him over.

"Is this man going downstairs soon?" Michael asked.

One of the nurses said, "We're waiting for the Cahill and Blake Funeral Home."

"Up in Hawthorne?"

"That explains why they're so late."

"Where's Dr. Katz?" he asked.

"If you'd like, we'll page him."

Michael said, "Please," and waited beside the body. He imagined Leah and Paul at their high school prom, dancing and kissing, Leah wearing a strapless dress and long black gloves. And Paul could dance, Jess had said. She said Paul made girls want to dance. He wasn't big or suave or tall but he possessed that glowing type of presence. Jess claimed that girls always wanted to be wrapped up in Paul's arms.

When Jacob Katz appeared, Michael explained the situation. The doctor, an old acquaintance, took in the details. He said, "I'll see what I can do." He stepped over to the nurses, talked to them quietly. One of the nurses said, "I'll take him." Then Katz walked back over to Michael. He told Michael that the nurse would bring the body downstairs. They'd keep him waiting in the holding room by the loading dock where the hearse would come.

He found Leah in the snack bar. She was sitting at the booth nearest the entrance, head in her hands.

"He's being moved," Michael said.

"Where?"

"He's heading down to a room beside the loading dock. The hearse won't be here for a while. If we go now we'll intercept them on the ground floor."

"Who did you have to bribe?"

Michael said, "No one."

Leah stood up beside Michael and smiled appreciatively. She kissed his cheek and said, "Thank you, Dr. Rubin."

He led Leah to the elevator, which they took down to the ground floor. For several minutes they waited outside a locked, gray metal door beside the loading dock. He kept his arm around Leah and said, "He'll be here." There was a hospital phone around the corner. If Paul did not show up in the next minute, he would go call.

To his relief, he heard the ding of the elevator. A nurse appeared behind the metal gurney that supported the covered body of Paul Haney. As she pushed the gurney toward them, she saw Leah and clearly understood the situation. Still she said, "Yes, doctor?"

He said, "Ms. Kleinfeld would like a moment with the deceased."

"Of course." The nurse stepped back. After a few seconds' hesitation, Leah stepped forward. She peeled away the sheet and plastic wrap that had been covering the face of her dead lover.

Michael could hear the droning of the heating system. Big, eerie metal pipes snaked across the ceiling. He watched Leah touching Paul's face. She started talking to him, calmly, her tone gentle and conversational. She said, "We're putting you in the freezer for a little bit. Then you'll wind up in a coffin, like you've seen." She stroked his head and said, "I love you, Pauly, you know that. You'll have to talk to them, explain it. And then make sure we meet up in the next life."

Leah stayed quiet for several minutes. She stood just looking at him, smiling, wiping tears off her cheek. After a while she kissed his face once more and reached out for the sheet. Before she covered him up for good, she said, "We must be crazy to have done this."

She placed the sheet over Paul's face. Then Leah stepped back and the nurse unlocked the metal door. They watched the nurse wheel the gurney into the stark, empty, well-lit room.

He saw the prom again, Paul and Leah dancing. He wondered why this wholly imagined vision kept returning to his brain. Maybe because the prom with Jess had been so awful. He had been twenty years old, self-conscious, and Jess refused to dance all night. She had looked stunning in her prom dress, her broad shoulders slouched, as always, frosty pink lipstick glossed onto her lips. After an hour, she went outside with her girlfriends. He sat alone for a while at a table, then left the gym and wandered around the parking lot. On the far side he found Jess and her two friends sitting with their shoes off. Jess had said, "Hi honey," and passed Michael the cigarette she was smoking, but he had still felt as if he was not there.

He heard the sound of Leah's shoes striking the hospital's granite floor. He turned and saw that she was walking toward the elevator. He followed after her and caught up as the elevator door opened. As they stepped in she took his arm and said, "The cider."

Michael said, "What?"

She said, "You left it in the lot, right on the ground beside my car."

"Oh, right," he said. "I'll walk you out."

"I hope the cider is still there."

She let his arm go when the elevator door opened. It was dark when they walked out through the hospital's front entrance. But as they turned into the row she'd parked in, he saw two silhouettes, the half-gallon jugs, sitting on her trunk. Someone had moved them. Michael pointed. He said, "Looks like the work of a Good Samaritan." In a sardonic voice Leah said, "Wonderful." But for reasons that Michael could not identify, the cider's presence filled him with quiet joy.

"Thank you again," Leah said, when they reached her car. "You've been a help. Now I'll go back to the motel and disintegrate."

He took the cider, one in each hand. He said, "I know you'll be okay."

She said, "I feel like I'm crashing up."

Michael said, "Cracking up."

"What?"

"You mean you're 'cracking up,'" he said. "Or else just 'crashing.'"

Leah smiled and said, "Whatever it is, I'm there."

Then she leaned forward and kissed his cheek again. Michael hugged her. It was difficult with the cider. She also didn't seem to want a hug.

"You should get home," Leah said. "I'll call you sometime after I get through this."

She turned away and pulled her car keys from her pocket. He knew to leave her. He said, "Take care of yourself," and headed across the lot. He heard her car start. He kept walking but glanced back in time to watch as Leah exited the parking lot. She took a right on Old Short Hills Road, then made her way into the darkness. She passed from sight and Michael thought: I'm crashing up.

HOCKEY PLAYER MYTH

Winter 1981–1982

ONE EARLY DECEMBER AFTERNOON before hockey practice, Anthony waited by the lunch room for Alex Brody, one of the three hockey team managers. He needed a roll of tape for a new stick. As he stood there, his linemate and team captain, Dave Delaney, walked up and asked if he wanted a ride to practice. Anthony told Dave he was getting a ride with Alex.

"Just didn't want you to be stuck with all those scrubs on the J.V. bus."

"I think I'm set," Anthony said. "But thanks for asking."

Dave said, "And hey."

"What?"

"No swimming before practice."

"Don't worry," Anthony said. "I know the rules."

Right at that moment, Alex appeared. She walked toward them with her usual brisk gait. Like certain players on the team, she always seemed to be carrying a great deal of momentum. She had her jacket on over some sort of elegant blue dress. Her black ankle boots made a clomping sound as she walked.

She was holding two sticks, a clipboard, and a key ring filled with keys. She looked at Anthony, smiled, and in a playful voice said, "Hey, number fourteen, will you please accompany me to the hockey closet?"

Alex cruised past them and kept going. Dave pinched Anthony's left shoulder.

He said, "Go easy. No swimming. You need to save something for practice."

"No swimming," Anthony said, and followed Alex down the hall.

+ + +

Even during Anthony's freshman year, everyone on the hockey team assumed that he was putting the moves on Alex. Or else that Alex was putting the moves on him. This never made any sense to Anthony. She was a junior when Anthony was a freshman. More significantly, she was dating Gary Weinstein, a senior who played shortstop on the baseball team. They had been one of the school's high-profile couples, always holding hands at recess and sometimes kissing in the Kraig Garden outside the senior lounge.

Alex and Gary were still together, even though Gary was now a freshman at Brandeis. This didn't seem to account for much with the other hockey players, or with the two other managers, Tina Bevona and Cammy Vincent. Even if Anthony denied it, no one believed that he and Alex weren't an item. They seemed to go together. At least that's what people seemed to think.

She was Jewish, after all. Not only that, she was in the highest school track, taking honors courses. She'd been the only junior girl who took physics, and as a senior she was taking AP biology. She claimed she wanted to be an emergency room surgeon.

Alex was hot, too—a sort of JAPpy hot: Designer jeans, short denim skirts, sometimes big rugby shirts from Benetton. She had long dark hair and a very athletic body. She had big brown eyes that tended to seem wild. And one amazing thing about her, at least to Anthony, was that she never wore any make-up. The other managers wore make-up all the time, the works: pastel eye shadows, base, even the shade of lipstick Dani would refer to as "fuck-me" red.

At the team party the spring before, the coach himself had brought it up. It was late and they had just given Coach Marino a framed and signed team photograph. The coach was holding the photo on his lap. They were all sitting on the couch at the house of last year's captain, Chris Ferreti. The coach had joked about how hard it was to work with Italian players, since the only thing they thought about was "swimming."

Then he said, "That's what makes Rubin a money player. He's got standards." He turned to Anthony, who was sitting there, trying to hold his own as the one freshman at the party. The coach said, "So, Antonio, where's Brody?"

He said, "She left with her boyfriend about two hours ago."

The coach said, "Hey, you listen to your coach here. Alex Brody, she is *perfect* for you. You wanna stick it out, you hear? I know she's onto you. And that tall guy of hers is gone next year. He's out of here. Some stupid school up in Maine."

"Massachusetts," Anthony told him. "He's going to Brandeis University."

"Right," Coach Marino said. "Now listen here, I really mean this. That Alex Brody could be your *wife*."

The coach was bombed, Anthony knew. He just said, "Coach, you really think so?" But still he knew what was going on. He knew the whole thing was a fairy tale, though he wasn't quite sure why. He often wished that what these people thought was true. He wondered if there was something he was doing incorrectly. Sometimes he even imagined kissing her—planting one right on her lips down in the hockey closet, then Alex saying something like, "Finally! I wondered when the hell you'd come around."

✦ ✦ ✦

On rides to practice Alex tended to drive fast. She had a Chevrolet Type-10 Cavalier, fully loaded. Her cassette player was expensive and could play songs very loud.

That afternoon Anthony was taping up his hockey stick while she drove. Alex was blasting Pink Floyd, and the song "Run Like Hell" resounded as they drove through the South Mountain Reservation.

Mondays and Wednesdays she would make detours through Mill-burn to bring Matt, her introverted little brother, to his karate class. Matt was just one grade below Anthony, but he always seemed much younger. He barely talked even when Alex asked him questions. After she'd dropped Matt off, she sometimes commented on her little brother's shyness and strange lack of personality. Then she would drive at excessive speeds over the winding road that S-curved through the wooded hills of the reservation. It was a well-patrolled road. Anthony felt sure she'd get a colossal speeding ticket at some point. But she was charmed, it seemed. They'd never seen a single cop in all the times Alex had raced through at breakneck speed.

That afternoon, just as they came around the bend by the Hawk Hill picnic area, she turned the music down and looked at him.

"What was that swimming stuff with David?" she asked. "I keep on hearing people say that, like there's a swimming hour in the pool now. What's the deal?"

"It's a joke," Anthony said.

"So what's the joke?"

He said, "It means . . . no getting laid. Dave made the rule up."

Alex just smiled and lightly bonked herself on the forehead. She turned to Anthony and said, "God, I am so *thick* sometimes. I'm sorry."

"No problem," he said, and continued to wind black tape around his stick blade.

"So Delaney thinks we're doing it. That's pretty funny, don't you think?"

"Everyone does," said Anthony, surprising himself. "I try to tell them but no one actually believes me."

Alex said, "Geez." She turned to Anthony, smiled, and said, "So people think I'm a real cradle robber. How do you feel?"

"I'm not so sure," he said, remotely hoping this was a turning point. "I once told Will Smithson I was a virgin. He just laughed."

Alex pulled up at a red traffic light where the two-lane road crossed South Orange Avenue. He watched her shift the car into neutral.

Then he said, "Well, what about you?"

"How do I feel?" Alex said. "About the idea that Smithson and Delaney think we're 'swimming' before practice? Or do you mean how do I feel about you?"

"Both," he said, and ripped the tape. He pressed the last strip with his palm against the stick blade. The light turned green but she didn't hit the gas pedal. She turned Pink Floyd down even more. They didn't move.

"Let's get something straight," said Alex.

Someone behind them started honking.

She said, "The thing is, there are certain things I know about you. Things that are obvious to me, but things you may not even be aware of."

"Such as what?" Anthony said.

"Such as the fact that you need a mother, or at least someone who can act like one."

The honks continued. Anthony glanced back and saw a bearded, long-haired man standing beside the open door of his Ford Pinto. "Would you get moving, for chrissake!" the man shouted, while still honking with one hand. Alex ignored him and continued the conversation.

"Hey," she said. "I've always liked you. But I'm still going out with Gary and I love him. I'm also not a slut like Tina 'Boner' Bevona or whatever they've been calling her these days. So, you should just think of me as your mother."

Anthony stared at her. Alex's eyes didn't seem all that maternal. The man behind them shouted, "Yo! You gonna move or do I have to ram your ass?"

"Oh Jesus Christ," Alex said. "Why don't they lock guys like this up?"

He started walking toward the car. Alex opened the power window, held her hand out, and calmly gave the man the finger. He yelled, "Fuck you! Fucking cunt!" and gave the finger back. He started jumping around wildly, giving the finger with both hands. Just as he reached the rear bumper, Alex floored it and screamed "Moron!" out the window.

As she hit forty or so she turned to Anthony.

She said, "And so, are we okay on this?"

"Fine," he said, still awed by the whole scene back at the light.

She said, "I like you, so you know. I mean, there are times when I want to jump your bones. But I just think you need me as a mother, see what I'm saying?"

He said, "Got it."

"Don't be so glum," Alex said.

"I'm not."

"How about this?" she said, and took the car up to seventy.

✦ ✦ ✦

Alex Brody was the team manager who knew the sport of hockey best. While Tina Bevona and Cammy Vincent mostly collected jerseys and filled water bottles, it was Alex who kept the stats and always made sure miscredited goals and assists were ultimately corrected in the scoring book. Coach Marino knew she had brains and poise, so she was also in charge of calling games in to the newspaper. As a result, she had been largely responsible for Anthony's notoriety during his freshman year.

Early on in that season, when he'd emerged as the team's main goal-scorer, Alex had dug around until she found out the state record for most goals ever scored by a ninth-grader. It was preposterously low: eighteen. Everyone guessed the record had been broken numerous times, but that no one had ever thought to report it. That year Alex alerted the *Star Ledger* to the record, which Anthony broke a little more than halfway through the season. Then for the first time in a while, the paper paid attention to Livingston games, most of which were lopsided losses. But Anthony frequently came up with two or three goals, and with his final total of thirty-one, the paper named him second-team all-state.

When it came down to it, Anthony understood that Alex had been

acting like his mother all along. From the first day of practice his freshman year, she had watched over him. She had made sure he iced his
calf after Hugh Strom hit him with a slap shot during practice. On
nights before games she sometimes called to make sure Anthony was
planning to get a good night's sleep. She'd even labeled herself "den
mother" of the hockey team, but not until now had he realized she was
consciously acting like a mom.

Throughout the fall of Anthony's tenth-grade year, the pattern had
continued. Alex drove him every day to practice. Once during a full-ice
scrimmage, he got his bell rung by Ralph Tortelli. He was out cold for
a few seconds. Alex had walked out onto the ice in her stylish ankle
boots. She helped him up and then sat with him on the bench. She
asked him all sorts of questions—what was the date, the year, the first
three decimal places of pi? Anthony only knew two decimal places, so
Alex asked him to call with the other decimal that night. After they
spoke on the phone—by then he'd memorized the first ten decimal
places—he said his father, who was a doctor, wanted to speak to her.
Anthony listened as his father asked Alex questions about seemingly
minute details of the injury. After his father hung up, he turned to Anthony. He said, "That Alex, she's terrific. How come you've never asked
her on a date?"

He told his father that Alex had a boyfriend, Gary Weinstein. He
told him Alex didn't fool around. His father asked him why he never
had any girlfriends, period. He didn't know what to answer. He said, "I
guess I'm just too focused on playing hockey."

One snowy afternoon late that December, Alex asked him the
same thing. Due to the wet snow that was falling, she drove slower than
usual through the South Mountain Reservation. They passed two cars
that had just had a minor accident, then an officer in a cruiser, its lights
flashing. She said, "Hey Anth, so what's the deal? Have you been secretly hoping I'll come around?"

"What do you mean?" he said, while rubbernecking. He saw a man
in a long overcoat, his arms crossed, sitting on his front bumper. Near
the other car a woman stood with a scarf that was tied around her ears.

She said, "I mean, why don't you have a girlfriend? You could probably date anyone you want. Except me."

"Yeah, right," he said.

"What?"

He said, "For instance, Bev Glasser had a crush on me—supposedly. When I walk by her in the hall she barely looks at me."

"Bev Glasser's in my grade."

He said, "I know. She's friends with Dani. That's how I knew she supposedly had a crush on me."

"What about girls in your grade? Or even ninth-graders? And why the hell would you think about Bev Glasser? She's just this goody-two-shoes waif who's kind of pretty. I think I've heard her talk three times in my life."

"But I might like her," he said.

"I doubt it. You would have done something. Maybe called her. When you like a girl you ask her on a date."

"My sister said that Bev lost interest."

"Sounds like you didn't give her anything to be interested in."

"Guess not," Anthony said.

"So is there anybody else?"

"Besides you?"

Alex said, "Stop that," and came to a red light. The thick, wet snowflakes looked exactly like the dust clumps that would miraculously form underneath his bed.

He said, "There is one person."

"Who?"

"My neighbor, Juliette Dimiglio."

Alex said, "*What?*"

"We sort of talked some in October. She bought a raffle. The thing is, she has this very scary boyfriend who would kill me. It's confusing. I don't even think she likes him."

She said, "Hello? Are we talking about the same Juliette Dimiglio? The nightmare junior who's dating that psycho football head? She's like...a Mafia chick or something."

He said, "I know her just because she lives next door."

In her dramatic way, Alex swerved into the lot by the Hawk Hill picnic area. It was empty, so she slammed on the brakes and skidded to a stop.

"Number one," she said. "If you go near Juliette Dimiglio again, I'll kill you. Number two, you need to get a clue."

He said, "We've talked. That's all that happened."

Alex said, "I don't care if she abducted you. The point is this—you have a problem. You just want fantasies. I get it. Because Bev Glasser's the same thing. You barely know her. You hear she thinks you're cute so then you just go off with some story in your head. And it makes sense, in a way, because you're so afraid of getting to know *anyone*."

"I know you."

"That's because I don't need anything!" yelled Alex. "It's because I act like your damn mother!"

"Well, you don't have to," he said.

"You just don't get it."

He said, "Get what?"

She said, "To be in a relationship, you have to *do* things. You can't just wait around for someone to swoop down on you. You can't rely on the goals you score in hockey to make people want to be with you. Because the thing is, that's not you. It's just some hockey player myth."

He said, "But Juliette's never even seen me play hockey."

Alex said, "Anthony, get over it. The best she'll do is break your heart. What about girls like Dana Kreisler? She's in your class. She might be perfect."

"She has a boyfriend. They've been an item since eighth grade."

Alex said, "What about Wendy Sherman? She has blond hair, for God's sake. Her mom's a WASP but she still had a bat mitzvah. She's like this perfect Jew-Goy combo plate galore."

"What about you?" Anthony said. "What if I really am just waiting around for you?"

"Then you're an idiot."

"Maybe not," he said. "Maybe I can't like anyone but you."

"Oh, Jesus Christ," Alex said, but for a second she turned and looked at him with something like surprise. He wondered if he had just spoken the magic words she had been waiting for. All Alex said was, "I told you to forget it."

✦ ✦ ✦

Over the next weeks, Anthony thought his father might be going crazy. He started playing his long-dormant clarinet. Sometimes he came home from work and went directly to his bedroom. Sometimes he played down in the basement for half the night.

Back when Anthony was very young, his father would often play all afternoon. He always liked to play "Moon River," which seemed to have some secret, deep, and heartfelt meaning for his parents. At times his mother would start crying when his father played the song.

But for more than ten years the clarinet had remained in the hall closet. He knew his father still sometimes listened to Benny Goodman, but that one afternoon—Dani claimed it was the day of the first moon landing—he took the clarinet apart and then abandoned what seemed to be his truest passion. For no reason anyone could pinpoint, he simply never took the instrument out again.

Once as a boy, Anthony pulled the case down. That was some time in the mid-seventies. The clarinet had sat untouched for at least six years. He had unfastened the metal latches, opened the case up, and gazed down at the bright red felt interior. Then staring at that array of interlocking clarinet parts, each snug and discrete within its matrix of inertia, he was reminded of a stone that, chiseled open, reveals a fossil.

But now the instrument was, once again, alive.

Anthony sensed something significant was happening for his father. He even liked being around him. But ever since his last romance-related talk with Alex, Anthony carried around his longing so intensely it had begun to feel like a form of music in itself.

He kept on praying, in a way—secretly wishing through every situation with Alex. She'd be collecting the team jerseys and she'd smile at him. He'd try to read something new into her smile. Once they got caught in traffic due to construction on Northfield Avenue. Alex reached across the dashboard and their hands touched. Anthony wanted their hands to touch again. So then he asked her for a Certs. She held her purse open. He reached inside and acted as if he couldn't find the pack of Certs. Alex reached in and searched around. Anthony playfully grabbed her hand. Inside the purse, she squeezed him back. She said, "There must be a black hole that likes wintergreen in here." Anthony waited to see if somehow this would alter the trajectory of their friendship. When Alex finally pulled her hand out, all she did was hand him the pack of Certs.

It was after the Morris Plains game that something finally changed with Alex. He watched it happen. It was obvious. Anthony knew what she had said about the hockey player myth, but still the only explanation seemed to be the goal he scored.

He'd snapped it over the goalie's shoulder with forty seconds left in the game. This gave his team a 3–2 win, their first nonlosing effort of the season. Right after the goal, a Morris Plains defenseman decked him. It was a cheap shot, and a vicious one. As Anthony raised his stick in celebration, the player cross-checked him from behind. He popped right up from the ice, furious, dropped his stick and reflexively began punching the player's head. They both fell down to the ice, still punching until the linesman broke the fight up. They were both thrown out of the game, but it didn't matter with forty seconds left to play.

When he stepped out of the locker room after dressing, Alex sprang down on him from the bleachers where she'd been waiting. She held her clipboard. She took his sticks in her free hand and draped her other arm and the clipboard around his shoulder. She said, "I just called the game in to the *Star Ledger*."

Anthony noticed his father moving toward them.

Alex said, "So, are you going to Bryan Howland's?"

"Who's Bryan Howland?"

"He's a senior. You want a ride?"

Right then his father broke through a small crowd and yelled, "Antonio!" He walked up close and shouted, "What a goal! High five!"

Anthony slapped his father five and prayed he'd leave. Of course, he didn't.

So he said, "Dad, do you know Alex?"

He said, "Of course," and they shook hands.

"Your son's a hero," Alex said.

"I saw it coming," his father said. "Right when you made that break-out pass to Dave Delaney on the wing. I saw you going hard for the blue line after you passed it. Then Delaney gave it back to you, right in stride..."

She surreptitiously grabbed his hand as his father went on with the recap. After a few seconds of squeezing, she let go. When his father stopped analyzing the goal, she said, "Nice meeting you, Mr. Rubin." She handed Anthony his hockey sticks and said, "I'll pick you up at nine."

That evening before Alex picked him up, he called his mother. He called a lot now—ever since the strange hiatus, when she switched numbers and didn't call them for a month. Most of the time his calls were motivated by a puzzling sense of nervousness. For instance, that night he'd felt nervous all through the hockey game. At certain times he'd almost been afraid to step out onto the ice. He called his mother while still feeling this sense of dread that did not seem to have an origin. When his mom answered, he launched right into his account of the winning goal.

He also told her he was going to a senior party with Alex, the team manager. He said that Alex was very nice to him—that she gave him rides to practice and had once hand washed his jersey after a game when someone bled on it. "Alex must like you," his mother said. "I hope you have a good time at the party." When he hung up he felt entirely confused as to why he'd called her. As usual, she had told him virtually nothing. And as usual there were fifteen other things he'd meant to say.

At five to nine Alex appeared at his front door. She wore black jeans and a dark purple corduroy shirt with snaps instead of buttons. From the first moment he laid eyes on the shirt, Anthony found that he was fixated. It was a ten-minute ride to Bryan Howland's, and the whole time he kept glancing at the snaps.

When they pulled up behind the last of the many parked cars on Rockledge Drive, Alex turned from the wheel and said, "Guess what?"

"What?" Anthony said.

She said, "Last night that slimebag Gary dumped me."

He said, "He did?"

"He screwed around on me. And told me. Guess I can't blame him for wanting out."

"What an idiot," Anthony said.

Alex smiled at him.

She said, "Thanks."

"What?"

"That was the answer I really needed. You're the best."

"Are you okay?"

Alex said, "Fine. I feel like getting really drunk."

He said, "You do?"

"Just hold my hand, okay?"

He quickly took her hand.

"I mean inside," Alex said. She turned and kissed him on the cheek. "We're here together, okay?"

He said, "Okay."

He felt self-conscious as they walked in, since by then Alex had her arm around his waist. On top of which, it was mostly seniors and not a very wild party. There were maybe fifty people there at most.

Anthony figured people would be stunned to see them, but when they entered no one seemed to notice. Even when hockey players saw them, they all just waved or said hello. They seemed to think it was only normal that she and Anthony would be there arm in arm.

As promised, Alex drank several beers, even once joining Cammy and Tina in a hockey manager chug. Shortly after that, a senior named

Stu Devlin asked her to dance. She looked at Anthony and said, "I'll be right back."

He assumed it would be one dance. He watched them dance to two songs by Foreigner and one Squeeze song, after which he decided to stop watching. He wandered off into the kitchen, where a group of long-haired seniors were getting stoned.

A slow song, Elvis Costello's "Alison," began playing on the stereo. He figured Alex would stop dancing, so he walked back into the main room. He saw her box-stepping with Stu Devlin and felt a hollow sensation in his chest. Any other couples still dancing were either making out or close.

He started wondering what he'd do if Alex started making out with Stu Devlin. He wondered why this thought was turning him into something like Swiss cheese. He stared at Alex on the dance floor, saw the snaps on her purple shirt. Then he felt lost, like he was floating. He walked back into the kitchen.

To his relief, someone yelled, "Anthony—you Anthony?"

He looked up at the group of seniors and said, "Yup."

"I'm Troy," said a guy he vaguely recognized. "Great goal tonight, man. That was so sweet. And when you pounded that guy afterward—that was *excellent*."

He said, "Thanks."

"You wanna hit?" Troy said.

"Sure."

He took a bong in his hands and heard the music change. The song that came on was "Shout," from *Animal House*. Several people in the kitchen heard the song and quickly headed to the dance floor. Troy lit the bowl for Anthony with a lighter. Anthony inhaled smoke until he began coughing.

"All right," Troy said. "We just got this hockey dude so stoned."

He felt a pair of arms slide under his. He turned around and said, "Thank God."

"You're getting stoned?" Alex said. "You?"

He said, "Not really."

She said, "You missed me, huh?"

"I figured you and Stu Devlin were about to get a room."

"You should have grabbed me," she said. "I'm drunk."

"You said you'd be right back. I thought..."

Alex said, "Let's get away from all these potheads."

She took his hand and pulled him back into the living room, which was now packed with people dancing to "Shout." He assumed Alex wanted to dance, but she kept pulling him through the people. When they got clear, she said, "I'm sorry. I'm very drunk. Let's go upstairs." She smiled. "Let's get a room."

She led him up to a bedroom where a queen-size bed was piled high with coats. Alex said, "Wow, so many coats. Good thing I left mine in the car." He kissed her ear and Alex turned. Soon they were kissing very hard. They mashed their tongues with a kind of fury Anthony hadn't ever felt before. Without thinking, he reached down and pressed his hand between her thighs.

"What's going on with you tonight?" she said. "It's just the way..."

But Alex didn't finish her sentence. She shuddered and he feared that he'd blown everything.

He took a step back, pulled his hand away. Alex reached out and took his hand. She brought it up to her mouth, kissed it. She put it back between her thighs. He smiled inwardly and felt a wave of calm pass through his body. Alex said, "God, let's hurry up and find a bed where we can totally just...swim."

They found an open room down the hall. There were no coats on the bed, so they went in. The room smelled like grape Bubble Yum. A giant poster of Duran Duran filled one entire wall. The thought of losing his virginity near this poster was disturbing, although he guessed it could be worse. He stood with Alex at the mouth of the door and waited. She closed the door and at first it was so dark he could not see.

"I'm locking this," she said, and pulled away from him. He felt weightless. He imagined he was part of a Duran Duran video. Then Alex, barely visible, was lifting up his shirt.

He felt her mouth, warm on his chest. He imagined things: her

face, her car, the rink. He saw the goal he'd scored and heard the way
the crowd roared when it happened. Then he was down on the ice,
fighting, hearing nothing. He felt the cold metal snaps of her shirt
touching his bare skin.

"This beats the hockey closet," said Alex.

"I wouldn't know."

"I think I'm going to devour you."

Anthony laughed and said, "And all this time you thought you were
my mother."

"I'm no one's mother," Alex said. "Not for a long time anyway."

His eyes adjusted to the dark. Now he could see her. She brushed
her fingers across his cheek with a touch that was so tender it almost
hurt.

"Can I do something?" he asked.

"What?"

He pulled the snaps on her shirt apart with a single motion.

He said, "I've waited the entire night to do that."

She started laughing. She smiled mischievously. Without warning,
she reached down and grabbed his crotch.

"You silly boy," she said. "Now I think Mommy's going to eat you."

Things became strange, almost surreal. She pushed him down on
the bed and stood before him. When she said, "Hey, number fourteen,
look at me," Anthony felt something shifting in the room.

"Look at me," she repeated.

She took her bra off. Anthony unsnapped her jeans and pulled
them down as she stepped out of them. "Like what you see?" Alex
asked. He nodded. She stood naked. Then she moved forward and
pressed his face between her legs. She told him, "Swim."

✦ ✦ ✦

For one day of his life, Anthony was in heaven. All through that Sunday
he imagined scenes with Alex. He pictured holding Alex's hand in the
senior lounge. He pictured Alex zipping his fly down as she drove at
high speed across the reservation. He imagined parking behind the

rink, the way he'd heard Dave Delaney sometimes did with Miranda Dixon.

But when he called Alex that night, her phone was busy. It was her own line, so Anthony tried repeatedly until midnight. The phone stayed busy and he finally gave up. Then on Monday Alex didn't come to school. Anthony knew she wasn't sick. He kept on waiting for her to show, for her to sneak up and wrap her arms around him in the hallway. But Alex never appeared in school. He wound up having to take the J.V. bus to practice, and only then did he begin to have a sense that things were not as he'd imagined.

When he got home, there was a message to call Alex. He dialed her number and she answered on one ring.

"Oh good, it's you," she said, which momentarily relieved him.

He said, "Where were you today?"

"I'm quitting," she said. "I had a revelation."

"Quitting the hockey team?"

"That's right."

Somehow he wasn't really surprised. Nor did it stun him when she said Gary had called the night before and pleaded with her until three in the morning.

"He kept on saying he deserved one get-out-of-jail-free card," Alex said. "Can you believe that? Five hours of hearing this dumb analogy. I finally yelled, 'Go build hotels on Park Place!' I didn't even know what I was saying."

"So did you make up?"

"Are you kidding? I told him get the hell out of my goddamn life."

"He deserved it," Anthony said.

"That's what I told him. I mean, the guy kept talking about Monopoly. It's not even a board game I liked playing."

He said, "Okay, so what's your revelation?"

"My revelation?"

"You said you had a revelation."

She said, "Oh, right. It's just that really there's no point to being manager of the hockey team. I like the game. I like the skating. Most of all I like watching you kick ass. But, you know, I want to be an E.R. doctor. I don't know why I never joined the rescue squad. Now I'm joining. I have to do some shifts on weekdays. I can't do both."

"The coach will miss you," Anthony said.

"I know he will," she said. "It's not so easy, but I think I have to do it."

"I'll miss you, too."

She said, "It's not like I'll be moving to Australia."

He got his guts up and said, "Then what's the deal with us?"

"What do you mean?" Alex asked.

He was afraid she would say that.

He said, "I mean, you have to tell me where I stand."

"I'm your friend," Alex said. "Just like I always was. You can still come with me into the senior lounge."

"So it's the same."

Alex said, "Right. The only difference is that now you'll have to ride that lousy bus to practice."

He said, "It's not the same."

"I know," she said.

"I like you a lot."

"I know."

"Let's try to be friends," he said.

She said, "Okay, let's really try."

There was a silence in which Anthony felt as if he were dissolving. Finally Alex said, "I'm sorry. I know I acted like a shit."

✦ ✦ ✦

For a few weeks they didn't talk, but then one morning Alex walked up to his locker. She said, "Hello, number fourteen." Somehow this managed to break the silence.

After that they sometimes chatted before homeroom or at lunch. Anthony kept her up to date with what was happening on the hockey team. Alex told him about her Livingston First Aid Squad adventures.

She had a radio, which she showed to him. Every weekend she was on call. She sometimes got called out at four A.M.

One afternoon in early March, just a week after the team's annual pulverization in Minnesota, Anthony had a seventh-period history test. Inexplicably, the teacher let them work overtime. Most students stayed an extra hour. After Anthony turned his test in, he looked up and saw that it was two-fifty. The practice bus left at two-thirty. He ran outside in a mild state of denial, but soon he realized that the team bus was long gone.

He ran inside and looked around for someone on the team who hadn't left yet. He even ran down to the hockey storage closet. He knocked in hope that someone was in there swimming before practice.

Then he sought out his last resort, his older sister. He knew she'd drive him, if he could find her. Of course she'd come up with some reason to be pissed off, but she still would. As he was sprinting down the hall toward Dani's locker, he and Alex Brody practically collided.

"Jesus, what's wrong?" Alex said. "Don't you have practice?"

"I missed the bus."

Alex looked down at her watch and said, "Meet me out front. I'll use my siren."

Before he'd said a word, she was jogging down the hall.

Anthony walked out front with his equipment. Within three minutes her car came racing around the building, a silent blue rotator light flashing on the top. It was the portable magnetic kind, for first aid squad volunteers. His first thought was that it wasn't technically a siren. He'd had this argument with Craig Kelby, whose brother Jamie was on the squad. Craig's father ultimately ruled that all sirens, technically, made noise.

Alex pulled up, opened the door. He saw the thin wire that was plugged into the cigarette lighter socket. He threw his hockey gear onto the backseat and climbed in front.

"Okay," Alex said. "I guess I'm going to break like fifteen major rules in my squad manual."

"I can be late."

Alex ignored him.

She said, "Just hold on tight. If someone hassles us, we'll tell them you have chest pains. But then I'll have to drive you to Saint Barnabas."

Alex burned out of the school parking lot, the blue light flashing on the left side of her roof. As she pulled onto the road she held her horn down. Several cars screeched to a halt as she cut them off.

Out on Northfield, in the stretch where the speed was forty, cars pulled over and let Alex pass at sixty. She ran red lights and passed several cars by driving on the shoulder. Anthony shouted at her but didn't dare touch the wheel.

As they came down the hill, Alex yelled, "Trust me!" Then something happened. Anthony actually stopped feeling afraid. He said, "Go faster." She hit seventy-five on a straightaway. For half a second the speedometer went as high as eighty. Then Alex slowed before the road curved. She took the curve at forty-five. He closed his eyes as Alex raced down the last straightaway. When she pulled into the South Mountain Arena parking lot, Anthony wondered if they were really still alive.

She said, "I've always wanted to do that."

"You're insane," he said. "We should be dead. Or at least in jail."

Anthony looked back toward the road, where he expected to see a phalanx of police cars speeding toward them. But all he saw was a bunch of passing regular cars, the golden arch of McDonald's rising behind them.

"Don't be a chicken," Alex said. "I was so totally in control."

"Sure you were," he said.

"I wouldn't kill my little boy."

He said, "Oh no?"

"No."

Alex reached over and touched his cheek.

"So can I kiss you one more time?"

He didn't answer. She kissed him on the cheek.

She said, "I'm glad I robbed your cradle. Aren't you?"

"I wish I knew."

Alex kept watching him for a moment. Then she said, "Well, we better get this siren in."

She hit the switch for the power window. She reached outside, pulled it in, and the whole car filled up with its blue light. She said, "Look into my crystal ball. If you look hard you'll see your future." Anthony looked and for a moment the light was blinding. Then it died. She had pulled the plug.

A BRIEF HISTORY OF SADNESS

March 1982

FOR THE THIRD DAY in a row, Jess Rubin was stretched out in her sister Leah's bed. She lay under the covers, reading. Leah and her husband were off skiing in Colorado. Jess was there house-sitting and taking care of Rufous, the almost Doberman. And though she wasn't really taking care of him, Leah's thirteen-year-old son, Timmy, was there as well.

Jess had come up to New Jersey to see Dani and Anthony. She hadn't told anyone, however, save Leah. And though she'd meant to call each afternoon and evening, when her ex-husband would not be home, she mostly lay in Leah's bed, feeling immobile.

In the mornings, she had been waking up with Timmy. He was a nice boy, shy and polite. He would eat cereal and then go outside to wait for the bus to school. They'd talked a bit about his older sisters, who were both in college. They'd talked about his classes. Timmy liked science. According to Leah, he scored extraordinarily high on all math and logic aptitude tests. He also had a pet iguana, which he fed carrots, mealworms, and live crickets.

By now, after a year and a half in Florida, Jess had snorkeled over manatees. She'd been on reef dives and wreck dives. She had visited the Everglades. She had gone kayaking off Key West. She'd had a short and confusing fling with her twenty-six-year-old scuba diving instructor. She was working as a bartender and sometimes waitress at Don Perry's, a swanky seafood place that overlooked the Gulf. Two nights a week she was taking college classes, and she was crying several times a day.

The extreme sadness she now felt had begun after her fling with Rob the Beautiful, as all the women in his scuba class had called him. The instruction ran two weekends and culminated in a third weekend of checkout dives. A few days after the final checkout, Rob came into Don Perry's for a drink while she was bartending. "Are you stalking me?" she asked. He told her yes and then invited her out to dinner.

On that first date he claimed to be enamored of older women. He also promised to take her diving in all the best places he knew. Jess felt a sense of dread that lasted throughout dinner, but she agreed to go out with him again. A few weeks later he got her drunk on margaritas. She let him take her back to his condominium. Rob proved to be the twisted, slightly sadistic type who like to dominate. From the outset, he left Jess whirling in wild torrents of adrenaline. He made her feel all the things that Michael never could.

At first she liked it, or at least she enjoyed the rush she'd feel each time Rob conjured up his tough voice, or his bastard voice, depending on how far she'd let him push it. But inevitably she would go home feeling horrified. At home alone at night she would sit naked under her covers, the blanket stretched over her head like a small tent.

She had a wild side, sure. She used to make Michael pull over on random roadsides, long ago. But the things Rob asked her to do felt different. They seemed to tap into some secret vault of feelings Jess had forgotten she possessed. The things she did for Rob seemed to come out of his desire to debase her. Jess sensed her willingness yet could not understand it. She hated being touched on her ass but let him spank her. She feared being restrained but let him tie her up.

It was the darkest time Jess could remember. She went into it without much hesitation. She saw him steadily for two months. The day he

helped her move into her new condo, she understood, without knowing why, that Rob was extremely dangerous. It wasn't any sort of physical danger, only some risk to her already damaged spirit.

After Rob left her in the new condo with all her boxes, Jess picked
the phone up to call Livingston and give her children the new number.
She got no answer but left no message. She didn't try to call again. Then
it went on more than three weeks. She didn't call them. She knew they'd
tried to call her disconnected number. She knew they'd looked her up
and found that her new number was unlisted. She guessed that Dani
hated her guts by now, that Anthony was a wreck. She meant to call
every night, but with each day she felt more paralyzed. And with each
day, she felt a stronger, more insidious pull toward Rob.

She sometimes wondered if in some way she was attempting to
compete sexually with Claudia. She'd always coveted Claudia's gen-
uine perversity. By nature Claudia was hurtful, whereas Jess sought
healing things, beauty, oceans—things that did not involve the energy
of two ravenous, lust-filled people. Jess wanted tidal pools and jetties.
She wanted reefs and high cliffs that looked out over shades of blue that
could seem infinite. But still she'd found this thing inside her—this
pull toward darkness. She was not sure where the darkness came from.
She half suspected that she wanted to be punished for her desertion of
her life.

Not that with Rob it was all punishment. He took her down a hundred feet to see the *Santiago*, a wrecked three-masted ship with rooms
that were now vaulted caverns of fish. Another time, after a Friday shift,
a month or so after she'd moved into the new condo, Rob showed up
with gear and took her night diving. They returned to Rob's sometime
past four and stayed up passionately screwing until dawn.

While they were lying in bed that morning, Rob said he would
have liked to know Jess back in her "innocent" years, in high school or
earlier. He would have liked to see what type of girl she was. She told
him how she'd been such an earnest cheerleader—and about how,
strange as it sounded, she had liked dressing up in a leotard, skirt, and
sweater, doing those kicks and jumps and splits in front of hollering

fans at games. Rob said it gave him an erection just to think of it, and that he wanted to take her shopping for new saddle shoes. Jess had assumed that Rob was kidding, but on their next date he did just that.

Rob took her to Randall's discount shoe store. She tried on three different pairs as he bossed a store clerk around with his tough-guy-bastard voice. Jess kept on chiding Rob for his rudeness, though she secretly found it funny. But by the time they left the store, she was feeling sick.

She kept the saddle shoes on while they ate dinner at an Italian place. Then they went back to Rob's condo, where he asked her to strip down to her shoes and socks.

"Why?" Jess asked.

He said, "I want to see you in your saddle shoes. I want to watch you until I can't."

She took her clothes off, stood before him. Rob smiled coldly as he walked up to her, examined her, and caressed her. He took a step back. He folded his arms across his chest and asked her to do a cheer. As if awaking from a spell, Jess simply stared at him and told him to go fuck himself. He went on circling her and talking, unaware that the game was over. Jess started putting her clothes back on and soon Rob seemed confused that she was not listening.

"What's the matter?" he said finally.

She said, "I think you're a weirdo prick."

"We're just playing," Rob said. "This is your favorite game. You know that."

When he stepped over and touched her back, she pushed him violently and said, "Don't you fucking touch me."

She drove back home. She sat beside her pond and watched the water rippling from the breeze. She had her saddle shoes on still and did not want to take them off. After an hour or so she went inside and lay down, fully dressed. She did not leave her condo for two days.

She called in sick to work both evenings. She hadn't given anyone her number, so the telephone did not ring. On the third day, she finally took the shoes off. She changed her clothes and realized she had not eaten since the dinner she'd had with Rob. She drove out to a takeout Thai place by the ocean and ordered noodles. On her way back from the Thai place something shifted. She wasn't sure if it was inside her or outside. She looked around and the trees seemed blurry. The clouds above the windshield seemed like a giant mouth. For a few seconds she expected something to happen. Some cataclysmic event or at least rain. She speeded up and caught three green lights in a row. By the time she slowed and hit a red light, this eerie sense of foreboding had subsided.

But then Jess witnessed a thing that made no sense. Passing the other way through the green light was a blue Honda Accord, four-door, just like hers. Jess caught a glimpse of the woman driving and felt light-headed. The woman appeared to be herself. She watched the car head down the road until it came to a curve and vanished. Jess smelled the Thai food and felt nausea coming on. She headed home.

She went directly to her bedroom and got into a hot shower. She leaned against the tile wall and felt weak. She started picturing the woman in the Honda. Herself or not herself. Whoever it was, she felt as if she could see this woman from far away. Inside her head she saw this woman buying groceries. She saw this woman lying alone, half asleep, on some very crowded beach. She saw the woman crying naked in her bedroom. Wearing a black shawl as she stood beside a taciturn mother in the kitchen. Watching the flames of the Sabbath candles. Sniffing the spice box after *Havdalah*. She saw the woman as a twelve-year-old. Very pretty. Crawling the length of an impossibly long table. Jess crossed her arms over her chest, got on her knees. She was throwing up. She saw the woman driving away, the blue car vanishing as if it were a hologram. As if she'd hit the exact angle where the image ceased to exist.

She quickly got out of the shower and called her sister. She told Leah she was starting to "go off." This was the phrase that she'd always used with Leah or Michael or former therapists—a simpler way of describing her dissociative and sometimes violent outbursts, which would usually come after prolonged depression.

Leah asked what had been going on. Jess hadn't talked with Leah for months. She quickly told her about Rob.

Leah said, "Okay, a real scumbag. How are things with Anthony and Dani?"

"I haven't called them in a month," Jess said. "I feel too dark and sick to be a mother."

"You're still their mother," Leah said bluntly. "And you should call them. That's your problem. You hate yourself right now because you should."

Leah had never been very patient with her. But still Jess knew her older sister's advice was valuable. Leah suggested she calm down, maybe go out for a walk, then call her children. When Jess hung up she was not calm, but she immediately made the call to Livingston.

Anthony answered on one ring. He seemed upset and kept on asking why she hadn't called to give them her new number. And why her number was unlisted. She said her life had been going a little crazy, that she was sorry. She said she couldn't talk long because she had to go to work.

He said, "It's night. I thought you're working at a nursing home."

She said, "Hey, listen for a second. I wound up quitting that job. It was too boring and depressing. Now I've been working as a waitress and a bartender."

He said, "Oh."

"I want to give you my new number. I have to rush off after that."

She gave the number. Anthony read it back three times to double-check it. She said she loved him and to tell the same to Dani. When she hung up, she called in sick again to work.

Later that night, Rob appeared outside her door. He said he'd driven by while stalking her and saw her car outside. And that he'd contemplated climbing in the window. Jess let him in and made him promise not to touch her.

She poured them drinks and he asked when she'd become so miserable.

"All of my life," Jess said. "This isn't really a new thing."

She started telling him about high school, about helplessly watching her perfect sister succeed at everything. How she both hated and loved her older sister. And how each time a teacher or boy or parent said, "You're not like Leah," Jess wanted to disappear.

She said the reason she liked cheerleading was that people finally noticed her. Girls were jealous and certain boys were dreaming about kissing her. Of course her parents were beside themselves. Games sometimes fell on Friday nights and she would go. Her parents threatened her and pleaded with her and pointed to Leah as an example. This turned her numb most of the time, yet every mention of Leah became a source of vindication.

By then Leah was gone and married to Mr. Orthodox Jew Moneybags. By then Leah had dumped Paul Haney, her truest love! And for once Jess had felt much smarter than her sister. She had a boyfriend who was now pre-med at Rutgers. All the star athlete boys would try to ask her out. She had a life that was her own, but still at night she would start crying and feel crazy. Each night she'd go to bed wishing she could wake up in a different life.

"There's something else," Rob said.

"What?"

He said, "I don't know. You tell me."

"What do you mean?" she asked.

"There's something else that totally fucked you up."

She said, "In grade school I went to a yeshiva."

"What's that?"

"The Jewish equivalent of Catholic school."

"What happened there?"

She told him, "Nothing, I just hated it."

"Did teachers paddle you?"

Jess said, "No. There wasn't anything like that."

"Then how did it fuck you up?"

She said, "I don't know. I turned cold."

She could feel tears coming up. She knew Rob saw it.

"Sometimes you're not cold," he said. "A lot of the time you're the opposite of cold. I think it's why when you get cold I get so horny. I want to conquer you when you're cold."

Jess started crying, very softly. He tried embracing her.

"I said don't touch me!" Jess yelled out, and pushed him hard.

He said, "I'm going to leave."

"Fine."

"Feel free to call me."

She said, "Don't wait by the phone."

Rob said, "You'll miss me. It will hurt a lot."

"Don't count on it," Jess said.

As Rob walked out she understood she would miss him terribly. She was already feeling physical pain from missing him. She also knew she would never see his face again.

In the weeks that followed, Jess regained touch with both her children. Dani called her the next evening. Then Anthony started calling collect a lot. He'd call from strange places. School. The hockey rink. McDonald's. He'd call to tell her stupid jokes or about hockey games. One night he called because he wanted to know whether she'd seen the TV news that night and watched the story about the rhino who'd escaped from a Texas zoo. He said a cop shot the rhino on a city street. Later the zookeeper said the animal was so tame that it would eat out of his hand. She tried to tell him not to worry, that it was awful but there were other rhinos and anyway this one lived in a zoo already.

Later that night she turned the news on. The eleven-o'clock hour covered the Texas rhino. She saw it running down a one-lane street. Two police cars pulled up in front of it and cut the rhino's path off. The rhino stopped, stared at them meekly. He looked confused and wanting only to be led back to his cage. They showed one officer raising his rifle, firing five shots or so into the panting animal. At last the rhino flopped over on his side. Jess watched this mesmerized and did not move until the segment ended. Then she went into the bathroom, got hysterical, and threw up.

Dani did not call as much. Sometimes when Jess called and she answered, Dani would sound detached and angry. Jess would attempt to ask her questions. During most conversations, Dani would finally come around and begin to talk. She once went on about her boyfriend,

Bobby. Another time Dani told her about the essay she had written for her UPenn application. Jess also talked with Michael, though always briefly, on occasions when he answered. He had once asked her to consider coming back. She had said, "No, Michael. We tried. I'd say a lot of it was good. There were some years when we actually *were* a happy family. But I just couldn't keep it together. I'm starting over and I need to be on my own."

In the wake of Rob, she found a dive group. All women. Her first trip with the Reef Explorer Girls was to Belize. A few months later to St. Thomas and St. John. One night in St. John she went snorkeling with her bungalow mate, Kisha. In moonlit darkness they snorkeled to an island half a mile off the shore. They sat on rocks and talked all night about failed marriages. They had swum back across the bay at sunrise. After that, Kisha and Jess were always dive buddies. They became friends outside the dive group, and it was Kisha who got them both involved in a statewide manatee census project. For a few weeks they made long drives to spots all over the state and volunteered for transects. In all, they'd counted almost two dozen different manatees. Nothing she'd ever done had made Jess feel as wonderful.

In late February Anthony called collect one evening. He said his team was about to go to Minnesota. He just wanted her to know that he would be away five days. Jess asked where Dani was and Anthony said, "I'm calling from a pay phone by the Shop Rite." Then he asked, "When are you coming up?" Jess had said, "Soon."

Jess hadn't told him that Leah would be gone in March. That she already was planning to come and house-sit. She meant to tell him the next week and the next, but she had not. The night she flew up, she planned to call from Newark Airport. But even though Leah was twenty minutes late picking her up—even though Jess stood by a phone for all that time—she could not force herself to dial.

+ + +

Now Jess had been carrying Leah's cordless phone around the house with her. After three days her plan, if she had any plan, was to call Livingston the moment she felt able to. It seemed crucial to always have the phone nearby. But all that day she had still not called. She was upstairs in her sister's bed, reading the paper, when Timmy knocked.

Jess said, "Come in, Timmy."

He entered, flanked by Rufous. He held a book in his hand and said, "Aunt Jess, can I ask a favor?"

She said, "Of course."

"Could you please read something?" he said.

Rufous jumped up on the bed and stared at her. He seemed quite menacing, but she knew better. Jess stroked his neck and Rufous flopped down on the bed.

Timmy held up a book that was entitled *A Brief History of Kabbalistic Mysticism*. He stepped over and sat beside her on the bed. He said, "It's this. Could you just read it?" He flipped the book open and pointed to a passage with his finger. He passed the book to Jess, and she read the following:

> A leader of the eighteenth-century movement called Hasidism, which is based on Kabbalistic principles, the holy master Baal Shem Tov was said to understand things that transcended human intellect. For instance, the Baal Shem Tov had the mysterious gift of *kefitzat haderek*, or "the shortening of the way." To the amazement of those who would accompany him, the Baal Shem Tov was capable of traveling vast distances in impossibly short intervals of time. Although his horses ran at no more than ten miles an hour, the Baal Shem Tov routinely traveled hundreds of miles in a few hours. It was said that his understanding of certain unseen dimensions is what gave him the gift of *kefitzat haderek*.

"So?" Timmy said.

"What?"

"So is it possible, the shortening of the way?"

"This is a story," Jess said.

Timmy said, "Yes, but could people really do it?"

She said, "Not now."

"But once could they?"

"Maybe."

He said, "The thing is, this happened once to me. We were all driving down the shore. It was an hour ride but we got there in . . . a *second*. My mother said I was asleep but I think it really was the shortening of the way."

"Maybe it was."

He said, "I know it was."

Jess told him, "Maybe you should study the Kabbalah."

"My mother says you have to be married and over forty."

Jess recalled something like that, that no true teacher of this mystical religion would teach anyone under forty or unmarried. She also knew you were supposed to be a male.

He said, "I want to write books, do you?"

Jess said, "Not really."

"I want to write one about this town. I'd call it 'A Brief History of Montclair.'"

Jess said, "That sounds like a good title."

"What would you write?"

She said, "Nothing. I hate writing."

"Why?"

"Some people just don't like writing. It's too hard."

"One more question," Timmy said.

"What?"

"What are you doing here? Usually Sam comes. He's my baby-sitter. Or else Emma sometimes on weekends."

"I'm just visiting," Jess said. "I'm leaving Saturday."

"You came up from Florida just to baby-sit?"

"Not exactly."

"How come you haven't gone to see Anthony and Dani? Aren't they home?"

"Timmy," she said.

"Yes?"

"You went to sleep-away camp, right?"

"Four years in a row."

"While you're away, do you talk to Mom a lot?"

Timmy said, "No. Like twice a summer. But she writes letters."

"Do you miss her?"

"Maybe a little, toward the end. That always happens."

"Is there one thing you like to hear when you first see her, after camp ends? Or something special you like to do?"

Timmy said, "No. I just want her to act normal."

Jess took this in. She thanked him. When Timmy left the room she picked up the cordless phone.

It was five-thirty. Michael would not be home. She knew she might hang up, regardless of who answered. She drummed her fingers on Leah's wooden night table as the phone rang. Dani picked up after three rings and said, "Hello?"

"Dani, it's Mom," she said.

"Oh, hi. Did you get my message?"

Jess said, "No. I'm in New Jersey."

After a silence, Dani said, "Where are you?"

"I'm at Leah's. I'm here till Saturday."

"You're in Montclair?"

"Yes."

"Can't you stay longer?"

"I have to work Sunday," said Jess. "I have to get back, but I'd really like to see you. Maybe tomorrow?"

"How about now?"

"You mean tonight?"

"We could watch Anthony play hockey. They're playing Whippany, the last game of the season. I can tell Bobby not to come."

Jess said, "It's fine if he comes."

"You'll go?"

She said, "I'll meet you in the lobby, by the pro shop."

"Be there at seven sharp?"

"Okay."

"I'll call up Dad now and make sure he doesn't go."

In her nervousness, Jess left for the rink too early. She realized this in West Orange, while driving past the Essex Green Shopping Plaza. Impulsively, she turned in one of the entrances. She used the time to buy presents for her children. Dani was easy. She went to Stern's and bought a vial of Chanel No. 5. It took three stores to find something for Anthony. She settled on a book about coral reefs.

At the rink she spotted Dani before entering the lobby. Dani was standing alone, arms crossed, wearing jeans and a mint-green sweater that hung down below her butt. She had on boots and was taller than most parents in the lobby. As Jess passed through the double doors, Dani caught sight of her and waved.

Dani stepped toward her and they hugged. "They're warming up now," Dani said. "I didn't get here in time to tell him you were coming. I told Dad, though."

Jess nodded. She reached down to her purse to give Dani the perfume. Before she could, Dani said, "Hey, I'm kind of starving. You want a hot dog?"

"Not really," said Jess.

"How about coffee?"

Jess said, "Sure," and went with Dani to the snack bar. She took her wallet out to pay for it, but Dani was already handing five dollars to the man behind the counter.

They went into the rink when they heard the horn that signaled the end of warm-ups. The rink was crowded and they had to climb far up, near the top row of the bleachers. When they found places to stand, Dani took Jess's hand and said, "I almost can't believe you're here."

"So where is Bobby?" asked Jess.

"I told him to stay home."

"Why?"

"Because," Dani said. "I thought it might be too confusing. I thought you might show up all teary-eyed, with presents and stuff. I didn't really know how you would be."

Jess didn't mention the perfume. She placed her arm around her daughter and looked out over the ice.

"So what's Anth's number?"

"Fourteen."

"The same as always."

"I'll never understand why he likes fourteen so much," said Dani. "It's so boring."

Jess said, "Fourteen was the first number he ever wore. His first game playing, when he was six. It was at the Ironbound rink in Newark."

"You were at his first game?"

Jess said, "Your father and I and Grandpa Max went. Fourteen was just the number he got handed in the locker room. On the way home we stopped at Hardee's and Max said, 'Well, Mr. Fourteen. What are you eating? Is that a number fourteen burger?' All the way home Max kept calling him 'Mr. Fourteen' in the car. You know how Max gets. It made Anthony love fourteen."

"Grandpa's so funny that way," said Dani.

"You'd think your father would have been more of a maniac."

"So where was I? At the Y, swimming?"

"I can't remember."

Dani said, "Wait, no. I was over at that girl Greta's house, on Thurston."

"Greta Poverman?"

"Yeah, the really weird one with gross teeth."

"Greta seemed nice enough to me, although you're right about her teeth."

"Anthony's line's on," Dani said, and pointed to her brother.

Jess saw him circling with the puck. He made a pass and someone knocked him to the ice. As he stood up, the whistle blew. There was a face-off. Jess never had much of a sense of what caused face-offs. She saw him glancing around at all his teammates as he stood outside the circle. She was surprised by how poised he looked, and how much stronger.

The puck was dropped and he pushed it through the other player's legs. He took the puck on his stick again and started forward, veering away from a gangly player who lunged toward him. He skated up the left side. He cut inward and faked out another player. Someone in front of Jess yelled, "Shoot it! Shoot the puck!" He didn't shoot. Jess watched him veer to the left, then turn in toward the goalie. He drew the blade of his stick back several inches. He snapped the puck to a teammate speeding toward the far side of the goal mouth. With a quick swipe his teammate batted the puck past the sliding goalie. Anthony circled behind the net and raised his stick above his head.

The rink erupted. Bunny Kane, as always, clanged her cowbell. Jess looked around and found Bunny, low in the bleachers. Bunny's son Brian had been playing hockey with Anthony for years. Jess stared back out over the ice. She watched the bright green clump of Livingston Lancers players avidly patting each others' helmets. Dani was clapping and yelling "Way to go!" as Anthony skated back for another face-off. She turned to Jess and said, "It's hard to believe that dunce brain is so good."

"He seems more confident," said Jess, and continued clapping.

Dani said, "So, are you coming back?"

"Back to New Jersey?"

"No, to Idaho."

Jess shook her head and said, "Honey, I don't think so."

She said, "Why?"

"I'm too unhappy here," said Jess. "It makes me crazy. Things aren't rosy for me in Florida, but I'm better. Here I just wind up feeling like I'm dead."

"I understand," Dani said. "I think I do. But maybe do you think that you could call more?"

She said, "I'll try."

"And could we visit? Don't you want us to come visit?"

Jess said, "Of course."

Anthony scored a goal in the second period. Jess wasn't sure how it happened. One of the biggest Livingston players blasted a slap shot, but it looked like he was aiming right at Anthony. Jess thought he'd dive out of the way but he just stood there. Then all the players started patting Anthony's helmet, giving him high fives, and smacking him on the shin guards with their sticks.

"What the hell happened?" Jess asked. "Did he just score?"

Dani said, "Yes, he deflected Ralph Tortelli's slap shot."

Though by then Livingston was losing five to two, Anthony skated off the ice with fans still cheering. Jess saw him sit down on the bench and tilt his helmet up in order to drink out of a plastic water bottle. He pulled his helmet down again and snapped the chin-strap.

"I think he saw us," Dani said.

Anthony scored another goal in the third period. He took a low, hard shot that found its way between the goalie's leg pads. But by then Livingston was losing by too much to stage a comeback.

After the game, Jess and Dani waited in the lobby. Jess was still debating whether or not to give Dani the perfume. Dani looked up and saw him first. She said, "Oh shit."

He crossed the lobby, waved, and said, "Hello there."

"I told you not to come!" yelled Dani.

"I thought I'd just stop by for the third period," Michael said.

Dani said, "Well, the game is over. You can leave now."

"I'm leaving soon," he said, and stared at Jess.

She said, "Hello, Michael," and felt strangely relieved that he had come.

"I hear you're at Leah's until Sunday."

She told him, "Saturday."

Michael nodded.

"Jesus Christ, Dad!" Dani yelled.

She turned away and stomped off toward the locker rooms.

"Looks like our daughter might hit the ceiling."

Jess didn't comment.

"I couldn't think of any other way to see you. I'd like to talk."

She said, "Don't start, Michael. Not here. Call me tomorrow at Leah's."

He said, "I'm sorry, Jess. I'm sorry about everything that's happened."

She said, "I know. I'm glad you came. But you should leave before I snap."

"What if I took us all out?"

She shook her head and said, "No chance."

"What if we..."

"Michael," she said.

"What?"

"Please get away from me right now."

Jess could tell several people were watching the encounter. She elected not to wait for him to leave. She turned away from him, crossed the lobby, and headed out into the cold chill of the ice rink. She made her way back to the bleachers. She started climbing. She turned around once to see whether Michael had followed. He had not.

When she got halfway to the top row, she sat down, put her face in her hands, but managed not to cry. After five minutes, she looked up again. She guessed that Michael had been smart enough to leave. She took the presents out and considered throwing them down with all the cigarette butts and hot dog rolls and cups beneath the bleachers. Before she could, she heard "Mom! What are you doing?"

She stashed the presents back in her purse, looked up, and saw Anthony. He jogged toward her with two sticks and his giant bag of equipment. He'd let his hair grow past his ears and he looked taller, as tall as Michael. Dani was following behind him, walking slowly, staring downward. Jess thought: Normal. Please God, once, let me act normal.

She walked back down to the rubber matting. Anthony dropped his bag and sticks and said, "I saw you. I saw you sitting there right after my first goal. You're here till Saturday?"

"That's right," she said, and hugged him.

Dani walked up and said, "Let's go out to that train place. I'm still starved."

"You hungry, Anth?" Jess asked.

He picked his hockey bag back up and said, "I haven't eaten anything since lunch."

"You had a great game," said Jess.

He smiled.

"You're that whole Livingston Lancers team."

"Not really," Anthony said.

But he was glowing inside, suddenly. Jess could see the plainly visible effect of her vapid words. He turned and shifted the giant duffel to his left shoulder. He seemed happy. Dani took hold of his two sticks and they headed out.

✦ ✦ ✦

Later that night, when Jess returned to her sister's house, she found a note on the kitchen table. Crossed out were the words *Went to the movies with the Jamesons*. Beneath the crossed-out words Timmy had written *Now I'm home*.

She put her purse down on the table. She unzipped it, took out the presents, and then searched for a pack of Tropical Fruit Life Savers she had purchased at the airport Monday evening. She found the Life Savers, took one out. It was the flavor Anthony used to call baked apple pie delight.

The Kabbalah book was sitting on the table. She picked it up, leafed through it. She read the chapter headings, titles such as "Mending the World" and "Magic Numbers" and "Ein Sof." She found the passage about "the shortening of the way," which was now underlined. In the margin Timmy had written *Phillips Avenue Beach, 1977*.

She read the passage about the Baal Shem Tov, then several about the sixteenth-century Kabbalist Isaac Luria and the raising of "holy sparks." She read about *Ein Sof* or endless nothingness. That God was really just an aspect of this endlessness. That God and all God's names were metaphors—representations of a far deeper, unimaginable mystery. Despite her flagrant repudiations of religion, Jess had the feeling that many things in the Kabbalah made perfect sense.

Before she went up to bed, she read:

Even the earliest practitioners of Kabbalah understood that
sublime joy went hand in hand with the deepest sadness. They
understood these things to be two different shades of the same
color.

This seemed so obvious on one hand. On the other, it was not obvious
at all. Jess went upstairs. She undressed. She slid her naked body under
Leah's covers. She knew that Michael would call tomorrow from his office. She figured Anthony would telephone from school. She'd see her
children again tomorrow. She guessed it wouldn't go as well. But for
the moment thoughts of Anthony and Dani filled her with quiet admi-
ration. She felt a joy that also made her want to weep with its painful
beauty. She understood that, somehow, they were fine.

WOLVES

Spring 1982

ONE MORNING IN EARLY APRIL, Juliette noticed Anthony by his locker. He was alone. Impulsively, she walked over. She leaned her shoulder against the locker just beside him. She wasn't sure what she was doing, though she was thinking about the day she had stood out in the pouring rain with him. When he looked up, Juliette said, "So, did I win the raffle?"

Anthony shook his head and smiled cautiously. In school, when they passed, he always seemed to keep his guard up. She knew this had something to do with Roland Malnick. Before that unfortunate incident, Anthony's in-school sociability with her had been bolder. Then Roland Malnick came to school with a purple face.

"No," he said. "They would have called you."

She said, "Oh well. I was hoping for that trip to Bonvini's Pizzeria."

She was about to leave when he reached out for the silver cross necklace she was wearing. This seemed unprecedented for Anthony, even reckless. He said, "It's nice," and let the cross fall to her bosom.

"Is it new?"

Juliette said, "No."

"I've always liked crosses."

"Not me."

"How come you're wearing it?"

"Guess I'm feeling very Catholic."

Anthony smiled his watchful smile. He pulled a book out of his locker.

"This was my mother's," she said.

Anthony nodded.

"Does that creep you out?"

He shook his head.

She said, "What does?"

"Creep me out?"

Juliette nodded.

After a moment, he said, "Nothing comes to mind."

That afternoon, Juliette discovered a folded note behind her steering wheel. Her name was written in printed letters. Someone had leaned it very carefully against the instrument panel's plastic shield. At first she wondered who'd know her car, but soon the answer became obvious. She unfolded the note and read: *It creeps me out to think that you're still with Tommy. You should break up with him already. Why do you wear your mother's cross?*

She dropped the note into her purse when she saw Tommy walking toward her in the parking lot. She fished it out again and quickly ripped it into tiny pieces. She stuffed the pieces deep in her purse, took out a brush, and fixed her hair in the rearview mirror. Tommy approached without expression and then got into her car.

He said, "I saw you walking out. You looked real cranky."

Juliette said, "Yeah, I feel like shit."

He slipped his hands under her shirt. She melted into him. He pulled the shirt up, moved her bra straps off her shoulders. He slid the bra down to her waist.

"Do you like this necklace?" Juliette asked.

"I like the way it hangs between your tits."

"But do you like it?"

Tommy said, "Yeah."

"This cross is magical."

He said, "How?"

"My great-grandmother, it was hers once. She trained a wolf to be her pet."

"Great pet," Tommy said, and slipped his hand under her skirt. He said, "So why do all loose Catholic girls wear crosses on their necks?"

✝ ✝ ✝

The silver cross was petite but somewhat heavy for its size. It was the one piece of Isabella's jewelry Juliette had wanted after she died. For six months she had kept it in her jewelry box. She hadn't planned to ever wear it. She'd never worn a cross and took care to eschew all things connected to her religion. One night that March she'd pulled it out, fastened the chain around her neck, and went to sleep with the necklace underneath her T-shirt. She hadn't taken it off since then.

It wasn't magical, so far as she knew, but Juliette liked to think it was. It had belonged to her maternal great-grandmother, Giulietta, after whom Juliette was named. Great-grandma Giulietta died when Juliette was one. Juliette's mother wound up with Giulietta's cross. Her mother rarely took the necklace off, though it was off the night she shot herself. Juliette found the cross lying at her place on the kitchen table. She understood that Isabella left it for her.

When Juliette was a little girl, she always liked to hear the stories about Giulietta's wolf. Her mom would go on and on. She sometimes sounded like she was reading straight from a book. Now it seemed funny whenever Juliette thought of it. She used to ask if she could be part of the wolf story. "You'd have to go back in time," was what her mother always told her. Her mother seemed to believe the story was all true.

Juliette's great-grandmother lived her childhood in the Etruscan hill country of Italy. As the story went, she once found a half-dead she-wolf in a meadow down the path behind her house. The wolf had gotten caught in a steel-jaw leg trap. To free herself, she'd chewed off the trapped leg. She lay collapsed on the ground, in shock, her severed foreleg still in the trap. Giulietta looked into the wolf's eyes, felt her terror, and ran home.

She returned to the clearing with an old wagon she had taken from the toolshed. She'd brought some gauze and tape and antiseptic to bandage up the stump of limb. Though she was only nine years old, she found a way to lift the full-grown wolf into the wagon. She took the leg out of the trap so that the trappers would not find it. She wheeled the three-legged wolf back to her house.

"Your great-grandmother had the gift of healing," was how Isabella put it. She'd kept the wolf alive somehow. For many years her family kept it as a pet. The wolf grew tame enough to keep inside the house. There was no mention of the necklace in the story, but Juliette would always ask whether the cross gave her great-grandma magical powers. Her mother typically said, "Who knows? She always wore it. She probably had it on when she found the wolf."

In the story, Great-grandma Giulietta's mother trained the she-wolf to eat mint leaves. She would feed mint to the wolf each day; otherwise, she said, the house would smell of wolf breath. Giulietta argued the mint was pointless. They'd trained the wolf to eat cooked chicken. It was not as if she were eating raw rabbits and weasels. But still her mother continued with the mint leaves, which appeased her sense of propriety enough that she came to love the three-legged wolf just like a daughter. She let the wolf sleep on the straw mat by the doorway, and in the early morning hours, Giulietta would sneak downstairs and curl up beside her. She'd smell her mint breath and listen as her tail swished softly across the floor.

Sometimes in darkness the wolf would rise on her three legs and begin howling. The neighbors often threatened to shoot her because the noise would wake them up. Still Giulietta's parents let the wolf howl all she wanted, and Giulietta would watch her staring out the window, her dark black nose pointed toward the sky. Her eyes would glow when the moon was bright and her plaintive howl was the saddest sound on earth.

Juliette knew it was a fairy tale. But still she thought about it as if the tale were real. She liked to think about the wolf howls. If she thought hard she could imagine how its fur would feel. She could imagine the peculiar grace of the wolf's three-legged posture. She could feel the cold, wet touch of the wolf's black nose against her face.

When the wolf died, Giulietta was almost twenty. She and her brothers buried the wolf out in the meadow. They marked the grave with a large boulder and Giulietta would come to visit the spot each day. She had gone on to become a nurse in the First World War. Every Italian soldier knew the story of Giulietta's three-legged wolf. They also knew that Giulietta had the gift of healing. After the war, she sailed to the U.S. with her first husband. Her husband died en route and she watched the crew toss his body into the sea. She came to live in Belleville, New Jersey, where she scraped by during the Depression. But she remarried, had five children, and had lived to be almost ninety. She was a legend still in Italy, but in New Jersey all that was forgotten.

✦ ✦ ✦

"Anthony," Juliette called, when she saw him wandering round his yard that night. He had a flashlight and it looked like he was shining it down onto some book or magazine.

"What are you doing?" Juliette asked.

She placed an unopened pack of cigarettes on the barbecue.

"Star-watching," he said.

"What?"

He said it louder. "I'm star-watching. Look *up.*"

Juliette looked up and saw more stars than she could ever remember having seen in Livingston, New Jersey.

"There was a cold front," he said. "And no moon. Perfect star weather."

"Show me some stars then," Juliette said.

She left the pack of cigarettes on the barbecue, skipped down the steps, and crossed her yard. Anthony climbed over his fence and made his way to her. He held the flashlight and what Juliette now realized was a star chart.

He said, "You're Leo, right?"

"How did you know?"

"I know your birthday."

"How?"

"I saw it that day you got your biorhythm at Friendly's."

"What a detective."

"Leo's out now."

Juliette laughed but felt surprisingly excited by the idea of seeing her own zodiac sign.

She said, "Okay. So show me Leo."

He put his hand on her arm and leaned his head in close to hers. He turned the flashlight on and used the beam to point out the different stars.

He said, "It looks like a giant lion with a mane. It's on an angle."

She couldn't see it.

He told her, "Low, by the Big Dipper. See the Big Dipper?"

She said, "No."

Anthony pointed with his flashlight. "Those stars that look like a big soup ladle."

She saw the soup ladle and said, "Okay. Where do you go from there?"

"Right underneath it," Anthony said. "That bright red star is its heart, Regulus."

She strained her eyes but at first could not see a lion. Then as if someone had suddenly focused a projector, the patch of stars she had been staring at took on the shape of a sitting lion. She said, "Oh, wait. Hey *wait*, I've got it. It really is big. Bigger than I was thinking."

He took his hand off her arm and said, "Leo's a good one."

"What are you?"

He said, "Aquarius."

"Show me that one."

"It's not out now, and anyway, it's not bright enough to see it from around here if it was."

She brought her eyes down from the sky and found him staring. She said, "What?"

"I was looking at your necklace."

She took the cross between two fingers and half-twirled it.

"Maybe I'll give you this necklace when I get sick of it. Then you can stare at it all you want."

He said, "You know, there's a constellation, Cygnus. It's a big cross, though it's supposed to be a swan."

Juliette said, "Where?"

"It doesn't come out till late June."

"You'll have to show me."

"I'll be gone."

"Where are you going?"

"I'm coaching hockey at a camp in Ocean County. Coach Marino runs the program. Will Smithson's going too."

"Who's he?"

"He's in your grade. He's a defenseman."

"Too bad you're going," she said.

"Why?"

"I don't know," she said, and let out a nervous laugh.

He said, "So why did you start wearing your mother's cross all of a sudden?"

Juliette said, "Why are you so concerned about this necklace?"

"There's something strange about it," he said. "Something that always makes me stare at it."

"You sure it's not just my boobs you like to stare at?"

After reflecting for a moment, he said, "No."

"At least you're honest," she said. "Anyway, before my mother got it, this belonged to my great-grandmother. She grew up in the hills of central Italy. I never met her."

Anthony nodded.

"She had a pet wolf," she said. "It had three legs."

He was still listening.

She said, "I like how the necklace feels, so I've been wearing it. In a few weeks I'm sure I'll throw it in a drawer."

He said, "How come?"

She said, "I told you, I don't like crosses. You wanna hear about my great-grandmother?"

Anthony nodded, so she told him the whole wolf story. He leaned against the fence and listened to her attentively, sometimes asking for explanations about details. She'd never told anyone the story and was amazed to find the whole thing intact inside her. She knew the story in the same way that her mother had. It was as if the words came through her, from somewhere else.

✦ ✦ ✦

Throughout that spring, Juliette and Anthony talked regularly. Sometimes in school they chatted before homeroom. At home they'd stand outside with a fence between them and talk about things Juliette rarely remembered afterward. It started feeling like they were friends.

One night he called her on the phone and made her come outside to see the planet Saturn. Juliette asked which was farther, Mars or Saturn, so he taught her the mnemonic My Very Elegant Mother Just Sat Upon Nine Porcupines. He always seemed to have great answers for the questions she would ask. But more and more Juliette wished he would just kiss her.

In June, just a few days before the school year ended, Juliette opened the *Star Ledger* and found a picture of two wolves. They had their heads poking out of a small cage that had been mounted on the rear bed of a pickup truck. One faced the camera, ears sticking out like bat wings. The other wolf was facing sideways, its tongue licking its big black nose.

She read the article beneath the half-page photo. The wolves had been delivered to the Turtle Back Zoo that weekend. They were both females, from Montana. They had been poisoned by a chicken farmer and rescued by a wolf-loving police officer. They had been nursed back to health on a not-for-profit wolf sanctuary near Telluride, Colorado. Somehow or other, the Turtle Back Zoo acquired them. When they were ready, they were shipped off to New Jersey.

The next day Juliette looked for Anthony at his locker. She couldn't find him. Then during lunch she couldn't get away from Tommy. He got all crazy whenever she wore mini-skirts. They wound up cutting classes and spending the afternoon out in his Firebird.

After school, he disappeared with his best friend, Nate, so she drove home. Her Chevy Nova now smelled like cinnamon. While she was wasting time at the mall over the weekend, she'd passed a kitchen gadget store that smelled of cinnamon. Juliette veered in, followed the smell, and soon found herself standing beside a barrel filled with cinnamon brooms. This seemed hilarious, in a way, but it was also a perfect way to block the odor inside her car.

As she pulled up Cherry Hill Road, Juliette saw Anthony. He was outside playing hockey in his driveway. She waved, drove past, and pulled the car in the garage. She took a shower, to scrub Tommy out. She changed into a pair of overalls and a T-shirt. She let the necklace hang outside her shirt where he would stare at it. She put on perfume, combed her hair, and wondered what she was hoping to accomplish. Then she got back into her car and drove the hundred feet to Anthony Rubin's driveway.

He was still outside playing hockey. He had on gym shorts and a T-shirt. He looked sweaty. She rolled her window down and said, "Hey, what are you doing?"

He slapped a tennis ball into a beat-up hockey net, turned, and faced her.

"Taking shots."

"You feel like going to the zoo?" Juliette asked him.

Anthony smiled and she could tell that he assumed she was just kidding.

She said, "I mean it. We'll go right now."

He said, "Since when are you interested in zoos?"

"Since last fall," she said.

"You went to the zoo?"

"Once."

"Why would you want to go again? There's nothing there."

"Didn't you read about the wolves?"

He said, "What wolves?"

"They got new wolves. You didn't see it in the paper?"

He shook his head.

She said, "Two gray wolves, from Montana. In the article they actually called them bitches. They ate some poison but they were rescued. So can I kidnap you?"

Anthony stared at her as if this were some riddle he had to solve. After a moment he said, "Wait, just let me put away the goal."

Inside her car he started asking about the cinnamon broom. Still wrapped in plastic, it lay as if asleep on the dark-blue vinyl.

He said, "It smells like a giant Atomic Fireball."

"I needed something to block out the smell of mildew. Nothing else worked."

They drove a little way in silence. She drove carefully, always putting on her blinker far in advance of any turn. At the intersection of Mount Pleasant and Shrewsbury, Juliette stopped at a yellow light.

"It's kind of funny," Anthony said. "You're such a slow and nervous driver."

"Why is that funny?"

He said, "I'm used to Alex Brody. She's a maniac and she drove me a lot to practice when she was manager."

"Are you in love with Alex Brody?" Juliette asked him.

He said, "No."

They each paid four dollars for admission. They received buttons that said TURTLE BACK ZOO SUPPORTER! Juliette immediately threw hers in the garbage.

"Oh look, a petting zoo," she said.

He said, "You sure?"

She said, "Why not?"

They bought some goat food and went into the children's petting zoo. She tried to feed several white billy goats. They showed more interest in the suspenders of her overalls. One started trying to eat her shirt. She said, "You little fucking shit," and punched the billy goat in the face. After that Anthony took her arm and led her out of the children's petting zoo. Juliette said, "God, I think I want to kill these goats."

They went over to the sea lions, which she liked better. She found some goat pellets that had fallen behind the front flap of her overalls. She threw them down into the pool and said, "Have some." Anthony told her that the sea lions ate fish.

"Is that a fact?" Juliette said. "Do you know everything?"

He said, "I know sea lions eat fish."

Juliette said, "Well, maybe I'll need you as my zoo guide."

She took a cigarette out and lit it. As she leaned over the rail she noticed an untied shoelace. She said, "Hey zoo guide, I need to tie my shoe. Can you hold my cigarette for a second or would that compromise your image?"

He held his hand out to take it between his fingers. He somehow fumbled it, tried to catch it, but wound up batting it right down into the sea lion pool. Juliette laughed and said, "Maybe they'll eat that." She tied her shoelace and stood up.

"Ever tried smoking?" she asked.

"Twice."

"What a bad boy," Juliette said. "You should be punished."

"It tasted gross," he said.

"It gets much better."

"I'll take your word for it."

She laughed and did not take out another cigarette. Instead she suddenly took his hand. This startled him, as she'd guessed it would. She said nothing and led him toward the wolves. She saw him glance once at their hands as they walked quietly past the yak cage. They passed the penguins and she stopped beside the tapir.

"I kind of like this guy," she said, but did not mention her zoo break-in with Jay Berkowitz. She didn't even mention Jay. She took her hand away from Anthony's. When he looked up at her his gaze seemed apprehensive.

He said, "Juliette."

"What?"

"What are we doing?"

"I don't know."

He put his palms down on the railing and watched the tapir. It lay asleep beside a patch of fake bamboo.

"He always looks so bored," he said.

She said, "He is bored, just like us."

She stepped behind him and slipped her arms around his waist.

"Are you afraid of me?"

He said, "Sometimes."

"But most of the time?"

"You're going out with Tommy. Most of the time I know I better leave you alone."

"Today you didn't though," she said.

"I guess I wanted to see the wolves."

She said, "What else are you afraid of, besides Tommy?"

"Maybe your father," he said. "I've heard some stories. I mean, I'm definitely scared shitless of your father."

Juliette laughed. Anthony turned around and faced her.

She said, "Hey listen, boy next door. Most things you've heard about my family aren't true."

"Like what things aren't true?"

Juliette said, "*Like,* my father isn't in the Mafia. He's just some peon with a really lousy desk job."

"Then how come everyone thinks he's in the Mafia? Everyone's *sure* he's in the Mafia."

"People invent what they want," she said. "My father looks like he could be part of the Mafia. He used to act like he was, so people thought he was. I mean, he's probably swindled a few people in his lifetime. He works for a big union in Jersey City. The whole thing's run by the mob but he doesn't qualify as a mobster. He's just Italian, and dumb. He has a temper but he's nothing to be scared of. As for my mom, she was just a depressed housewife who decided to blow her brains out."

Anthony nodded. He seemed amazed.

"So your mom wasn't..."

"Don't even say it."

"Was she a dancer?"

Juliette said, "Yes."

"What kind of dancing?"

She said, "Show stuff. She was once in a Broadway show called *Spangle,* in the sixties. She gave it up so she could marry the great man of her dreams, my father."

He said, "My mom gets depressed, too."

"At least we have one thing in common."

"So do you miss her?"

"No."

"That isn't possible."

"You're not me."

"I know you miss her," Anthony said. "Even if you think you don't, you miss her."

"Well, if I do it's out of guilt," she said. "Maybe I miss her because I drive her shitty car. I also wish I could have figured out how to like her. I know she killed herself partly because of me."

"I doubt that's true," he said.

"It's true."

"But can't you love her even if you didn't like her?"

Juliette said, "No, I really don't. Something went wrong with me, unfortunately. Why the hell else would I be dating Tommy Lange? I don't love *anyone,* okay? I don't know how to. I guess I'm damaged or I'm evil or cruel or something."

"You might feel a lot less damaged if you dumped him."

"Well, I'm not planning to," she said. "Now can we drop this?"

He said, "Sure."

He turned around and resumed staring at the tapir.

Juliette said, "Hey, would you please look at me?"

Anthony turned and she looked into his eyes. She said, "Wake up."

"What do you mean?" he asked.

She said, "I mean wake up before I'm gone."

"Where are you going?"

"I'll be gone sometime."

She slapped his face just hard enough to tingle.

"What was that for?" he asked.

"To wake you."

Juliette kissed him where she'd slapped him.

"Okay, come on," she said. "Let's find these wolves."

She took his hand and they ascended a sloped path, past a big cardboard sign that said GRAY WOLVES. They passed an empty pen and came upon the wolf cage. She saw a low wooden fence that they could lean against. Beyond it, a chain-link fence rose above them twenty feet.

No other people were around. Two wolves were sitting on hardpacked dirt beneath a wooden lean-to. They both had thick gray-brown coats and the long snouts that always got exaggerated in cartoons. One of the wolves had her snout resting on the fur of the other's neck.

She sensed these wolves were bored and miserable. They did not seem to be enjoying their new residence. She knew that wolves slept during the daytime. She knew the zoo had in some way saved them. But still it angered her to see them there, so listless and pathetic. "I can't believe it," she said. "I can't believe this is what I get in my life for wolves."

"What do you mean?" Anthony asked.

"For all my life I think of wolves like as...*magical*. Howling at moons. Eating mint. I get two trauma victims lying around this shitty cage."

"I'm sure they howl," he said. "And they're still magical. They're wolves."

Then he stared brightly, almost ethereally. It was as if he had two different types of gazes. Sometimes his face came up like this—strikingly beautiful, angelic. Mostly it came up tense and anxious. He had green eyes.

She grabbed his collar and pulled him toward her. She pressed her chest against his and liked the way his muscles tightened. "Kiss me," she said. She drew him close to her face and tilted her head to kiss him. She felt his lips and his tongue, but Anthony's mouth never came to life.

She released him, faced the wolves, and then turned back to him. "I don't get it," she said.

"What?"

"You're so damn tense you feel like you'll blow up."

"That's how I do feel," he said.

"Then what's your problem?"

He said, "What's yours? Why won't you ever break up with Tommy?"

"Goddamn you," she said.

"What!"

"Do all things have to be the way they always are in your stupid head? You have to own me, is that it? If you had any brains at all, you wouldn't *want* to be my boyfriend. You'd want to screw around until I disappear like your goddamn mother. Only when I disappear, you'll never hear from me again."

He turned away from her. She'd hurt him. She had a knack for it, she knew. She rolled her eyes and said, "Hey. Let's not start crying here."

"I'm not."

She said, "Hey, neighbor boy. Look. Do you know why I dragged you to the zoo today? I dragged you here because I like you. Do you know that?"

He said, "Yes."

"Okay," Juliette said. "I'm glad we have at least that straight."

He looked squarely into her eyes. His gaze was stronger than she'd expected. She felt a lot from his gaze in ways she could not explain. She felt a lot when he kissed her softly and pulled her head against his chest. It was as if some sort of energy field was rising off his body.

Before they left they both bought Cokes and sat to drink them at a table near the entrance. She understood he was still upset. She wondered how long it would linger. She looked away and decided she would avoid him from now on. She lit a cigarette, looked up. She caught him staring at her necklace, or else her breasts.

"Hey," she said.

"What?"

"Try not to drop it this time," she said, and handed Anthony her cigarette. He took it carefully and then watched her. She reached behind her neck with both hands and unfastened the silver chain.

"I'm getting tired of this thing, just like I said I would," she told him. "I hope you'll keep it somewhere safe. But I don't care if you throw it out."

She placed the cross in his hand and took the cigarette. She watched his eyes for a spontaneous sign of recklessness. She saw none. She could see anguish in there, strength, and the callow innocence of resolve. Juliette leaned forward and put her elbows on the table. She let her chin rest on her hand. She said, "Wake up."

Angels Like
Audrey Hepburn

Here we are.

We're here.

We're in the airport and I'm almost done with volume two of Malory. It's been a good week with my mother. I've seen her life after three years, but now I'm ready to go home.

My mother stands and says, "I'm going to get a soda. Do you want one?"

I tell her, "Sure, I'll take a Coke."

She walks away, across the airport gate's blue carpet. My plane to Newark has been delayed two hours, so we have plenty of time to kill. Right now we're caught between two feelings—the inconvenience of the late plane and the fact that I'm going home. Also, my mother doesn't know how to do this. I know she wondered if maybe she should just leave me. After all, I'm busy reading about King Arthur. She has to be at work at five o'clock. But then she figured she should stay. She bought a *Redbook* and a magazine that has to do with diving. We've both been reading. From time to time she'll just look up and stare and seem surprised that I'm still here.

When she returns she isn't holding a Coke or anything for herself.

She says, "Guess what, Anth? There's a hockey game. It's on the TV in the bar."

"Who's playing?" I ask.

"One team has orange shirts."

"The Flyers."

"They have some food you can order, too," she says. "I ordered a plate of wings. Aren't you hungry?"

I say, "For buffalo wings, sure."

I close my book and slip it into my backpack. I follow my mother into a crowded airport bar. We take two seats facing a television. The Flyers are playing against the Capitals—my two least favorite teams in the NHL. Still it's hockey and I am always very happy to watch hockey. All things that happen on a hockey rink seem fluid and make sense.

I say, "It's strange to see a hockey game in Florida."

"They have a game-of-the-week each Sunday."

"You watch hockey?"

"Sometimes I'll watch when I'm flipping channels," she says. "It makes me think of you."

An attractive bartender brings our drinks out. I can't help staring as she places my Coke in front of me. She looks to be in her late twenties. She has red hair and a tight shirt. Most notably, she's wearing a silver cross around her neck.

After she leaves, I face my mother. By now I've told her almost all I have to say about Juliette Dimiglio. I've told her things that already seem like stories, and things so boring I'm amazed she even listened. She sips her Diet Coke with lemon. I tell her, "Juliette had a necklace like that bartender's. It belonged to her great-grandmother. I still have it. I sometimes wore it, though I never let people see."

"Really," my mother says.

Her gaze turns inward, the way it does when she's deducing things.

"I'm sure she loved you," she says offhandedly.

I give a laugh and say, "I doubt it."

"In her own way she did," she says. "I'm sure you know that."

She gets a look in her eye—too vulnerable and urgent to mean nothing.

After a moment I say, "Yeah, maybe I do."

The pretty bartender returns and brings our buffalo wings. She places the plate down with an odd gentleness. I look once more at her cross necklace, then make sure not to look again.

The Flyers score. It's a nice shot from the point. My mother points to the TV with a buffalo wing and says, "That was a slap shot, am I right?"

I say, "You're right. That's what it was."

"I always loved it when you took slap shots."

"My slap shot isn't so great," I say.

"Well I still like how it looks," she says. "And you once had that great goal when you were playing for the Chiefs. You shot it in right off the post. I think maybe you were twelve. It was in Newark at that rink in the scary park just off 280."

"Branchbrook," I say, and I'm amazed that she remembers this. It was the first time I had ever scored on a slap shot. The puck bounced off a defenseman's skate and came right to me in the slot. I just wound up and blasted it without looking.

I'm about done with my Coke when someone walks up behind my mother. I assume he's trying to get a drink because the bartender is standing right in front of us. But then I realize he's tapping my mother's shoulder. My mother turns and he says, "Excuse me. Are you, by any chance, Jess Adelman?"

For a few seconds she just stares. Then she says, "Eddie. Eddie Fischer?"

He says, "That's me."

"Eddie, how *are* you?" my mother asks. "It's been so long."

He says, "It has been a long time. You sure look great though."

"So do you."

Eddie keeps standing there behind her as she smiles over her shoulder. He is a very handsome man. He's six-foot-three with a big nose and

curly hair that's just beginning to go gray. He wears a powder blue but-
tondown, tan slacks, and a lightweight leather jacket. A floppy tennis
bag with a racket hangs over his left shoulder.

"Guess we're the only Jews in New Jersey who don't like Boca
Raton," he says. "Where did you stay? I was in Siesta Key."

She says, "I *live* in Sarasota. And this is Anthony, my son. His plane
to Newark is delayed."

"Anthony," he says, and holds his hand out.

I shake his hand and say, "Nice to meet you, Mr. Fischer."

Eddie stares at me and smiles. He says, "You've got your mother's
eyes."

"Pull up a seat," my mother says. "How much time do you have
to kill?"

He says, "Unfortunately, not much. Just maybe time for one quick
drink. God, if I knew I'd see you I would have booked a later flight.
How could I know?"

My mother says, "You couldn't."

Eddie's eyes fill with something I don't recognize. It's more than
longing—it's delirium and abandon. I've never seen anyone look this
way at my mother.

"Where are you headed?" she asks.

"Back to New York," Eddie says. "La Guardia. I recently moved out
to Long Island."

"Why did you move there?" my mother asks.

Eddie hesitates. He says, "Linda, my second wife. She's from there.
She owns a flower store in Great Neck."

My mother looks away to hide her disappointment. When she turns
back, she says, "That's great." Eddie nods strangely and motions to the
bartender.

"I'll take a Beck's," he says. "Another Diet Coke for the lady and a
Coke for the young man."

"You don't have to," says my mother.

He waves his hand in the air and says, "My pleasure."

My mother smiles with resignation and says, "It's Eddie. The big fish. How has your life been?"

"I can't complain," Eddie says. "I have two daughters. My oldest one just started Yale."

"You always wanted to write," my mother says. "Did you grow up to be a writer?"

He shakes his head and says, "Not me. I wound up taking over my dad's business. Not much choice when it came down to it, though a part of me still imagines going to Hollywood, writing screenplays. Maybe I'll do it when I retire."

"You always wrote such good essays," says my mother. "I still remember that one about the Seashell Diner's drive-in window. I remember when Mrs. Seelye read it out loud."

"Those were the days," he says. He looks at me and says, "I knew your mom in high school. All us dumb guys were always following her around. She was an angel." Eddie nods.

I say, "So how was she an angel?"

Eddie glances at my mother. He laughs and says, "We used to call your mother Hep. That's because she acted just like Audrey Hepburn. That kind of angel."

"Who's Audrey Hepburn?" I ask.

"Tell me you're kidding."

"She's an actress," my mother says. "She's still in movies sometimes now, but in the sixties she was more famous. She's gotten older."

"She was like no one on this earth," says Eddie. "You took one look at Audrey Hepburn and your head would spin."

"I've never seen her," I say.

"You never heard of the movie *Breakfast at Tiffany's*?"

My first reaction is that I have, but then I realize that I'm thinking of the Supertramp album *Breakfast in America*.

I say, "Guess not."

"You ever hear the song 'Moon River'?"

I say, "My father used to play it all the time on clarinet."

"Well, that's the movie where the song came from," Eddie tells me. He smiles pleasantly, turns to my mother, and says, "Goddamn it, Hep. We must be getting old."

The bartender brings our drinks. I watch the game as Eddie starts to ask my mother questions about her life. She tells him about her new-found love for diving; about Dani and then Dad—she says, "I split up with Michael about three years ago."

"You're not remarried?" Eddie says.

I turn and see my mother shaking her head shyly.

"That's such a crime," Eddie says. "That seems impossible. Maybe I'll call up Manny Berman. Remember Manny?"

My mother nods.

"Well, Manny's wife died last year. He's a big partner in a law firm and he's loaded, but now he's miserable."

She says, "Hey, Eddie, I'm just fine. I do okay here by myself, so don't go fixing me up with Manny. If I remember, he's a nutcase."

"He's calmed down some," Eddie says.

Then Eddie laughs and says, "Damn, if I just had another life."

My mother smiles and I can tell she feels much more than she is showing.

She says, "You don't have two lives, Eddie. But I thank you for the compliment."

I get this feeling I should give them some time alone, so I tell them I have to use the bathroom. I glance up at the hockey game. The third period has just started. It's 4–2 Flyers, as would be expected. I try to act like I care about this hockey game, though I don't.

I leave them sitting at the bar. I pass some pay phones and the near-est set of bathrooms, which are too close. I keep on walking until I find another set.

As I go in, I keep on wondering things about my mom and Eddie. Such as—What if my mom had married him? Would she be happier right now? That's when it hits me. I know who Eddie Fischer is. He played basketball. I know because I've looked at my mother's high school photo albums and scrapbooks. She used to keep them right out in the hallway bookshelf. The day she drove off to Florida, they were gone.

There was a cut-out photo from a newspaper. I used to stare at that one photo all the time. My mother's sitting on Eddie's shoulders. She's in her cheerleading clothes and holds two pom-poms in her left hand. Her right hand's touching Eddie's neck, keeping her balance, though it looks like she's almost falling. Eddie's all sweaty and young and tall, with that same nose and curly hair. He's in his basketball shirt and shorts, and there are people crowding the court behind them.

I flush the urinal and head back out into the corridor. Now I walk quickly, almost jogging. When I get back to the airport bar, Eddie is standing. It's that same tall, dignified stance as in the photo.

Eddie says, "Anthony. Son, it was nice meeting you. I'm glad I got the chance to say goodbye."

"Nice to meet you," I say. "Have a really good flight back."

"Thank you," he says, and turns back to my mother. He says, "Well, Hep, it was nice. It's just too quick. I feel so . . . God." He starts to look like a total wreck.

My mother stands up and says, "Hey now, it's okay. Most things in life are too quick, but it's okay."

"Maybe I'll stay."

"Of course you won't," she says.

"I'd stay one night at the hotel in the airport. We could have dinner."

"You have to go."

"We'd just have dinner."

She says, "No."

He looks away, then back, and says, "I'm sorry. It's just nice seeing an old friend."

"It really was nice," says my mother. "Now you take care. Have a good flight."

"Oh, Christ," Eddie says and puts both arms around her neck. After an awkward, non-reciprocated moment, he releases her. He tells her, "Seeing you made my day."

"Mine too," she says.

"Alright then."

"You take care," she says again.

He walks away from us. He looks back once and waves before he passes out of sight.

"Stay here," my mother says.

"Where are you going?"

She says, "I need to walk this off before I faint."

She heads off in the direction opposite Eddie. She quickly vanishes into the shapeless crowd. Just as I turn back to the hockey game, the score flashes. I'm shocked to see that it's 4–4. Not only that, the Capitals have a power play. I watch a flurry of missed shots. One hits the post. Another seems like it's going in, but the Flyers' goalie somehow snags it. I keep on watching this strange animal, momentum, which I've felt a thousand times.

Of course, it happens. They score a goal. It's on a blast from the point that gets deflected. The goalie's following the shot's angle, but it changes and zips by him. All the Capitals raise their sticks. I can't help cheering. The red-haired bartender walks up and says, "Good game?"

I am about to start explaining all of hockey when my mother comes up beside me. Now I expect her to be calm, but it's the opposite. She seems frantic.

I say, "What's wrong?"

She says, "Nothing. How's the game?"

I say, "The Capitals came back."

She waves her hand to the bartender and says, "Check, please."

I say, "So tell me about this movie, *Breakfast at Tiffany's.*"

"I really am amazed you never heard of it."

"What's it about?"

She says, "Well, Audrey Hepburn, she's this woman who wants to marry a rich millionaire. She also has this cat. And the thing is, she's sort of like the cat, since she has no one. But then this other guy, the one who she sings 'Moon River' to, not the millionaire—he rescues her. It's pouring rain in the last scene, and the last thing they have to do is save the cat because she left it in an alley. What kind of cold bitch dumps a pet cat in an alley, tell me that? Of course they live happily ever after, since it's the movies. Even the cat lives happily ever after. You have to trust that it didn't catch pneumonia."

"So do you act like Audrey Hepburn?"

"Maybe a little," my mother says, and gives the bartender her MasterCard. "But no, not really, I don't think so. I don't know why all those people called me Hep."

I watch the bartender move the plastic piece that slides across the track that holds the credit card. She slides it back, pulls out the slip and card, and hands them to my mother.

"Pen?" my mother says.

She hands my mother a black pen. She tries to sign but I can see that her hands are trembling. It takes my mother a good three seconds before she manages to put the pen to paper.

I say, "We still have an hour to kill."

She says, "Look, honey. I have to leave now. I have to leave before that man comes back. He's coming."

"How do you know?"

"Because I know him. He used to date my best girlfriend, Roz."

"Is it so bad if he comes back?"

She says, "He's taken. Just like twenty-five years ago."

"Maybe he's not so happy in his marriage."

She says, "Please, Anthony, there's more to this. I can't get into it."

She rips the slip and grabs her card.

I say, "But Mom..."

"Tonight I'll call you."

I say, "Wait, Mom," but there's no stopping her. Not when she wants to disappear.

We walk together to the gate. My mother kisses me for shorter than she hugged Eddie. Then she's gone. I feel this thing go off inside me, almost as if it's me who's vanished.

I walk over to the pay phones. I try calling up my father. He isn't there so I leave a message saying my flight's delayed. I know this message is irrelevant. He always calls to check on flights. Next I try Dani at her apartment in Philadelphia. A machine picks up and beeps without a voice message preceding it. I say, "Hi, Dani. It's me, Anthony. I was just sitting in the airport and thought I'd call you. Nothing urgent. Maybe I'll try you again later."

As I hang up, I turn away from the phone and see him, Eddie Fischer. Now he's talking to the bartender. My Mom was right. He skipped his plane, or else the plane got delayed like mine. At first I'm tempted to walk over and point out where my mother went. But even if Eddie caught up with her, I know that she'd just tell him goodbye again.

I watch Eddie as he looks around that airport bar. And then what happens is I feel him. I feel exactly what he's going through. He keeps on looking as if maybe she'll be behind a chair or underneath a place mat. He even orders another beer, sits on a stool, and seems to wait for her. He chugs down half of the beer, gets up again. He talks again with the bartender. Just as I think it's time to break down and go speak with him, he hands some money to the woman and heads off.

Eddie walks quickly and I don't follow. Then I feel better—maybe because I'm not the only one she's vanished on. I sit down by the gate.

I take out Malory and start reading again. I'm near the end, at the part where Lancelot and Guinevere speak for the last time. Arthur has died in his fight with Mordred, his son by Morgause, his half sister. Lancelot comes to see Guinevere in a nunnery. At the sight of the knight, she swoons. She is so filled with restraint and longing she can barely hold herself up.

She commands Lancelot never to lay eyes on her again. Her exact words are, "I require and beseech thee heartily, for all the love that ever was betwixt us, that thou never see me more in the visage." She says, "Mine heart will not serve me to see thee, for through thee and me is the flower of kings and knights destroyed." She urges Lancelot to take a wife, live happily, and pray that God allow her to amend her own "misliving." Lancelot vows that he will never take a wife and asks her for one last kiss. The queen refuses, so he departs. He mounts his horse and rides away through the forest, weeping all day and night.

I keep on reading this chapter, over and over. It's just three pages. It seems to me the most painfully beautiful scene I can imagine. I understand that the queen has broken her own heart, and that this truest of knights, Lancelot, is a passion-enslaved buffoon. Yet in some way I understand that I love them. That these two characters aren't really people. That they are somehow part of the air I breathe.

My plane to Newark pulls in, finally. I close the book and watch the people coming off the plane. Soon there's a crowd around the gate and no more passengers deplaning. I am just starting to wonder when they'll board when a voice says, "Anthony."

I look up.

And then it feels as if I'm dreaming. I see my mother. She stands in front of me. The magazines are sticking out of her bag.

She says, "I'm sorry, Anth. I think I sort of panicked just before."

My mother sits in the chair beside me. She lets her bag fall to the carpet. We hear the boarding call. She laughs.

"I'm glad I got here," she says. "Even if it was for only thirty seconds."

I say, "Me too," and we stand up.

It isn't strained, the way it might be. We stand and hug for a few more seconds. We let go. As I am walking away I turn. I see her scanning the many faces in the terminal. I meant to tell her Eddie returned. Of course she knows, and knows he's gone—but she is not one to test fate. She turns again to me, waves quickly, and then flees.

PART FOUR

THE FIGURE 5
IN GOLD

July 1982

"I'M GOING DOWN THERE," Dani said.

"When?"

"Sometime in August. Before I have to be at college. You should go."

"I'm coaching here until the sixth," Anthony told her. "We could go down right after that."

He had called Dani from the lobby of Camp Manahawkin's ice rink. He was wearing skates, a helmet, sweatpants, a sweatshirt, a silver whistle around his neck. His gloves and stick lay on the rubber floor matting. Dani was home that summer, working as a lifeguard at the Livingston town pool.

"Then we'll go August seventh or eighth," she said. "There's a cheap flight that I can book."

"Okay, then book it. I'll call and tell her."

"She went away today," said Dani. "She went diving with her dive group. But she gave me her American Express number."

Anthony saw Will Smithson crossing the lobby with his skates on. Coach Marino popped out from the rink. He said, "Hey Rubin, we got the ten-year-olds, your specialty."

Anthony nodded and held one finger up.

"When does she come back?" he asked Dani.

"In like twelve days. She said she'd call."

The coach barked, "Rubin," and headed out through the lobby door. Will Smithson followed.

"I'll call tonight," Anthony said. "I better go."

When he stepped onto the ice, the coach and Will had already set the kids up in a skating drill. The coach was hollering, as usual, telling the players to keep their heads up and look alive. Will was sitting on the boards, his two legs dangling in the air. Anthony skated up and said, "I was just talking to my sister."

Will said, "Man, your older sis is such a babe. How can you stand it?"

He said, "Stand what?"

"Just living in the same house with her. What happens when you see her in her underwear?"

He said, "Nothing. She's my sister."

"But she has such an amazing ass."

The coach's whistle blew. He called out, "Forwards down with Coach Rubin for stick skills. Defense with Smithson for a twenty-minute power-skate. Goalies, get rid of your sticks and come with me."

Will jumped down from the boards and skated toward the nine or ten boys who considered themselves defensemen. The other thirty or so hightailed it to the far end of the ice. Anthony grabbed the orange cones and a puck bag from the bench. About six boys were down on the ice wrestling when he got there.

He skated over, blew his whistle, and barked, "Save it, unless you feel like power-skating all practice." The half-dozen boys separated quickly. Anthony dumped the puck bag. "Everyone take a puck," he said. "Skate in a circle inside the blue line, stick-handling, head up at all times. When I blow the whistle, speed up."

All the boys hungrily took pucks and began skating in a circle. After fifteen seconds Anthony blew his whistle and yelled, "Faster!" He blew the whistle again ten seconds later and yelled, "Slow!" Meanwhile he set the orange cones up for the next drill. He placed them down in three zigzagging lines between the goal line and the blue line. Then he skated with the forwards for five minutes, dutifully speeding up and slowing down along with them each time he blew his whistle.

"Weave through the cones," he said, while explaining the next drill. "Not fast. You want to keep your head up while you're stickhandling. Think of the cones as players who will cream you if you don't."

He blew his whistle. He looked down the ice at Will and his core group of defensemen. In general, they were better behaved, more serious, and willing to work harder. There were a few serious forwards, but the rest of them were clowns.

"Kyle, kill him!" someone yelled. "Punch his face in!"

Anthony turned. He saw Kyle Miller, a very reckless boy, pummeling Scott Brown in the goal crease. Scott Brown was homesick and kept crying, and now he seemed to be getting beaten up every day.

He skated toward them, whistle blowing. Just as he reached them, Kyle knocked Scott down and a cone slid off in Anthony's direction. Somehow it found its way directly under Anthony's right skate. He put his weight down on the cone just as he saw it and felt his right leg slide out to the side.

He heard a pop. Then he was down on the ice, confused but unalarmed. He turned away, tried to get up, but his knee buckled. He fell down onto the ice again.

Some of the forwards started laughing. He blew his whistle. One boy said, "Coach, are you okay?" He answered, "No." The other two boys were still rolling around together in the corner.

Coach Marino yelled out, "Rubin! What are you doing?"

Anthony turned himself around with his hands and saw Coach Marino striding toward him. He felt embarrassed and had no idea how to explain what happened.

The coach flew past him and raced into the corner, where he stopped sharply and sprayed the fighting boys with a cloud of snow. He grabbed Scott Brown by the head, dragged him away and flung him toward the blue line. He picked up Kyle, hoisted him fireman-style over his left shoulder. He skated up to the boards and heaved the leg-flailing boy into the penalty box.

Then the coach skated back to Anthony. He was still trying to get up. Will Smithson was crouched beside him, asking him questions about what he thought had happened. The coach crouched down and said, "Christ, Rubin, just tell me it's not your knee."

✦ ✦ ✦

After the surgery at the Lenox Hill Hospital in New York, Anthony lay doped up on painkillers, a cast up to his thigh. The six-inch vertical incision had been closed with metal staples, which itched like crazy. The painkillers sometimes seemed to paralyze his muscles while he slept, and upon waking he would not be able to move until he concentrated hard.

His dad and Dani visited every day. For the first four nights, when Anthony was on morphine, Dani stayed over with him. When she got tired she would sleep on the vacant bed. From time to time, he would wake up and start to yell about the pain. If six hours had gone by since the last shot, Dani would chase down a nurse and ask her to give Anthony another. If not she would sit next to him, douse his brow with a wet washcloth, and start telling him bad jokes.

One evening, when he was half awake, he looked up and saw Dani in the bathroom. She hadn't closed the door all the way. Dani was sitting on the toilet. He thought of Will and how long ago Camp Manahawkin seemed, though it had been less than two weeks since he'd left.

"Close the door," he called.

Dani just laughed and said, "I didn't know you were awake."

"Will Smithson thinks you're hot."

She said, "Too bad he's a dumb shit. I prefer geniuses like Bobby."

"Will you and Bobby keep on going out this fall?"

"We'll be in college."

"So?"

"Maybe we'll try, but I doubt that it will work."

She flushed the toilet and stepped out.

He said, "I think I'll die soon if I don't manage to find a girlfriend."

Dani said, "Well, there's always some hot girl who has a thing for cripples."

After four days the doctor took him down from morphine to Demerol. Later that morning, a nurse wheeled him over to Therapy, where a physical therapist taught him to use crutches. When he first stood, his knee felt hot, as if the blood inside were boiling. He imagined red pulp under his kneecap. He walked around the room on crutches several times and considered how this would be in the school hallways come September. Then he sat down in the wheelchair and put his leg up. The knee was throbbing as if somehow it had grown its own small heart.

When he came back from physical therapy, he had a roommate. His father was there, waiting outside the room to explain the situation. He said the roommate was quite sick, but Lenox Hill was overcrowded. It was a fluke that he'd had no roommate for the first four days he'd been there. He said this all in a hushed voice, then wheeled him in.

Inside the room, he said, "Anthony, meet Chris. And Chris's mother, Mrs. Robbins. This is Anthony."

Mrs. Robbins said hello and Chris just nodded. On first sight, Anthony felt queasy. Chris weighed no more than sixty pounds. His limbs were sticks. He had intravenous tubes hooked to one hand.

His mother sat beside his bed. A husky, broad-shouldered, forlorn woman, she was reading *Newsweek*. Anthony said hello and tried to engage Chris in a conversation. The boy would only give one-word answers. His mother kept on saying, "Christopher, be nice."

Later that day, when Dani came to visit, she was feeling playful. She took Anthony out in his wheelchair and said, "It's time you got a guided tour of the hospital. And time you ate something besides that so-called food they keep on bringing."

"It doesn't matter, I can't eat," he said. "All the painkillers make me nauseous."

"You want to wind up like your roommate?" Dani asked him.

She wheeled him around a corner, just fast enough that the turn felt smooth.

He said, "What's wrong with Christopher Robin?"

Dani said, "Robbins. He's anorexic."

"What can they do for that?" he asked.

She didn't answer. Dani wheeled him into the empty elevator. Though he could tell that she was thinking about Chris Robbins, she said, "First stop is the fourth-floor terrace. Then we go down to the café for a milkshake."

They reached floor four and he heard a ding.

She said, "I came up here before with Dad."

She pushed him out and again Anthony said, "So, what can they do for anorexia?"

"Not a whole hell of lot. It's psychological."

She turned a corner with the wheelchair. She pushed him through a door that led to the outdoor terrace. He felt the warm air; he heard cars. The only view was the side of another building.

"So then what happens?" he asked. "Isn't Chris seeing a psychiatrist?"

She said, "He's starving to death, I think. Dad says he's probably going to die."

✦ ✦ ✦

Another day went by and Anthony lay despondent and uncomfortable. It took a lot of effort to move. From time to time he would try to read one of the books his father brought him, but after five or ten minutes it made him sick. Sometimes he'd take Juliette's necklace out from his wallet, flip the cross around, and play with it. He'd imagine Juliette finding out about his accident, taking a train in, and surprising him with a visit. He'd imagine Juliette as his nurse, spending the night there the way Dani had. But mostly he would sleep or watch TV.

Chris liked to watch TV as well. It was the only time they ever really communicated, now and then making offhand comments or suggesting another channel. That evening Anthony woke to the Daily Double noise on *Jeopardy*. He closed his eyes but heard Chris whispering the answers. Somehow the whispers were more distracting than if he'd been there playing an accordion.

"What is China?" Chris whispered with great urgency. "Who was the Archduke Ferdinand?" Anthony glanced at him and saw that he was pressing his palms together. He appeared to be doing some sort of isometric exercise while he watched.

"Are you a history buff?" Anthony finally asked him.

In his nasal voice, Chris said, "Not really. But I would probably win on *Jeopardy*."

"How do you know things?" Anthony asked.

Chris said, "I read a lot of books."

The conversation seemed to be going nowhere, so he dropped it. Chris was still vigorously pressing his palms together. Anthony sat up and watched the show. The last remaining questions on the *Jeopardy* board were all in the category "Famous W Poets."

This transcendentalist was the editor...

"Who was Walt Whitman?" Chris whispered, long before the clue was finished.

"I Wandered Lonely as a Cloud" was this...

"Who's William Wordsworth?" Chris said reflexively.

"Wow," Anthony said. "You're like a talking encyclopedia."

In a meek voice Chris said, "There aren't many famous W poets."

This much-loved doctor, writer, and poet lived in Rutherford, New Jersey...

Chris called out, "Who was William Carlos Williams?"

"You're kidding."

Chris said, "What?"

"A famous poet lived in New Jersey? In the Meadowlands?"

"He wrote weird poems," Chris said. "They're weird but nice, such as, 'Among the rain and lights I saw the figure 5 in gold on a red firetruck, moving, tense, unheeded, to gong clangs, siren howls, and wheels rumbling through the dark city.'"

"That's the whole poem?"

Chris said, "Lots of his poems were short. He had to type them in between his patients."

"Say it again," Anthony said.

"'Among the rain and lights I saw the figure 5 in gold on a red firetruck, moving, tense, unheeded, to gong clangs, siren howls, and wheels rumbling through the dark city.'"

"That's neat," Anthony said, and he could see it in his mind. A golden 5 on a bright red firetruck. He saw the rain and lights and the dark city. He heard the sirens.

"So you like poetry?" he asked.

"Certain poets. I like Williams. What do you like?"

He said, "Hockey."

"Is that how you broke your leg?"

"I tore my knee," Anthony said. "It's my anterior cruciate ligament."

"Did someone check you?"

He said, "I stepped on a cone. I fell. It was idiotic."

Chris said, "The knee is the most poorly constructed human joint. That's what I read somewhere."

"Terrific."

"So are you good?" Chris said. "Do you score goals?"

He said, "This year I was supposed to be team captain for my high school."

Chris said, "You look like you'd be good. You have that hockey-player look."

"Thanks," Anthony said, and stared at Chris, who was still doing his isometrics. He tried to think of something nice to say, but couldn't. He thought: You look like you're about to disappear.

✦ ✦ ✦

Chris had a fight the next morning with his mother. She had come to visit and found that in the night Chris had pulled the IV out of his hand. She'd called a nurse but Chris refused to let the IV go back in. Mrs. Robbins kept saying, "Damn it, do we have to call your father?"

Finally Chris gave in and let the nurse connect the IV once more. Then he sat up and put his head in his hands, the left one black and blue from the IV. His mother sat in the chair beside him while Chris cried and vented hatred for his father.

Late that night, Anthony's last night in the hospital, he woke and sensed that Chris was wide awake. He felt the pain in his knee and pressed the button for the nurse. It took ten minutes for her to come, but she'd already brought the Demerol. She turned him over and asked which was the less sore cheek of his butt. He said the right and felt the momentary sting of the syringe.

When she went out, he could hear Chris's awake breathing sounds. He felt too awful to start a conversation, so he just closed his eyes and waited for the painkiller to affect him.

As he was starting to nod off, Chris whispered, "Anthony?"

He said, "What?"

"Are you awake?"

"I am now."

"I have a question."

"What?"

"When did you first start playing hockey?"

"I was like six," Anthony said. "Or maybe five when I first took lessons. The next year I started playing on a team."

Chris said, "That's neat. I always wished I could play hockey."

"Then why didn't you?"

"I have no coordination. I like to run though, a lot. I'm on my school's cross-country team, and track team."

"Where do you live?"

Chris said, "Tarrytown."

"Where's that?"

"It's in New York, just up the river. It's really nice there."

"Can I ask *you* a question?" said Anthony.

"What?"

"How come you won't eat food?"

"I'm not sure," Chris said. "But I just can't now."

"You might die."

"That's what my mother says."

"Doesn't it scare you?"

"I won't die if I don't want to."

Anthony heard Chris sitting up. He turned his head and looked at Chris's enshadowed face. He was unwrapping the tape on his left hand again.

"My dad's a doctor," Anthony said. "He told my sister that you probably will die."

"I won't die," Chris said.

"My dad's a doctor."

He said, "I won't."

"How do you know?"

He felt the drug taking effect, turning him into a body-shaped mold of Jell-O.

"Because I know," Chris said.

Anthony felt like he was floating around the room.

"When we get out of here, maybe we'll see a Rangers game," said Chris. "My dad gets tickets, for his clients. We go a couple of times a year. One time I even caught a puck in warm-ups. But then my dad made me give it to this lady who was right near us. It rolled right to me, but she wanted it. I knew my father didn't think that I deserved it."

"Deserved the puck?"

He said, "Yeah. She was very pretty. Blond and thin. She kept on saying it was her puck."

"But it was yours. I mean, you caught it, right?"

"That's right."

"So what's the deal?"

He said, "No deal. I gave the puck to her. She wanted it."

"What a bitch."

Chris said, "I know, but my dad made me. For a few months afterward I thought about that puck. What would I do with a puck, though? I don't play hockey. I don't have any actual friends. I might have given it to you, though. You seem nicer than most people."

"You seem nice too," Anthony said, and understood that Chris would not be getting better.

Chris told him, "Thanks."

He said, "You're welcome."

He heard Chris unwrapping the tape. It was a loud sound that now seemed to be drowning out his voice.

+ + +

On his way home from the hospital the next morning, Anthony sat with his cast stretched across the backseat of his father's BMW. Dani sat up in front, wearing red sunglasses. It was the last day in July. He'd been an inpatient for seven days, but by now Camp Manahawkin seemed like another lifetime.

They were passing through the Lincoln Tunnel. He saw the painted double line that indicated where they'd crossed into New Jersey.

He said, "Hey Dad, you ever hear of the poet William Carlos Williams?"

His dad said, "Sure. He was a doctor. He wrote about the Passaic River."

"Do you like him?" Anthony asked.

"I've never been much of a fan of poetry."

He spied a tunnel cop sitting in one of the claustrophobic tunnel booths. He tried to get his mind off Chris.

"So what the hell will I do at home?" he asked. "This cast stays on two months."

"You'll do what everyone does when they first get out of the hospital. You'll sit around. You'll get better. You'll drive us crazy."

"Not for long," his sister said.

Dani was going down alone to see their mother. She would be leaving for a week on the eighth of August. A few weeks after she returned, she would be leaving for UPenn.

"There's a big package from Mom," his father said.

"She got home Friday," Dani said. "She must have gone shopping right after we hung up."

"She'll call tonight," his father said. "I told her all about the hospital, your surgery, and your roommate."

He said, "You told her about Chris?"

His father said, "It just came up."

He pictured Chris back in the room. They'd shaken hands before he left. Chris wished him good luck in hockey. He had said, "Thanks. It was nice getting to be your roommate." He waved to Chris and the nurse wheeled him into the hallway. Then he said, "Wait, I have tell him one more thing."

Chris looked right up when Anthony reappeared at his bedside. As their eyes met Chris smiled brightly for a moment. He turned away and stared down at the floor. "I'll try to look for the figure 5 in gold," Anthony told him. Chris's IV hand was now wrapped up like a bear paw. He raised the paw to his face and rubbed his cheek. When he looked up once more at Anthony, his eyes seemed luminous. Then Chris said, "Good. That's kind of funny. I always look for the figure, too."

The car emerged from the Lincoln Tunnel. They passed the toll booths and began curving up the ascending road that doubled back and led down to the Turnpike. Anthony stared off at the skyline of New York. He was about to ask something more about his mother, but the whole view caught him off guard.

He saw the Empire State Building, the World Trade Center, a ferry crossing the river. He said, "Drive slower," and stared over the calm water. His father slowed and said, "Wow, look at the view."

Anthony didn't really know what he was looking for. He suspected he was looking for Chris Robbins, or else a firetruck rumbling through the heart of a dark city. What he saw was the sunlight sparkling on the water, all of Manhattan under a perfect summer sky. It all looked quiet, in a way, as if the city were at rest. He knew this distance, like all distances, preserved things. He sensed that somehow he was trying to preserve Chris. "Okay?" his father said. "Can I speed up now and change lanes?" He told him, "Sure," and the car rose quickly above the skyline. Craning his neck to look out through the back windshield, Anthony watched until the view was blocked by cliffs.

B'SHERT

August 1982

MICHAEL RUBIN'S FATHER, Max, had lived for four years at the Pine Manor Home for the Elderly, in South Orange. He was a passionate, well-informed man. A former high school English teacher, he'd been a widower nine years. He'd lived alone until he started having heart problems. He had protested when Michael moved him. He was depressed, at first, but then he started playing chess and reading philosophical books about "time."

They would have Max over to Livingston on holidays. Michael tried to visit him weekly at Pine Manor. He would play chess with him, lose badly, and receive long explanations of his poor strategy. On occasion, Max would discuss what he was reading. He was predictable, for the most part, but then one afternoon he introduced Doris Schulman.

Doris had come to Pine Manor a few months before because she'd started falling. She was a heavyset woman, strong and dignified, with straight white hair and a slightly crooked nose. She'd survived Auschwitz and sometimes gave talks to Jewish youth groups and continuing education programs at local synagogues. She claimed her vision sometimes got blurry, that the floor would start looking like a river. Ever since coming to Pine Manor, she'd used a walker.

Michael was sitting with Doris and his father over breakfast on a

Friday. Doris sat quietly beside Max while he went on and on about the American culture's ludicrous misconceptions about time. "We think that time just flows outside of us," he was saying. "But it flows in us too, you see? It can flow slower on the inside, or else faster. It's all relative, just like Einstein figured out."

Doris was eating a bowl of fruit salad.

She said, "Your father thinks too hard."

"There's relativity in the body," Max said emphatically. "That's why you feel like you've stopped time when you fall in love. And in some way, you really *do*."

Doris said, "Max is the last eightysomething romantic left on this planet." She ran her hand across his head, which was mostly bald except for two white winglike strips that ran down the sides. She kissed his head in a way that impressed Michael with its tenderness. Then Doris rose and said, "I've always gone for nuts."

She went upstairs to her room and Michael agreed to play one game of chess with his father. They set the board up in the sitting room outside the cafeteria. On his second move, Michael took his queen out.

Max said, "What are you, meshugah?"

Michael just laughed and said, "I thought I'd try something different."

His father shook his head, moved out a pawn, and smiled at his only living son.

He said, "So Michael, I'm falling madly in love with Doris."

"I'm glad to hear it," Michael said. "You've been so solitary since Mom died."

"I never thought I'd want another woman after your mother. I thought I'd had everything I needed, good and bad, but I was wrong. As I tell Doris, I feel like a young rooster. Now I'm just pullulating with passion and love and all those things I haven't felt forever."

"What does pullulate mean?" asked Michael.

Max said, "Oy, doctors. Too busy charging a thousand dollars an hour to make any time to read a book."

Michael chose not to indulge his father's somewhat righteous life-long obsession with multisyllabic words. If he remembered the word an hour from now, he'd find the dictionary in his office and look it up.

"Doris is not much like Mom," Michael said, and moved a pawn out.

His father quickly moved out a bishop and said, "Cover your queen."

"Mom was less sure of herself," said Michael. "Doris seems like someone you can't ruffle."

"Your mom was spoiled. Doris is not. Now I just wish I'd saved some of the money I spent buying your mother things she didn't need."

Michael said, "Don't you worry about anything."

His father stared at him, his deep brown eyes unfathomable, as always. He said, "The thing is, I want us to get married."

Michael said, "Dad, you're eighty-one years old."

"But I'm in love," Max said. "After so many years of living, my *b'shert* appears. As she must. Because your mother, she was *not* my *b'shert*. We stayed together for you and Daniel. And after Daniel died, the only thing to do was be a family. It was the right thing, with Miss Wrong. But now I finally find Miss Right."

"But you can't marry at your age, Dad. If you get married, one of you loses Social Security."

"That would be me, the high school teacher," he said. "Doris made more as a librarian. So I lose nine-hundred-eighty dollars a month is what it comes to. Is this enough that I'd give up the chance to marry my heart's desire?"

Michael said, "Yes."

"You're just like Doris," Max said, and took his queen.

Michael said, "Dad, you live in the same facility. You eat your meals with her. You'll see her every day for your whole life."

Max told him, "Doris will come around. She understands the beauty of the spirit."

Michael looked down at the chessboard. He moved out another pawn. He said, "It's not as if the two of you could leave this place, so what would be the difference?"

"You don't understand," said Max.

Michael said, "What's to understand?"

"Love is the only thing there is," Max said. "The *only* thing that ever cuts across the grain of time. When real love comes, you don't subvert it. You don't treat love like a commodity."

"But you can love her without marrying her, or losing Social Security."

Max said, "I'm sure you will understand this better when you're old."

✦ ✦ ✦

Later that week Dani returned from visiting Jess in Florida and immediately broke up with her boyfriend. She claimed it was a mutual decision, and only logical because she and Bobby were going off to different colleges. Michael was stunned by her poise and nonchalance until one evening, a few days later, when he heard Dani sobbing in the bathroom.

On that same night, while he was playing clarinet, Dani walked in and sat down on his bed to listen. He was just practicing scales, so he stopped playing. He said, "Is everything okay?"

"Fine," she said.

"Don't worry."

"About what?"

"About Bobby," he said. "He obviously wasn't your *b'shert.*"

"What's a *b'shert?*" she asked.

"It's Yiddish. It means your fated other spiritual half. In other words, the romantic partner who you fit with, and should stay with."

"But Bobby might be my *b'shert,*" she said.

"I doubt it."

"Why?"

He said, "Because, you'll know it when you meet him."

"What do you do then?" she asked.

He said, "You love him. You don't part."

"So who was your *b'shert?*"

"I obviously haven't found her."

"How do you know?"

"Because you know," Michael said. "It's destiny. I think that's the whole meaning of the word."

He picked his clarinet up and began to play again. Dani sat listening for a while, and Michael sensed that the music made her calmer. Ever since he'd resumed playing, he had noticed this in his children. It was as if he had brought some lost thing back to them. And it was all he had found to give back to himself.

That August, Anthony had been miserable. In the weeks following his knee surgery, he had spent most of his time sitting on the couch. He'd started reading poems and short stories by William Carlos Williams. He was deep into Williams's autobiography, which seemed to be the only thing keeping him sane.

He kept a pad and would scribble down quotes and phrases. Michael would look at the pad from time to time. He'd try to infer meanings from the things his son had scribbled out. On the top page of the pad, the first quote Anthony had copied was the following: *What I believe to be the hidden core of my life will not easily be deciphered, even when I tell, as here, the outer circumstances.*

Though Michael had never read any of the poetry or stories, he had always been somewhat fascinated by Williams. He was intrigued by the man's hybrid abilities. Of the competing poles of his two vocations, doctor and writer, which Michael also knew were not so far removed. But in his own case, the art had been a heartbreak. He'd never felt the obligatory drive as a musician. Perhaps he'd never possessed the required talent. So he had opted for a reliable career, a way to provide, an eminent profession. He'd had a family, just as he wanted. Beautiful children. A tall, beautiful, and volatile wife. Then after seventeen years everything had exploded. He never knew if he had wrecked things, or if some vital, fundamental bond with Jess had simply never been created.

Jess was a diver now, he knew. She had been diving while Anthony was having reconstructive surgery on his knee. She had told him all about it during their last telephone conversation. After discussing the operation, he'd said, "So, what are you doing down there in Florida these days?"

Jess had said, "Nothing too exciting. Just surviving." Then she said, "Oh, and lots of diving. I have some girlfriends. We have a dive group, the Reef Explorer Girls. We take trips like the one we all just took to the West Indies. I go whenever I have money for a plane ticket."

Michael said, "How was the West Indies?"

She became more animated after that. Her voice grew stronger. She said, "We went to three different islands. And on our last day on Barbados, we took a boat to a reef called Jaws of Death. It used to be called South Reef, but no one went there. So they changed it. We saw a manta ray. It swam right over us, so big that it got darker for a second from the shadow. Kisha, my dive partner, was scared and held my arm tight as we watched it. But I was wishing I could grab onto the thing and go with it, wherever it would take me."

Now when he thought about Jess, Michael would picture her underwater. He would imagine what it would be like diving with her, while also knowing that, in his lifetime, such a thing would not occur. So it became a kind of dream, a half-formed jealousy, to think of Jess underwater. He'd never go that far, he knew, or be that free and unrestrained. Yet despite what he or anyone could say—despite the easy, justifiable perception that she was crazy—he had the nagging sense that Jess had found a richer and more authentic life.

A week or so after Dani returned, Michael called up Jess's sister, Leah. They agreed to meet for an early dinner. Ever since their chance meeting the night Paul Haney died, they had gone out from time to time.

Leah didn't talk about Paul much when they went out, but Paul was there in ways that Michael could always feel. They would have coffee or a quick bite. Once they went to see an early movie. There was a clandestine quality to their meetings, but interactions never strayed beyond the bounds of an affectionate, if unconventional friendship.

They would hold hands sometimes, but Michael understood that Leah would never kiss him. They had kissed once, years ago, but now a kiss would be too complicated. There was a charge that could ignite for reasons Michael always wrestled. She was the sister of Jess and he was the man who'd held her through the death of her secret lover. She was still married to a man who took good care of her, and bored her. She had voluptuous curves and predatory eyes.

They went to Via Veneto, an Italian place in Orange. It was Leah's favorite restaurant in the universe. Her husband, Barry, would never take her because the neighborhood was unsafe.

They ordered fried mozzarella and stuffed mushrooms as their appetizers. They were each on their second vodka. Leah was looking at him with melancholy, which lately seemed to be the way she looked at most things. But with Leah it was a soft, somehow complacent form of ennui. He had the sense that she was happy to be with him, even if there was nothing that she wanted.

He told Leah about Anthony's operation and Dani's breakup. He told her Dani had just come back from visiting Jess in Florida. He said, "I called Jess a few weeks ago, just to let her know the details of the surgery. She'd been away somewhere. Barbados. Now she's a diver. She got certified in scuba. Did you know that?"

Leah said, "Yes, she told me she took lessons."

"She goes on dive trips with her girlfriends. The Reef Explorer Girls."

Leah smiled strangely, with a haunting look of empathy. She said, "My little sister always was a diver."

"What do you mean?"

Leah laughed. She said, "Jess always liked to play under her bed. She would take all of her stuffed animals down under there. She would pretend they were all swimming around underwater. I'd say, 'You ass, what are you doing?' Jess would say, 'Leave me alone, I'm having fun.' So I would leave her there, talking to her stuffed animals. It made me mad sometimes. I don't know why. I even once brought my best friend Anne into her bedroom. We both kicked Jess but she still would not come out. And you know once when we were watching TV, Jess and I turned to this program about frogmen. I must have been fourteen, so Jess was ten or so. She said she wanted to marry a tall frogman, or else be one."

Michael said, "Well, I guess she didn't marry a frogman."

Leah said, "Now you know why everything went wrong."

"Do you think she'll find one?" Michael said. "Some nice tall frog-man down in Florida?"

Leah said, "Maybe. Though right now I think she'd rather be alone."

Before the main dishes came, Leah got up to use the bathroom. He watched her walking across the restaurant, her striking figure catching a few eyes. He didn't want to think about her body. He didn't want to think of Jess playing frogman under her childhood bed. He took a sip of his wine and wondered what it was that he was doing. Why did he go out with Leah when he could not have her? Was it Leah or Jess or something else entirely that he wanted?

Leah returned just as the food came. She poured more wine for herself, then poured a glass for Michael. Before she picked up her fork, she took his hand, as she sometimes did.

"You seem upset tonight," she said. "What is it?"

"I'm not sure," Michael said. "I think I'm starting to feel very, very old."

"I wouldn't worry," Leah said gently. "You'll never be as old as me."

She let his hand go, took her fork, and twirled the tines in her bowl of pasta.

"And I'll get older," said Leah. "I'll be a hideous old crone. I'll let my hair grow to my butt. I'll have those crow's-feet by my eyes and tons of regular old wrinkles. Someday I'll even stop plucking out my whiskers. You'd hate to look at me."

"How do you know you'll get so old?"

She smiled, shrugged, and said, "It's something I just know."

"You won't be hideous," he said.

He watched her chewing and sensed that Leah could tell what he was thinking.

She said, "I hope that we'll be friends for a long time."

"But there's more to it."

She said, "Of course there is. And nothing good would come of it."

"You can't be sure."

She said, "Then maybe I'm too exhausted, or just too jaded. So many years of meeting Paul in motels was taxing, to say the least."

He said, "It's not only sex I'm talking about."

"Then what?"

"You know it's more."

She said, "Now listen to me, ex-husband of my sister. Unlike most people, I'm done with love. At least I am until I decide I'm not. I have a husband and three children. I had one true love who's dead, and who I weep for all the time. That doesn't mean I don't enjoy it when you stare at me. It doesn't mean I don't enjoy being adored. I also like you very much, and I like going out to dinner. In certain ways, I think this helps you too."

"Maybe it does, but I want *love*," he said. "I almost don't even know what love is these days. I look at you and it's the most I've ever felt."

"I know," said Leah, and took his hand again.

"You do?"

She said, "I feel it. I appreciate it, too."

He said, "It frightens me. This loneliness. Sometimes I feel so afraid I'm up all night."

"But you're just starting."

"How?"

She kissed his hand and put it down.

"You might have loved Jess but it wasn't the kind of love that ever lasts. I thought you figured it out in college, when you dumped her. Then six months later you got crazy, drove your car over, and said 'Marry me' one cold, rainy, idiotic night on our front doorstep. If I'd been there I would have done my best to stop it. I could have told you that same night it wouldn't work. And I can tell you it would never work with us. This much I'm sure of. But you have time, you know?"

Michael said, "What do I have time for?"

Leah said, "Time enough to wind up being happy. You let it come to you, I promise love will come."

———

A few mornings later, Michael was with a patient in his office. Nan, his receptionist, popped her head in and said, "It's Max. He says it's urgent."

"Tell him I'll call back in ten minutes," Michael said.

"He's at the airport," said Nan. "He says he doesn't have much time."

Michael stepped out of the room and took the phone call.

He said, "Hey Dad, Nan says you're calling from the airport."

"I'm here with Doris," he said. "In Newark."

Michael said, "What are you doing there?"

He said, "We're flying to Las Vegas to get married."

Michael said, "What?"

"We're getting married, in Las Vegas."

"How did you get out of Pine Manor?"

"It's not a jailhouse. I called a cab."

"But Doris falls," Michael said.

"She has her walker."

He said, "You can't just go get married. What does Doris say?"

Max said, "You want me to put her on?"

He said, "We talked about this, Dad. I thought we talked."

"You just informed me that I couldn't marry Doris. That's not a talk."

"I said you'd have to combine Social Security. I informed you that it wasn't in your best interest."

He said, "You think I care about this money? So now we'll lose my nine-hundred-eighty a month. All I've been doing is saving up though I have nothing I need to save for. You do the paying for Pine Manor. What do I need with the extra money?"

He said, "But Dad, that money was for security. In case you get really sick, beyond whatever your health policy can cover. That's why we set up your account."

"I want to marry her," he said. "If I can marry then I'm happy to die tomorrow. Now could you call up the people at Pine Manor?"

Michael said, "Why should I call Pine Manor?"

"I doubt they've noticed we're gone," said Max. "The daytime staff, they're not too bright."

"When are you coming back?"

"Two days. We get back Thursday, at four o'clock. It would be nice if you would meet us at the airport."

"So what did Doris's children say?"

"They never talk. They had a rift."

"Do you have all your medication?"

He said, "Of course. You think I'm nuts?"

"I need to know what flight you're coming back on."

Max said, "United. At four o'clock. It would be great if you could meet us with a wheelchair. You know, for Doris. She gets tired. We have to board now."

Michael said, "See you in two days."

After the phone call, Michael saw three patients. At last his lunch hour came. He called Leah, the only person he knew who might remotely understand his father.

Leah said, "Well, your father always was a lunatic. I remember how he danced around at your wedding. I thought he might have his first heart attack right then."

"I hoped you'd tell me that my father isn't crazy."

Leah said, "No, Max is definitely crazy. He'll wind up losing his monthly check."

"I tried to tell him," Michael said. "He didn't care."

"You can still get it all annulled."

"My dad would shoot me."

She said, "How much is his monthly check?"

"About a thousand."

She said, "Okay, then it's what? You lose twelve thousand or so a year? If he lives ten more years, that's just... a hundred twenty thousand dollars."

"He might live twenty. Should I stop this?"

"I think you already know the answer."

Michael said, "Yeah, I must be out of my mind too."

"Throw him a party," said Leah.

"A party?"

"A little party, at the home. It would be nice."

"Who would come?"

Leah said, "No one. Just all the residents. You and the kids."

"My father likes parties, that's true. How did you know this?"

She said, "I know things. I know Max. And I know you."

+ + +

Long ago, when Michael was a young boy, his father took him into the woods behind the Concord, a resort hotel in the Catskills, where they had gone for a week's vacation. They had been saving for two years for the vacation, and as it turned out, Michael's younger brother got very sick. Half of the week, Daniel was in the hospital with what appeared to be some virulent form of stomach flu.

Michael's father argued that Daniel wasn't sick enough to check into a hospital. He thought they all should just get into the car and drive back to their house in Fair Lawn. But still they stayed in the Catskills the whole week while Daniel vomited. One afternoon Max took Michael into the woods.

It was a cloudy summer day, and when they'd stepped under the shadow of the trees, his father said, "Son, there is a word for what I feel. It is tenebrium, dark and gloomy, from the Latin word *tenebrae*, which is darkness." He said this spookily and held Michael's hand as they walked.

"Life will have woods and it will always have tenebrium," said his father. "You will get lost unless you understand you *can* get lost, you see?"

They kept on walking through the trees. "You have to cross," his father said, his homiletic voice leading them through a thicker section of brush. Michael could never understand his father. But he kept nodding and pushing through the forest. Then they stepped into a small clearing, where a circle of green grass took up the space between the trees.

"And this is it," his father said. "You look for clearings. This is what life is all about. And when they come you stay inside for as long as possible. You look for openings and clearings, in your life."

✦ ✦ ✦

Michael went alone to meet Max and Doris at the airport. Meanwhile his children were busy setting up Pine Manor. They had hung streamers and ribbons from the ceiling. They covered four long tables with white tablecloths. Dani's one brainstorm was the flowers. Bobby's cousin owned a flower shop in Millburn. For a hundred dollars they filled a van with fresh-picked flowers, which they carried into the dining hall in piles, then put the residents to work making garlands and bouquets.

They set a stereo up in the dining room. They found Michael's big-band hit records, Frank Sinatra albums, Cole Porter. They piled flowers on the speakers. They also purchased a large, square, most likely tasteless cake, which Dani covered with purple irises and roses. Before he left, Michael saw all this happening—Dani directing operations like a foreman; Anthony hobbling around on crutches, talking with Len, the manager of Pine Manor. And the ex-boyfriend standing by miraculously. At one point Michael saw them talking, Bobby and Dani, in the hall. Bobby reached out with his finger and moved a strand of hair off Dani's forehead. In that one instant, Michael worried. He wondered whether it was actually possible to break up with one's *b'shert.*

He had a wheelchair waiting at the airport gate. When he saw Doris and his father, he waved and pointed. His father nodded as Doris, using her walker, slowly made her way out of the gate.

In the car they talked nonstop about Las Vegas. They'd gone to dinner after they got married. They'd seen a show. They seemed excited, which was good. Michael had worried they would be tired.

"There was this waterfall," said Doris. "It was a waterfall *inside* our hotel."

"And all those blinking signs," said Max. "It was like being at a space-age Coney Island."

"The food was awful though," said Doris. "And what prices! I had the lamb chops."

They were still talking when Michael pulled into the driveway of Pine Manor. He went around back, to the rear entrance. There were some flowers hanging from the eaves.

"That's very nice," Doris said.

Michael stepped out, peeked once inside. Then he helped Doris from the car. He got her walker out. He opened the door. Doris stepped up and went into the building.

"There's a surprise for you inside," he told his father.

"I need surprises?"

He said, "We're throwing you a party."

Max said, "You're kidding. That's very nice." He said, "Hey, Doris"—but she was already inside. Max turned to Michael, his face beaming with the delight of a little boy. He even seemed somewhat shy, but clearly thrilled to be coming home to a celebration. "What a good day this is," said Max. "I know a good day when it feels like I woke up sometime last week."

Michael helped him in and then heard one of his Frank Sinatra albums. They followed Doris and her walker down the hall. They turned the corner and saw the flowers festooned all around the lobby. Michael saw Doris whisper something to his father. Max just nodded and continued walking forward. Soon all the Pine Manor staff and residents were around them, kissing Doris and patting Max on the back. Max's best friend in the home, Hiram, actually wept when they shook hands. Finally Max yelled out, "So, I am insane! Here's Doris Rubin!"

Later, after the party, which didn't last long, Michael was downstairs cleaning up with Dani. His father and Doris had gone upstairs. They were both tired and were resting in their own rooms. Anthony was sitting on a couch in the TV room with his bad leg up. He was watching a Jacques Cousteau special with several residents of the home.

At one point, Michael stepped into the TV room. He saw two divers moving through a school of yellow fish. "Take five," he called to

Dani. Dani walked in and they sat with Anthony to watch the last bit of the program. "Could you massage my neck?" she asked, and then sat down on the floor in front of him. Michael massaged his daughter's neck as they watched a sea turtle gliding past the divers. For the first time in what seemed like eons, he felt calm.

DINOSAURS

September 1982

JULIETTE WAS STANDING on the smooth asphalt of a driveway in Roseland's expensive new development, Shale Hill. Only one group of houses had been completed. Beyond the driveway, she saw construction sites for two or three new homes. Beyond that, it still looked like a rock quarry. The former quarry had been closed now for two years.

She'd never known what kind of rocks they excavated, but she had heard about the dinosaur footprints. The shale in Shale Hill was filled with them. Supposedly, there were still dinosaur footprints everywhere. When the construction first got under way, teams of geologists had raced out and hauled off the fossilized footprints by the dozens. Teams came from everywhere—Australia, Israel, Finland. Juliette read all about it in the paper. The funny thing was that the Essex County Parks Museum had collected hundreds of footprint specimens, most of which were piled in wooden bins in the basement. Back in grade school, Juliette's class once took a field trip to the museum. They had so many dinosaur footprints that every kid in the class was given one to take home.

She saw her boyfriend, Tommy Lange, walking up the driveway with his friend Nate. She had driven her own car to the party and had been waiting. She was wearing only a T-shirt and a skirt, and she felt cold.

It was September and the school year had just started. Again she wondered what she was doing dating Tommy. What need he filled and whether this need was useful. At times she found herself amazed to be in Livingston. She didn't fit here, Juliette knew. Tommy seemed to know it too. Lately he'd started calling her Kryla, after some evil ice queen alien he had read about in a comic book. Kryla could disappear anytime she wanted, snap her fingers and wind up in another galaxy.

Juliette's father was talking again of leaving. He kept on saying they were going to head out West. Juliette imagined things like rock bridges and river canyons and wolf howls. She would imagine herself becoming someone different. Or else she just imagined herself vanishing.

"I'm fucking freezing!" she yelled to Tommy.

"Then why the hell are you wearing a fucking skirt?"

She said, "For you, so can you stare at my damn ass. Where the hell were you?"

"Getting a keg," he said, and pointed down the steep incline of the driveway. "Here it comes."

A black Trans Am turned in and barreled up the driveway. She was prepared to dive aside, but then the car screeched abruptly to a stop. Toby Williamson, the driver, rolled down his window and spat onto the driveway. He said, "Yo, helmets. Get over here and help me with this keg."

A girl got out of Toby's car. She was a tenth-grader, Laura Bennett. Juliette wondered what she was doing with Toby Williamson. He popped the trunk and then Tommy lifted the keg onto the driveway. He and Nate carried it inside.

When Toby went to park his car, he left Laura standing on the driveway. Juliette walked over and said, "Hey, don't you go out with Jeff Holloway?"

She seemed surprised Juliette knew her. Her hot pink lipstick was smeared all around her mouth.

She said, "We broke up, today."

"What did he do?"

Laura said, "Nothing, we broke up because I dumped him."

Jeff was a diver, Juliette remembered. A wiry short guy who did flips and twists and always looked like he was squinting. He was also slightly famous in school for doing back flips during homeroom. People would ask him, so he did them. He would just stand up, do a back flip in his loafers, and then sit down.

"Why did you dump him?" Juliette asked.

Laura said, "Well, because I started dating Toby."

"Then you're a fool."

"Why?"

Inside her head Juliette pictured Jeff Holloway. She'd always found Jeff interesting and sexy. He kept to himself and didn't seem to care what anyone else thought of him. He also had amazing muscles on his chest.

"Jeff's a great guy," Juliette said. "Toby's an asshole."

Laura said, "Maybe I like assholes."

"Take it from me," Juliette said. "You should get over it."

"Why?"

"You'll find out soon enough."

Inside the party, Tommy was punching walls in. Meanwhile Toby and Nate had taken a pile of albums from the stereo. They were making "smash hits" by flinging them against some wooden basement cabinets. It was a junior named Jason Beck's house. He went to Livingston, Juliette knew, but now he lived with his rich father just over the Roseland line. She'd heard his father was away on business somewhere in Europe. If Jason had any brains at all, he would be calling the police right now.

She stood with Laura and watched the boys.

Toby yelled, "Styx, a bunch of fucking fairies!"

"I kind of like that one song 'Babe,'" Laura said.

"You would," Toby said, and hurled the record like a Frisbee. It hit the wall and seemed to burst into a thousand shards of vinyl.

Juliette walked over to Tommy, who was now standing more or less motionless with his arms crossed. He and Nate did this a lot. The idea was to trick people into looking at them funny, or maybe saying something, then body-slam the person to the ground.

"Another DABS party?" she said.

She kissed Tommy, although he still had not moved.

"You want a beer?" she said.

He nodded. "Keg's in the kitchen," he said, but remained frozen with his arms folded over his chest.

Juliette walked across the finished basement. The room was huge, more like a ballroom in a catering hall. At least a hundred people were inside and the room still did not seem crowded. She climbed the stairs and found herself in a living room. She saw a silver, white-carpeted spiral staircase and a big picture window that looked out on next door's construction. She saw a single bluish light that glowed somewhere on the far side of the former quarry. She thought of dinosaurs moving out there, shadowy ghosts the size of buildings. And for some reason, the idea filled her with emotion. For some reason, the idea made her happy.

They'd put the keg on the kitchen floor, right over a fancy inlay of tiles. A bunch of people were sitting around the table, playing quarters. Others were milling around with beers. She saw one tall boy with a goatee and somehow knew this was Jason Beck. He held a cigarette and looked nervous, though he was desperately trying to act cool.

Juliette crouched down by the keg. Someone above her gave the tap a few pumps, then walked away before she had even started to fill her cup. The beer was foamy, so she pumped it herself. She grew aware of her ass sticking out behind her. She pulled it in and stared down at the mosaic of colored tiles. She thought of dinosaurs again and almost smiled at the fact that they kept coming into her head.

She felt a finger touch her shoulder and said, "One second. I'm almost done."

She spilled some foam out and stood up. She turned around and found herself ten inches from her neighbor, Anthony Rubin.

He was on crutches still, from his accident. He was wearing baggy brown pants with a drawstring, and the leg that had the cast looked like a log. His hair was longer than it had been before the summer, and he'd lost weight. Even his face had gotten skinnier. Surprised to see him, she said, "Hi. Was that you tapping on my shoulder?"

Anthony nodded. He said, "I saw you. I just wanted to say hello."

He smiled and Juliette could tell he was not afraid of her. She wondered what he had done with her cross necklace.

"So how's your knee?" she said. "I heard you hurt it."

He said, "It's healing."

"Will it be better in time for hockey?"

He shook his head and leaned forward on his crutches.

She said, "Too bad."

"I saw that Tommy's here."

"Hard to miss Tommy," she said. "So who are you here with? Some doting manager of the hockey team?"

He said, "I came with my friend Craig and his girlfriend, Vicki Coleman. They're in Craig's car though. They've been out there for an hour."

"Well, can I get you a beer or something? It must be hard to do anything with those crutches."

He said, "I'm taking Tylenol with codeine."

"So?"

"I shouldn't drink."

"Then you should hold one, at least. Girls always like to talk with guys on crutches who have beers."

He said, "Okay," and shifted his weight back again.

She turned to put her own beer down. She grabbed a cup and crouched beside the keg to fill it up. Anthony stepped up behind her, leaned down over his crutches, and started pumping. She said, "You really don't have to do that. You're not even going to drink it." He kept pumping. When she had filled the cup, she rose and said, "You've lost a lot of weight."

He said, "I know. It's from the surgery. Lately I'm trying to eat like crazy."

"Well then, keep eating," she said. "I have to go."

"I'll be around if you get bored," he said. "I might have to wait all night for Craig and Vicki."

Juliette laughed, though somewhat nervously. She recalled her vow to stay away from him.

She said, "Okay, maybe I'll find you if Tommy gets too drunk to talk."

She walked away and felt quite sure that she and Anthony would not speak again that night.

✦ ✦ ✦

A little later there was a band. It was "Eclipse," a bunch of tenth-graders. They set their amps up in the basement and started pounding out songs that sounded all the same, guitars and drums completely drowning out the singer.

"These guys are amateurs," said Tommy.

Juliette said, "Yeah, they're in tenth grade."

"They fucking suck. I want to kill the drummer."

Tommy was obviously drunk. He and Nate had each downed five or six shots of tequila. Juliette kissed him and said, "I think it's time to go upstairs."

She got him out past Nate and through a crowd of people dancing in the basement. They went upstairs and then up the spiral staircase. The stairs ended at a long shag-carpeted hallway.

They searched around until they found the master bedroom. It had a king-size bed with a satin canopy, a big-screen TV, and fake Greek columns in two corners. It had oak floors and Persian area rugs. Artwork covered the walls and dresser. Juliette said, "Wow, this is just like my room at home."

"Watch this," Tommy said.

He took a night table and heaved it at a full-length wall mirror. The mirror shattered and one leg of the table broke as it crashed down to the floor.

"That must have cost a lot," she said.

She quickly walked back to the bedroom door and locked it.

"What about this?" Tommy said, and took a painting off the wall. "You think it's worth much?"

She said, "It's hideous. I can't believe anyone would've paid more than five cents."

She felt a pang of guilt as he heaved the painting against another full-length mirror. She also felt unbelievably aroused.

"Do something," he said.

"What?"

"Break something."

Juliette picked up a blown-glass vase and threw it. It shattered against a wall.

"Good thing that music's so loud," she said.

"Why?"

"No one can hear us," she said, and wondered if Tommy's brain was bigger than a pea.

"Break something else," he said.

"Why?"

He said, "I like it."

Juliette took a crystal elephant from a dresser. She threw it hard at Tommy's chest and he said, "Shit!" as it bounced off him. It hit the floor and then lost most of its crystal trunk.

She said, "Come on, Tommy. Me."

Tommy said, "What?"

"You can do anything you want."

He said, "You know I have a tough time when I'm shitfaced."

"Then you can kiss me," she said. "How about that?"

"It's not the same."

Juliette said, "Christ. I might as well go fuck Nate."

She turned to leave the room, but Tommy grabbed her. He lifted Juliette from behind and rammed her into the nearest bedroom wall. She felt his chest holding her up, crushing her back while he took his pants down. He slid her underpants down and they were ripping. She felt his hands gripping her ass, lifting her skirt, spreading her legs. She felt him trying to put himself inside her, three or four times, but it didn't work.

+ + +

When they went downstairs Tommy quickly vanished, as expected. She didn't bother looking around for him. She just leaned up against the wall and watched the band. She noticed a bunch of people dancing. She saw that Anthony was engaged in something slightly stupid—dancing around on one leg with his crutches. A petite, attractive girl danced near him, but by her posture and the distance between their bodies, Juliette knew this was the girlfriend of his friend.

Juliette waited for Anthony to stop dancing. She watched him crutch off from the dance floor and lean up against a wall. The girl now danced with the boy who was undoubtedly her boyfriend.

Juliette saw that Anthony was leaving. He was crutching his way toward the basement stairs. She watched him put both crutches in one hand and use the banister to walk up without putting weight on his knee. He was methodical and careful now, unlike when he was dancing. It took forever to ascend the fifteen steps.

Juliette followed him, assuming she would find him in the kitchen. But when she got there, she saw Nate, Toby, Laura, and Jeff Holloway, the diver. Tommy was there as well. He stood leaning against the edge of a kitchen counter.

"Do a flip," Toby was saying. Juliette realized Jeff Holloway was cornered. He wouldn't do one, although Laura said, "Just do it! Please, I'm sorry!" Jeff didn't look at his former girlfriend. Toby said, "Do a fucking flip or I'll flip you out that picture window."

Juliette could see where this was going. She was about to leave the room when Tommy saw her and said, "Juliette, check this out. We're gonna make this little diver shit do a flip."

She saw Jeff Holloway's foot sail forward and connect squarely with Toby's balls. He doubled over and Jeff Holloway drove his knee into Toby's face. Toby went down as both Tommy and Nate sprang up and went for Jeff. Nate sent a fist into Jeff's head, then slammed him hard to the floor as he staggered backward. Tommy picked Jeff up and threw him against a wall while Laura screamed.

Juliette stayed quiet at first. She leaned against a kitchen cabinet and felt numb. Something was happening to her now, something she knew she was not in control of. It was like crying, but the tears would not come out of her. She felt like someone else was crying very deep inside her body.

She crossed the room, behind the tumult. Somebody's blood was all over the kitchen tiles. She kept on walking, found a door, and pulled it open. She pushed a storm door out and stepped outside.

She crossed a raised wooden patio. She followed wooden stairs down onto a back lawn. There were no woods behind the yard, just an expanse of flat cleared land and then a hill that sloped down into the former quarry. She saw the same blue light she'd seen when she was staring out the picture window. She felt as if she could be anywhere, any time or place—as if she were looking out onto a landscape of centuries ago.

Juliette sat on the cold grass. She felt it touching her bare legs. She pulled her skirt as far down her thighs as it would go. She remembered going to the Essex County Parks Museum. She had not cared at all about the dinosaurs or their footprints. She remembered taking a footprint home, throwing it outside in the shrubbery beds, as if were an ordinary rock.

"Juliette?" someone called.

She turned her head. The voice was far too gentle to be Tommy's. She saw the silhouette of a body and two crutches on the porch. She saw him hopping down the steps, holding the railing. She noticed that the music from the band had stopped.

He crossed the grass with rapid, long strides of his crutches. With each stride he swung them forward almost to the point of falling down. But then the crutches would plant and his whole body would arc toward them. She'd never seen anything as wildly graceful as the sight of her neighbor moving toward her full speed on his crutches.

He said, "I saw you go out. Are you okay?"

Anthony came to a stop next to her. He breathed rapidly.

She said, "Why wouldn't I be okay?"

"Tommy and Nate and their other friend took off," he said. "And someone called the police."

"Is that kid Jeff alive?"

"Yeah, although his face looks pretty bad."

She said, "I hate these goddamn DABS parties."

"What's a DABS party?"

She said, "It stands for Drink And Break Shit. It's Tommy's favorite kind of party."

Juliette stood and saw that the lighted kitchen was now empty. She could hear cars pulling away—people absconding before the police appeared. She had the sense that she and Anthony were in some place they'd never find again. She touched his face and said, "Why are you here?"

He said, "I saw you go out. And I just thought..."

"You thought what?"

He said, "I saw you..."

She moved her mouth toward his and kissed him. She stepped up closer, between his crutches, and was relieved when he leaned against her. She felt his mouth come to life in the way it hadn't beside the wolf cage, but he still would not touch her with his hands. They kept on kissing and soon she realized that the problem was the crutches. She realized Anthony was not touching her because he could not move much. She also sensed that for the moment he was trusting her.

She said, "You're like a great big dinosaur, you know that?"

He said, "How?"

She said, "I'm not sure. You just are."

She heard a door slam and then someone was on the deck. She saw him walk out to the rail and said, "Oh shit" under her breath. At first she felt positive it was Tommy. When the boy lit a cigarette, Juliette practically collapsed in her relief.

She said, "That's Jason Beck, our host. We'd better go. I have my car."

"You'll drive me home?"

She said, "Yes."

"I should tell Craig."

"You should tell no one."

"But he might worry."

"Then you can let him stay up all night."

He said, "My coat's in Craig's car."

"I'm leaving right now. Do whatever you feel like doing."

She hoped like hell that he would follow, because she needed him. She started walking across the yard, staring down at the blue light across the quarry. When she had taken maybe five steps she looked back. He was still standing there. Before she knew what she was saying, she yelled, "Jesus Christ, Anthony, *come on!*"

He said, "Okay," and thrust his crutches forward. Juliette felt something she had never felt before. She felt a person moving toward her, a person frightened by this movement but still moving. She watched him move and for the first time in her life felt something sacred. When he caught up to her she turned and walked beside him, saying nothing.

She put her arm around his back but he moved too fast, so she just followed him. Anthony stopped where the yard ended. He turned and said, "So where's your car?"

When she caught up to him, she kissed him again and knew they weren't playing. Now they were close to the thing they'd wanted. Close to this thing that had seemed impossible. All of a sudden it seemed so easy that she stirred with trepidation. She felt afraid to move or speak for fear of entering and passing through—whatever this was—too quickly.

JULIETTE WAKES
ANTHONY AT DAWN

Fall 1982 — Winter 1983

JULIETTE WAS NOT his girlfriend. From the start Anthony knew that this was something else entirely. Sometimes she visited him at his locker in the morning. She'd stand by talking to him and holding his hand in ways no one could see. When she walked past him in school with Tommy Lange, she'd flash a smile but barely look at him. Each day when Tommy began practice, she'd pick him up near the school's side entrance and drive him home.

Dani was off at college, so Anthony had taken her downstairs bedroom. He planned to stay there until he was off crutches. No one was home after school. His father rarely came home before seven. Dani's bed was low — a queen-size mattress and a box spring but no bed frame. Juliette could sit on the floor and help him take his pants off. She'd slide them carefully over his full-leg cast, then fling them back over her shoulder.

Juliette was rough with him, yet careful. Careful and rough was how she kissed him, how she touched him, how she moved over him when they maneuvered into either of the two functional positions they'd discovered. The more erotic way was standing, Juliette bent over Dani's desktop, Anthony balanced on one leg. Or he could lie back on his bed, the bad leg propped up on two pillows. This way was actually much harder, but he liked staring into Juliette's dark eyes.

She'd make him eat all the time, since he had lost weight following the surgery. Sometimes she'd even drive out to the Village Bakery. She would come back with a half-dozen chocolate éclairs. Roger would follow her around. She wouldn't feed Roger éclairs, but she would give him plenty of dog biscuits or carrots. Roger loved carrots the way zoo elephants love peanuts. He went crazy if you gave him a whole carrot. He was a pound dog. He was old. He'd had a secret life or two and he loved carrots. Juliette found this quirk of Roger's remarkable. Each time she walked in and Roger jumped all over her, her first words would be, "Roger, want a carrot?"

Roger also seemed to know when they were screwing. Most of the time he was fine alone, but when they had sex Roger would always get upset if they locked him out. He'd scratch the door and pound his head. Anthony figured this was because all of their human noises scared him. Juliette guessed Roger just thought it was time to play. But neither theory seemed to work. They'd let him into the room and he'd sleep quietly in a corner. He wouldn't look at them or want any attention. He would just lie there, happy to be near them. When they were finished, he'd pick his head up. If Roger heard his name, he'd jump up on the bed.

Anthony found that he could have sex as much as Juliette would allow it. And she allowed it. All the time. She seemed delighted by his stamina and interest. The problem was that it got addicting. Sometimes when Juliette wasn't with him he would feel panicky and his stomach would get knotted. When she was out on dates with Tommy, he would feel sick. One night when she returned from a date he went outside and threw stones at her window. She came out wearing sweatpants and a nightshirt. Anthony said, "I'm all confused. You have to tell me what this is." She kissed him softly and pulled his head against her. "I was with Tommy," she said. "You know exactly what we do and that it's nothing to get upset about."

A few nights later, he was surprised to hear Juliette knocking on his window after midnight. He let her in and she explained that she was nervous because her father was out gambling. He led her into Dani's room and she lay in bed beside him until dawn.

In school that morning, at his locker, he felt afraid of her. He had her necklace on and Juliette slid her hand beneath his shirt. She said, "What's wrong?" and started playing with the necklace. He took her hand away and said, "You're like a test." Juliette asked what kind of test—did he mean essay or just fill-in-the-blank questions? "Essay," he said, but knew she understood the meaning of the statement. She was a test of his strength, will, and his ability to let go.

Anthony finally got his cast off in late September. Although by then he had gained back his normal body weight, most of the muscle in his right leg had disappeared. The skin was sickly white yet covered with hair much darker and longer than on the other one. There were still sores where the fifteen staples had been. He could not bend the knee at all.

He started seeing a physical therapist three times a week right after school. His father said he'd arrange for rides, but Anthony said a friend had volunteered to take him. Who was the friend? his father asked. He made a name up. Larry Gelb. If he said someone like Craig Kelby he knew his father would call to thank Craig's parents. So every Monday, Wednesday, and Friday, Juliette would drive him to see a private physical therapist out on Northfield. Juliette read magazines while waiting and always acted like his girlfriend.

He would go into a small room and lie prone on a padded table. With almost violent force, the therapist would push and attempt to bend the knee. Anthony sometimes yelled and screamed until his throat was raw. He would hear scar tissue popping and sometimes worry it was his ligament. But eventually he'd feel the euphoric rush of endorphins, and, incredibly, the pain would disappear.

On the last bend of each session, the therapist would take out his little tool, a goniometer. He would measure the furthest angle to which

Anthony could bend. Each week he gained a few degrees. He would have full range of motion by late winter if all went well. At home each day he would lie prone, hook a belt around his heel, and pull. Because of the pain, he could not pull as hard as the therapist. Sometimes he'd ask Juliette to push and not to worry while he made all sorts of noises. Besides the therapist, his parents, and maybe Dani, Juliette was the only person who'd ever heard him scream his head off. She often ribbed him, but the screaming did not ever seem to upset her.

He lifted weights with his leg to rebuild his muscles. He was supposed to lift weights three times a day. Instead he lifted weights six, seven, sometimes a dozen times a day. He watched his muscles get bigger week by week, but never big enough. He watched the red vertical scar on his knee turn pink.

He still used crutches, but now he wore a metal knee brace. He didn't take it off, except when he took a shower. One afternoon, when he was rolling around with Juliette, the knee brace cut her. She wound up bleeding from a gash on her leg and went home wearing a strip of Band-Aids.

He tried to get her to read the poetry of William Carlos Williams. She didn't read, she said, but she would listen when he read to her. He read "The Great Figure" and "The Red Wheelbarrow" and several other poems he'd recently come to love.

"I know one poem," Juliette said. "You want to hear it?"

Anthony nodded and then she spoke with an affected, funny attempt at a British accent. Juliette said:

> *Cold hearted orb that rules the night*
> *Removes the colors from our sight*
> *Red is gray and yellow white*
> *But we decide which is right*
> *And which is an illusion*

He said, "What's that?"

She said, "The Moody Blues. I'm horny."

She took her shirt off and unhooked her bra. Her breasts spilled out before his eyes.

"Wait," he said.

"What?"

"Could you say that poem again? I liked it."

"You're such a weirdo," Juliette said. She put her hand on his cheek and gazed into his eyes dramatically. She said the words again without the British accent. When she was finished Anthony felt sure that he loved her.

They sometimes argued, of course. She would come out with things. Why was he such a spoiled brat? Why was he not more aware of how damn easy his whole life was? One day she asked why he never talked to his friend Jay Berkowitz. "How the hell do you know Jay Berkowitz?" Anthony asked her. She said she'd met him last fall, the night she planned to watch his hockey game but didn't. She said, "We broke into the zoo to see the tapir. Don't ask me why."

"You and Jay broke into the zoo?"

She said, "I happened to run into him. He's a lunatic and made me see the tapir. He also told me all about you. So why the hell aren't you friends?"

"We just trailed off," Anthony said. "Now his family moved to West Orange."

She said, "That isn't the real reason. Did you guys fight?"

He told her, "No."

"Then what's the reason?"

"Our parents had an affair."

"That's still a crappy reason not to be friends with him."

"His mother hangs up if I call."

"You're both dumb idiots," Juliette said. "But I forgot that all you Jew-boys always listen to your parents."

"It isn't that," Anthony said.

"Okay, what is it?"

He didn't have another answer. He said, "I guess we just trailed off."

One afternoon after school in late fall, Juliette drove out to Shale

Hill, the new development in Roseland, where two months before they had kissed at a wild party and stayed up most of the night talking in her car. She said she wanted to look down at the former quarry. She pulled up to a spot just beyond the most recent construction site. Then she told Anthony that lately she had been thinking about the dinosaurs. She said the fact that New Jersey once had dinosaurs astounded her. He had assumed she'd parked the car so they could neck. He tried to kiss her. Juliette took his hand and said, "Hey porn star, not right now."

On the way back, he made her stop at a bookstore by the traffic circle. His secret plan was to buy her a book about dinosaurs. He left her browsing the 1983 calendars while he sought help from a store clerk. As it turned out, there were no dinosaur books for readers beyond the age of six.

"What are we doing here?" she asked, when he returned after twenty minutes. Anthony disclosed his failed plan. She said, "That's sweet," and held a bag up. She said, "I wound up getting you something. It was just $3.99 on the sale table." Juliette handed him the bag and he pulled out Sir Thomas Malory's *Le Morte d'Arthur*.

She said, "You're just like that knight, Lancelot. You can't resist me even though you tried to. And I'm like Guinevere, the queen. Well, you know, sort of."

"How do you know about King Arthur?" Anthony asked her.

"I saw the movie on TV."

"*Excalibur*?"

"No, the old one."

"You mean the musical? With that totally awful theme song?"

"Don't remind me," Juliette said. "I liked that song about the lusty month of May though. And I was looking at this. Wait."

She grabbed the book back and leafed through until she found the page she wanted.

"This popped right out when I opened it. The whole chapter's about the month of May and lust. Who would have thought that song came from a real book, but there it is. It kind of thrilled me."

Anthony looked and saw a two-page chapter entitled "How true love is likened to summer." He read it all while Juliette stood watching.

The same night, Anthony saw her leaving with Tommy Lange at dinnertime. From his upstairs bedroom window, he kept on watching for her return. A big black boat of a car pulled up at one point. Two men got out and went inside. They stayed for close to half an hour and then drove off.

It was near ten when Tommy dropped her off. Anthony saw them kiss goodbye—a very short kiss—and then Juliette went inside. Five minutes later she was barreling out of her garage in her mother's Chevy. Her dad was with her, but Juliette was driving. He watched the car race down the street and he felt panic filling his heart.

She returned long after midnight. He wasn't sleeping. He heard the car. As he debated the pros and cons of throwing stones again, Juliette tapped lightly on his window. He let her in and they tiptoed back into the bedroom.

Juliette sat down on the bed and put her hand over her mouth. She started crying, trembling and shaking, her hand still over her mouth so that she wouldn't wake his father. He didn't know what to do. He just stayed near her and caressed her. She pressed her mouth into his chest.

When she was calmer she just sat there with tears running down her cheek. He said, "What is it? What the hell happened?"

She said, "I had to take my father to the hospital. They beat him up and something ruptured. I think that maybe he could have died."

"Who beat him up?" he said.

"The loan sharks. He owes money again, I guess."

"Money for what?"

She said, "He must have borrowed money for whatever he couldn't pay."

"So did he pay the loan sharks back?"

She said, "He must have paid them some."

"I thought your father wasn't in the Mafia."

"He isn't," Juliette said. "He's just dumb enough to borrow money from these loan sharks. Any fool can manage that."

"Is he staying in the hospital?"

Juliette said, "Yes. He'll be okay though. That's what the doctor said."

"I'm sorry."

"I'm cracking up," she said. "I *never* cry. I don't know what I'm doing."

"You can stay here," Anthony said. "And I'll just be here if you need me."

"Okay, I need you," Juliette said. "God, I need you."

He wrapped his arms around her body. Juliette wept softly, on and off, for about an hour. After that she just seemed drained. She curled up next to him, her face against his chest, and talked in whispers. They talked until the morning twilight began seeping around the window shade. Then she dressed quietly and slipped out of the house.

✦ ✦ ✦

The first and only time Anthony set foot inside her house was in December. Juliette called on a Sunday evening. She said, "Come over here right away," so he walked over with his crutches. She let him in and said, "Look, I'm really sorry. I have to go get my father and I want you to come with me. I'm kind of scared though it's not dangerous, I promise."

She said her father was down in Atlantic City. At first Anthony assumed he'd been arrested for drunk driving. He said, "This happened to my mother once. They might not let him out of jail until the morning."

But Vince Dimiglio hadn't been arrested. Juliette told him that her father had temporarily lost his Cadillac in a card game. Now he was waiting at the bus station with no money. He still had to pay someone back. He'd called to tell her that she could find a pile of cash under his mattress. He'd pay the money he owed and get his car back. Then they'd drive home.

On the drive down, Juliette smoked cigarette after cigarette. In an attempt to cut the smell, Anthony kept her cinnamon broom on the floor beneath his seat. He'd never been to Atlantic City. He imagined glitzy casinos and Vince Dimiglio holding a big cigar. He wondered whether his own father had ever gambled. He also wondered if his father knew he'd lied to him. He had left messages at the office and at the hospital. He said he'd gone to a Devils game with Larry Gelb.

Vincent Dimiglio, as planned, was waiting at the bus station. He seemed nervous. When he saw Anthony and his crutches, his first words were, "Who the hell is this?"

"Anthony Rubin," she said. "Our neighbor."

"Jesus H. Christ," he said, but seemed too exhausted to get angry.

Juliette said, "I needed someone for the ride."

A few miles inland, they made a stop at a dark and seedy-looking motel. There Vince Dimiglio dropped off the money he still owed. When he came out again, he held his car keys. He said, "They put it in the Tropicana's parking garage." He pulled five one-hundred-dollar bills out of the envelope Juliette had brought him. "You keep this," he said. "Besides ten dollars for the tolls, it's all the money I have till Friday. And if I ask for it back by the casino, you either drive away or shoot me in the head."

Juliette nodded. She took the money. She said, "Pop, are we okay?"

He said, "We're fine, Julie."

"You look like shit."

"Just get me to my car and we'll hit the road."

They drove to the Tropicana Hotel and casino. Its towers rose above the Atlantic City boardwalk. Beyond the buildings Anthony saw the darkness of the ocean. He saw the moon in the sky above it but no stars. He worried because situations like this in movies did not end well. In a movie, Vince Dimiglio would have to kill someone to get the car back. Or else he'd wind up getting shot himself. But to Anthony's relief, Mr. Dimiglio was gone less than ten minutes before emerging from the parking garage. His big black Cadillac seemed fine. He blinked his lights as he pulled in front of Juliette. She put her car in gear and followed her father back to the Atlantic City Expressway. They stayed behind him until they got onto the Parkway.

A little more than an hour later, Juliette decided she was hungry. So she pulled off at the next exit, which was Long Branch. They found a Friendly's. They hugged and nuzzled in the car for a few minutes, after which they went inside and took a booth.

Juliette said, "So, what can we order for five hundred dollars?"

"I'll have the Fishamajig," said Anthony.

Juliette smiled and said, "What the hell's a Fishamajig?"

"I always order it," he said. "It's a fish sandwich, with cheese and tartar sauce."

Juliette said, "Good, I'll have one too."

A short while after they had ordered, while they were sipping their drinks and waiting for their Fishamajigs, Anthony told her they were near Allenhurst, the town where they used to rent a shore house with Jay Berkowitz's family. He said the shore was where he had first kissed a girl. And it was where his father once taught them the Yiddish constellations. He said, "One night, when we were sitting on the porch. The sky was filled with stars but no one knew them. So then he made things up like Sophie the Kvetch and Maury the Disappointment. I still know where those fake constellations are."

Juliette smiled and leaned across the table. She kissed his cheek and said, "I love the way you hold things."

Anthony felt like his whole body was made of liquid. He took a breath and said, "I think that I love...you."

"No you don't," Juliette said, and seemed alarmed.

He said, "Why not?"

She said, "Oh Christ. Because you *can't*."

"Why can't I love you?"

"You're not allowed."

"Don't you love me?" Anthony asked.

Juliette stared with a pained look of compassion that bewildered him.

"No," she said.

She leaned across again and kissed him very gently.

"No?" he said.

"I don't love anyone."

"But I can feel it."

"Then you're deluded."

He said, "But Juliette..."

"What? I told you this. Something's wrong with me, remember?"

He said, "But you and I..."

"What?"

Right then the waitress appeared. She put their Fishamajig sandwich platters down in front of them. After she left, Juliette got up to use the bathroom. Words started racing through his head—thoughts such as: Juliette never was my girlfriend. Thoughts such as: dinosaurs and cold hearted orb and how true love is likened to summer. When she came back, he still hadn't touched his Fishamajig. She said, "Oh well, we've lost our appetites." She paid the check with a one-hundred-dollar bill. Then they drove home.

Two evenings later, when Anthony was still wondering what the fallout of their awful meal at Friendly's was, Juliette called him from a pay phone. "What are you doing?" she asked. He told her, "Nothing." She said she wanted to grab a bite and would pick him up in his driveway in an hour.

She arrived after only forty minutes. He was upstairs in his own room and wasn't watching for her yet. His dad was downstairs playing clarinet. Anthony heard the music stop abruptly. He heard his father climbing the stairs and then his footsteps in the hallway. After a knock, his father stepped into the room.

"There's someone here to pick you up," he said. "Out in the driveway."

Anthony nodded.

His father said, "It looks like Larry Gelb."

He felt a whirling sense of confusion—half of it coming from his

own need to lie, the other half from his father's not-yet-discernible reaction. Then the sensation passed and Anthony felt surprisingly un-
guilty. He said, "I didn't want you knowing. I'm not sure why."

"It's very nice of her to take you to your therapy."

"Juliette is nice," he said. "She's much nicer than you'd think. Also,
her dad isn't really in the Mafia. People just think that. Can we talk
about this later?"

"Where are you going?" his father asked.

"To get a bite somewhere. I doubt we'll be out long."

"Take some money," he said, and handed Anthony twenty dollars.
"I'd like to hear more about this when you get home."

He crutched downstairs and out the door. He heard his father re-
sume playing his clarinet. He made his way across the porch and down
the three cement porch steps. As he approached Juliette's car he saw Jay
Berkowitz sitting in the passenger seat. He waved, confused. Jay
shrugged his shoulders. "I had this idea last month," Juliette said, as she
helped Anthony into the backseat of her Chevy. He stretched his leg
across the seat and moved the broom.

She walked around and got into the driver's seat.

Jay said, "I had no idea what she was up to."

"What is she up to?"

Juliette began backing down the driveway. She said, "I just thought
it was time that you two talked."

"She called and asked whether I wanted to get *pizza*," said Jay. "I
haven't eaten, so I met her by the rink. She didn't say she was taking me
to your house. And how the hell should I know that you were *dating*?"

"We aren't dating," Anthony said.

Juliette made a right on Tiffany.

"Well she just said you were and I have to say you're crazy. Roland
Malnick..."

Juliette yelled, "Hey! Can you shut up about Roland Malnick?
Tommy's not hiding under the seat, okay? If I hear Roland Malnick's
name again I'll..."

"What? Will you beat us up?"

Juliette said, "Look. We're just going to get pizza."

"You said we're dating?" Anthony asked her.

"I told him 'sort of.' Jesus, aren't we?"

"We've never had an official date."

Juliette said, "What the hell does 'dating' mean? No one *dates*, for God's sake. It's just a word."

Jay turned around in the front seat and stared at Anthony. He said, "You're crazy. I mean, you're out of your goddamn mind. I know we haven't talked for like six decades, but you should really think about how nuts you are."

"Hey!" Juliette yelled. "Would you like to get out of this car and walk home?"

Jay said, "No thank you."

"Then shut up."

Jay said, "Just don't go to Bonvini's or any other place in Livingston."

"Maybe we'll go have pizza in Bergen County."

"That would be fine," Jay said. "Although you'd have to take the Parkway. There are tolls."

"How about Millburn?" Anthony suggested. "There's that good pizza place next door to the golf range. My mother always used to bring us there."

Jay said, "Oh *yeah*. I remember going there that time your mother took us to the flea market."

Juliette said, "Fine, we'll have pizza in Millburn. Someone direct me."

"Just take Mount Pleasant," Anthony said, and placed his left hand on her shoulder. "Go toward West Orange. When we get down the hill we'll tell you where to turn."

They drove across the South Mountain Reservation. When they came out in the town of Millburn, Anthony directed them to the pizza place. By then they'd figured out it was called Pompeii. Anthony had not been there in five years, possibly longer. He found it next to the Millburn driving range, exactly where he thought it was. Only Pompeii was now a home appliance store. They were all starving, so they ate at the golf range snack bar.

They had hot dogs with sauerkraut and mustard. Then Juliette paid four dollars for a bucket of fifty golf balls. She brought three drivers and the balls back to the table. She said, "And what? Do we just hit them? What's the point of that?"

Jay said, "It's golf. I think there isn't any point when it comes down to it."

They all tried driving, which proved comical. Both Juliette and Jay kept hitting spastic grounders. Some of Juliette's drives went no more than ten feet. Leaning his weight on a crutch, Anthony swung one-handed and hit long, slicing drives into the side netting. Two other serious-looking golfers kept on scowling. When one complained to the boy who was handing out balls and drivers, the boy just shrugged and said, "This isn't Baltusrol."

They didn't manage to finish the whole bucket. Juliette offered what was left to the man who had complained. She said, "Hey, hot stuff. Have some golf balls." He seemed annoyed but took the bucket. After that they all sat down again at the picnic table. Juliette smoked as they watched a man in a strange vehicle drive around the range and gather up the balls.

Before they left Juliette said, "So, I want you both to promise you'll start talking again." When no one spoke she said, "It's not going to kill you. You can agree at least to talk every now and then."

"Does tonight count?" Jay asked.

"What are you, five-year-olds?"

"Why are you so concerned?" asked Anthony.

"I'm not concerned. I just think you should talk."

Jay said, "We've been through a lot, you know?"

She said, "Like what?"

Jay said, "For instance, his mother once went wild and smashed all of our windows."

Juliette said, "So? Isn't all that between your parents?"

"She has a point," Anthony said.

Jay said, "It is true that our parents can be imbeciles."

A loud clang echoed across the driving range. After a moment, they all realized that a golf ball had struck the ball-collecting vehicle. "Nice shot," Juliette called out. Jay added, "Asshole," but said it a bit louder than he meant to. The man they'd given the extra balls to turned and suddenly looked violent. They all took off for the car, Anthony hopping as fast as Jay and Juliette were running.

✦ ✦ ✦

Just after the New Year, Anthony began walking again. He still had to use his crutches, but he could now take steps with both feet, using the crutches to bear part of the weight on his bad knee. He started biking in the school training room and swimming. He'd gotten most of his range of motion back and sometimes dared to walk without his crutches around the house.

By then the hockey team had played seven games—five of them losses, one win, and one tie. He had gone to the first two games. He'd sat on the bench with all the players, trying to act like he was still, in some way, captain. Then he stopped going to games—even after Juliette yelled at him. Her exact words were, "What the fuck is all this bullshit?" He knew she couldn't understand that watching hockey now made him physically sick with longing.

He always tried to find ways of being preoccupied on game nights. He would find things to do with Juliette whenever she was available. On one occasion, he called up Alex Brody, who was at college. He even told her about Juliette. Alex just laughed and said, "Well, is she taking care of you?" He felt a jolt and said, "Not the same way you did." After the call ended, he stared at the wall and pondered their conversation. Then he decided, in one very quiet moment, that he needed to grow up.

A day later, Tommy Lange went to visit relatives in Ohio. Anthony took this as a sign that it was time to do something radical. He called up Juliette and asked if she would go on a "real date."

"And what the hell is a real date?"

"We just go out somewhere, on purpose."

Juliette said, "Fine. We'll have a date. How's six o'clock tomorrow evening?"

He said, "That's great. I'll figure out a place to go."

When Juliette picked him up, she was wearing "date" clothes. A short black skirt and a tight sweater. Lipstick, eye shadow, and mascara. Her hair was still wet from a shower. He hadn't thought she would dress up. He was wearing jeans and a rag-wool sweater. Anthony looked at her and suddenly felt unsure about his date plan. His idea was to go bowling in East Hanover.

"Go right," he said, as Juliette reached the light at Tiffany and Route 10. They drove through town and she stopped for gas at the Sunoco station. As she pulled out, she said, "So, what are we doing on our date?"

"How about bowling," he said, "at Hanover Lanes?"

"You're joking."

He said, "Why not?"

"No way in hell I'm going bowling. What was plan B?"

He hadn't thought of another plan. Up on the left he saw Bonvini's Pizzeria.

"Turn here," he said reflexively.

"Bonvini's?"

"You can try their mussels marinara."

"Tommy's friends come here to play video games. They would kill you."

He said, "Just turn."

Juliette turned and they sat idling in the parking lot. She said, "I think we should drive to Calabria's. It would be safer."

"They don't have mussels."

"Then how about we drive up Riker Hill and park?"

"That wouldn't count as a real date," he said, and opened the car door.

"We can't go in here..."

"We'll be safe," he said, and felt completely sure of this.

They went inside and a strange calmness overcame him. They took a table in the corner. They ordered pizza and mussels and then got up to play Centipede and pinball. They stayed an hour, and as he paid the check, it struck him: He was crazy. He took her hand and quickly led her to the car.

A few days later the temperature dropped to fifteen, though there still had been no snowfall. After school Juliette drove Anthony home and came inside. By then he'd moved back into his own bedroom. They went upstairs and Juliette began looking at his trophies.

"This one says 1973. League champions. You were seven."

"I was in Squirt league."

She said, "Funny I didn't know you when you were seven."

"I always felt like I knew you."

"That's because you always stared at me like a psycho."

"Maybe I am one."

Juliette laughed and said, "I know."

"Then so are you," Anthony said.

"Guess that explains why I keep staying with my father."

Anthony found this last comment somewhat peculiar.

He said, "Where else could you go?"

She shook her head, rolled her eyes, and said, "My aunt Camille, in Short Hills. Her husband's loaded. Ever since Mom died she's been saying I should come live with her. And she's right, of course, I should. I should go tomorrow."

"Will you?"

"No."

Anthony pulled Juliette close. As he slipped his hands under her wool sweater, they heard scratching. "He has a sixth sense," Juliette said. She stepped back and pulled her sweater down. She folded her arms across her chest. Anthony opened the door for Roger, who walked in and quickly lay down in the corner. He turned to Juliette. She seemed guarded and uneasy.

"Is there a problem?"

She said, "No."

"Can we go back to what we were just doing?"

Juliette laughed, but he felt her heaviness. Inexplicably, something had changed in the days following their date. The only notable thing she'd mentioned was that two days before she'd had a talk with her father. She said her father had promised to give up gambling. She wouldn't tell him anything else.

He stepped up close and slid his arms around her waist. She let her arms drop to her side, so he tried kissing her. She stepped back.

She said, "You know, you're going to have to do something."

"What?"

"Get over me."

"I'll do it when I have to."

"If I were you I'd start to do it now."

"Will you stop talking like it's doomsday?"

Juliette nodded. After a moment she took his hand and said, "I'm sorry. I'm acting weird." Then she stepped close again, kissed him, and said, "I hate when I get this way." She pulled him down onto his bed, but he knew something had just shifted. Even when all of their limbs were entwined in ways that seemed impossible to unravel, he felt his body crying out and understanding that Juliette would disappear.

✦ ✦ ✦

Anthony was sleeping. Up in his room, on his old pro-hockey sheets. He was asleep and who knew what he dreamt as dawn broke over his backyard? Maybe he dreamed of hockey, or of his mother down in Florida. Or of the days when he and his friend Jay Berkowitz had crabapple wars outside. Maybe he dreamed of his neighbor, Juliette Dimiglio—of Juliette picking dandelion clocks, blowing them and counting, "One, two, three, four, five, five o'clock!"—then tossing the naked stem into the wind.

A snowball struck the glass behind Anthony's closed window shade. Anthony stirred but did not wake. A second snowball struck the glass. Then a third one and a fourth one and then finally he woke. He sprung down off his top bunk, landed hard on his good leg without bothering to use the ladder. He was no longer on crutches. He wore his knee brace at all times. He pulled his window shade up, opened the window and the storm window. It was late February and a feathery snow was floating down over Livingston. He felt the cold against his naked chest.

Anthony saw Juliette. She was standing in his backyard, wearing a ski parka, mittens, and ripped blue jeans. Cream-colored longjohns peeked through the knees and other places where her jeans were torn. Maybe a half-foot of new snow covered all the yards that he could see. Juliette stood there, exhaling mist, the vapor rising around her face.

She motioned with her hand. Anthony nodded, closed both windows. He rifled through the clothes inside his dresser, found his longjohns, a turtleneck, and wool socks. He grabbed a sweater from his closet. Leaving a pile of clean clothes on his floor, he ran downstairs.

He searched madly for his ski parka. He couldn't find it so instead he grabbed his Livingston Lancers hockey jacket. He also couldn't find gloves or mittens but decided he'd live without them. He found a ski hat and boots, raced through the kitchen, and darted out the back door.

Juliette waited there, arms folded, leaning against the Rubins' barbecue. The snowflakes flecked her dark blond hair, which hung uncovered below her shoulders. When she saw Anthony she walked toward him, each breath visible as she stepped quietly through the snow. Then she stepped close enough that together they breathed a cloud that they could stand within, concealed, as the snow fell dustlike over Cherry Hill Road, over Livingston, and all of the northern suburbs of New Jersey.

"You're a sound sleeper," she said.

"What time is it?"

"Just after six o'clock."

Juliette's mitten passed over a wooden table by the barbecue. She brushed away a swath of snow and flakes immediately began to fill the space in.

She said, "We're leaving. That's why I woke you."

"Leaving for good?"

She said, "Yeah. I know you knew I would be leaving. I wasn't totally sure I should say goodbye."

"You would have left here without saying goodbye? That's crazy!"

She touched her mitten to his mouth and said, "I didn't. I'm right here."

"Where are you going?"

"My pop is talking about some place right near Los Angeles. I guess I'm going to be a California girl."

"You'll finish high school in Los Angeles?"

Juliette laughed, almost lightheartedly. She touched Anthony on the shoulder with her mitten. She said, "I think I'll get by without more high school. I'll get a job. It's not as if school ever helped me. I won't be missing much, you know? I don't have brains like you or anything. I have these, you know, boobs. That's about it."

"You have a lot more than boobs," said Anthony.

She said, "Like what? The nasty temper I inherited from my father."

"You have strength," he said. "And poise. And believe me, you have brains. Maybe you're not great in school, but that's because you couldn't give a crap. You're smart in ways that most people only wish they could be. I'm sure you're smarter than most people you'll ever meet."

Juliette said, "What? Is this that angel movie where what's-his-face finds out that he's not so worthless after all? Spare me, okay? I'd really rather you keep staring at my boobs, the way you always do. That's what I'm used to, okay? So don't turn into a little pansy on me now."

"What did Tommy say when you told him?"

"He doesn't know," Juliette said. "Give him a week or two, he'll figure out I'm gone."

She let out a pained laugh, bordering on a sigh.

She said, "You know, now Tommy's doing that dumb cheerleader. Kelly McDowell. MacDowell. Whatever her stupid name is. The whole school knows."

"I've heard about her."

"What? That she's given at least half of the team blow jobs?"

"Something like that," Anthony said. "I think she also did that science teacher, what's his name, who coaches J.V. football."

"Tommy knows how to pick the winners," she said. "The stupidest, most moronic, dumbest thing is that I'll miss him. I think I hate the guy, and I'll miss him. I'll miss him maybe as much as I'll miss you."

He felt his stomach turn upside down. He felt his heart contort, his knees buckling, his brain starting to swirl.

"What?" he said.

"I'll miss you."

He said, "You'll miss me?"

"It's six A.M. and I'm out here throwing snowballs at your window. I'm standing out in a goddamn snowstorm, freezing my butt off. My father's waiting in there, wondering what the hell I'm doing saying goodbye to our Jew neighbor's kid—and you can't figure out I'll miss you?"

"Okay," he said. He stared at Juliette and tried to gauge the things that were happening inside him.

"You shouldn't feel me this much," she said. "Goddamn you."

Juliette tackled him. He landed hard in the snow with Juliette on top of him. He grabbed her head with his ungloved hands and started kissing her. They rolled over and he kept kissing her and squeezing every part of her. He caressed Juliette's face and soon he could no longer feel his fingers. He felt as if they were both dead somewhere, some lost place, where he'd almost rather stay.

He looked across his own backyard. He saw snow covering the ground of every yard that he could see. He watched the tiny, ugly flakes falling all over that snowy wasteland. And for one eerily lucid moment, he beheld it all as if from a great distance. He saw a place that was both beautiful and horrible, a place both magical and empty, and from which Juliette was now about to leave.

"So," Juliette said. "We better cut this before my father begins hollering out the window. We also might want to get up before we freeze to death."

Juliette rose and Anthony glanced upward. He saw the underside of her face and found it strangely unfamiliar. After he stood he reached out to brush her hair off. He said, "I'm glad you came over to say goodbye."

She said, "I'll think about you, Anthony. I'll imagine how it might have been to get to know you."

He said, "You do know me."

"Maybe," she said. "Thank God I finally had someone tell me that he loved me. I'm really sorry I got upset."

"Come in here," Anthony said. "Come in my house for just one second."

"Why?"

"Just come."

He led her to his back door and then opened it. "Come in," he said again, taking her arm and leading her inside. He wasn't sure what he was doing, but before he could speak she started kissing him again. They stood there kissing in his kitchen, a place where Juliette's presence now seemed to be defying some fundamental principle of the universe.

Then Juliette stepped back, unzipped her coat, took his right hand, and slid it under her wool sweater. He felt the smooth cotton of her turtleneck. Still wearing mittens, she pressed his frozen hand against her breast.

"Keep this," she said.

"What?"

She told him, "You keep my heart, since I won't need it. I should get going now, I think. There's really nothing else to say."

"Wait," Anthony whispered.

"What?"

"Can I give *you* something?"

"Make it quick."

"How about my Lancers hockey jacket?"

Juliette groaned and said, "No way."

He said, "Then how about a puck?"

Juliette laughed. She told him, "Sure, give me a hockey puck."

Anthony opened up the freezer, where for years he'd kept a stack of pucks ready for pond hockey. He reached inside and pulled out a frozen rubber puck.

"It'll thaw out," he explained. "Keeping them frozen makes them slide better."

He handed Juliette the puck.

"I don't believe it," she said. "A puck."

She smiled and slipped it into her coat pocket.

"That's very sweet," she said, and kissed him again. "I think I really better go now."

"How's your dad's Cadillac in snow?"

She said, "It sucks. I was hoping that we'd leave it."

"You're taking both cars?"

She said, "Yeah. I'm looking forward to driving through fun states like Iowa and Nebraska."

Anthony took her hand and squeezed it. He pulled her mittens off and pressed both of her hands between his own. It seemed so simple and yet now so monumental just to touch her.

She said, "Okay, so even though you just took my mittens off, and even though I'd love to stay for breakfast, now I'm going."

He said, "I know."

"I don't write letters, so don't expect any."

"I wasn't," Anthony said.

Juliette said, "Well, it was nice being your neighbor."

"Have a good life," Anthony said.

"You have a good one, too," she said, and pulled him close once more.

They stood there kissing for a moment, until Anthony heard his father lumber into the upstairs hallway. And until Anthony could physically let go of her. Then Juliette put her mittens on and walked away forever.

THE LOST LEGENDS
OF NEW JERSEY

ONE WINTER LONG AGO, my parents decided to take waltz lessons. They signed up for a class at a small studio in Millburn. Classes were Tuesday nights at eight. I remember this because I sometimes got stuck waiting at the studio. That year my Chiefs practices were Tuesdays at six-thirty. They'd pick me up and race across South Mountain Reservation to their lesson.

They were both tentative at the start. Even my mother, whose idea it was, seemed shy for the first few weeks. They got the hang of it pretty fast though. Of the four couples in the class, they quickly proved to be the most adept and graceful. They also seemed very happy to be waltzing.

At home they'd practice downstairs. They'd put on music in the living room. They'd dance from room to room, waltzing around in a big circle. The dining room and living room both had hardwood floors. The kitchen floor was smooth ceramic tile. I can still see it—their bodies rising and falling, sometimes twirling, my father calling out things like "diagonal center" or "against the line of dance." They would play songs you might not think were waltzes, including some I recognized from the radio. But as my father once explained to me, any three-four time signature is waltz tempo, even if the song is "How Can I Be Sure?" by the Young Rascals.

The waltzing did not last long. They kept at it for a few months after hockey season ended. They still practiced from time to time that summer. By the next fall they seemed to have lost interest.

I started wondering: What was the point of waltz lessons? I asked my mother this one day, about a year after they'd stopped. She said, "We tried it. We got bored."

"You didn't look bored," I said.

"We're good at faking."

"It didn't seem fake."

She stared at me.

"Maybe not."

They weren't faking. That's for sure. You can't fake waltzing the way they waltzed. And even now, though they don't talk much, I know something is real between them. They'd say this something boils down to me and Dani, but it's more than that. You'd see it if they waltzed.

✦ ✦ ✦

This is what I know: My parents fell in love quickly. They fell in love, and then they fought, and then it ended for a while. But then one rainy December evening he changed his mind and appeared on her front doorstep.

He had come back from college for the weekend. He was at home in Fair Lawn with his mother. He told his mother, "I want to marry her." His mother tried to talk him out of it. "You'll be unhappy," she said. "The girl has problems. All you will do is take care of her and get nothing." He left the room.

He knew the rain was pretty bad. He knew the roads would be terrible. He got into his little Volkswagen. The snow was melting from the rain, and so the roads were full of slush. Millburn would be a far drive on the bad roads but he didn't care. Though he felt nervous, he felt good. He felt that this—making decisions—was what life was all about.

When he turned onto her street, he wasn't sure what he should do. Should he park there, by the curb, or should he pull onto the driveway?

Or should he park two blocks away, so that she didn't see him coming? She couldn't hide then, if she saw him. Would she hide? Maybe she would. Or she might lock the front door. She'd stand behind it and listen to him beg, but refuse to open it. Maybe she'd talk to him with the door closed. She might tell him to go away. But once she faced him, he knew, she would have trouble resisting. She would say yes, if she just faced him. All would be fine if he could get her to just open the front door.

He parked quietly on the street beneath her front yard, headlights off. He saw the oak tree and the beech, dark silhouettes at the base of her steep front lawn. He saw the acorns by the curb. He put his raincoat on and stared down at the dashboard. He saw his Pall Malls, winter gloves, two quarters, and the ring. He'd bought the ring three months before from a jeweler in New Brunswick. He'd changed his mind once in October but did not return the ring. He hadn't spoken to her since June, when he broke things off a few weeks after his junior year ended. He thought: My life is on this dashboard. He slipped the ring into his pocket and stepped outside.

✦ ✦ ✦

Right now it's twilight and I'm on my way to Newark. The plane is somewhere over Maryland or Delaware. I have just spent a full week with my mother. She is at work now, pouring drinks, feeling exhausted from my visit.

When I see Dad I know he'll also feel exhausted. He'll say he's tired from work but really he'll be tired from thinking about my mother. They've become "friends" now and he understands he's happier without her. But he still dreams of her. I'm sure of this. Why wouldn't she still haunt him?

✦ ✦ ✦

He wound up waiting on the doorstep in the rain for fifteen minutes. He rang the doorbell three times, heart racing wildly. Her mother came to the door, finally, and said, "I'm sorry. She won't come down."

"What did she tell you?" he asked.

"She's up there crying."

"What should I do then? Can you talk to her?"

"I think you should go home."

He said, "I drove here all the way from Fair Lawn. It's freezing cold out here. It's raining."

"That's not my problem," her mother said. "I'm sorry."

She shut the door.

So he walked back down to his Volkswagen, his heart broken, his head aching. Now it was hailing. The air seemed colder. He got inside and lit a Pall Mall. When he inserted the key, the engine would not start.

He punched the steering wheel several times and then got out. He took a long drag from the cigarette. He threw it in the gutter. Then he collected himself and walked back to her doorstep.

He couldn't know that she was waiting there and watching as he returned. She had been watching from her window. She saw him get into the car. For all her life she would wonder why she felt pain as she watched him. She had intended to feel relieved, but she kept thinking: Please come back here. Please don't leave.

She'd seen the glow from his cigarette. She'd watched him step out of the car. She saw him waver for an instant before he walked up to her door again. And then she sprinted down the stairs. She had to force herself not to burst outside and tackle him on the lawn.

And when she opened up the door, she saw him drop down on one knee. He didn't care about the rain. He bowed his head and said, "I'm here because I want you to be my wife."

She didn't answer, and he looked up. Then he said, "So, will you be my wife?"

She stepped outside, into the cold. She had her nightgown on, and slippers. She said, "It's freezing out here. Get up." She took his hand. She led him inside, slammed the door closed. Then she kissed him with all she had. She said, "What made you drive out here in this weather, are you crazy?"

He said, "No."

She said, "Come over here. Get these clothes off." She took him into the downstairs guest room. She said, "I'll be back with dry clothes. Get in the shower before you catch pneumonia." She shut the door and stood there listening, until she heard him turning on the water.

Then she went up to her older sister's room. Leah was married now and lived on Upper Mountain Avenue in Montclair. She knew Leah's husband, Barry, had left clothes there and was roughly Michael's size.

She found a pair of men's pajamas and a sweatshirt. She brought them down into the guest room. Then she went up again and knocked on her mother's door. She stepped inside. She saw her mom on the bed, reading. She was amazed not to feel even the slightest hint of indecision.

She said, "His car broke down. It's late. I told him he could stay over."

Her mother said, "It's not such a good idea."

"Why?"

"Your father won't be back until tomorrow."

She said, "His car. It won't start. And it's an hour's drive to Fair Lawn in this weather."

"Do you plan to marry him?"

"Yes."

"He won't keep kosher."

"I couldn't care less," she said. "You know that. Why would you even bring it up?"

"Because I have to," her mother said.

She sighed and turned her eyes back to her magazine.

✦ ✦ ✦

At Newark Airport my father will be waiting down in Baggage Claim. He rarely waits at the gate the way my mother does. He's more practical. It's also possible he got tired and decided to send a car service.

If he is there, he'll be with Roxanne, his new girlfriend. They began dating last winter, a few weeks after Juliette Dimiglio left New

Jersey. They met one night at the Short Hills mall. Roxanne is not much like my mother, though she does have a mysterious, edgy, sultry kind of presence. My father always seems to be going for these larger-than-life women. Still, I think Roxanne may be safer than my mother. At forty-two, she is a widow. She has two daughters, Jen and Mariel. She is a bond trader and, amazingly, an artist. She paints landscapes that look a lot like tables. It always looks like there are table legs, or stilts maybe, holding the landscape up.

Possibly Roxanne and my father are *b'shert*. I like to think so, but who knows? When Grandpa Max married last year, he said that Doris was his *b'shert*. Still I'm not sure you can really know *b'shert*, except in hindsight. You just vault into things, I think, and then you hope.

✦ ✦ ✦

He was still in the shower. She stood there sitting on her sister's bed and listening to the water. She kept on hearing her mother sigh, which made her angry and afraid.

She knew her father would start hollering when she told him—but she would. Because she loved this Michael Rubin, this clarinet-playing half-intellectual, who, thank God, would never want a kosher home. This brash boy wonder who still swaggered and always stared at her as if she were his princess. She slipped her nightgown off and let it fall onto the floor outside the bathroom.

He still had soap in his hair and didn't hear her when she entered. She pulled the curtain back and smiled. She stepped under the water. She let her hair get wet and started kissing him and crying. He didn't know that she was crying, because the water washed her tears away before they reached her cheeks.

And so he thought this was as good a time as any to ask again. He said, "So anyway, do you think...have you considered what I asked you?"

"Would you just hold me for a while, under this shower please," she said.

And then he put his arms around her. He held her tight and did not say another word.

✦ ✦ ✦

Sometimes I played hockey in the driveway with my father. I shot hard, which was okay. I figured nothing could hurt my father. He had no face mask, but I shot low. He used to play shortstop in baseball, so his glove hand was amazing. All of my friends were impressed and would say, "Wow, Mr. Rubin, what a goalie."

He couldn't skate very well, of course. It was much different on the ice during the Chiefs' annual father-and-son hockey game. He wasn't goalie because Richie Owens's father was a goaltender in college. We couldn't score on Mr. Owens. That's why the fathers always won. I saw my father very differently when both of us wore ice skates. I saw him trying to keep his balance. I saw him crashing into the boards.

I still think sometimes of the Sunday I first knew that things were definitely ending. When I returned from an early-morning hockey game, my mother was there waiting. She asked me how the star anise had worked for face-offs. My father went out to buy bagels. He took a long time and Mom got all hysterical when he returned. I never understood what triggered my mother's episode that morning. The only odd thing was that Dad came home with doughnuts instead of bagels.

I called Jay Berkowitz to play goalie, though he was terrible. I knew he'd dive for every shot. If I shot high, I'd always score. Jay's mother wouldn't let him come over. But then my father appeared outside while I was shooting in the driveway. He grabbed the goalie stick and a catcher's mitt from the bin in the garage. He stepped in front of the beat-up net and said, "The goalie's here. Just keep it low, okay?"

I took a slap shot. I wasn't aiming. The yellow tennis ball flew right into his glove. "Shoot stick-side," he said. He dropped the ball and kicked it to my stick. I kept on hoping he'd say something about the goal I'd scored that morning. It was the game winner, my second goal. I scored it with eight seconds left to play.

I took a slap shot. Wide and high. It caromed off the garage and I had to chase it down the driveway. When I got back, he said, "Antonio, you're winding up too much."

I've always hated being called Antonio. I'm not Italian to begin with, though I happen to like Anthony. I've always wondered what life would be like if they had named me Eric, like they planned. But just a month before my birth, my second cousin died. So I became the only Jew named Anthony in America.

I saw my father look at his wristwatch. I waited until he looked up again. I took a slap shot and shot stick-side and I scored. He said, "Nice shot." He kicked the ball back and I blasted it on the fly.

I watched it go. I saw it rise. I saw it clock him in the face and then I wondered why I did that. I said, "Oh Christ. I wound up. Sorry." He dropped his stick and threw the glove down. He said, "We're done for today, Antonio." I started wondering what was going through my head.

✦ ✦ ✦

"Take these pajamas," she said.

He took them. They were alone in the downstairs bedroom. He slipped his towel off and put on the pajamas.

He said, "I have something to give you, okay?"

She smiled gently and said, "Okay."

He took his wet pants off the chair where they were hanging. He took a small box from the pocket and then placed it in her hand.

He said, "I bought this with the money I earned last summer."

She took the ring out. A small diamond set in a thin gold band. She slipped it on and said, "Yes, I want to be your wife."

Then they went into the kitchen. There were three pots filled with dirt, several forks and knives sticking out of them. He asked her what they were for. She said, "To purify. They touched both milk and meat." And then she laughed.

They sat down at the antique kitchen table. Her mother had gone to sleep and they stayed up talking about the future. They talked about where they would live, and how they'd struggle for a while. He'd go to med school after Rutgers. After he finished maybe she would go to college.

They'd have a kid in a few years, or maybe sooner. They wanted two kids, or else three. Maybe he'd work as a doctor in Pennsylvania. Maybe New Jersey. Boston. Anywhere. Who could know?

They planned their honeymoon in New England. Soon they were trying to decide between the Berkshires and Lake Placid. After an hour of debating, she said, "Hey, we have a lot of time to plan this." They both quieted. She smiled impishly and kissed him on the cheek.

"My mother's sound asleep," she said. "Do you feel tired?"

He said, "Not really."

"We can go out on the porch and share a cigarette."

He said, "Okay."

She took one cigarette from her mother's porcelain box in the living room. She found a blanket and some matches. She held his hand and led him out to an enclosed porch.

They heard the rain as they shared the cigarette. At some point they started kissing. At some point they made love. It was not the first time, or the last. It was not the best and not the worst, but they made love until the rain stopped and the oak trees framed the first light of the morning.

✦ ✦ ✦

There is no way I can tell you everything, though I'd like to. One of the problems with all stories is they have borders. Then you extrapolate, like in algebra. You use the things you know to guess at what is left outside the border.

Will I see Juliette again? Not likely. But this is something I leave you to extrapolate. All I can say is that I don't feel like she's gone. As for my parents, I believe they'll both calm down as they grow older. They will talk less and less until they don't have anything but old stories to keep track of.

Now I can see all the lights of Newark, Jersey City, and Elizabeth. From the air these ugly cities always look like a big carnival at night. We start to circle and I see the Manhattan skyline for a moment. I see the Staten Island bridges, the Verrazano and the Goethals. As we come round I see the runway, all lit up.

Listen to me, okay? I want to tell you one last story, about my grandfather—Grandpa Max. Years ago, when he still drove, he took me out to see my grandma Lilly's grave. Dani was somewhere off with Mom, shopping for school clothes, I think. My father was on call for that whole weekend.

So it was just me and Grandpa Max. We had to drive to a Jewish cemetery on Long Island. He made me follow our whole driving route on a map. We took the George Washington Bridge and then the Throgs Neck. Then we drove east and south and found our way to Pinelawn, a strange town that was mostly graveyards. I had been there when she was buried, but I was young and don't remember much of it. He parked the car and we walked out on a winding path through endless headstones.

Max had brought two dozen roses for my grandmother. At her grave, he handed me a dozen. We dropped them one by one over the area where her coffin had been buried. When we were finished, he said, "Your grandma was a strong, stouthearted woman." He took my hand and said, "Let's go and visit Daniel."

Until that moment, I had forgotten about my father's brother, Daniel. My father very rarely spoke of him. I hadn't even known that he was buried there. We crossed a dozen plots or so and then we came to Daniel's gravestone. Max stood there quietly. Something was different. I turned to look at him and saw that he was trembling.

Before I spoke again, he fell to his knees, weeping. He just broke down, totally lost it. He had his hands pressed to the stone and within seconds he was sobbing uncontrollably, making raspy sounds and shuddering, as if something inside him had just broken. I didn't know what to do, so I stepped forward. I touched his shoulder. This pulled him back from where he was and he calmed down. It happened quickly.

After a moment he got up. He looked around and then again at Daniel's headstone. He wiped his face and said, "What a lousy graveyard. They're supposed to plant new ivy and geraniums each spring."

We looked for pebbles and each placed one on Daniel's headstone. We left the graveyard, headed home, and made a stop at the Tick Tock Diner on Route 3. We didn't say another word about Daniel. I doubt my grandfather was even thinking about the graveyard anymore. He started talking about pastrami, how in the old days the pastrami at this diner was renowned. But I was still thinking about Daniel, wondering who he would have been if he were living. Would he be married and would I have three more cousins and would I like them? I looked at Max and understood that we all lose things. That loving anyone means having to face the pain of separation. That we can fall on a lost son's grave and then go out for pastrami on rye with mustard. Now we touch down. Newark, New Jersey. The airplane rumbles along the runway, racing the river of cars out on the Turnpike. Soon the plane loses its breakneck speed. The airport buildings come into focus. It's always strange to me that all this is so comforting. And yet it is.

I'm home.

Acknowledgments

My heartfelt thanks go out to my editor, Jane Isay, and to the agent team of Dan and Simon Green. For invaluable feedback, particularly on early drafts, my deepest thanks to trusted readers Nancy Pick, Leslie Pietrzyk, and Lisa Sheffield. Thanks to the members of my writing group: Stephen Philbrick, Constance Talbot, Wilmot Hastings, Colin Harrington, Antonia Lake, Rosemary Starace, Antonia Palfrey, and Charles Morey—who generously listened to almost all of these chapters, as well as many that were discarded. To David Hough, many thanks for tireless patience and camaraderie during the copyediting process. And to Chrysler Szarlan, thanks for fielding endless questions about everything from eye make-up to nutcakes.

I am also grateful for many pieces of factual information, advice, feedback, inspiration, and general assistance I received along the way. Another round of thanks go out to: Leigh Weiner, Lorie Stoopack, D. A. Feinfeld, Jon D'Alessio, David D'Alessio, Michael D'Alessio, Abe Loomis, Sandra Benter, Brant Cherny, Nancy Gannon, Doris Hartman, Norine Philipp, Monika Giacoppe, Cailin Cammann, Peter Weinstein, Alison Simpkins, Stephen Listfield, Rick Seto, Tim Ehrlich, Ronnie Lambrou, Karen Rosenblum, Michael Waldron, and my grandmother, Vivian Fishco.

Finally, a big thanks to two keepers of many arcane facts and pieces of New Jersey lore: my father, Samuel Reiken; and my mother, Michelle Reiken.

READING GROUP GUIDE

1. What is the significance of the title? Can the chapters be considered "legends?" In what way, for instance, is the chapter entitled "Constellations" a legend? What about "Lost Meadows"? "Romeo and Juliette"? "B'shert"? "Juliette Wakes Anthony at Dawn"?

2. What are some of the specific geographical details that Reiken incorporates into the book? What particular locales emerge most distinctly? What else helps to establish a sense of place? How are the characters connected to the geography and culture of northern New Jersey circa 1980?

3. Both Michael and Jess Rubin might be said to be flawed characters, yet they are presented in a sympathetic light. How does Reiken's characterization process strike this balance? What is the effect of the book's use of multiple character perspectives or changing "point-of-view"?

4. Is Vincent Dimiglio really a mobster? Is there any evidence that Isabella Dimiglio ever was a prostitute? How does the book present the idea of mythmaking in regard to these and other characters?

5. In the chapters "Anthony Sells Juliette a Raffle" and "Wolves," Juliette contemplates her feelings toward her mother. What are they? What about her father? Aunt Camille? Why do you think she continues to date Tommy Lange?

6. In "Lost Mothers," Anthony wonders whether finding his mother "dead and bloody," as Juliette has, might be easier than having a mother who is still alive but absent in his life. How does Anthony's predicament compare with Juliette's? How do their responses to having a "lost mother" compare or contrast?

7. Is there any way to account for Jess's erratic behavior and obvious problems with relationships? Does she have an identifiable mental health disorder? In "A Brief History of Sadness," why does she begin and end an affair with her scuba diving instructor?

8. What is Joeyland? Is it a place specific only to Claudia? Why does Claudia decide to leave Joey Malinowski? How do her actions toward Joey compare to Leah Kleinfeld's actions toward her own high-school sweetheart, Paul Haney?

9. What does the inclusion of Leah Kleinfeld and Max Rubin, two secondary characters, accomplish for the novel? How do their respective stories treat the notion of love? How do their understandings of love compare to those of Jess and Michael?

10. In Yiddish the word *b'shert* literally means "meant to be" and is often used idiomatically to refer to one's destined romantic partner. How does the chapter "B'shert" play on this idea of the possibility of a destined "true love"?

11. The novel depicts characters from three generations. How does each character's age influence his or her opinion on marriage and the

appropriateness of a particular mate? Do you consider Max's views to be atypical of his generation?

12. The novel makes allusions to the legendary doomed romance of Guinevere and Lancelot in the chapters "Angels Like Audrey Hepburn" and "Juliette Wakes Anthony at Dawn." How does this reference pertain to Anthony and Juliette? What about Jess and Eddie Fischer? Are there allusions to the Arthurian legend in other chapters?

13. Is there a logic to the sequence in which the chapters narrated in first person are arranged within the more prevalent third-person chapters? What is the effect of the first-person chapters on the overall shape and structure of the book?

14. Are there any distinct moments when something shifts or transforms during Anthony's visit with his mother in Florida? In "Sanibel," why does he focus on her gold jacket? What is the significance of the tunnel they swim through in "Atlantis"?

15. In the last chapter, Anthony notes that "One of the problems with all stories is they have borders." What does he mean by this? Which particular story lines feel like they continue beyond the borders of *The Lost Legends of New Jersey*? How does the book achieve its sense of closure?